THE FIRES OF TREASON

MICHELE QUIRKE

ISBN 978-0-578-77875-4

For Ed, the one person I can always count on to walk through fire for me.

THE FIRES OF TREASON

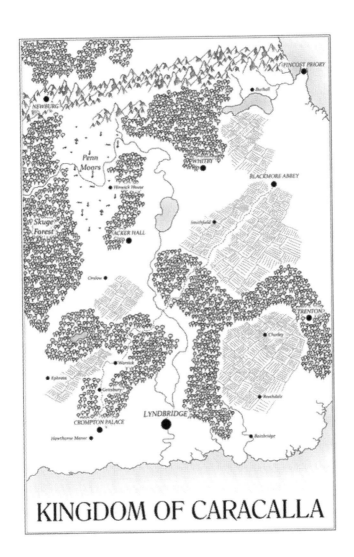

KINGDOM OF CARACALLA

CHAPTER 1

Kingdom of Caracalla
Summer 1595

*A*s General Howard approached the edge of the cliff, his fingers itched to rip his sword from its sheath and behead the Prince of Caracalla. He'd find no greater pleasure than throwing Prince Gregory's corpse over the side of the jagged precipice.

Howard sneered as he imagined the buzzards swarming the fresh meat, their beaks ripping through flesh in the scorching summer sun.

There'll be nothing left but bare bones. He smiled, rejuvenated by his fantasy.

General Howard long believed the prince lacked the necessary skills to rule a prosperous nation, and the inefficient way he'd handled the rebellion in the north was further proof of that.

Rather than obey the king's order to put each one of the mutinous bastards in the ground, Prince Gregory hanged only the leaders of the insurrection and made an unauthorized truce with the rest. Less than forty men were sentenced to death when the actual number of traitors reached well into the thousands.

By showing lenience toward the participants of the rebellion, Gregory had turned his back on his kingdom. In Howard's opinion, the prince was now a traitor himself.

The general yearned to inform King Charles of the prince's insubordination in hopes of elevating Princess Bernadette over *Gregory the Merciful*. Once she replaced her incompetent younger brother as His Majesty's heir, Bernadette would be compelled to reward Howard's support with titles and land.

That hopeful thought alone saved Gregory's life.

With his teeth clenched, the general glared at the armored prince. He knew to act now would bring forth his own demise. Patience was all he needed. Why should he stain his hands with Gregory's blood when the king's wrath upon his treacherous son would lead to the same fatal outcome?

"The horses are tired." Howard interrupted the prince's solitude as they gazed at the red-brick palace in the lush valley below. "I'll have the men set up camp for the night." He turned to give the order to the soldiers.

"No." Prince Gregory rounded on him, eyes narrowed. "You won't."

Howard drew in a slow, steady breath and met the prince's heated glower head-on. He straightened his back and squared his shoulders as a touch of impertinence darkened his tone. "Your Highness–"

"We'll keep moving," Prince Gregory commanded. "The horses can have all the sleep they want in a few hours."

Howard's pulse pounded in his ears as the prince lifted the reigns of his stallion and began the slow journey down the side of the mountain. Gregory twisted his head to look at him over his shoulder. "Now!"

General Howard struggled to suppress his temper as he raised his arm to signal for the infantry behind him to move forward. To his annoyance, the soldiers clapped and cheered. They were going home.

CHAPTER 2

*T*he melodic tune was a gentle whisper in the background as Princess Elizabeth and her ladies sat beside the pond, each engulfed in her own preferred method of relaxation.

"This is my favorite song." Elizabeth glanced over her shoulder at the musician and smiled in approval. Her interest in his music emboldened the shy lute player who straightened in his chair and plucked the strings with expert precision.

Elizabeth tapped her foot in rhythm with the tune and returned her attention to the canvas with a sigh. For over an hour, she'd attempted to depict the serenity of the swans paddling on the water but failed to capture the true calmness of the beautiful birds. She dropped the brush in the cup of water next to her easel and stared at the artwork before her. "It looks as if a child painted it," she pouted.

Lady Jane, the princess's second cousin and favorite of her two female attendants, glanced up from the book of French she was studying. "I think your painting is lovely."

"Then you're blind." Elizabeth let out an unladylike snort.

4

"See how long I made the neck? It's more like a fat giraffe than a swan."

Lady Jane rose from the blanket and made her way over to the edge of the pond. Her mouth fell agape as she inspected the canvas.

"Your Highness, the realistic skyline and reflections in the rippling water make this one of the best landscapes I've ever seen. It'd be a sin to speak against it."

"Jane, I want advice on how to improve my work, not to be showered with praises for it. Look at the swan. Don't you see the problem?"

Lady Jane examined the painting again and issued a resigned sigh. "I suppose it's *a bit* long," she muttered after a pause. "You could make the body bigger until you feel it's balanced."

"Hm. That's not a bad idea." Although there wasn't a speck of sincerity in her attendant's voice, Elizabeth was mollified and excused Lady Jane with a casual wave. She dipped the brush in the paint and was in the process of making the swan's body larger when one of the servants approached.

"What can we do for you?" Lady Charlotte tossed aside her embroidery hoop and puffed out her enormous bosom. "Have you come to invite me on a romantic stroll around the pond?" She batted her eyelashes at him.

Charlotte will throw herself at the feet of any man who so much as glances at her. Elizabeth rolled her eyes and returned to her painting. *Pathetic.*

Lady Jane stuck her nose back in her French booklet. "He's betrothed, you know."

"That has never stopped me before," Lady Charlotte chirped with a wink. "It can be our secret."

Awkwardly shuffling his feet as the color rushed to his

cheeks, the servant directed his attention to Elizabeth. "Your Highness," he greeted with a low bow. "I've come to inform you that Prince Gregory and his army were spotted at the top of the mountain."

"Already?" Elizabeth squealed with delight as she dropped the brush in its holder and leapt to her feet. The moment her bottom left the chair, the back of her dress popped back out as the whale-boned farthingale beneath her skirts retook its circular shape. "They weren't expected to return for another week."

Lady Jane stepped forward to smooth out the wrinkles in Elizabeth's elaborate teal-colored gown and checked the girdle belt around her waist to be certain none of the pearls had gotten tangled.

"What's their estimated arrival time?" All smiles, Elizabeth bent her knees as Lady Jane reached up and repositioned the pearl diadem atop her head.

"His Highness should be entering through the main gate in no more than two hours," the servant replied.

"Two hours?" Elizabeth clasped her hands together and bounced on her toes. "I assume my brother's household has been informed of his early return?"

"Yes, Your Highness. His lodgings are being dusted top to bottom, and a fire will be lit in every hearth, per your instructions."

"Good. The last thing he needs after so long an absence is to find his chambers dirty and cold. I want it to look as though he never left. Is that clear?"

"Of course, Your Highness."

"Splendid!" She flashed an appreciative smile, unable to stem her exhilaration as she practically shooed the man down the cobblestone path.

Elizabeth rounded on Lady Charlotte next. "Go to the

kitchens and make sure the cooks followed my orders to have a pot of rabbit stew prepared for the feast. I know they've been busy, but the stew is a priority. It's Greg's favorite."

"Yes, Your Highness." Lady Charlotte lifted the hem of her dress and sped off toward the kitchens.

"Come now, Jane. The breeze made a mess of my hair, and there isn't much time to fix it. I was still a child when Greg left, but I'm an adult now. I must look the part."

"It's a shame he missed your sixteenth birthday," Jane remarked, tucking her arm into the crook of Elizabeth's elbow. "I bet he'll hardly recognize the woman you are now."

Prince Gregory led his men into the crowded courtyard where they were greeted by the cheers of courtiers and servants alike. Flowers flew through the air as the soldiers dropped their bags and rushed into the arms of their lovers and families. To their delight, the revolt was over at last.

Despite the swords and thick breastplates the soldiers were equipped with, it still took more than six months for the rag-tag army of rebel farmers to be oppressed. *Six months.* A chill traveled down Gregory's spine as images of the carnage he'd witnessed flashed through his mind. Sent by King Charles and accompanied by hundreds of soldiers, Gregory had traveled north to slaughter his citizens and bring about a quick and easy end to the rebellion. However, nothing about the suppression had been quick or easy.

It's all over now. He breathed a heavy sigh of relief as he scanned the faces in the crowd. When he spotted his little sister rushing toward him, his mouth broke into a wide grin and a feeling of weightlessness washed over him. In his haste to dismount from the saddle, Gregory disregarded the clashing and banging of his armor. For once, the sinister noise didn't bother him.

"Greg!" Elizabeth dashed forward and threw her arms around him before his feet even touched the ground.

"Bess," he murmured in a choked whisper as he enveloped her in a hug.

"I'm so glad you're home," Elizabeth sniffled. "I missed you terribly!"

"It's been a long six months." Gregory kissed her forehead, then stepped back and bequeathed her with a playful grin. "So long, in fact, I think you've grown a few inches taller in my absence."

"And you've gotten much too thin." Elizabeth's face crumbled from glee to alarm as she inspected his appearance. "Didn't they feed you up there?"

Gregory shrugged, unsurprised by her reaction to his weight loss. At least ten pounds had vanished from his frame, and even he recognized how loose his clothing fit now compared to when he'd left in January.

"They fed me enough," he lied.

Elizabeth's voice thickened as she gawked at him through wide, worried eyes. "This armor barely fits you anymore."

Gregory shuffled his feet and fiddled with the scabbard belt around his waist.

"But don't worry, the solution to that problem is waiting for you in the Great Hall." Elizabeth stood tall, beaming. "A huge feast has been prepared in your honor. Rabbit stew is just one of the many dishes being served. It's a good thing, too. I can see how much you need the nourish–"

"Welcome back, Your Highness." A pair of groomsmen advanced on him, one on either side and both intent on removing the cumbersome suit of armor right there and then. "We'll have this off in no time at all."

Gregory breathed in through his nose and forced what he hoped to be a pleasant expression as he waved them away. "I'll take it off later. Right now, I plan to spend some time with my sister."

The smile Elizabeth sported expanded at his words and as a result, a genuine grin stretched across Gregory's face as well. His sister's happiness was rubbing off on him, despite his heavy conscience.

"So, tell me, Bess. Was the rabbit a decent size?"

She pressed her lips together. "I don't know. I didn't participate in the hunt." She sounded equally disgusted and offended by the idea.

"Of course you didn't." Gregory chuckled. Elizabeth possessed such a tremendous soft spot for animals he'd been forced to forbid her from accompanying him on his hunts. Otherwise she purposely scared all his prey away. "Still hate the idea of taking a life? You're going to have to get over that someday if you ever want to earn His Majesty's approval."

Elizabeth's face dissolved into misery, and the look she gave Gregory tugged at his heartstrings.

"You misunderstood me, Bess. I only meant–" His explanation died in his throat when a group of courtiers swarmed in on him.

With all the excitement and vigor of a litter of puppies surrounding their bowl at mealtime, the nobles welcomed him home with appreciative pats on the back and handshakes. Gratified by their words of encouragement and show of support, Gregory forgot about the issue Elizabeth had taken with his previous comment.

The crowd eventually dispersed and Bartholomew, the stable master, was next to approach. "Welcome home, Your Highness. It's good to see you back at Crompton Palace, safe and sound."

"Thank you, Bart. It's good to be back." Gregory's lips composed into a smile and his voice was buoyant.

Elizabeth must've thought so too, because the sadness that tinged her face a moment ago vanished as she linked her arm with his. "Greg's return is like a balm for the troubled soul," she announced, jovial once again.

"Well said, Your Highness. His presence has certainly been missed these last few months. Tempers have a tendency to run high when Prince Gregory isn't here to maintain the peace."

Elizabeth nodded. "That's because my brother is the only person brave enough to oppose the king. Without him here, the door is left wide open for the devil to walk through. This whole place falls into the depths of hell when he's not around."

Bartholomew blanched and a bead of sweat dribbled down his brow. Gnawing on his lower lip, he directed his gaze to Gregory. "Look at me, rambling on when I'm sure you're aching to get inside. Would you like me to return your horse to the Royal Mews?"

"I'd appreciate that. Thank you."

"You're welcome, Your Highness. Good day."

As Bartholomew took the reins and led the stallion to the stables, Gregory cast his sister a reproachful glare. "You need to stop speaking out against the king in front of the servants," he ordered in a low undertone. "Don't you see how uncomfortable it makes them?"

She shrugged. "The words were out before I could stop them."

"That's no excuse."

"If it makes you feel better, I'll try not to let it happen again."

"Please do." Gregory wrapped his arm around Elizabeth's

shoulder and led her inside the palace. "So, how have you been spending your time these past few days? It's been almost a fortnight since your last letter came."

Elizabeth's brow creased. "Really? A fortnight?"

"I was starting to think you forgot about me." He feigned a pout.

"Of course not! I sent at least three letters a week. If you haven't been getting them–"

He chortled and held his hand up. "Relax, Bessie, I was teasing you. It's likely the messenger turned back when he saw the army was on its way home. Don't worry, the rest of your letters found me."

Gregory was dealt a good-humored punch to the arm, which encouraged him further. "Ouch! First you forget about me, and now you're beating me up? I'm starting to think I shouldn't have come home at all."

"You're such a dolt." The mirth in Elizabeth's eyes gave her away. "Now, you asked how I've spent my time lately. Do you want me to tell you or not?"

"I do."

Elizabeth wasted no time filling him in on the latest court gossip. During the short walk to his apartments, Gregory half-heartedly listened as she informed him —with no shortage of details— that the royal falconer's son had gambled away all his father's wealth when he bet on an unlucky racehorse last week.

"That's a shame." Gregory sympathized with the man's plight. However his compassion soon turned into disappointment in Elizabeth's lack of sensitivity. "You shouldn't find amusement in spreading gossip of other people's misfortune. It's crude."

"But–"

"It's *crude*."

"Well, it's quite the scandal and everyone's talking about it." Elizabeth trailed him into his bedchamber, where a tall, gangly young man with short red hair and a face dotted with freckles waited to help him out of his armor.

Gregory dropped his knapsack on the floor and stood in the center of the room, his arms held out to the sides as the servant darted forward to remove his gauntlets and bracers.

"It's rumored His Majesty plans to banish their entire family from court as punishment." Elizabeth heaved a troubled sigh. "It's unfair Master Brock will be sent away, though. He's the victim in all this since it was his money lost. Not to mention, he was the finest falcon trainer I ever met. Wouldn't you agree?"

A brief moment of silence passed before Gregory realized she asked him a question. "Pardon?"

"Never mind. It's not important."

Gregory threw her an apologetic frown. He felt bad for not giving her his full attention, but there were more important thoughts weighing on his mind than court gossip. *The upcoming feast, for one.*

While he was being helped out of his armor, Elizabeth took a seat in the chair beside the hearth. She sat with her back straight and her fingers interlocked on her lap, just as her governess taught her. With her chestnut-colored hair done up in curls and adorned with her favorite pearl coronet, Elizabeth was a picture of demure regality. Gregory, however, knew her well enough to see through the façade. The last word he'd use to describe his little sister was demure.

"It's amazing you can move around so easily while wearing that." Her eyes scrutinized him and rather than sounding impressed by the observation, her tone was one of forced nonchalance.

Gregory searched Elizabeth's face. He wasn't sure where

she was going with this, yet he was certain he wasn't going to like it. "It takes practice," he said simply.

"I see. Plus, you've completed much more...*difficult* tasks while wearing it. Am I right?"

"Yes." He kept his expression guarded as the servant knelt down to take off the cuisses that protected his thighs and knees. "Armor serves a valuable purpose. A morbid purpose."

A loaded and uncomfortable stillness followed.

"That's true. However, before you left you told me if being a good leader meant murdering hundreds of your own subjects, you had no interest in taking the throne." Trepidation dripped from Elizabeth's voice. "Your comment earlier about the inability to gain His Majesty's approval without ending a life scares me, Greg. It gives me the impression you changed your mind."

Elizabeth shifted in the chair, her face indecipherable. Her fingers shook as she fiddled with her pearl necklace. "I can't imagine you killing anyone. Nor do I want to."

Gregory stayed silent as he tried to think up a way to address her concerns with honesty while also keeping the positive image she had of him intact. Unlike their older sister, who was infamous for her harsh treatment of both enemies and allies alike, Gregory had always harbored a desire for peace so strong that many of the nobles perceived his disposition to be 'too soft for kingly affairs'.

However, despite this preference to solve problems with words rather than violence, Gregory was the one who'd been ordered to squash the rebellion. As much as he wanted to assure Elizabeth he hadn't returned from his six-month journey as the man his father always wanted him to be, he wasn't sure he could.

What if his time as a soldier had, in fact, molded him into a *trained killer?* After twenty-two years of resisting it, had

Gregory finally given into His Majesty's hope to have a son with less aversion to violence? He shuddered to think it.

"You said you were going to do everything within your power to end the rebellion without slaughtering all the participants." Elizabeth lowered her gaze as angst colored her face. "So, I can't help but wonder, were you able to overcome those feelings and complete the task you were sent to do?"

While his attendant unbuckled and took off the pauldron from his shoulders, Gregory considered his answer. After a moment of contemplation, he found his voice. "The battle at Crafton lasted hours, but the rebels were outnumbered and were eventually forced to surrender to us. By the end of the day, I'd executed thirty-six of their leaders."

"Thirty-six? That's it?"

"Thirty-six is plenty," Gregory spat. "It was hell, and I'm ashamed to have been a part of it."

"You let the rest go?"

"Yes."

Relief rose in Elizabeth's face. "You only killed a tiny fraction of the rebels, proof you've held onto your humanity. I can't tell you how proud I am of you."

Gregory gave her a thin smile as a second groomsman emerged from the wardrobe closet, carrying a fresh change of clothes. With a respectful bow, he put them on the bed and exited the prince's lodgings without a word.

I'd forgotten how little privacy there is here.

"Nevertheless, my mind isn't altogether eased." Elizabeth's cheeks took on a grayish sheen. "If anything, I'm more terrified now than I was while worrying you'd be corrupted. Now that I know you aren't a coldblooded murderer–"

"Corrupted? Coldblooded murderer?" He jerked his head back, his jaw tight. "Is that what you think of me, Bess?"

Elizabeth drained of color.

"Pardon the interruption," the servant's voice was small and hesitant, "but could Your Highness please relax your posture? I'm having a difficult time with the clasps on the breastplate."

With effort, Gregory loosened his muscles and stood motionless as the metal that protected his chest was removed.

"That was the wrong thing to say, and I apologize, but you were instructed to smother the revolt by killing *everyone* involved. His Majesty insisted this would change you, and like a fool, I believed him. Then you made that comment about me being unable to earn his approval if I still hated the idea of taking a life and...well, it worried me."

"I didn't mean–"

"I know. I never should've doubted you. Forgive me?"

Gregory swallowed, letting go of the unwarranted umbrage he'd taken at her misgivings. "There's nothing to forgive. Honestly, there are times I too wonder if the role I played in suppressing the rebellion changed me."

"It didn't. You're still the compassionate, merciful brother I know and love. But while *I'm* relieved by that fact, His Majesty won't be." Her voice shook as she crossed her arms over her chest and chewed the inside of her cheek. "What will he do when he learns of your clemency toward the rebels? You only executed thirty-six men when you were sent to kill them all."

"*Only* thirty-six?"

"You know what I mean." A contrite frown tugged at her lips, and her voice dropped to a whisper. "He's going to be furious. Have you given any thought to what you're going to say when he asks why?"

"No. All my thoughts are spent reliving those terrible, drawn-out deaths. I thought hanging would be the most humane way to execute them. I was wrong. Some were lucky enough to die straight away, but most times the rope failed to snap their necks, and they continued to kick and squirm long after the board was released beneath their feet. They suffered for ages, and all the while I had to watch, knowing *I* was the one who sent them up to the gallows. I called each of their names, one at a time. I ordered their deaths."

"No, you didn't. You were following the king's orders. You didn't have a choice."

"*Everything* is a choice." He looked into her supportive gaze. The brown eyes staring back at him were dark, but when filled with such tremendous compassion, they seemed to shine brighter than the sun. "I made the wrong one."

Gregory leaned forward so the servant could pull the final bit of armor, the chainmail, over his head. Once it was off, he was able to take in a full breath of air for the first time since his return. It was far easier to breathe when his movements weren't hindered by the weighty suit.

"I know you feel guilty." Elizabeth's voice was laced with sympathy. "But if you wouldn't have sentenced their leaders to death, surely His Majesty would've accused you of being a rebel sympathizer. Your reputation is unstable enough without the dangerous accusation of treason hanging over your head."

"My reputation isn't half as important as the lives I took," Gregory argued as the groom retrieved his clothes from the bed.

Elizabeth's lips pressed together into a tight scowl. "Greg, I hate to tell you this, but three weeks ago Bernadette proposed to the council that she replace you in the line of succession. Half of them agreed. Even the king appeared to fancy the outrageous suggestion. I opposed, of course, but you have no idea how often your name has been dragged through the mud during your absence."

"My name is quite accustomed to being sullied." While

the servant held his red doublet up for him, Gregory slipped his arms through the sleeves. "Why's this any different?"

"I just told you! The lies are working. Half the council already– "

"Bernadette's supporters have always invented new calumnies to spread about me. It's nothing new."

"This is different!" Elizabeth's shrill voice rose a few more octaves. "Don't you understand? She's poisoning the entire court against you. Her rumors spread like wildfire, and it's all I can do to extinguish them. Now it's time for you to grab a bucket and help me put out the flames!"

Gregory shook his head as the groom pulled little puffs of black fabric through the slashes in the sleeves of his doublet. "You're wasting your time. Haven't you learned by now that any rumor we oppose will be replaced twofold? It'd be best to–"

"Are you daft? My God, you can be so infuriating at times! If you don't intervene, you're going to lose all your supporters."

Gregory drew back. The sudden suspicion that there was some truth to Elizabeth's words made his heart soar into his throat. His tone bubbled with worry as he asked, "Do *you* believe anything you've heard?"

"Of course I don't! The fact that you even feel the need to ask is incredibly offensive. Do you truly believe I'm so feebleminded I'd believe anything Bernadette says about you?"

Gregory relaxed, and although Elizabeth was now ripping into him, her outburst roused a smile from him. He was confident that with his fiery sister on his side, he'd be more than capable of withstanding any rumors their older sibling threw at him. Even when the whole world turned against him, Elizabeth remained by his side. She was his biggest supporter.

"But I must be honest," she continued. "Just because I turn a deaf ear doesn't mean everyone else will. You must help me put an end to these wretched rumors. We both know what Bernadette's ultimate goal is. Your reputation is all that matters right now."

"Bess–"

"Listen, I'm sorry the burden of ending the rebellion was placed on you. It wasn't fair, and I know you're haunted by your part in it, but you're still a good man. I refuse to stand idly by while Bernadette turns every member of the council against you. The crown belongs on your head, and I'll be damned if I let anyone steal it from you."

Upon receiving her colorful words of support, Gregory felt a sharp twinge of guilt brewing in the pit of his stomach. Instead of feeling honored or pleased that she so faithfully admired him, he was swarmed with the painful awareness of his unworthiness. He always aimed to be the person Elizabeth believed him to be, but consistently fell short. He didn't deserve her patronage, yet she never failed to offer it.

"Greg?"

"Yes?"

"I'm scared of what'll happen during your meeting with His Majesty."

"So am I, but let's not think about that yet. I've been gone for six months, and right now all I want to do is enjoy a few minutes of peace before entering the lion's den. Deal?"

Elizabeth acknowledged his request with a glum nod.

"I'm finished, Your Highness."

Gregory blinked, confounded to find himself fully dressed already. He'd been so distracted by the conversation with Elizabeth that he'd forgotten what was going on around him. As usual, the servant faded into the background, completing his task in silence.

"Is there anything else you would like me to do for you?"

"A cup of ale, please."

With a deferential bow, the groom headed into the next room to get the beverage.

"Greg, there's a whole feast waiting for you in the hall."

Hence my need for the ale. "I know, but that can wait a bit longer. I have something to show you before we go down."

CHAPTER 3

*P*rincess Elizabeth practically fell off the edge of her seat as she leaned forward and rubbed her hands together. "Really? What is it?"

"Here you are, Your Highness."

Greg took the cup from his servant, drank a hearty gulp, and reached into the travel bag at his feet. His eyes aglow, he pulled out a small bundle.

"A gift?" Elizabeth bounded off the chair and took the tiny package from Greg's hand. She eagerly untied the red ribbon and when the cloth unfolded, a stunning emerald ring was revealed. Her jaw dropped as she twirled the piece of jewelry in her fingers. "Thank y–"

"I'm going to propose to Lady Rochester tonight." Greg set the cup on his bedside table and plopped onto the mattress, his arms crossed behind his head as he stared up at the ceiling with the stupidest grin on his face. "I wanted you to be the first to know."

Elizabeth's smile evaporated. Feeling as though she'd swallowed a rock, she rewrapped the engagement ring and walked back to the fireplace, then deposited it on the mantle.

She chewed her lip and stared into the flames. Despite the heat, Elizabeth's skin turned to goose flesh. The time had come for the conversation she'd been dreading. She hated herself for what she was about to do to her brother. It had to be done, but she'd hoped to postpone the admission until after the feast. She'd rather suffer another of her father's thrashings than be the one to deliver this heartbreaking news.

"Well?" Behind her, Greg's tone took on a slight edge. "It's common knowledge that you aren't fond of Lucy. Nevertheless, I expected you to say something positive about my intent to propose marriage. A simple congratulations will suffice."

Elizabeth tutted. *Not fond of her? I hate her.*

"You can't propose to her tonight." Her voice was flat, no hint of regret. Chin held high, she twirled around to face her brother. "I've sent her away."

Greg jolted upright and swung his legs over the side of the bed, his veins straining against his mottled skin.

"Before you get angry–"

"I'm already angry!" he hissed. "What possible reason could you have for–"

"I'd prefer to speak about this in private." She cast a scowl at the servant who lingered as he poured more ale into Greg's already-full cup. "This isn't a conversation I want anyone else to overhear."

His eyes sharp as needles, Greg reached for his glass. Ale spilled over the rim as he ignored the groom's presence altogether. "You had no right to cast her out, Elizabeth. Tomorrow morning I'm going to retrieve her, and you'll apologize as soon as we return. Do you understand?"

Elizabeth snorted. *There's no way in hell I'm apologizing to that whore!*

She felt no remorse for the terrible insults she'd thrown at

Lucy upon discovering her affair. Nor did she regret the slap across the cheek that she'd dealt the strumpet for her lewdness. In all honesty, that harlot deserved much worse!

"All I'm asking is for you to be civil. Is that so difficult?"

"Yes!" Elizabeth set her mouth firmly and met the hostile glare in her brother's eyes, hoping she looked less timid than she felt. "There's something you need to know about–"

"Unless you're going to say how happy you are for me, I don't want to hear it."

"Please." She stole a glimpse at the redheaded servant who now stood beside the door with his eyes forward and hands behind his back. He'd remain rooted there unless he was dismissed. Stoic and silent, yet no doubt hanging on every word. "Will you please speak with me alone?"

"No. I'm well aware of your distrust in Lucy, but I care about her, and I hope you can set aside your differences and offer us your blessing."

Elizabeth took a deep breath and sat down on the bed next to him. "There's no easy way to say this, so I'll just come right out with it. She's been unfaithful to you, Greg. I've had my suspicions for a while, so when I noticed her sneaking out to the gardens a few nights ago, I followed her. She went deeper into the labyrinth than I ever dared go by myself, but she obviously memorized the route because she didn't hesitate at a single turn or fork in the path."

Greg's face turned a deeper shade of red with every word she spoke, but Elizabeth didn't let his flaring nostrils or twitching jaw preclude her from saying more. He deserved to know the truth, and no matter how much it pained her to be the one to break it to him, it was best he hear it from her.

"I trailed her for at least ten minutes, and when she finally reached her destination, Thomas was there, waiting for her.

I'll spare you the details but suffice it to say that I witnessed their intimate relations firsthand. I'm sorry."

The color in Greg's cheeks rose and his fists clenched atop his lap. "That's impossible. It couldn't have been Lucy."

"I'm sorry," Elizabeth repeated, sincere in her words. "I really wanted to wait until tomorrow to tell you, but–"

"Enough." The spit that had been building up in the corners of Greg's mouth sprayed across the space between them, showering Elizabeth's cheek. "It wasn't Lucy."

"I saw them with my own eyes. I crouched behind the hedge, but since I didn't know the way out, I had to wait until they–"

"I said that's enough!" Greg jumped to his feet. His outburst reverberated off the walls and the servant guarding the door flinched. "I will not have you speak of her in that way."

"It wasn't just that once," Elizabeth continued, her tone as sensitive as her own impatience would allow. "I asked around and others admitted to witnessing similar occurrences. She made no attempt to be discreet."

Greg's chin jerked. "You're lying."

"I am not!"

He took a step toward her, leaning so close their noses almost touched. "I thought you of all people would be happy for me."

Lucy is the one who betrayed his trust, yet I'm the one he's angry with?

Elizabeth's eyes misted and she twisted her hands, wishing she had something to clutch onto. "I would be happy if you were marrying *anyone* else," she explained in a placating tone. "But Lucy is a strumpet who wants nothing more than to be married to the future king of Caracalla. She wants the wealth and influence that comes along with being your queen."

"You're wrong. I'm not sure what she did to deserve your hatred, but I'm marrying her. Do you offer your blessing or not?"

Elizabeth kept her gaze trained on her lap, shaking her head in refusal. "I can't. I won't bless a marriage that's based on greed and lies." She spoke in as level a voice as she could manage. "You deserve so much better. You deserve happiness, and Lucy isn't going to bring you that. She's an unfaithful, power-seeking, she-devil. I'm sorry, but I can't support this."

Greg's lips pulled back as he darted over to the hearth and snatched the emerald ring off the mantle. "Lucy is to be my wife, and if you don't support her, then you don't support me. I'm giving you one last chance to take back your lies."

"Please don't do this." Elizabeth's voice cracked, but she refused to recoil in the face of his anger. "That's not fair. I've always supported you, but she doesn't deserve–"

"I'll ask one more time, Elizabeth. Will you support my marriage or not?"

With a drawn-out sigh, she straightened her shoulders and boldly looked into Greg's incensed eyes. "I will not."

"Then you're dead to me."

Elizabeth let out a gasp as her brother's words sliced through her heart, cleaving it in half. Cold shook her to the core, and she clutched at her pearl necklace, breathless. "You don't mean that." Her throat burned as a procession of hot tears slid down her cheek. "Greg–"

"Yes, I do." With his terrible remark polluting the air, Greg thrust a finger at the door. "Get out."

"But–"

"Now!"

Crestfallen, Elizabeth ignored the groomsman's flabbergasted stare as she stood and tearfully excused herself from the room.

～

Gregory collapsed onto the edge of the bed and rubbed his hands through his dark hair. His mind ached, but despite the gossip, he refused to acknowledge his relationship with Lucy as a failure. If he believed what Elizabeth told him, even for a moment, then he'd have no choice but to admit defeat.

It's not true. Gregory's reflection glared back at him from the full-length mirror across the room. *She's in love with me.*

He fell backward onto the mattress, trying hard to ignore the terrible thoughts dancing in his head as he closed his eyes and envisioned Lucy's flawless face.

"Your Highness?"

"What?"

"Don't you want to join the feast? It was prepared in your honor, and everyone is eager to welcome you home."

Not everyone. "I'll head down shortly." His stomach was a bundle of knots and perspiration anointed his brow as he got up and quaffed back the entire cup of ale. "Tell me honestly, how's His Majesty's mood today?"

"Foul. I recommend you make haste."

I'd be more excited about getting a boil lanced. "Noted. You're dismissed."

"As you wish, Your Highness." With a swish of his cloak, the groom spun around and closed the door behind him.

Gregory's breathing was labored, and the alcohol sat like a rock in his stomach. He splashed water from the basin on his face, steeling himself for whatever suffering was to come.

The king didn't tolerate disobedience on his best days, but

on his worst days he punished his son's infractions with a number of fresh bruises. That said, Gregory was no longer a child. At twenty-two years old, he was a grown man, strong enough to defend himself against his father's abusive tirades. No matter how livid he was, King Charles had to know his son could easily overpower him now.

Gregory's fear melted away as the realization that he was untouchable sunk in. If the king laid a hand on him or his little sister ever again, Gregory wouldn't hesitate to snap their father's wrist in half.

His lips curled into a perverse little smile as he made his way into his closet and rummaged through the wooden chest that contained his dozens of hats. The soft fabric was drastically different from the suit of armor he'd worn during the last six months, and it felt good to be able to move about without the loud clanging and banging to announce his every step.

He placed a red velvet hat on his head and a golden chain adorned with a pendant of his sigil, the Tree of Life, around his neck. Satisfied with his reflection, he strutted to the Great Hall, confident he could handle whatever reproach he was about to receive.

CHAPTER 4

*P*rince Gregory held his head high as he strode into the large, rectangular hall. Its walls were adorned with glorious tapestries woven of golden thread, and the ornate, hammer-beamed roof stood sixty feet tall. Sunlight poured in from the high, stained glass windows and glistened on the wooden floor.

The Great Hall was the heart of Crompton, the most impressive room inside the palace, and served as the center of activity and entertainment at court. At present, the tables on either side were so crammed that the feasters couldn't lift their fork to their mouths without elbowing the person next to them. This often led to drunken feuds and brawls amongst the nobility, but not today.

As Gregory advanced up the middle of the hall, marching toward the raised platform at the opposite end, the lively music ceased, and a sudden hush blanketed the room.

"Welcome home," King Charles greeted from his place at the head table. His hawk-like eyes slid toward his son and settled on him in an expression of wintery condemnation.

"Thank you." Gregory's automatic reply didn't possess a tinge of gratitude. He bowed in front of the king, but it was his younger sister his gaze landed on.

She too was seated at the head table, her features darkened as she stabbed at her plate and sank her teeth into whatever it was she'd speared with her fork. He tried to catch her averted eye, but it was no use.

He'd never said anything so horrible to her and now he profoundly regretted the harsh words he'd spoken. He'd been angry, yes, but to say she was dead to him was out of line and unreasonably cruel.

Gregory shot her an apologetic frown, but since her attention was directed at her plate of food, Elizabeth remained unaware of his efforts to make peace.

"It's about time you graced us with your presence." King Charles looked down his nose as he assessed his son. "This is *your* homecoming feast, after all."

"His Majesty doesn't like waiting," Princess Bernadette chimed in from her place adjacent to the king's left hand. "It's almost as if you aren't excited to see us." Her eyes burned into him as she clicked her tongue. "You should apologize at once."

"My apologies," said Gregory, fighting the urge to roll his eyes. He stepped forward to take his seat in the chair to the right of the king. The honored spot belonged to him, the heir directly after King Charles in the line of succession.

"Stay there." His Majesty pressed his lips together and glared down at him.

Puzzled, Gregory stopped dead in his tracks.

"I wished to wait until *tomorrow* for this." The king sneered at the general, who immediately dropped the turkey leg he'd been gnawing on and wiped the sauce from his mustache. "However, General Howard insisted we discuss your accomplishments in the north while we have food in our bellies. He seems to think I'm not going to like what you have to say."

You're not. Gregory's mouth went dry as he eyed the exits.

With a wave of his hand, His Majesty motioned at Howard. "Make it quick."

The general hopped to his feet and yelled loud enough for the people at the back of the hall to hear. "Your Majesty, in my professional opinion, nothing has been accomplished. The entire campaign was a waste of time."

Damn it. Here we go. Gregory inhaled through his nose and puffed out his chest.

"Excuse me?" The king's mouth twitched. "You were away for six months, and you claim *nothing* was accomplished?"

Howard paled a bit. "I say this because after the rebels surrendered at the Battle of Clafton Point, most of them were permitted to go home. I predict another uprising by summer's end."

Fists clenched, King Charles's veins strained against his skin.

"Your Majesty, I tried to persuade him, but he's so stubborn. He refused–"

King Charles raised his hand in the air, stopping Howard midsentence. His attention shifted to Gregory, and he stared at him accusingly. "Is this true?"

Sweat sprang out on Gregory's neck. "Somewhat."

His Majesty drew in a great breath. "Don't play coy with me, son. My orders were clear. 'Snuff out the rebellion and teach those ingrates a lesson the whole kingdom will remember'. Either you obeyed my command, or you didn't. Success or failure. Which was it?"

Gregory's aplomb sank with all the speed of an anchor plummeting down to the bottom of the sea. His eyes darted toward Elizabeth, the only person he'd admitted his 'failure' to, but her countenance was unreadable.

Bernadette, on the other hand, watched this interrogation through giddy eyes. To her, Gregory was a mere insect that needed to be squashed if she wanted to achieve her maximum potential. She said so often.

"Look at me, and answer the goddamn question!"

Gregory lifted his chin and looked his father squarely in the eyes. "Hundreds of rebels were killed in the battle, and after their surrender, I personally dealt with the *leaders* of the rebellion. Suppressing the rebels and ending their revolt was a great victory, but it seems that still isn't adequate proof of my worthiness to inherit the throne. What more do I have to do to prove myself?"

King Charles narrowed his eyes until they were mere slits in his face. "You disobeyed me."

Gregory kept his response brief and to the point. "It would've been senseless and unconscionable to massacre them when they'd already given themselves up. It was over."

"It's *not* over," the general piped in. His nasally voice made Gregory's ears ring. "Thousands of men raised the treacherous banner against our beloved realm." For dramatic effect, Howard took the flag he'd seized in battle and thrust it in the air. Gregory ignored the gasps of the courtiers as they viewed the bloodstained fabric.

"And they suffered for it! In the six months we were at war, more than half the rebels died at the end of our swords. The terms of the truce were that their army would disband for good in exchange for the lives we'd spare. It was a reasonable arrangement."

"They were to be an example!" The general threw the flag

onto the ground and stomped on it. "Killing those who rebel against our sovereign is essential if we truly intend to teach the rest of the kingdom a lesson. Otherwise, what will stop their army from assembling again tomorrow?"

Gregory was fed up with this man's ignorance. "The leaders were all judged and executed for their crimes. Any more deaths would've been unnecessary. I made them a deal, and I trust they'll honor it. I'm telling you, the rebellion is over."

A thunderous bang echoed throughout the tension-filled room, silencing all.

Gregory saw Elizabeth flinch when their father's clenched fist slammed onto the table, but as she took a sip from her cup, not even a shred of emotion seeped into her blank expression.

"I gave you orders!" The king's red face contorted, and the veins on his neck enlarged. "I told you to exterminate the rebels. How dare you disobey my direct commands in order to honor the unsanctioned agreement you made with those lawless insurgents! I told you to kill them all, and you spared their lives in the interest of a peaceful resolution I didn't agree to! You are a disgrace to the House of Cavendish!"

The members of nobility were soundless as King Charles shot to his feet and leapt off the side of the platform. He stamped over and put his face inches from his son's.

"How many leaders did you hang?" His Majesty's voice boomed throughout the hall.

As the eyes of the nobles bore into him, Gregory squared his shoulders and straightened his spine. "Thirty-six. But as I said before, hundreds were slaughtered at Clafton Point before they surrendered. Plus, they suffered heavy losses in all the previous battles. The complete number of casualties—"

"Thirty-six?" King Charles repeated the number in an ear-splitting howl and directed his attention to General Howard. "How strong were the rebel forces?"

"At least twenty-five hundred men fought against us, Your Majesty."

Bernadette burst into a fit of laughter and all eyes in the room turned her way. "It seems as if my brother's math is a little off," she snickered. Moving with purpose and grace, she rose from her chair and descended the steps of the dais. She marched up to her father's *right* side and declared, "Either he's a fool…or he sympathizes with the rebels."

Her accusation hung in the air like an odorous gas, poisoning the minds of all those who'd allow it.

Gregory's jaw tightened as he met his elder sister's virulent gaze head-on, but he dared not open his mouth for fear of being sick. Like everyone else, he waited to see what would come of Bernadette's inexcusable attack upon his honor.

Only a few seconds passed before the charged silence was broken by General Howard. "I judge Princess Bernadette's assessment to be correct. After traveling with him for the past six months, I have come to one conclusion…"

The general paused, and Gregory's entire body stiffened.

He won't complete that sentence. His breath hitched, and he panicked for a moment, but he settled when he realized the deceitful accusation of treachery would cost the general his position in the Royal Forces. No one would believe the impossible lie, and Howard would be expelled from Crompton for suggesting such a thing. Was the general really foolish enough to risk everything he had just to satisfy Bernadette's lifelong goal to discredit Gregory?

Eager to bring a swift end to the ghastly predicament he now found himself in, Gregory lost all patience. "Dispense with the dramatics, Howard. If you have something to say–"

"You are a traitor!"

The public denunciation served as a verbal punch to Gregory's abdomen, knocking the wind out of him and turning his knees to jelly. He opened his mouth to contest the allegation made against him, but his astonishment at being so overtly vilified overtook his ability to speak.

Noisy chatter erupted throughout the crowded hall as the courtiers shared their opinions with one another. While many of them seemed to think Howard had gone mad, quite a decent number of them appeared to take the general's words to heart.

"Nothing could be further from the truth," Gregory argued, a ring of terror in his newly found voice. Barely able to be heard over the frenzied chaos, he raised his volume. "I'd never do anything to betray my kingdom! This is outrageous!"

His brain was on fire, and it felt as if the air itself was strangling him. Once you were branded a traitor, there was no going back. A full-scale trial would ensue, and it could take months to clear his name. The sudden awareness that imprisonment would be his fate in the meantime swelled up inside him, and his blood pressure rose with every thump of his heart.

A cold sweat washed over him. He was outnumbered. There were plenty of council members who considered Bernadette to be Gregory's better, and they'd happily accept the accusation as truth.

"Listen to me! I'm not a traitor!"

Frantic, he looked to Elizabeth for support. He immediately wished he hadn't, for when his eyes found hers, he was overwhelmed by a suffocating, frosty surge of despair. Instead of offering him reassurance, Elizabeth's stone-cold gaze stared straight through him, as if she didn't see him at all.

No emotion leaked through her tough demeanor, and it was then that Gregory realized he'd lost her. If this had happened an hour ago, she would've jumped to his defense the second the accusation surfaced, and every noble in the room would've listened to her. She was the favorite of many of them, even above Bernadette, and Gregory knew she could raise her own private army if she ever got the inkling to do so.

But it was too late. The nasty words he'd spoken to her earlier shredded any ounce of love she had for him. He was the one now dead to *her*.

Gregory's heart sank. He was alone. His one and only ally had quit on him, and he had no one to blame but himself. The realization brought a sob to his throat, but he pushed it back down with a desperate gulp and redirected his attention to the king. He could practically see the flames roaring in his father's eyes.

"Silence!" As King Charles demanded, an eerie hush fell over the Great Hall. No one made a sound as their sovereign visibly thought about what the princess and general had just said. It felt like an eternity had passed before the stillness broke. "Gregory, for showing mercy to the traitors, I have no option but to declare you a traitor as well."

Again, the members of the king's court exploded in uproar. Those loyal to Bernadette whooped and cheered, while the rest were suspended in a petrified state of alarm.

"You're sentencing me without a trial?" Gregory couldn't believe his ears. Had His Majesty really just denied him, the Prince of Caracalla, the right to a trial? Even peasants were given the opportunity to defend themselves in court.

"Your behavior speaks for itself. You are a traitor."

"Your Majesty! No!" Elizabeth's horrified outburst was the only sound Gregory picked up. It seemed this had finally gone too far for her to handle, regardless of her wounded feelings.

To be branded a traitor meant death. The hairs on the nape of his neck bristled as his imagination painted vivid pictures of his demise in his mind. He could almost feel the axe coming down on his neck already, and he wrestled with his natural instinct to run. Even if his feet weren't boulders holding him down, he had nowhere to go. The King's Guard was vigilant and would have him pinned to the ground before he took three strides.

"Your Majesty?" Elizabeth's voice was hoarse, as if she too was about to be sick. She cleared her throat and tried again, this attempt louder than her last. "Your Majesty, this is unjust!"

King Charles raised his voice to drown her out as he continued with grim resolve. "As you are my blood, I'll grant you life. However, if you ever set foot on my land again, you'll be hanged, drawn, and quartered. Your lifeless body will be an example to all of those who wish to defy me. Let it be known that rebels and their sympathizers won't be tolerated in my kingdom. Your title is hereby revoked, and Princess Bernadette is now heir to the throne. You're exiled from this realm."

"Greg's not a traitor!" Elizabeth shot a fleeting glance toward him as she got up from her chair. This time, when her brown eyes met his, they weren't polished and cold but brimming with unshed tears. "Your Majesty, please, reconsider. You're making a grievous mistake!"

King Charles ignored his distraught daughter's pleas and motioned for the guards to seize Gregory. They didn't hesitate. Gregory's sword was ripped from its sheath, leaving him defenseless.

"Let go of me!" His attempts to escape the firm grasps of the guards were ineffective. There were four of them, and every time Gregory managed to shake one off, another jumped in to take his place. "Unhand me!"

"Greg!" Elizabeth raced over to the steps, but she was blocked in an instant by Captain Blanchard, a burly man whose crotchety face lacked even the tiniest glister of charity. She lifted her skirts and ran back the other way, only to be trapped atop the platform when more retainers surrounded her. "Move! Let me through! Greg!"

As she hopped around like a wild hare cornered by a pack of wolves, Gregory locked eyes with her, and she stopped. He intended to promise her everything was going to be fine, but when his lips parted, a pathetic little croak was all that emerged. His attempt to reassure her floundered, badly. Elizabeth broke eye contact with him and resumed her harried efforts to push through the guards encompassing her.

With his arms restrained behind his back, Gregory's captors pulled him backwards, farther away from the head table and his sister.

"Get him out of here!" King Charles swatted his son away like a pesky fly.

"Greg!" Elizabeth screamed again, much louder. "Greg!"

The king's face turned purple and the vein on his forehead throbbed as he reeled on his youngest. "I suggest you shut your mouth unless you crave a thrashing!"

"This is lunacy," she shot back at him. "You know he's not a traitor!"

Enraged, King Charles raised his fist, shaking it at Elizabeth. "Silence that hole in your face before I silence it for you! Say one more word, and I'll strike you so hard you won't even remember your name. Do you understand me?"

Gregory didn't see what happened next, for he was dragged out of the hall by the armed guards and tossed out into the humid summer evening.

CHAPTER 5

*I*t was almost daybreak when Hawthorne Manor came into view.

His mood bolstered by the sight of Lord Rochester's estate, Gregory pushed himself to keep moving through the thick wall of morning fog. He knew if he stopped for even a moment, his legs wouldn't permit him to begin again. He'd been walking all night, refusing to take a break even as storm clouds poured heavy rain upon him.

With an overwhelming sense of accomplishment, Gregory passed through the vaporous, dew-covered meadow that led to the mansion in the distance. His stomach growled, and he wondered if Lucy would have the cook prepare breakfast for him. The notion helped quicken his steps as he approached the front door.

The closer he got to the entrance, however, the louder his second thoughts screamed for him to stop. He'd been doing his best to ignore them, but now that he was here, his doubts demanded to be heard.

What if Elizabeth is right?

Has Lucy been unfaithful?

Does she even care about me at all?

Gregory pushed up his sleeves. *I need to find out.* He threw his shoulders back and strode around to the back of the house where a large oak tree stood. The thick branches led right to an open window.

He grinned at his luck. If he could sneak inside and catch Lucy unaware, she wouldn't have time to formulate a lie when confronted about the supposed affair. By springing the question on her, he'd be able to gauge her reaction with his own eyes. She'd be forced to tell the truth, whatever it may be.

Either way, I need to know for sure.

He took a deep breath, then reached for the lowest branch. As a child he'd mastered the art of climbing trees, and although a number of years had passed since his last tree-top excursion, Gregory made his way up the trunk with ease.

He did his best to stifle a grunt as he pulled himself onto the rain splattered windowsill. Out of breath, he climbed inside, grateful to whoever had opened the shutters this morning. His feet landed on the slippery floor with a careless thud and like a wide-eyed stag in the forest, he froze in place. Gregory's gaze darted around the room and came to rest on the bed in the corner. It was empty.

The dolls on the shelf and rocking horse in the middle of the carpet indicated this was the bedchamber of Lucy's younger sister, Millie. Gregory released the air he'd been holding in his lungs. Like most noble children, she was probably practicing her morning prayers with her governess, downstairs.

His wet boots squeaked as he went over to the door and peered into the corridor. He waited with bated breath and strained his ears for any indication that his intrusion had been discovered. To his relief, it wasn't.

Now it was time to face the next problem. He'd never visited Lucy's home before. She preferred to live at court, attending lavish parties and showing off her fanciest dresses. As Gregory contemplated which way to go in these unfamiliar halls, the single comment Lucy had made regarding her life at Hawthorne Manor sprouted in his memory. *Back home, every wretched day is the same. The sun's blinding rays shine through my bedroom window, waking me far too early for a day I've already lived a thousand times before.*

Eager to be the change Lucy so desperately craved, Gregory had invited her to live at Crompton Palace in his next breath, gifting her with permanent lodgings overlooking the Base Courtyard. She settled into court life straight away, attending every banquet, sporting event, and show with the happiest smile illuminating her face. Like the sun, Lucy was born to shine. His Majesty's court was her sky.

She'd packed her trunks without a second thought when asked to trade the monotony of Hawthorne Manor for the excitement of Crompton, but would she be willing to pack them again in order to join him in exile?

His steps guided by the morning sun, Gregory swallowed those fears as he tiptoed through the halls toward the east side of the house. He'd have his answer soon enough.

He paused every so often, listening for footsteps that never came. His own anxious breaths were the only sound he heard in the deserted corridors.

In a great estate such as this, the halls should have been bustling with activity as servants prepared for the day. There were always linens to wash, fires to stoke, meals to cook, and shelves to dust. It seemed Lord Rochester's servants weren't quite as disciplined as His Majesty's early-risers. Then again, there was an enormous difference between running the household of a baron and servicing the hundreds of courtiers who resided in the court of King Charles.

Gregory skulked along the corridor with the light of dawn glimmering through the windows to his right, his attention drawn to a handmade sign hanging on one of the doors. The name *Lucy* was carved neatly into the wood, and Gregory cracked a smile, pleased to see the entrance to Lucy's private room adorned with his own handiwork.

He placed his hand on the latch and was about to open it when the sound of lustful moans reached his ears. His blood boiled in response to the erotic noises, and he whipped the door open so hard, it slammed against the wall.

Alarmed by the intrusion, the startled couple broke apart and struggled to cover their sweaty, naked bodies with the blanket.

"Lucy…" Gregory's breath clogged in his throat, and as his eyes shifted to the man beside her, his heart was clawed out of his chest.

Elizabeth was telling the truth.

The rage expanded inside him, and he reached for his sword, forgetting it'd been stolen from him the night before. "Thomas," he spat with venom.

With her disarrayed blonde hair hanging loose past her bare shoulders, Lucy's voice trembled. "L-let me explain."

Gregory sniffed. His head spun as an entire army of questions charged rampant through his mind. He gave voice to the most pressing one. "How long?"

Lucy's sapphire eyes filled with tears. "Greg–"

"How long?" He was so intent on Lucy he didn't even hear the steward behind him. Without warning, the head servant wrapped his arm around Gregory's neck in a choke hold.

Gregory grabbed the man's forearm and stepped to the

side, leaving his opponent's vulnerable area exposed. He swung his fist back and struck him in the groin. The man's head flew forward with a grunt. Gregory then jerked his elbow up, smashing it into his enemy's jaw.

Satisfied by the loud crunch, Gregory twisted around and escaped the arms of the steward. "Answer the question." His gaze shot back to Lucy as he held the servant steady in a headlock. "Now."

"Five months," she confessed with a shudder.

"Five months?" The thought scalded his insides. "You couldn't even wait more than a month after I left?"

Thomas rose from the bed, unclothed and making no effort to cover his private piece. "She never loved you," he sneered. "She seduced you, as her father instructed. The Rochester family wanted more power, and what better way to do that than to put one of them on the throne?"

"Watch your tongue," Gregory advised through clenched teeth.

"It was the crown she envisioned as she bedded you."

"Shut up!"

Arrogant as ever, Thomas chuckled. "She loves *me*."

Gregory shoved the steward away and let loose with his fist. A sickening crack filled the air, and Lucy screamed as blood leaked from Thomas's nostrils.

In that brief moment of chaos, the steward lunged forward and thrust a dagger at Gregory. Jumping aside, he avoided the blade.

The steward spun and charged again.

Gregory braced for the dive and maneuvered around it once more, then shoved the servant's head into the wall. He collapsed onto the floor in a disgraceful heap. Gregory kicked the weapon out of reach and frowned at the unconscious man at his feet.

"You'll pay for this." Thomas threw a punch while Gregory was distracted, aiming for his turned head.

Gregory ducked and delivered one of his own to his cousin's abdomen.

Holding his stomach as blood flowed from his nose, Thomas spat a crimson glob onto the floor.

Gregory's lips curled into a sneer. "Need a moment?"

Foaming at the mouth, Thomas rushed forward and rammed his shoulder into Gregory's waist. He wrapped his arms around Gregory's hips and pushed him backward into the bookshelf.

Pain sizzled down Gregory's spine as his back slammed into the wood and half a dozen silver candlesticks were knocked to the floor with a deafening clatter. Pressed against the furniture, he jerked his knee up, gratified by the agonized groan it evoked from Thomas as he leaned forward, clutching his exposed crotch.

Gregory put his fists up, ready to strike again. "Next time put some clothes on, imbecile."

Thomas growled, wincing as he set his back straight. All of a sudden, he launched himself at Gregory, sending him flying backward. Lucy's earsplitting screams echoed through the house as the cousins landed on the floor with a unified *thump*.

Thomas scrambled on top of Gregory and started raining hammer fists down on him. Pinned and blocking his head, Gregory shifted side to side to avoid the blow. A few landed, and he knew he had to get out from under Thomas. He grabbed a hold of his cousin's waist and pulled him down, then wrapped his leg around Thomas's foot, trapping it. He hooked his arm over Thomas's and flipped him over onto his back.

Gregory jumped up and licked his bloodied lip. "Had enough?"

"No," Thomas spat back, his breathing ragged as he pushed himself off the floor. "I won't have my fill until you're dead."

Gregory clenched his hands into fists. Stabbing pain coursed through his arm, and he relaxed his hand, hoping none of his fingers were broken. He masked his pain behind a challenging stare.

Thomas's deranged gaze flicked to the steward's discarded knife.

There was a second's pause, then a flash of movement as both men dove for the weapon.

The ensuing tussle was over before Gregory even realized it'd begun. He couldn't say how it happened, but Thomas lay sprawled out on the floor, a slow, ominous puddle of red seeping from a puncture in his gut.

Shit. Gregory's head whirled, and bile climbed into his throat. "Tom. I didn't mean to–"

"Thomas!" Lucy slid off the bed and pressed her hands into his stomach to stop the bleeding. She whirled on Gregory, eyes wide and teeth bared. "You stabbed him!"

Gregory dropped the blade and fled.

CHAPTER 6

*P*rincess Elizabeth's sadistic sister was obsessed with fire. Bernadette often spoke of her love for the element, admiring the way it could appear peaceful and warming one minute and burn someone alive the next. Since this was her congratulatory celebration for being moved up to first place in the line of succession, she'd been permitted to select the entertainment. Alvin the Fire Lord was a fitting choice.

The buff, shirtless man leaned his head back and slid the flaming sword down his throat. The audience roared with applause upon seeing such a daring spectacle. Even the king grinned as he sipped his beloved canary wine.

"Amazing!" Bernadette jumped to her feet and clapped, her eyes sparkling. Upon receiving a charming wink from the performer as he prepared for his next dangerous act, she fell back into her seat with a contented smile plastered on her face.

"I wonder what he'll do next." She sounded half-anxious and half-admiring as she gawked at the Fire Lord. "Fire can be very uncontrollable."

Elizabeth pursed her lips, saying nothing as she kept her hands folded in her lap. It was getting progressively more difficult to hold her tongue though, for the unabated exuberance in her sister's voice made her sick with resentment.

Sitting atop the dais as the mindless courtiers allowed entertainment to distract them from the unfathomable plight of their prince, Elizabeth despised herself for attending this wretched event at all. She should've held firm in her boycott of it, refusing to submit even after His Majesty threatened to punish her insolence by having her put in the pillory overnight.

"Your disagreeable behavior is dampening my mood," Bernadette grumbled, making zero effort to hide the displeasure Elizabeth's sullenness caused her. "This is the happiest day of my life. Could you at least try to be amiable?"

Elizabeth swept her icy gaze over Bernadette and wondered how it was possible for the two of them to have the same blood running through their veins. "Forgive me. I wasn't aware your mood was so heavily influenced by my personal distaste for…this." She motioned toward the performer who was now doing cartwheels through iron rings that had been set on fire.

"He's a legend." Bernadette directed her attention to the muscular man and dreamily added, "No one can do the things he can."

As the reflection of the fire glowed in Bernadette's eyes, Elizabeth was reminded of a painting she'd once seen of Satan biting the head off a child. The unnerving comparison gave her chills, and she returned her gaze to the show taking place in the center of the hall.

Unlike the other spectators, Elizabeth wasn't impressed by the man's ability to set things on fire. Of course, a week ago she would've been delighted by the show, but everything was different now.

Just yesterday, her innocent brother had been charged with treason and banished. So how could the intolerable usurper possibly expect Elizabeth to be amiable toward her? Did she really expect her to sit here and act like she was happy that "*Burn*-a-dette" had been given Greg's rightful title?

"Ooo, this is the part I was telling you about." Bernadette elbowed her in the arm to get her attention. "This is his encore!"

Elizabeth groaned and rubbed her now-throbbing arm as she looked up to see the lunatic lowering himself into a tub of black pitch. She'd heard rumors from her lady's maids that the performer was going to light himself on fire at the end of the show, but she'd denied the plausibility of such a thing.

However, it now appeared as though there was some truth behind it.

"He's a madman." Elizabeth straightened in her seat so she could get a better view. Despicable as this cursed celebration was, she couldn't stem her curiosity. Like everyone else crammed together in the Great Hall, her eyes were wide as she watched the shirtless, pitch-covered man climb out of the tub.

Bernadette shook her head. "Not mad, courageous."

Elizabeth bit her tongue, for not even in her indignant state could she deny he possessed great courage. The performer's entire body was coated with the thick, black substance as he stepped forward.

"Princess Bernadette," he called to her as she smiled down at him from atop the royal dais. "Would you do me the honor of setting me ablaze?"

Bernadette hopped to her feet and rushed down the platform steps. She pulled one of the candlesticks out of its holder and took her place in the middle of the large room, next to the performer as she impatiently waited to be given the cue to light him on fire.

Men with buckets of water surrounded the audacious Fire Lord. Counting the men, Elizabeth prickled with unease. Five. There were only five. She was no Fire Lord, but she doubted five buckets of water would be enough to put out the blaze.

Building the tension, as well as his audience's excitement, Alvin the Fire Lord gave a quick speech about the severe consequences one would endure if they ever tried to copy the hazardous act. "I've practiced the art of fire manipulation for many years," he boasted, then turned to Bernadette. "Light me up."

Just as she stretched her arm out to do so, a man charged into the Great Hall, waving his sword into the air in a display of hostility. He stomped forward in such a fury that the crowd was compelled to part so he could pass. He was clearly in want of the king's undivided attention.

Letting out a yelp in response to the invasion, Bernadette dropped the lit candle on the floor as a group of guards surrounded her.

Also encircled by a ring of security, Elizabeth shot up from her chair with all the gusto of a racehorse hearing gunfire for the first time. She stood on her tiptoes and craned her neck in an effort to see what was going on.

"I demand an audience with His Majesty!" To unsheathe your sword in the presence of the king was a crime punishable by death, but as always, the Duke of Salvatore thought himself the exception to the rule. "I won't be turned away!"

"I'm right here." King Charles dismissed his guards with a casual wave of his hand. They stepped back, but remained watchful, ready to jump to their sovereign's aid in case his brother-in-law should attack. "Your Grace, this uncouth intrusion has disrupted your niece's Succession Celebration."

"It can't wait!" Salvatore's scorching gaze scanned the faces in the crowd. "Where is he?"

King Charles raised his brow. "Who?"

"Prince Gregory!" His murderous eyes locked squarely on Elizabeth. "Where's that monstrous brother of yours?"

Elizabeth gulped, horrified by the hatred glaring back at her. Even if she did know where he was, she certainly wouldn't give that information to her uncle!

"He's not here," the king answered. He held his goblet in the air and offered the Duke of Salvatore a drink. "Please, join us. We were about to witness a true test of bravery."

"The prince assaulted my son, and you offer wine? I want revenge!"

King Charles slammed his fist down on his armrest. "Enough! I've been more than tolerant of this outburst thus far, but I warn you, my patience is waning. Any other man would've been dragged out and hung from a rope by now. You know that, don't you?"

As though he suddenly remembered his place and to whom he was speaking, the Duke of Salvatore folded into a bow so low his nose all but touched the floor. "Yes, Your Majesty. I beg your pardon for my reprehensible behavior."

The king shrugged with indifference. He'd always favored the late queen's youngest brother, and in this case, Elizabeth knew that was the only reason the Duke of Salvatore was still standing. Like he'd said, a lesser man would've earned himself an execution for this sort of outburst.

"Now tell me," His Majesty said, sounding curious. "What is it you've come here to seek revenge for?"

Salvatore perked up. "As you well know, Prince Gregory

was away for quite some time. In his absence, Lady Lucy Rochester sought affection elsewhere and fell in love with my Thomas, your faithful and loving nephew. When His Highness discovered the two of them together this morning, he acted out in a jealous fit and stabbed Thomas. The physicians are with him now and doing all they can, but it's possible Tom will die of his injuries."

Elizabeth choked on a laugh, powerless to wipe the grin off her face even after her uncle threw her a fierce look of rebuke.

Thomas was one of the cruelest young men Elizabeth knew, and she'd always hoped fate would deal him the blow he so desperately deserved. He was a vicious monster, to say the least. Tears still sprang to Elizabeth's eyes whenever she recalled the day many years ago that her cousin had climbed up a tree and plucked a handful of baby birds from their nest. With his mouth twisted into a demonic smile, he'd forced the helpless girl to watch as he slammed their little bodies onto the ground. He chuckled with pleasure as he killed the poor creatures for no reason other than boredom.

That was the sort of wicked man Thomas was.

Nevertheless, Greg never would've stabbed him. He didn't use violence as a means of retribution, ever. He always turned the other cheek and took the high road. He believed it was better to show self-discipline than to let oneself be governed by their emotions.

Greg insisted that stooping to the level of one's enemies compromises one's own character. Therefore, even if he had accepted the truth about Thomas and Lucy's affair, he'd never react that way. He was above that sort of behavior.

This accusation was laughable.

"Are you certain you've got your story straight?" Skepticism flooded the king's face and when he continued, his words were a perfect echo of Elizabeth's thoughts. "I find it difficult to believe Gregory would've committed such a violent act. My son's distaste for bloodshed is the precise reason he's no longer the prince."

"I'm absolutely certain! Lady Rochester bore witness to it and gave me every detail. I urge you to punish him for his crime!"

"This interruption has dragged on long enough." Bernadette lifted the hem of her emerald green dress and barreled through the circle of guards, closing the space between her and the duke in just a few strides. Her radiant blue eyes sparkled with triumph and her voice hummed with pleasure as she asked, "Haven't you heard the news, uncle? Or have you been too busy coming up with more ways to ruin my special day?"

Salvatore's face registered confusion. "What news?"

"Ugh!" A look of resentment flickered across Bernadette's countenance as she threw her hands in the air. "Even when he's gone, that traitor still finds a way to steal the attention that rightfully belongs to me."

The creases in the duke's forehead deepened. "I don't understand what—"

"You've come seeking justice, correct?"

"Yes."

"Trust me, dear uncle, I understand your need for revenge, but alas, Prince Gregory can no longer be found here at Crompton Palace. In fact, *Prince* Gregory will never again be seen anywhere. He no longer exists. Yesterday, he was condemned as a traitor when it became clear to us he chose to side with the rebels over his own kingdom. Gregory's title was revoked, and he was banished. He's gone."

"Banished?"

Bernadette's face lit up. "Yes."

"His title was revoked?"

"That's what we're celebrating." She swept her arm across the crowded room in a gesture of grandeur, a malicious grin spread across her face. "I'm next in line for the throne. One day, I'll be queen."

The duke pondered this shocking news aloud. "So, if a prince is no longer a prince, what does he become?"

"Nothing," Bernadette declared. "He is nothing."

Elizabeth cleared her throat at this, purposely making an effort to call attention to herself. With her lips pursed and her brow set in a scowl, she made her disagreement with this statement obvious.

Paying her no mind, Salvatore regarded Bernadette a moment. "I see. I'm curious though…what would the consequences be if I were to deal with this problem myself?"

Bernadette gaped at him. "Meaning?"

"Say I wanted to get rid of him for good?" Salvatore's voice was smooth and unburdened, as though they were discussing suitable picnic spots and not planning the murder of a prince. "Could I be punished?"

"Yes!" Since no one else seemed motivated to stand against this injustice, Elizabeth took it upon herself to be the single voice of reason. "You can't just go around killing–"

"People die. It'd be impossible to investigate every death that takes place in our kingdom." Bernadette's eyes sparked with malice.

A quiver of fear pulsed throughout Elizabeth's entire body. She dreaded whatever awful thing her depraved sister was going to say next.

"In fact, why not hire an assassin to do the job cleanly?" With all the fervor of a youngster asking for a piece of marzipan before supper, Bernadette looked to her father for approval. "What do you say, Your Majesty?"

With a subtle nod of his head, King Charles gave his consent. "I see now that I should've executed him straight away. God knows what sort of hell that traitor will raise if he's permitted to roam free. I treated him with mercy, and this is how he repays my kindness? By attacking one of our own? Clearly he won't stop until he exacts his revenge on all of us."

Elizabeth's jaw dropped. This had to be a nightmare…

"Sadly, we cannot change the past," King Charles rued with a shake of his head. "I allowed sentiment and blood ties to prevent me from doing what needed to be done, but I won't be played for a fool a second time! He must be destroyed *before* he makes his move against me."

Elizabeth was overwhelmed with such terror that her breath stopped, a small whimper being the only protest her constricted throat could manage.

"Salvatore!" The king's eyes smoked with resolve as he stared at his late queen's brother. "You've come here seeking justice for the crimes against our family, and I applaud you for that. Permission is granted. Having attempted to take the life of a noble, the traitor has dug his own grave. You may hire an assassin."

"I'll even pay the bill," Bernadette interjected with mad humor. "How does that please you?"

"I appreciate the generous offer, Your Highness, but I must decline. I'd much rather take care of him myself."

"Have it your way," Bernadette said with a careless shrug. "As long as he's dead I'm happy."

Unsteady on her feet, Elizabeth broke into a cold sweat. Her vision was blotched by little black dots that flashed across her eyes, expanding and growing into a total darkness that threatened to consume her. She collapsed into her chair and buried her face in her hands, all too familiar with this sickening sensation. If she didn't calm down, she was going to faint.

Lady Jane was at her side in a flash. She shoved a cup of hippocras into Elizabeth's hand and vigorously fanned her. Knelt down beside Elizabeth, the attentive handmaiden leaned into her ear and spoke in a voice so soft it couldn't even be classified as a whisper. "Bernadette is arranging the murder of her own brother, yet she's to be our queen some-day? If she's cold-blooded enough to do that to a member of her immediate family, what will she do to the rest of us?"

Elizabeth didn't answer, but her clammy skin bristled with apprehension. Her father's reign had been horrific enough for his subjects to bear, yet there had always been hope in knowing that Greg would bring them a brighter future. He offered Caracalla the chance for a renaissance, a future where arts and peace would be embraced and blood-shed eschewed. But with Greg gone, there seemed to be no end to the Cavendish family's atrocious reign.

A fresh parade of chills slid down Elizabeth's spine as she drew up a mental picture of Bernadette perched atop the throne, calling for the heads of everyone who offended or provoked her. The Kingdom of Caracalla would be vacant in a matter of weeks.

Like her lady's maid, the crowd of courtiers standing around the room also appeared staggered by Bernadette's murderous solution to the duke's problem. Nervous murmurs were exchanged between the women, and the men glanced amongst one another with dread.

"It's settled then." Bernadette's shimmering blue eyes were alight with victory, a victory she'd mercilessly sought to obtain since she was old enough to comprehend the power Greg's birth had stolen from her. "Don't come back here without my brother's head."

"I won't. Thank you for your most unexpected and appreciated cooperation." The Duke of Salvatore bowed, his mouth curved in a devilish grin as he strutted from the Great Hall.

Unable to control her anger any longer, Elizabeth stood up, pushed through the guards encircling her, and descended the steps of the dais.

Bernadette's face was split by a smile radiant enough to outshine the sun, and with an over-exaggerated sigh of accomplishment, she bent down to pick up the candlestick. "Now let's get back to–"

Elizabeth advanced on her sister. Fueled by rage and her own yearning for vengeance, she slapped Bernadette right across the face with all the might she could muster. The force of the impact was so great, Bernadette staggered backwards, a red handprint stamped on the side of her cheek.

Elizabeth was aware of the gasps of surprise from the dozens of members of nobility who'd just witnessed her unladylike conduct, but her reputation was the last thing on her mind.

"How dare you! He's your brother! Do you realize what you've done?"

Bernadette's eyes watered as she pressed her hand against the imprint on her cheek. The expression of bewilderment on her face made her look like a ferocious lion that had just been attacked by a timid mouse. But Elizabeth wasn't a mouse, and she definitely wasn't timid. If anything, she was the lion, and she was ready for round two.

But she wasn't alone in this.

"You bitch!" An evil blaze in her eyes, Bernadette lunged at her without warning. The collision propelled Elizabeth backward, and both princesses tumbled as one to the floor. Scratching at each other's faces and yanking hair as they rolled about, the women continued their violent brawl even as the King's Guard stepped in to pull them apart.

"Everyone get out now!" His Majesty's voice was tense with fury as it bellowed throughout the hall.

Quick to obey, the courtiers fled from the room in a rainbow of colorful fabrics and gems. The sisters were released from their captors, but their father's paralyzing scowl guaranteed that neither of them moved a muscle.

Elizabeth locked eyes with Bernadette as the hall cleared, refusing to show any sign of the fear she felt inside. She took deep, calming breaths in hopes of lowering her heart rate. It felt as if her chest would burst.

Once they were the only three souls left in the room, she put on her bravest face and rounded on her father. "Your Majesty, how could you allow such a thing? You're willing to have your own son killed?"

"He's a traitor." The frigidness of the king's tone implied that he wasn't going to tolerate further discussion of the topic, but Elizabeth didn't care.

"He's your *son*," she persisted, glad her fear couldn't be heard in her winded voice. "You can't let Salvatore murder him. Please, Your Majesty, this isn't right."

The king's provocation was written all over his pinched face. "I wear the crown. I can do anything I want. So, unless you wish to be banished as well, I suggest you never mention his name again. Do you understand me?"

Elizabeth stood there, her chin tilted up in defiance, and said nothing.

Apparently, her silence wasn't a suitable response, because King Charles grabbed her by the shoulders.

Feeling the fire of her father's wrath as he shook her, her head bobbed back and forth. Her brain was thoroughly rattled by the time he finally stopped.

"Do you understand me now?"

"Yes." Whimpering, Elizabeth chomped on her bottom lip to prevent the tears from rolling out.

"Yes, what?"

"Yes, Your Majesty. I understand."

King Charles unclamped his fingers from his daughter's shoulders. "I should've expected such a reaction from you. Ever since you could walk, you've followed that gutless boy around like a lost puppy."

"It's an embarrassment!" Bernadette held onto her cheek as she took a single step closer. "You're sixteen years old, Elizabeth. Why do you still have the notion that Gregory is some sort of champion?"

"I think those days are over," His Majesty told his eldest with his eyes pinned on Elizabeth, a grin of satisfaction stretching his mouth. "The mask has slipped off and his true face has been revealed, hasn't it?"

"What do you mean?" The question belonged to Bernadette.

"I mean, Elizabeth's opinion of the seditious mongrel has been altered. Why do you think she didn't follow him into exile? Didn't you hear how he treated her upon his return? He accused her of being a liar and told her she was dead to him."

Elizabeth felt a coil of sorrow twist around her heart, and she thought it might break all over again. "Gossip sure spreads quickly," she replied with distaste.

Bernadette's mouth fell open. "I heard whispers, but I didn't believe–"

"He was awful to her." Although King Charles put on his saddest face as he said this, Elizabeth sensed it was all for show.

He wanted to make Greg look like a villain in her eyes, and this reminder of his mistreatment toward her was a blatant attempt. It was useless, though. No matter how much sympathy her father inserted into his voice or how pronounced his frown lines became, Elizabeth could still see right through his charade.

"The pedestal on which she has placed Gregory for so long was shaken by his cruelty toward her, and now that his acts of treason have been brought to light, he has fallen off it completely. Elizabeth's eyes have been opened, and her loyalty can be placed with me instead, where it belongs." A nasty smile played on the king's lips. "Isn't that right, Elizabeth?"

She dropped her gaze to the floor, and her mind raced as she considered her best plan of action. She'd spent her whole life defending Greg's every move. She spoke out against anyone who criticized him. But this was different, more serious. Her big brother had been accused of treason, and if she defended him at present, she might as well go ahead and place her head on the chopping block right now.

She needed to be careful this time. Unless she wanted to be locked in this palace forever, with no hope of warning Greg of the duke's plan, her true thoughts needed to remain a secret.

The king's mouth turned down in impatience as he waited for her response. "Answer me. Does your loyalty now belong to me, your sovereign?"

Hoping the thought of her shifting loyalty, no matter how inaccurate, would urge her father to show forgiveness rather than implement the punishment she deserved for creating such uproar in front of the entire court, she decided to acquiesce. She held out the sides of her dress and lowered herself into a deep curtsy, making sure to keep her gaze lowered in a show of complete submission. "My loyalty belongs to you,

Your Majesty. I apologize for my ignoble behavior. It won't happen again."

The king's shoulders relaxed, and his demeanor softened. "Good. I'll grant forgiveness this time, but I swear, if *either* of you ever pull a stunt like this again, you'll both be horse-whipped and confined to your apartments for a month. Am I understood?"

"Both of us? I didn't do–" Bernadette's words were stopped midstream by her father's pointed glower.

"I'll have no more of this shameful feud, do you under-stand me? My own son committed treason. The Cavendish family needs to put on a unified front, now more than ever. We don't have the money or resources needed to suppress another rebellion, and if the people think we're vulnerable, they'll revolt. You two are the future of this kingdom. Start acting like it."

Elizabeth nodded. She'd gotten off easy. It appeared either luck was on her side or alcohol was absent from the king's belly. Either way, a bud of relief sprouted from the seed of terror that had dug its roots deep into her chest. That little bud bloomed into a full-fledged blossom of joy when she was dismissed from the Great Hall without a single new bruise.

Now the real work would begin.

CHAPTER 7

*O*nce the palace was shrouded in darkness, Elizabeth slipped a brown servant's dress overtop her long-sleeved chemise. With her hands on her hips, she stared at her reflection in the looking glass.

I look like a penniless pauper. Her nose wrinkled as she scrutinized the drab fabric of the dress, and she wished she'd found something more flattering in the laundress's basket of dirty linens.

Doomed to look like a lowly peasant for the next few days, Elizabeth hoped the handprint she made on Bernadette's cheek was equally as dreadful. *It would serve her right.*

A smirk curved Elizabeth's lips as she relished in the trea-sured memory of slapping her sister across the face. If she was brave enough to do that, then wearing the stained, previ-ously-owned kirtle should be no problem at all.

She gathered her wavy brunette hair to the side and twirled it into a hasty braid before snatching the final touch to her peasant disguise off her bed. She tied the strings of the white apron around her waist and adjusted it in the mirror, her own disapproving frown looking back at her all the while. *Hideous.*

She dragged her feet to the edge of her apartments and poked her head out into the gallery. It was well after midnight and, as she'd predicted, it was abandoned.

Equipped with a single candlestick, Elizabeth set off toward Greg's lodgings. As she tiptoed down the long halls, she prayed she wouldn't be seen. His apartments were on the opposite side of the palace, across from the chapel, and getting caught wasn't an option.

She crept along with increasing haste, every step full of care and consideration. Her desire to leave Crompton without issue was the driving force behind her caution, yet she also had a second reason for sticking to the shadows: pride. She was quite certain she'd drop dead of humiliation if anyone were to lay eyes on her while she was clothed in these dreadful rags.

That was unlikely to happen, though. Her flickering candle scarcely emitted enough light to see her own feet. Besides, if she heard approaching footsteps she'd simply blow out the tiny flame and run in the opposite direction. The darkness would make no difference to her anyway. The layout of these corridors was embedded in her brain, and she reckoned she could find Greg's rooms with a blindfold on.

As a young child, Elizabeth had suffered from terrible nightmares. Her father often visited her dreams, giving her no respite from his cruelty and abuse. Every time the nightmares came, she'd scamper across the palace in the middle of the night, seeking protection and comfort in her big brother's presence.

Greg had always been her indestructible shield, and now it was her turn to protect him. It was her responsibility to warn him of their uncle's murderous intentions and *nothing* was going to stop her from accomplishing that goal.

That is, unless she couldn't find him. A pain rose in her throat as she held back her tears.

The only fragment of hope she had rested in the slight possibility that Greg was heading to Nestle, a trade port in the north where men went to start anew. Nestle itself was a deplorable hive of corruption and filth, but its docks were loaded with ships waiting to take explorers across the ocean.

Regardless of the fact it was an unattainable dream for the crown prince of Caracalla, Greg often fantasized about traveling to the New World. Elizabeth could still hear the excited hitch in his voice as he told her all about the men who volunteered for thrilling, yet dangerous expeditions to the Americas.

While Greg's eyes radiated a rare happiness every time he talked about exploring uncharted lands, Elizabeth's stomach plummeted whenever this fanciful hope of his was discussed. She once got so distressed by the idea of him abandoning her that she broke down in tears, shamelessly sobbing on his shoulder even as he promised never to leave her behind for some silly pipe dream. Since that day, Greg had never mentioned Nestle or the New World again.

But everything was different now. He had been expelled from his homeland while she did nothing to stop it. If Greg was under the impression no one here cared about him, why wouldn't he cross the sea and follow his craving for adventure in faraway places? Yes, Nestle was Greg's destination. Elizabeth was certain of it.

Once she crossed through the galleries and chambers that led to Greg's private quarters, Elizabeth closed the door behind her and placed the candlestick on the bedside table. She immediately spotted his rucksack on the floor and dumped the contents of the bag onto the bed, spreading them out to get a better look. Greg had been ordered out of the palace with nothing but the clothes on his back, so he'd be in dire need of supplies.

Inside his bag, she found a small fire-starting kit with some flint, a cloth square, and a piece of steel in it. There was also a pouch of almonds, a detailed map of Caracalla, and a change of clothes that included a spare chemise, a pair of black breeches, and one doublet.

The travel sack also contained a stack of envelopes so thick that the strip of leather tied around them barely held. *He saved my letters.* The corners of her mouth rose up in a smile. She'd written him so many that the narrow piece of binding looked about ready to turn to dust. With a light chuckle, she set the pile aside and continued to rummage through his belongings for anything that would be of use.

Her vision was drawn to an ivory-handled dagger. Confusion swirled inside her as she pulled it out from under the doublet. Elephants were Greg's favorite animal, so what was he doing with a weapon made from one of their tusks?

Lucy probably gave it to him. Elizabeth snorted. Even on the few occasions when she actually tried, that she-devil didn't understand him at all. Yes, he liked elephants. No, he wouldn't appreciate a weapon made of its tusk.

Elizabeth rolled her eyes as she removed the sheath and inspected the blade. The edges were a bit dull, but she knew the importance of a weapon, and after reinserting the metal into its sheath, she placed the dagger in the front pocket of her apron for safe-keeping.

Satisfied with the collection of items, she was in the process of stuffing the chemise back into the bag when a golden locket fell out from the folds. She reached her hand out, grasping the jewelry just in time to prevent it from falling to the floor. "Phew."

She held the long chain in her fingers. The proper thing would be to put the locket back where she found it and continue about her business. Greg had often reminded her that snooping through someone else's personal items was both disrespectful and sinful.

But as usual, Elizabeth ignored her conscience and allowed her curiosity to guide her fingers as she opened the locket. Appalled, she instantly regretted her decision, for the image smiling up at her was of Lucy's sapphire eyes and plump pink lips.

Elizabeth scowled at the portrait. It had been done a few days before Greg left, as a reminder of what he was leaving behind. Perhaps he should've left a painting of himself for his promiscuous whore. Maybe then she wouldn't have been so quick to jump into the arms of another man.

Grateful Lucy's deception had been brought to the surface before it was too late, Elizabeth tossed the wretched trinket into the rubbish bin with a pleasing clunk.

That's the end of that. She banished the harlot from her thoughts once and for all and refolded the chemise, placing it back inside the knapsack with the rest of the supplies.

With the straps secured over her shoulders, Elizabeth grabbed the blanket off Greg's bed. Since it was impossible to fit it into the sack, she folded it into a tight square and carried it in her arms as she made her way back to her own apartments.

Once she returned to her bedchamber, all she had to do was grab her own blanket and add her personal provisions to Greg's bag. Only four items made her list: a freshly laundered chemise, a vial of lavender-water and musk perfume, a hairbrush, and a bar of scented Italian soap. Just because she was disguising herself as a pauper didn't mean she intended to smell like one.

Next, Elizabeth slipped on the shoes she'd pilfered from the servant's supply closet and fastened a stolen cloak around her shoulders. She then scurried across the courtyard and made a brief stop in the Great Hall, just long enough to deposit the rucksack and blankets behind her father's throne, before making her way into the kitchens.

Though the hour was late, a few of the scullery maids had yet to finish washing the dishes and were chattering like a flock of honking geese. Their vexing presence forced Elizabeth to rely on stealth and use the shadows for cover.

The first prize she filched was a wicker basket that was left unguarded atop the counter. She crawled on the floor and hid under tables with the basket in hand, putting various food items inside as she went. She grabbed anything she could get her hands on without being spotted by a member of the kitchen staff.

By the end she'd managed to steal five eggs, two lemons, three pears, a bunch of grapes, two carrots, a jug of wine, half a block of cheese, and an entire loaf of wheat bread.

Elizabeth was bursting with pride as she returned to the Great Hall with the basket full of food and jug of wine in hand. After retrieving the blankets and travel bag, she snuck outside and hurried toward the stables.

With the rucksack on her back, the blankets in her arms, the basket of food hanging from her left wrist, and the jug of wine grasped in her right hand, Elizabeth was sweating by the time she arrived. She released an exhale of breath as she dropped everything on a wooden bench and wiped the perspiration from her brow with her sleeve.

She glanced around the interior of the building and smiled as her eyes rested on the mound of tent-rolls the soldiers had brought back from their journey north. She knew each light-weight, cotton canvas had its own set of pikes rolled up inside, and Elizabeth squealed as she grabbed one. She was lucky they hadn't been put away yet. The need for a shelter while traveling hadn't even crossed her mind until she saw the tents right in front of her face.

I hope I'm not forgetting anything…

But she *had* forgotten something. Or at the very least, overlooked it. She pressed a hand to her temple as her gaze bounced from Lavender, the gentle mare Greg had gifted her with last Christmas, to the reins and saddle hanging on the wall.

What was she thinking? She had no clue how to saddle a horse. Unless she found help, she wasn't going anywhere.

Elizabeth scratched her chin as the solution to her dilemma drifted down from the loft in the form of the stable boy's snores. She hiked up her skirts and strutted toward the ladder.

"Are you certain you don't require payment?" Elizabeth asked the stable boy for the third time since she'd woken him. "My perfume is worth at least—"

"You needn't bribe me, Your Highness." He double checked to make sure the saddle was secure and handed her the reins, yawning. "I'll not tell a soul you were here. You have my word."

"When my absence is discovered, His Majesty will know you readied my horse for me. You'll be punished." She held the vial in front of her. "Please, take it."

He glimpsed down at the perfume, yet even as the jewel-encrusted bottle glistened in the candlelight, he made no move to take it. "I've been whipped before, Your Highness. Rest assured I can handle whatever consequences my involvement may bring."

"Whipping?" Elizabeth scoffed. "I suppose there's a chance His Majesty will be lenient enough to reduce the sentence to that, but I wouldn't count on it."

The boy paled.

"However, if you sell this, the profit should amount to at least six months wages, possibly more. It was a birthday gift from the Queen of England, and she has very expensive taste."

A sudden glow ignited in his eyes as he gawked at the perfume. "Very well. I accept."

"And?"

He nibbled his lip. "And I hereby tender my resignation?"

"Indeed. I think that's wise. What's your name?"

"Robert, Your Highness. Robert Nolan. My friends call me Robbie."

"Do you have any parchment, Robbie? And some ink?"

With a nod, he sped off toward the stable master's office, and returned a few moments later with the items in hand. "I'm afraid I can't read," he confessed as Elizabeth knelt down in front of the bench and dipped the quill into the ink.

"That's fine. Do you have any family nearby? Anyone who depends on your earnings?"

"No, Your Highness. My parents died when I was eight. My uncle took me in and was the one who procured this job for me. He passed away last summer."

"I'm sorry for your loss." Elizabeth scratched away at the parchment, scrawling a quick letter to her cousin. Once finished, she blew on the ink to help it dry faster. "Here. Take this letter to Daymon House in Lyndbridge. It's owned by my uncle, but it's his eldest son, Henry, who lives there and runs it. Give this to him, and I trust you'll find yourself employed once again. I've instructed him to be discreet, and I advise you to do the same. No one can know you worked here, understand?"

Robbie's face broke into a grin. "Yes. Thank you!"

"No, thank *you*. Now go. You'll want to be long gone come morning."

"Quite right. Farewell, Your Highness. I wish you and Prince Gregory the best of luck." With that, Robbie climbed the ladder to gather his belongings from the loft.

With a heavy sigh, Elizabeth put her arms through the straps of the knapsack and took a handful of apples from the pail. She dropped all but one into the basket of food hanging from the saddle. "Here, girl. It's time to go."

She held the fruity treat in front of Lavender's mouth and giggled when her horse extended her lips to snatch the apple out of her hand. "Good girl. Now, let's go find Greg."

CHAPTER 8

*I*t was past midday the following afternoon when Elizabeth was awakened by the sound of raindrops landing on top of the tent.

The small shelter was a godsend in this weather, and she was grateful for the camping trips Greg dragged her on each summer. Despite the insects and utter lack of comfort to be found on those annual outings, she had to admit his instructions on how to pitch a tent and start a fire were quite helpful now that she was on her own.

It had taken her half an hour and plenty of obscenities to get the tent set up, but that feat never would've been possible if it wasn't for Greg's lessons.

Rubbing her eyes, Elizabeth pushed the blanket off and watched the small drops fall from the sky, thankful she had enough common sense to bring all the supplies under the canvas with her. The rain had just started, but she knew it'd probably get worse as the day progressed.

"I'm glad you're enjoying yourself," she mumbled to her horse. Lavender didn't seem to be bothered by the rain in the slightest. She was content, grazing on the grass.

Elizabeth weighed her options and decided she'd need to move on, even if it meant getting wet. Knowing Greg, he'd keep traveling no matter what, so if she wanted to catch up to him before the duke, then she needed to do the same. She'd already slept far too long.

Elizabeth massaged her neck, cursing herself for not bringing a pillow as she dug through the knapsack for the map. To her estimation, she was less than a day behind him. Greg's visit to Hawthorne Manor would've added a few hours to his journey, and since she'd gone straight north toward Nestle and was traveling via horseback, she should be trailing close behind.

Should be. In reality, there was no way to know for sure.

With a loud yawn, she crawled out from under the canvas and stretched. The triangular tent kept her dry, which was fortunate, but it was hardly big enough for a dog to sleep in. She could scarcely believe the soldiers had slept in such confined spaces for six months straight.

Elizabeth slipped into her shoes with as much speed as her cramped back and stiff legs would allow. Lacking the luxury of a looking glass—she knew she'd forgotten something important—she brushed her hair and gathered it into a loose braid. That was the best she could do.

In an attempt to freshen her breath, Elizabeth chomped down on one of the lemons she brought along. Her mouth rinsed, she spat the sour fruit out. The fresh citrus scent invigorated her as she tore down the tent and rolled all the pikes up inside the canvas.

Once the tent and blankets were secured to Lavender's back, Elizabeth fed the horse another apple. She shot an irritated glower at the grey, drizzling sky and climbed into the saddle.

Against the advice of her physician, who claimed that

eating raw vegetables brought on evil humors, she grabbed a carrot from the basket and munched the uncooked vegetable as Lavender carried her north.

～

Shivering in front of the stone cottage while the howling wind twisted her clothes, Elizabeth rapped on the door. Lightning flashed and illuminated the sky as sheets of icy rain fell like needles from the clouds.

Although showing up on a stranger's doorstep this late at night went against Elizabeth's better judgement, the torrential downpour offered little alternative. What began as a light drizzle had turned into one of the nastiest storms she'd ever seen, making it impossible to build a fire or erect the tent.

This little house in the woods offered refuge from nature's wrath. At least, that's what Elizabeth told herself as she pounded her fist against the door. With an impatient huff, she wrapped her cloak tighter around her shoulders and waited for an answer.

She could hear someone moving around inside, and a moment later, the profuse scent of mint leaf slapped her in the face as the door flew open. An elderly woman wearing only her chemise and a single sock on her left foot emerged.

"Dear child." The old woman with leafy-thin, age-spotted skin wrapped her lanky arm around Elizabeth's shoulder and pulled her inside. "Come out of that rain before you catch a chill."

"My horse…" It took a moment for her eyes to adjust to the brightness of the small, one-room cottage. The fire glowed in the hearth, illuminating the room.

"I'll put your horse in the barn." The woman placed her hands on Elizabeth's shoulders and herded her toward the chair in front of the hearth. "You sit down and warm yourself up." She exited the house without her shoes, mumbling about the foolishness of the youth these days.

As Elizabeth sat down and waited, her eyes wandered about the home. In the far-left corner was a large, unmade bed with a thick green blanket hanging off the edge.

After the quality of sleep she'd gotten the night before, it took all Elizabeth's strength not to jump in the bed and curl into a ball. Although, if she did that, she'd likely never get up again.

Beside the bed was a round table with a vase of yellow daisies on top. Elizabeth recalled how her own bedchamber in the palace was always brightened by the presence of fresh flowers. Her favorite was lavender, which made Bernadette sneeze. Just to irritate her sister, Elizabeth also bathed in water filled with the purple plant. Bernadette refused to go anywhere near her when she smelled of lavender and therefore, Elizabeth bathed with it almost weekly. That is, until she ran away. Now who knew how long it'd be before she could have another bath.

"A wash tub!" The wooden tub was tucked away in the corner. Elizabeth couldn't contain her excitement.

"That animal is starved," the old woman muttered as she hobbled back inside. "I gave her some hay…dear?"

Elizabeth peeled her eyes away from the tub. "Thank you for feeding my horse. I'm Dorothy." She stood up and politely curtsied before her hostess. "What's your name?"

"Mary."

"Pleasure to meet you. I'm sorry to disturb you at such a late hour. I'll leave soon. The wind was just–"

"No need to explain." Mary poured some steaming syllabub into a mug. "And you won't be leaving until morning. Here."

Elizabeth accepted the hot cup of spiced milk and sat back down, burning her tongue as she sipped it. Her gaze again focused on the tub.

Mary must've noticed, because the next words out of her mouth were, "Fancy a bath, dear?"

"I wouldn't want to impose."

"Nonsense." The old woman pulled the tub to the center of the room and dumped a bucket of water into it. "I must go to the well and—"

"I'll get it." Elizabeth jumped off the stool as if she'd been sitting on hot coals. The pungent scent of the mint leaves on the table assaulted her nostrils, and she needed a breath of fresh air.

She grabbed the empty bucket and made her way out into the rain. It took her a moment to locate the well through the darkness, but once she spotted it beside the barn, she sprinted over and lowered the pail into the water below. The rope burned her hands as she pulled it back up, and she muttered a few obscenities into the night, already dreading the blisters that were sure to develop.

Out of breath, Elizabeth unhooked the overflowing bucket and used both hands to carry it toward the cottage as water continued to spill over the rim. After dumping the liquid in the tub, she repeated the process five times and it was still only half full.

If she'd known it was going to cost her this much effort for a simple bath, she would've allowed her hostess to do it for her.

"Now you see why I never bathe," Mary said as Elizabeth opened the door and stumbled inside.

She forced an indulgent smile, unsure if Mary was joking or not, and dumped the water into the tub.

How did my chambermaids manage to do this without

passing out? Elizabeth dripped with sweat by the time it was filled. Having earned this bath, she eagerly freed herself of her clothes and all but jumped into the tub.

Mary laughed and knelt down to pick the cloak, dress, chemise, and soaked shoes off the floor, then hung them over the back of a chair to dry. "You're not modest, are you?"

Elizabeth shook her head as she lowered herself into the cold water and poured it over her naked breasts. She was used to bathing in front of an audience. Back home, she had maids to undress, wash, and dry her off. All she had to do was lean back and enjoy the fragranced water.

This was the first time she'd ever lathered soap onto her own arms, and she adored it. The pleasant aroma of roses filled the air as she rubbed the imported square of scented wondrousness all over her body. She then leaned back and dunked her entire head under the cold water.

She stayed in the tub for a good hour, pouring the refreshing water down her back over and over, relishing in the joy of it. All the while, she and Mary conversed.

The woman rambled on and on about her past, telling her everything from what it was like growing up during the great famine of 1534 to how proud she was when her younger brother became a well-respected priest in their local parish.

"A priest? That's quite an admirable accomplishment."

"Yes, he's worked very hard…Oh! You must accompany me to mass tomorrow. He'll adore you!"

Elizabeth bit her lip. Greg was in danger, and she had to warn him. She couldn't waste any time kneeling in front of an altar.

"I'm afraid I have prior commitments," Elizabeth stated.

Mary pouted. "You can't spare an hour or so? It would bring me great pleasure."

"I simply don't have the time to sit through–"

"It starts early," Mary assured her.

Elizabeth frowned at this. "How early?"

"You'd be on your way by mid-morning. Please?"

Uncertain, Elizabeth pondered Mary's request for a moment. She wasn't accustomed to rising before the sun, so in all honesty, going to the mass would be beneficial. At least then she'd be sure to wake up at a decent hour. Otherwise she might sleep in again and risk the chance of not reaching Greg in time.

Besides, her hostess wasn't asking much in return for a place to sleep. For these reasons, Elizabeth accepted the request, much to Mary's delight.

Yawning and already regretting her decision to wake at the crack of dawn, Elizabeth climbed out of the tub. She dripped water all over the floor as the grey-haired woman handed her a fresh towel and dry chemise.

"You can wear this while yours dries."

"Thank you." Elizabeth wiped herself down and slipped the undergarment on, then dried her hair with the towel. "Where shall I sleep?"

"With me." Mary's eyes crinkled with mirth. "I have a bed made for two."

"I see..." Her displeasure leaked into her tone, and Mary's smile faltered as a result.

"Or there's a trundle bed tucked underneath if you'd prefer to sleep on that." The halfhearted offer was delivered with a frown. "It's not quite as comfortable as mine, but it'll do in a pinch. Would you like me to pull it out?"

At first, the thought of sleeping beside the old woman disgusted Elizabeth, especially considering she smelled as if she'd been sweating outside all day. However, Mary's obvious disappointment persuaded her to decline the use of the spare bed.

"No need. We can share yours. I could probably sleep on the floor and still wake up better rested than I did this morning."

"Tell me, child. Why are you knocking on random doors at this hour?" Mary climbed into the bed and pulled the thick cover up to her neck. She smiled with all the exhilaration of a young girl having a slumber party with a close friend.

Elizabeth climbed in next to her and cuddled up under the blanket. "I'm looking for my brother. Someone wants to hurt him, and I need to warn him."

"You don't know where he is?"

The rain crashed against the thatched roof, and Elizabeth wondered if Greg had been lucky enough to find shelter too. She pictured him lying on the cold ground, freezing in the rain. Granted, a tiny part of her felt like he deserved it for the way he'd spoken to her.

"No!" she grumbled, forcing the sinful thought from her mind. How could she possibly think that, even for a second? No, Greg didn't deserve any of this!

Mary's eyes narrowed and lips tightened.

"I mean…" Elizabeth softened her tone. "I mean, no. I don't know where Greg is."

"Greg?" Mary stared intently at the young woman next to her, and a moment later, a look of understanding washed over her wrinkled face. "That's it!"

"That's what?"

Her mouth curved into the merriest grin as her excitement spewed out in a rush of words. "Since you first stepped into my cottage, I've been convinced you and I have crossed paths. You looked so familiar, but my senile mind couldn't quite place where I knew you from. I was certain I've seen your young, cheery face before, and for some reason, the memory of my visit to the king's court popped up as we talked. Now I know why."

Elizabeth's chest tightened. A lump formed in her throat, precluding her from saying more than a simple, "Oh?"

"Your regal curtsy was the first reason for suspicion, and the way you bathed in front of me without a speck of reserve while expecting me to pick up after you was the second. Mentioning your brother, however…that did it. Gregory is far too uncommon a name. So uncommon, in fact, that there's only one man I know of who goes by that name."

"It's not that uncommon." Elizabeth's tongue fumbled over the lie, anxiety trembling in her voice. "I know plenty of–"

"Your brother is *Prince* Gregory!"

"That's absurd!" Elizabeth's cheeks flushed. She'd only been outside the palace walls for a day and already slipped up…with the very first person she came in contact with!

"I'm right, aren't I?"

"No–"

"Yes! When our church caught fire two years ago, I accompanied my brother to Crompton Palace. While there, he made a formal request for King Charles to support the reconstruction, and although the king refused to contribute funds for the rebuilding of a *Catholic* establishment, the charitable prince donated £250 to the cause. That's where I first saw you."

Elizabeth shook her head in firm denial even as the memory of that day surfaced in her mind. As much as she wished Mary was wrong, the truth was that she had been present when Greg handed over the money.

Ugh, of all doors to knock on, I had to pick one where I'd be recognized.

There was no way to wheedle herself out of this one. Nevertheless, she still had to try.

"Your vision must be on the decline if you think I look anything like a princess. Didn't you notice the rags I was wearing? They're hideous. Besides, I said *Peg.* My brother's name is Peg." Gnawing on her bottom lip, Elizabeth couldn't believe she made up such a foolish name.

"No. Your brother is Prince Gregory, and you're Princess Elizabeth. Ole' Mary never forgets a face, especially a face as pretty as yours."

Elizabeth felt her cheeks redden. "No, no. You're wrong. My name is Dorothy, and my brother is Pegasus, you know, like the flying horse in Greek mythology? We call him Peg for short, not Greg. It was a slip of the tongue, a mere mistake. I'm not the princess."

"Very well, child. Relax and go to sleep, I'll not mention it again."

Breathing heavily, Elizabeth rolled over and faced the hearth as the heavy wind blew against the side of the house. The storm that'd been brewing all day finally arrived, and it was relentless. She wondered how stable the cottage was and hoped it wouldn't topple over.

She muttered a quick prayer and begged God to watch over her brother. She also prayed that she'd be able to find him before her uncle did.

"The Lord will protect him," Mary promised, overhearing Elizabeth's words to God. "Prince Gregory is a good man, a kind and generous man. News of the mercy he showed in the north has gotten around, and I don't see treachery in his acts. He's still the rightful heir in my eyes."

Elizabeth's mouth fell open. Not only did the old woman's proclamation prove Greg had supporters despite the lies about him, but it also meant news of his supposed acts of treason had reached this random little cottage in less than three days' time.

This discovery shouldn't have surprised her, though. Bernadette's thirst for power was insatiable, and her sole purpose in life was to usurp Greg. In all honesty, she probably sent out at least a dozen heralds the moment he was sentenced to exile. Bernadette wouldn't have hesitated to flaunt her victory over him.

Incapable of denying that she'd been found out, Elizabeth promised herself she'd be more careful to hide her true identity next time. But since it was already too late in this particular instance, she whispered back, "I'm grateful for the kindness you've shown me. It's good to know there are people out there who don't see mercy as treachery. My brother is no traitor, of this I'm certain."

"I know he's not," Mary pledged. "We all do. Don't worry, for I sincerely believe after His Majesty has a few days to think about what he's done, he'll realize what a terrible mistake he made. The king needs some time to calm down and get over the embarrassment of having been publicly disobeyed. His pride was wounded, but everything will soon go back to normal. You'll see."

That hopeful thought allowed for the semblance of a smile to appear on Elizabeth's face. After rolling over to give her new friend a gentle kiss on her wrinkled forehead, she laid on her back and closed her eyes.

Basking in the warmth of a blazing fire while the storm continued to rage outside, she allowed herself to believe the childish hope that all would be well again as soon as her father's embarrassment subsided.

CHAPTER 9

*G*regory huddled closer to the tree trunk, desperate to protect himself from the vicious storm. It had been sprinkling all day, but soon after the sun went down, the rain began falling as stones, and the wind grew strong enough to pull the sturdiest trees from the earth.

Leaves and large branches whirled all around him, and Gregory wondered if the oak would be able to withstand the gale. Younger, less stable saplings were being ripped from their roots and discarded all over the road. With the uprooted trees lying on their sides and leaves littering the soggy ground, the storm left a titanic mess. It was as though Mother Nature herself was throwing a wild temper tantrum, and it was only a matter of time before his oak became another victim of her relentless gusts.

The rain stung his skin like thousands of tiny barbs as it smacked against him, but he was strangely fine with it.

He deserved it. He deserved all of this.

Gregory sank to his knees and buried his face in his hands. Sobs of hopelessness racked through his body as tears streamed down his cheeks, falling unnoticed in the pouring rain.

He was no stranger to feelings of defeat and misery, but for the first time in his life he experienced something else as well. A*bsolute* loneliness.

Only two people had ever stood by his side and as it turned out, one of them was never really there at all. Lucy's love for him was nothing more than an illusion.

Elizabeth, on the other hand, was his one true ally and friend. She'd always given him the strength he needed. But now his toxic words had shoved her away from his side for good, and the realization that he was utterly alone thickened in the blustering air. The crushing weight of his isolation pressed on his chest, breaking and fraying his will to live.

Lightning cracked in the distance as the wind's eerie howls were joined by the earth-rattling rumbles of thunder overhead. Gregory sniffled and tilted his face up at the gathered storm clouds, a silent plea for God to strike him down. He longed for one of the bright bolts to light him up from the inside and take away his pain.

There was no way out of this desolation otherwise. It was pointless to look for shelter because there was none...not from the storm *inside* of him. There was no escaping the darkness that had corrupted his soul.

First, he murdered Caracallan citizens simply because his ruthless father told him to.

Then he hurled cutting words at his faithful sister, telling her she was dead to him despite the fact that she was the one person who gave him something to live for.

And lastly, he allowed jealousy to provoke him into a fight. He stabbed his own cousin, probably killing him.

Gregory's list of infractions was unforgivable. No one,

not even God himself, could possibly still love him after everything he'd done.

Shivering, in the middle of nowhere and soaked to the bone, Gregory felt dead inside. He rolled onto his back, spreading his arms and legs out as he allowed the cold rain to pour over him. With any luck, he'd drown.

Precipitation splattered his face for the next few minutes, washing away his melancholy little by little as he came to his senses. As the thunder roared and the wind whipped debris all around him, Gregory knew he was acting like an overdramatic child. He was acting like Bernadette.

With a disapproving shake of his head, he wiped the water from his face, rose to his feet, and covered his head with his arms. It was time to stop this lunacy. It was time to face his future.

Hell, now I'm free to have whatever future I want. Sudden enthusiasm coursed through Gregory's body, and the knot of depression in his stomach loosened. As his earlier surrender gave way to determination, he faced the tempest with newfound purpose. *I alone command my destiny.*

Gregory's lips quirked up in a smile. Right now, he needed to find a safe place to wait out this wild storm, but tomorrow he'd head forth to Nestle. The New World awaited its newest explorer.

When he arrived in the next town, Gregory's legs burned with fatigue as he passed by an aged, crooked sign along the road, informing him he was now entering the village of Gettsbury.

It was no wonder he'd never heard of the place. Gettsbury was a quiet little community with deserted streets, and as far as he could see, no tavern. It seemed everyone was fast asleep in the comfort of their warm beds, sheltered from the rain by the slanted roofs above their heads.

The streets weren't so fortunate. The fountain in the plaza overflowed with rainwater, drenching the dirt roads and turning them into a muddy mess.

Gregory passed half a dozen closed shops without a second thought toward the growing puddle of sludge at his feet. His mind was firmly centered on his plan to travel to Nestle and start his life over. In a few short weeks, he'd reach the port and board a ship destined for the exotic and mysterious New World.

Imagining all the wilds of a strange new land, Gregory struggled to ignore the feelings of guilt that seeped into his brain. He tried not to think about how distraught Elizabeth had been the last time they discussed his dream to become an explorer, but it was no use. The memory sank its teeth into his resolve, weakening it one bite at a time.

Gregory massaged his forehead as he recalled the way she'd wept, her voice trembling as she begged him not to go. She couldn't seem to comprehend that a prince-turned-explorer was a laughably unrealistic dream.

To Elizabeth, the mere idea that he *wanted* to join an expedition was terrifying enough to send a series of sobs ripping through her. No matter how much Gregory assured her that it was nothing more than a flight of his imagination, she wasn't consoled.

His ensuing promise echoed in his ears, booming louder than the heavy thunder as he sloshed through the streets of Gettsbury. "*More to the point,*" he'd told her, "*even if it was feasible for me to travel to the New World, which it isn't, I'd never consider getting on the boat if it meant leaving you behind. I won't abandon you, Bessie. You have my word.*"

A chill passed over Gregory and he used all his willpower

to shove the memory from his mind. Warring with his conscience, he knew he had to avoid dwelling on the fact that he was breaking that promise. He was abandoning his sister, leaving a sizeable chunk of his heart behind in the process.

But the sad truth was that he'd been sentenced to exile. Elizabeth and the kingdom of Caracalla were part of Gregory's past, while his future was across the Atlantic Ocean.

So, as he trudged through the muddy streets, Gregory buried the ache deep within his chest and distracted himself by filling his mind with exhilarating images of unusual creatures and strange looking plants. About to embark on a grand adventure, he was determined to enjoy every moment of it.

The sight of a bakery, however, broke through Gregory's mental barrier and stopped him in his tracks. His stomach growled, and he turned his head from side to side, inspecting the empty lane as another flash of lightning darted across the sky.

Although he didn't relish the idea of becoming a thief, his current hunger far outweighed his lifelong adherence to the moral code. He needed bread, and one way or another, he was going to get it.

Gregory dashed over to the window and lifted the latch on the shutters. When his efforts to open them proved ineffective, it dawned on him that they were most likely barred from the inside as well.

His fists curled, but then he noticed a pile of bricks beside the outdoor kiln and picked one up. He rolled his shoulders and, with a deep breath, he hammered the brick onto the shutters.

A mixture of joy and remorse coursed through him as the wood snapped, but he didn't let the latter keep him from following through with his robbery. Gregory moved with haste as he climbed through the opening and grabbed as many loaves of bread as he could carry.

With his arms full and another loaf clenched between his teeth, he fled from the scene of the crime. He left a trail in the mud along the way, much to his stomach's aggravation.

A ripple of pain shot down Gregory's leg as he wandered through the streets, but he couldn't stop moving until he found a safe place to chow down on his stolen supper.

His clothes were soaked through and as quakes overtook his whole body, the wind rattled his bones. Frozen to the core, Gregory kept his head down as he fought against the ferocious storm.

Calling on what little reserves of strength he had left, he pushed his body forward in a fight against earth's wrath. Rain dripped down his forehead, pooling in his eyes and obscuring his vision. He was teetering on the verge of collapse when he spotted refuge at the top of a small hill. The sight summoned an instant grin. Never before had he been so pleased to see a house of worship.

His boots squished in the thick mud as he followed the mucky path that led up to the top of the knoll. He slipped often, landing with his face in the sludge a few times along the way, but his grumbling stomach persuaded him to continue on despite his exhaustion.

The stone church was a guiding light, like a beacon of hope on the shore to guide swashbuckling sailors home.

As he reached the top of the hill and stood before the church's arched doorway, Gregory's stomach dropped, and he let out a long, dejected exhale. The door was bolted shut, shattering what little morale he still possessed in one final, defeating blow.

His supper grew soggier by the second as the storm continued to drop buckets of rain on his already soaking wet treats, but he no longer cared. He shuffled back down the hill toward the cemetery.

A tiny wooden shed stood out among the headstones, and to Gregory's surprise, it was unlocked. He crammed inside the tight space, thankful for an escape from the storm. Finally, something had gone right.

His first order of business was to take off his doublet and twist the water out. He hung it on the wooden handle of a shovel to dry, and then feasted on what remained of the mushy bread. For days he'd eaten nothing but a handful of wild berries and a small catfish he caught in a stream, so this was a welcome addition to his empty stomach.

Nevertheless, Gregory was burdened by his plunder. He felt like a hypocrite as he took another bite of the sopping bread. He'd never stolen anything before tonight, but Elizabeth had.

When she was nine years old, she coveted the stable boy's favorite marble. She spoke of it often, telling Gregory that if she had a marble like that then she'd be the happiest girl in all of Caracalla. She grew obsessed with the toy and eventually obtained it through thievery.

It fell out of her pocket during a game of bowls, and Gregory confronted her about it. *"We're royalty, and as such, it's our job to lessen the hardships of those less fortunate than us. We should generously give all we can to our subjects, not take what little they own merely because we want it for ourselves."*

Throughout the course of his lecture, Gregory didn't once tell her to give it back. Instead, he opted to trust that she'd do the right thing and return the toy to its rightful owner. Elizabeth proved worthy of his trust when she owned up to her sin that same day, giving the marble back to the boy with a heartfelt apology.

As far as Gregory knew, she hadn't stolen again since. Yet here he was, years later, devouring the bread he'd destroyed the shutters to steal.

Although his inner voice was in a state of upheaval, the grumbles of his belly were silenced for the first time since leaving Crompton Palace. Gregory leaned his head back against the wall and shut his eyes, drained. The fierce wind whistled outside the shed, lulling him to sleep as the weight of his remorse slowly trickled from his shoulders.

CHAPTER 10

*E*lizabeth dragged her feet as she followed Mary along the muddy path. Despite her reluctance to attend the religious service, dawdling wasn't an option. The morning fog was heavy, and straying more than a few feet was sure to leave her disoriented. Unless her wish was to become lost in these unfamiliar woods, Elizabeth had no choice but to hasten her pace.

As if the dense fog wasn't enough to contend with, the clouds overhead continued to darken, threatening to unleash buckets of water upon anyone foolish enough to brave this miserable weather.

It was a terrible, horrible morning altogether. With its ominous cover of rain clouds looming in the sky, the earth itself made a point to demonstrate to all its inhabitants that no one in their right mind should be up this early. Yet as the pair entered the town and the sound of excited voices reached their ears, it soon became clear that everyone living here was, in fact, completely irrational.

The town's noise level was far too high for the early hour, and it wasn't long before the source was located. As they approached the square, Mary and Elizabeth discovered a crowd had gathered in front of the bakery.

"I wonder what all the commotion is about." Mary pulled Elizabeth toward the group, ignoring her moody protests along the way. "What happened? What's going on?"

A tall, freckled mother holding a baby to her chest was the first to offer a reply. "Someone broke the shutters." There was a bit too much enthusiasm in her chipper tone. "The baron is livid!"

A smile played at the corners of Mary's lips. "Yes, I'd imagine he is."

While Mary and the redheaded woman reveled in their shared delight at the noble's expense, Elizabeth watched as the bakery's owner accused each one of his fellow townspeople of the crime. She too found it hard not to suspect a few of them, for as she observed the faces around her, Elizabeth discovered that almost every person was grinning with unabated amusement.

Seeing their strange reactions, she was curious as to what the baron could've done to make an entire town loathe him so much. Didn't he offer handouts for the hungry from his kitchens? Didn't he invite the townsfolk to his manor each Christmas to enjoy the bounteous feasts of baked goose and plum pudding? If so, perhaps his taxes were too high, or he was reluctant to allow the townspeople to wed whomever they wished.

While Elizabeth considered these possibilities, a more prominent question danced around in her head: Why would a noble choose to waste his time running a bakery? There were plenty of more appropriate hobbies for a baron to partake in.

Regardless of his reasons for investing in such a simple business, Elizabeth was on the brink of pitying the baron until he pointed his long finger at her.

"You are a good-for-nothing criminal, and I'll have you locked up for this!"

"Me?" Elizabeth gasped. The insult struck down any sympathy she'd built toward him.

"You're jealous of my success!" Malice flashed in the baron's eyes as he glared at her. "You knaves are the scum of the earth! You leech off the hard work and ambition of your betters!"

"My betters?" Elizabeth spat back. Her pulse quickened at the very idea of this lowly noble calling her, the Princess of Caracalla, the scum of the earth. Her father was King Charles!

Mary's hand squeezed Elizabeth's shoulder in warning, but it did nothing to stop the familiar flame of rage from flickering within her. Just as she was about to open her mouth and expose her identity…

"Enough, Father. Keep this up, and you'll chase away the few customers we have left." A tired-looking young man appeared in the bakery doorway and stepped onto the packed street. His sandy blonde hair fell in tousled wisps over his forehead, and Elizabeth was amazed by the strong family resemblance.

Although the well-dressed baron was a mean looking scoundrel with cold eyes, it was obvious he would've been handsome in his youth. Like his son.

"That's Joshua," Mary whispered in Elizabeth's ear, pointing to the younger of the two men. Unlike his scowling father, who was dressed in a fashionable black hose and velvet doublet with slashed sleeves, Joshua donned a simple brown tunic and faded leather shoes. The significant contrast between their outfits made it obvious that whatever income the bakery brought in, the baron's son didn't receive a penny of it.

Elizabeth's heart went out to the young man, for it wasn't a stretch to assume Joshua was the one kneading the dough while his father reaped the reward. And he had the nerve to call her a leech?

"He's the only reason any of us still go to the bakery," Mary continued in a hushed murmur. "As you've seen, his father's a real troll, but Josh is sweet as honey."

Elizabeth nodded, losing interest in Joshua the moment the clouds released their tears upon her head. Now that she was getting wet, she didn't care how unfairly Joshua's father treated him or why his curious gaze flitted away from hers whenever she glanced in his general direction. All she wanted was to get out of the rain.

"That's wonderful, but we're going to be late." She pulled the edge of Mary's cloak to get her attention, but the old woman paid her no mind as she turned to the lady with the baby.

"When did this happen?"

"Sometime last night." The mother shrugged, patting the infant on the back. "Whoever it was didn't steal much, just a few loaves of bread. The pouch of money behind the counter wasn't even touched."

Elizabeth closed her eyes and lifted her chin into the air. The droplets dampened her face as she begged the Lord to grant her patience. As expected, it didn't work. "Mary, it's raining," she huffed. "We really must be–"

"What sort of thief would leave the money?" The wrinkles in the old woman's forehead intensified as she stood on her tiptoes, craning her neck to obtain a better view of the broken shutters.

"A brainless one," Elizabeth answered.

Mary frowned, eyeing her with an expression of sharp rebuke.

Elizabeth decided to try again. "A moral one?"

"Perhaps. The poor soul was probably hungry. It's a shame, though. Josh already had enough trouble keeping the business afloat with his arse of a father refusing to help–"

"Mary!" Elizabeth was shocked by the profanity the old woman had uttered.

The blood drained from Mary's face. "Did I say that out loud?"

"Yes, but don't worry." She giggled. "I've said more than my fair share of curse words as well, so I can't judge you for it."

Mary shook her head and turned toward the church. "We both have some repenting to do. Come, let us beg for forgiveness."

Elizabeth rolled her eyes. If uttering a single curse word was the only sin Mary had to repent for, she was an angel compared to her.

With one last quick glance over her shoulder as she walked away, Elizabeth couldn't help but notice Joshua's hazel eyes still lingered on her. She had to admit that for a baron's son, he was quite attractive.

To her disappointment, he looked away and busied himself with inspecting the broken shutters the moment she caught him staring. Suspicious of his refusal to make eye contact with her, Elizabeth made a silent prayer that he didn't suspect her true identity.

Exhausted and famished, Gregory plopped down on a fallen log to rest. He leaned forward and buried his face in his hands as he tried to ignore the rumbling of his stomach. His eyesight was blurry, and he knew it was from hunger. The bread he'd stolen in the early hours of the morning helped a little.

In the four days since he was removed from the palace, Gregory had consumed one catfish, an apple, a few handfuls of wild berries, and the bread. That wasn't enough food to keep a twenty-two-year-old man alive.

He focused on his breathing in an attempt to recover from the sprint he'd just made.

A few minutes ago, he tried to steal some asparagus from a small garden on the outskirts of town. Before he had time to grab one, he was shooed away by a plump woman armed with a rake and a terrible attitude. As she chased him down the road, she screamed after him that he was foul vermin who should be exterminated for attempting to steal her crops.

The woman's poisonous words sank into Gregory's sweat-dampened skin as he rose and continued down the muddy road. Try as he might, he couldn't deny the accuracy behind her accusation. The truth that he was *worse* than vermin burrowed itself deep into his center.

Gregory hated the person he'd become. He'd give anything for the opportunity to do things differently.

But as he mulled it over, he came to realize that even if it was possible to alter his actions in the north, he wouldn't. Although it made him sick to think about the role he played in squashing the rebellion, he now saw how beneficial his involvement was.

Those men had acted out against their sovereign with no regard for the repercussions. Whether their reasons were justified or not, they opposed the natural order and if Gregory hadn't been in command of the army, every single one of them would've been slaughtered. He showed mercy by allowing them to disperse in peace and return home to their families. If Howard had his way, they'd all be dead.

Gregory may have executed thirty-six of the rebel leaders, but he also prevented a blood bath for the rest. Therefore, even if it was possible to change the past, his time in the north wouldn't be where he directed his efforts.

He would, however, change the unforgivable way he'd treated Elizabeth.

His insides squirmed as he reflected on the painful awareness that no one other than her had ever cared about him, not really. To his father, he was simply an heir. To Bernadette, he was unwelcome competition. To the servants, he was their master. And to the courtiers and nobility, Lucy included, he was a way of gaining advancement. No one truly loved the real Gregory...except Elizabeth.

While Bernadette grew up being worshiped like a goddess, Gregory's early years were filled with loneliness and insignificance. Nothing he did was good enough to save him from the eternal criticism of his father and ruthless ridicule from his older sister.

However, the cyclone of misery in his life started to fade when he first laid eyes on his new baby sister. Gazing down upon the cooing infant, Gregory swelled with hope as he recognized the opportunity Elizabeth's pure, innocent soul represented for him. Unlike everyone else in his life, she didn't harbor any ill thoughts against him. Her opinion of him was a clean slate, and because of this, the six-year-old prince believed she could one day grow to love him. Fond of the possibility, he formed an unbreakable attachment to the child.

After their mother succumbed to childbed fever and their father became a heartless drunk, Gregory felt it was his responsibility to look after his little sister. Of course, as a princess she was entitled to an entire household full of caretakers. In her infancy there was always an army of nursemaids with her. Next came the governess and finally, a slew of tutors had been employed to ensure she received the level of education expected of a royal.

Yet despite all that, Gregory made a point to be just as involved in Elizabeth's upbringing as they were. Whatever time he could steal from his own busy schedule was spent with her.

He was the one who taught her to write her name when she was five years old. When Elizabeth first discovered her love of painting, Gregory was the one who encouraged her and accepted each piece of canvas to proudly hang on his wall. Every time she mastered a new song on her lute or harpsichord, Gregory was the one she played it for first.

He showered Elizabeth with kindness and protected her from the evils of court. He showed her what it was like to be loved, and she returned the favor.

Elizabeth was the one person who treated him as if he had something special to offer the world. She believed he could do anything and challenged anyone who said otherwise.

Gregory was Elizabeth's defender and teacher while she was his supporter and follower. The two of them depended on one another for survival. They needed each other.

We used to need each other, the harsh part of Gregory's brain amended. He took in a deep breath, but the heaviness in his chest prevented him from filling his lungs with air. Regret welled up inside of him instead. *Now she's probably better off without me.*

Elizabeth had been stuck to his side since the day she was born, yet when she came to him with news of Lucy's perfidy, he repaid her honesty with a knife in the back. Now he'd never get the chance to redeem himself for that. He was never going to see her again.

As that disheartening truth coiled itself around his stomach, Gregory lumbered along in a mindless trance. He was vaguely aware of his feet moving, but nothing else registered as he stared ahead.

By the time he reached a point where the road was flooded over, he was acting out of pure instinct.

The water from the swollen tributary flowed across the road and poured with vigor into the field. It moved with great speed, and he knew attempting to cross it would be dangerous. The trees that had once been safe on the bank of the stream now fought to stand against the current surrounding them.

A calm breeze blew, and Gregory heard a strange sound coming from the bank. His whole body tensed, and he strained to locate the source. The low growls originated in a pile of large rocks beside the water and as he made his way over, the angry snarls grew in both volume and intensity.

A few seconds later, Gregory laid eyes on the culprit. A full-grown badger had somehow wedged itself between the rocks and was fighting to escape the current. A fraction of him felt bad for the creature, but he needed to eat.

It's you or me. Gregory bent down to pick up a stone and in one fluid motion, put the animal out of its misery.

He yanked the badger free from the boulders, bled it, washed the carcass in the stream, then set to work organizing what he needed for the fire.

It'd take some time to light one, especially since most of the sticks and twigs scattered about the forest floor were wet from the storm. He gathered the best ones and arranged them in a vertical structure so the fire could feed itself as it burned upward.

As he waited for them to dry off, he skinned the badger with the knife he'd taken from the shed in the graveyard. After he removed all the fur and entrails, Gregory was finally ready to light a fire and cook his breakfast.

He struck the steel knife against the flint he'd found in the woods, unable to stem his excitement when a spark caught on the tinder. He blew on the tiny flame and nudged it under the sticks he'd arranged earlier. A minute or so later, he was the proud creator of a large, blazing fire.

Tapping his foot, Gregory grabbed the badger off the damp grass and cut the meat into sizable chunks. He slid the pieces onto long branches and held them over the flames, rotating the spits every few minutes.

Good enough. Saliva dripped from his lips as he removed the first portion from the stick. He tossed it into his mouth without bothering to check if it was cooked the whole way through and sighed with contentment as he chewed. It wasn't the tastiest food he'd eaten, but it was edible.

It seemed he made a wise decision, for once all the chunks of badger had been scarfed down, Gregory felt full for the first time in months.

Next it was time to make a raised, makeshift bed so he could lie down and give his heavy limbs a break. It was still early, he guessed around seven in the morning, but he'd gorged himself almost to the point of nausea. He longed to curl up in a ball right then and there, but it was important to stay off the cold, damp ground if he had any hope of getting decent sleep and warding off illness.

Gregory scanned the forest floor for three thick, fallen logs and placed two of them parallel to each other on the ground. He put the third log in the middle to add stability.

His abdomen cramped as he plodded through the trees and gathered long pieces of deadfall. He'd eaten too much, too fast, and his stomach was eager to proclaim its displeasure. Reminding himself to slow down and chew his food next time, Gregory scraped the moist bark and moss off the limbs and laid them on the platform. The final step was to shave off the small branches from coniferous trees and put them on top to add insulation and some comfort.

Arms folded, Gregory stepped back to admire his work. He had to admit, for only a minimal amount of effort, the bed looked rather respectable. He climbed in for a nap and heaved a heavy sigh of relief when the whole thing didn't crumble apart beneath his weight.

Cushioned on the bed with his belly now full, he fell asleep within minutes.

CHAPTER 11

*E*lizabeth wondered if she'd ever find her brother. Who could even say if he was traveling to Nestle, he'd stick close to the road like she was doing? Or what if the time she'd wasted at Mary's allowed him to get miles ahead of her? Or what if her uncle had already–

No! Stop! She didn't permit herself to finish that wretched thought.

"You're faster than Greg, aren't you?" Elizabeth leaned forward to pat Lavender on the back of the neck. "Surely we should've caught up with him by now."

The rainclouds had cleared, and she closed her eyes to bask in the warmth of the sun. She'd left the cottage about half an hour ago, after eating a light breakfast of eggs and buttered bread with Mary and her brother, the priest.

Father Timothy had bombarded her with questions about the future, most of which she couldn't answer. He was particularly interested in how she thought Greg would react to his banishment. *"Will he fight for the crown? Surely he won't take this lying down. He has a duty to the people of this kingdom."* Elizabeth told him her only concern at present was to save her brother's life, and once her meal was finished, she promptly took her leave.

As she reveled in the summer heat, she clicked her tongue for the chestnut-colored mare to pick up the pace. Greg had trained the horse, and Lavender's swift obedience proved he'd done a magnificent job.

The road curved up ahead and as she rounded the bend, Elizabeth's heartbeat quickened when she noticed grey smoke. She brought Lavender to a halt and climbed off, then led the horse down the road at a measured, yet steady pace. Soon the orange flames of the fire came into view.

Please be Greg. Elizabeth approached the campsite with as much caution as her racing heart permitted. There was indeed a man sleeping next to the fire, but since his back was toward her, she was unable to tell if it was Greg.

He was dressed in a red doublet and black breeches, same as Greg had been when he was removed from the palace. However, from this distance, it was impossible to tell if the fabric of this one boasted the same elaborate, gold designs as her brother's doublet did.

Without making a sound, she pulled her dagger from its sheath and approached the man. She was about to call out to him when he let out an agonized groan.

Elizabeth jumped back and watched as he awoke. She held the blade in front of her, ready to strike.

The stranger moaned and tried to push himself off the crude bed of logs and sticks he'd been sleeping on but fell back into a heap.

Elizabeth took one slow, hesitant step forward at a time. Whoever this man was, he was clearly suffering as he writhed on the bed in the fetal position, clutching his belly.

"Greg?" Her brow crinkled as she scrutinized the man's

face from a safe distance. Sweaty and twisted as it was, she'd recognize those sharp features anywhere.

He glanced up at her in disbelief and uttered a strangled cry. "Bess?" He audibly swallowed and licked his lips. "What're you doing here?"

"Greg!" She rushed forward and knelt by his side, her mouth agape as she gawked at him. His face was contorted in pain and his short, dark brown hair was soaked with perspiration. His pale skin was a sharp contrast to the dark shadows under his eyes, and Elizabeth's breath caught as she surveyed him. "What's wrong? What can I do?"

"I'm fine," he croaked as he pressed his hands against his stomach and made a sorry attempt to get up on his own. He managed to sit up, but his strength was expended before he got any further.

Elizabeth placed her hand on his sweat-soaked back as she scrambled to help him to his feet. "What happened?"

"I ate–" Greg clamped a hand across his mouth and held his abdomen as he staggered away from the campsite. He didn't make it very far.

Coughing and gagging, he leaned forward with his hands on his knees and vomited, violently purging the contents of his stomach in loud, noisy retches.

Unsure what to do, Elizabeth rushed over to her horse and led the animal to the fire. After tying Lavender to the trunk of a cedar tree, she grabbed the jug of wine. It was vital for Greg to stay hydrated.

She passed the remains of some sort of dead animal on her way back to the fire and suddenly had a good guess as to why he was sick.

Greg wiped his mouth with his sleeve, then tottered back to the bed and collapsed, shaking with chills.

"Here, I brought this for you." Elizabeth placed one of the thick blankets under his head as a pillow.

"Thank you." He gaped at her for a moment before a regretful frown broached his lips. "Elizabeth, I'm so sorry–"

"Don't talk. Drink this." She'd been so worried about getting to him before their uncle that she'd thought of little else, but now that she knew he was safe, the betrayal she felt rushed back into her like a roaring river through a broken dam. He'd called her a liar *and* told her she was dead to him. Elizabeth wasn't sure if it'd be possible to forgive him.

Her blood ran hot as she lifted the back of Greg's head and tilted the jug to his mouth. "Sorry," she said without remorse when some of the cool beverage spilled down his neck.

Greg swallowed and waved the jug away. "Bess, I need to apolo–"

He bolted upright and leaned over the side of the bed just in time, for a mere second later, more vomit flooded from his mouth. He moaned, rubbed his stomach, and retched again.

Elizabeth waved her hand in front of her in a wasted attempt to blow the odor away from her nose. "What the hell did you eat?"

"A badger. I don't think I properly cooked–" Again, he heaved. His clammy face was as white as the underbelly of a fish. His breathing ragged, he removed his doublet and tossed it on the ground, then fell backwards onto the wooden bed. "Don't give me that look, Bess. I know how disgusting it sounds, but I was desperate. The badger was all I could find."

Elizabeth sighed. If only he'd waited a few more hours. Of all the supplies she brought from the palace, she'd eaten just two of the carrots, a handful of grapes, half the bread, and a few bites of cheese. Everything else was still nestled in the wicker basket.

"I brought you food," she told him. "It should be enough to last a few days. I also brought some of your clothes and–"

"Wait." Greg sat up, but judging from his grimace, that was the wrong thing to do. He brought his hand to his mouth and lines of concentration plagued his sallow face as he fought to keep another wave of sickness at bay. "You're leaving already?" he asked at last.

"Yes."

"You came all this way just to bring me some food? How long were you traveling?"

"A couple days."

"So, you left the palace and traveled alone for days to find me, all so you could give me a basket of apples? That doesn't make sense."

"It was never my intention to stay." Elizabeth ignored the sadness in his eyes as she added, "I only came to warn you."

Greg's forehead creased. "Warn me about what?"

"Our uncle came to the palace. He said you stabbed Thomas when you found him and Lucy together." A flicker of guilt crossed Greg's face, answering her next question before she even had the chance to ask it. "You did do it…"

"Yes. I did."

Her posture stiffened at the coldness in Greg's tone. A sour taste entered her mouth and she turned away, chewing her inner cheek. Her mind raced at his confession, as well as his harsh delivery of it. For once in his life, Greg wasn't brooding or beating himself up. In fact, he seemed fine with what he'd done to Thomas, and that was what troubled her most.

Elizabeth's stomach twisted and it took her a moment to dislodge the lump in her throat. "Why don't you sound the slightest bit remorseful about it? Don't you feel any guilt?"

Greg shrugged, his loose limbs and flat voice proof of his

indifference. "Why should I? Thomas is the scum of the earth; you've said so yourself on countless occasions. Besides, he came after me, and I acted in self-defense. His death isn't my fault."

"He's not dead."

A muscle in Greg's jaw twitched. "He's alive?"

"He was when I left."

"That's–" His voice splintered, and he sat in silence a moment, still and rigid as he processed this information. "That's good. I'm glad murder can't be added to my list of crimes. Treason is bad enough."

Blown away by her brother's nonchalant attitude, Elizabeth scoured his features, finding an unusual gleam in his eye that made her stomach churn. There was no way to know for sure, but she was under the distinct impression that the gleam was one of satisfaction. To her dismay, Greg appeared to be *proud* of what he'd done.

"You really don't feel bad about this? At all?"

"What's there to feel bad about? He tried to kill me. I stopped him."

Elizabeth bristled at the smirk marring his face, and when she managed to locate her voice, it shook with worry. "I understand you were acting in self-defense; I had assumed as much. That's not the problem here. The issue I take is with your apparent lack of repentance. I refuse to believe you're fine with what you've done. Surely you feel–"

"He had it coming." Although his tone was controlled, Greg's curled lip was evidence of his mounting temper. "Thomas deserved it."

"Perhaps, but did I?" Heat flushed through Elizabeth's body as she glowered at him. "Did I deserve the way you treated me?"

Greg shook his head, the corners of his mouth pulled into a deep frown. "Is that what this is about?"

"No." Elizabeth crossed her arms and fought to keep her face passive. Her tone was steady, belying the ache in her heart as she faced him head on. "It does make me wonder, though. If you can attack our cousin and feel no worse for it, do you even regret what you said to me? Did you mean it when you said I'm dead to you?"

"Of course not, Bess. I never should've–"

"Who *are* you? When did you become this person?"

Greg drew in a long breath, then released it slowly. "What person?" The question was asked through clenched teeth, with a restraint Elizabeth could see was forced.

Her resolve wasn't shaken. "Someone who hurts people and feels no guilt for it whatsoever. The brother I knew six months ago never would've doubted my word and certainly wouldn't have told me I'm dead to him. You're no longer the same man, are you?"

Greg's lips twitched, but no words came out.

Unease bubbled up in her and her eyes drilled holes into the ground as she avoided his gaze. "You were right. The rebellion did change you."

There was no denying that anymore. It was hard to believe this impenitent stranger was the same man who'd taught her to swim, taken a beating for her when she spilled ink on their father's fur coat, and read every single one of the silly stories she'd written about nonsensical animals from her imagination. Where was *that* man?

Elizabeth sniffed as she met Greg's eyes once again. "I don't even recognize you anymore."

His shoulders drooped and his gloomy expression was a perfect match to Elizabeth's inner turmoil. "I know. I wish I could say I'm still the man I was six months ago, but that'd be a lie. I'm not the person I was then, and although I won't apologize for what happened with Thomas, I need you to know I'm deeply sorry for the way I treated you. You didn't deserve it. That, I do regret, more than you could ever know. I'm sorry, Bessie."

Elizabeth's anger dissipated in response to Greg's open display of remorse. Not yet ready to forgive him, she shook off those feelings of sympathy. "No matter. That's not what I came here to discuss. The only reason I'm here is to let you know Salvatore's coming after you."

"Coming after me?"

Elizabeth dropped her gaze.

"He wants me dead, doesn't he?"

"Yes. He plans to kill you himself."

Greg's whitewashed skin gave the impression he was going to be sick again. "I'm guessing His Majesty granted permission for this."

Elizabeth nodded and peered into his eyes, stunned by the fear she found there. "Yes, but Salvatore no longer has the element of surprise. Our uncle doesn't stand a chance now that you know he's coming. You're the greatest swordsman in Caracalla. You'll be fine."

She reached into her pocket for the sheath, slipped the dagger back into it, then tossed it on the ground. "I know it's not a sword, but it'll do. There's a map and some other supplies in the knapsack, and I'm leaving Lavender with you. You weren't difficult to find, so I advise you to stay off the roads."

"So that's it?" Greg's mouth tightened into a taut line. "You're leaving, just like that?"

"I've said what I needed to say."

He cocked an eyebrow. "And how do you plan to explain

where you've been these last few days? You can be sure your absence was noted."

"I won't go back to Crompton right away," Elizabeth answered. "I'm going to visit Clara in Ephrata for a while. You and I both know our cousin has no qualms about stretching the truth, so she'll happily lie about the date I arrived if necessary. No one needs to know I searched for you first."

Greg's eyes were unreadable. "Sounds like you've thought this through."

"I have." Elizabeth looked down and kicked her toe into the dirt. "And what about you? I assume you're heading to Nestle? You must be thrilled you can finally leave this place behind and have the life you've always wanted."

For the briefest moment, Greg seemed ruffled by her curt tone. A shadow of grief passed over his face, but he cleared his throat and all traces of sadness vanished.

"Yes," he said, his expression carefully blank. "I am."

The words landed like a rock in Elizabeth's chest and she bit down on her lip. "Farewell, Greg. Stay alert."

"Bess, wait." Greg's voice quaked. "Would you just listen to me for a minute?"

"No. I'm done here." Elizabeth pursed her lips and ignored her screaming conscience as she spun around and marched away from her best friend without a backwards glance.

However, while the distance between them grew, Elizabeth's resolve shrank. Her feet grew heavier with each step and as the painful sting of tears formed behind her eyes, doubt burned in her chest.

She'd warned her brother of Salvatore's plan, provided him with supplies, even gave him her own horse. But was it enough?

Her shoulders drooped. What more could she do? She couldn't possibly join him in exile. Could she? Though her thoughts were in turmoil, they were disrupted by the sound of hoof beats galloping up the road.

Elizabeth scurried to hide under the branches of a nearby willow tree. She peeked through the low-hanging limbs and watched as the Duke of Salvatore flew by on the back of a black stallion.

She glimpsed the determination on his face, but it was the bow and arrow strapped to his back and the two swords hanging from his belt that gave away his purpose with no room for doubt. He was prepared to kill... and he was headed straight for Greg's campsite.

The blood drained from Elizabeth's head as she pushed the branches out of her way and ran after him. She knew when her uncle rounded the bend up ahead he'd be able to see the smoke from the fire.

One of her shoes flew off, then the other, but she kept running. She sprinted through the mud back to the campsite, fighting through the pain as fallen branches dug into her feet.

Her heart pounded, and she prayed she'd reach her brother in time.

The emotional sting caused by Greg's words had blinded her to the seriousness behind all this. Her anger was real, but she'd overreacted and underestimated the danger he was in. It'd be her fault if he died, and she'd never be able to forgive herself if she was too late.

CHAPTER 12

*G*regory reclined on the bed of branches, battling numerous bouts of nausea. As his stomach whirled, he had the strange sensation he was being watched. He tried to convince himself it was just Elizabeth's words getting in his head, but he couldn't shake the feeling. "*He plans to kill you himself*," she'd said. "*Stay alert.*"

A chill swept through him, and he snatched the dagger off the ground. He then rose to his feet, his eyes narrowed as he scanned the forest for anything out of the ordinary.

A twig snapped in the trees, and he twisted around to locate the cause of the soft noise.

"Who's there?" Gregory did his best to keep his tone steady as he held the dagger in front of him. "Show yourself."

There was no answer save for the shrill cries of the cicadas in the trees.

It's only the wind. Nothing to worry about…

As Gregory stared into the wood, he heard the unmistakable sound of a bow snap, followed by a loud *whish*.

The arrow pierced his abdomen, just under the ribs, and

ripped its way through the right side of his torso. Gregory dropped to his knees, wheezing in agony.

Dizzy and disoriented, he glanced down at the tail-end of the shaft. The tip had forced itself through to his back, but slowed by the wall of flesh, the arrow was stuck inside him, causing excruciating pain with every shallow breath he took.

He struggled to keep his eyes open, but the unbearable burning under his rib took its toll, and he lost the strength to remain upright. Unable to support his own weight, Gregory crumpled sideways onto the ground.

The clumsy change of position disturbed the arrow and sent a surge of fire throughout his entire being. Though his hands quavered, he held the shaft in place, desperate to keep it still.

Every twitch of movement provoked the wound to launch a new assault, but he refused to let that stop him. To stay there was to die, and Prince Gregory of Caracalla wasn't about to let Salvatore best him. *This isn't how my story ends.*

Gregory released a guttural roar as he peeled himself off the soggy grass. He scraped together what little vitality he had left and used it to push himself onto his hands and knees. He'd almost succeeded, too, but the intense aching below his ribs dragged him back down to the forest floor with all the power of a thousand cannons.

Gregory's heart thudded in his chest. His body went limp, and he lay helpless on the ground as his uncle emerged from the trees.

Elizabeth rounded the bend and dove into the cover of the trees as soon as the smoke came into view. Like a cautious fox, she used the forest to her advantage and darted from trunk to trunk without being seen.

She approached the campsite to find Salvatore towering above Greg, and she slapped her hand over her mouth to smother the sob in her throat. Goosebumps speckled her skin as she absorbed the precarious scene.

Curled up in the grass with an arrow lodged in his torso, Greg sucked in long, desperate wheezes. As blood seeped from the wound through his white undershirt, the area below his right rib was painted an unnerving shade of red. His eyes were murky and weighted yet alert enough to follow Salvatore's movements.

A prideful smirk slinked across the duke's face as he walked circles around his victim, much like a hungry vulture inspecting its meal. The grim comparison made Elizabeth's heart thump so hard against her chest, she was certain it was going to betray her presence.

Betrayal. Now that was a concept she was familiar with and, unfortunately, guilty of. She'd left Greg alone to defend himself even though it was obvious he was in no state to fight. Less than ten minutes ago he'd been choking on his own refuse, yet she abandoned him anyway. Like a vindictive child, she allowed anger and hurt to direct her behavior.

A blade of guilt slashed through her as she acknowledged the horrible truth. Greg's blood was on her hands. Bernadette may have sent Salvatore, and Salvatore may have sent the arrow, but Elizabeth was the one who'd done nothing to stop it. If Greg died today, it'd be on her. *She* betrayed *him.*

Fully prepared to lose her life in this effort to save him, Elizabeth fixed her uncle with a cold, gritty stare. He was so distracted by the simplicity of his attack that he had no idea he was now the one being watched, hunted, stalked.

"This is almost too easy." A pinch of disappointment snuck into the duke's voice as he assessed Greg's colorless face. "Like snapping a twig."

Greg clenched his eyes shut, and with a sharp intake of breath, slowly reopened them as he lifted his head to greet Salvatore's stare head on. "Get it…over with."

"Patience, my boy," Salvatore snickered. He bent down to retrieve the small, ivory-handled dagger from the ground.

Elizabeth's heart sank. Minutes ago, she'd given the weapon to Greg so he could protect himself, but now she feared it'd be used *against* him.

"The blade is a bit dull. No matter, I'm sure it'll do the job. Even you have to admit that dying at the end of your own dagger is poetic. Yes, this will do well enough."

Elizabeth kept her gaze trained on Greg as she crept closer. Luckily, she avoided any branches that would alert her uncle of her intrusion. Her frazzled mind worked to formulate a plan, but she was at a complete loss. The only weapon she'd brought along from the palace was now in enemy hands.

"You have no idea how much pleasure this brings me." Salvatore seized a fistful of Greg's hair, and with a fierce tug, yanked him to his feet.

The anguished, primal wail Greg issued raised the hairs on Elizabeth's neck. She clutched both hands to her mouth to quiet her own horrified screams. She squeezed her eyes closed to ward off the black spots that blurred her sight.

When she reopened them, Salvatore had his arm snaked around Greg's neck and the dagger against his throat.

Greg twisted and gasped for air in a feeble attempt to break free. The arrow in his side jerked along with him, and after a few seconds, he slumped against Salvatore in defeat.

Elizabeth's gaze darted around the forest in search of her

uncle's horse. When the animal whinnied from behind a tree trunk, she tiptoed toward it and the assortment of weaponry strapped to its back.

The prickled weeds and sticks made her wince with every barefooted step, but she wouldn't stop even if there were hot coals at her feet.

"I've pictured this a hundred times." The duke cackled as he pressed the blade harder against Greg's neck. "I've imagined all the ways I could end your life. Slitting your throat will bring a much quicker death than I'd hoped, but I'll play it over and over in my mind for years to come."

Greg's eyelids fluttered closed as he faded out of consciousness.

Salvatore jerked him upright in a choke hold. "You're nothing. You threw in your lot with the rebels, and now no one cares what happens to you. You're alone."

Elizabeth clenched her fists so tight her nails dug into her palms. "That's not true," she snarled.

Greg's eyes shot wide open and sweat beaded his forehead. "Bess. Leave."

Elizabeth's gaze flittered to him as she advanced. Her stomach dropped. Greg's face was flooded with panic–for her.

She severed eye contact with him and shifted her focus to Salvatore. "Greg is still the rightful heir, and armies will rise up to defend his claim. You'll see. Drop the dagger, Uncle." She planted her feet in a wide stance. Her jaw set as she glared at the duke and braced herself for the crime she was about to commit.

"Don't be naïve," Salvatore spat. "His Majesty branded him a traitor, therefore he *is* a traitor. Interfere with my work here and you, too, shall be guilty of treason."

In spite of the fear building in her chest, Elizabeth took a deep breath and held her ground. She tightened her grip around her weapon, a primitive rock sling paired with a handful of stones. Although a rock sling wasn't the first weapon one thinks to bring into battle, it was the only one she had any experience with. In fact, her handiness with this particular instrument was quite impressive, and she was prepared to prove that should her uncle force her.

"Bess." Greg's troubled gaze sought hers, and when Elizabeth caught sight of his face, an uncontrollable shudder swept through her. The tendons stood out in his neck as he said, "Leave. Please."

The alarm in his voice made Elizabeth's heart pang.

"I'm not going anywhere." She swallowed, trying to maintain her veneer of bravery as the cracks in her voice exposed her underlying fright. "I won't let him hurt you."

The duke's eyes shifted toward the sling in his niece's hand. "Is that how you plan to stop me?" His face broke into a crooked grin. "A shepherd's sling? Henry must've put that in my bag as a joke."

"Interesting you should mention your son." Elizabeth placed one of the rocks in the leather pouch and slung it in a threatening circle above her head. "Henry is the one who taught me how to use this *puny thing*."

A spasm of apprehension swept across Salvatore's face.

"We used to hide in the garden." Elizabeth stole a peek at Greg. Despite his efforts to remain lucid, he was fading fast. "We'd put buckets of tar and goose feathers in the trees and use our rock slings to knock them down on the courtiers below. Correct me if I'm wrong, but I believe you were once a victim yourself."

Salvatore's face went pasty. For the first time since Elizabeth's appearance in the clearing, he seemed to question his wellbeing.

She pushed on. "Need I remind you I was the one who knocked the bucket of feathers down on your head? You of all people should know the accuracy of my aim. After all, I spent *years* perfecting it."

The duke gulped. "I should've expected you to intercede on your brother's behalf. Your admiration of him has always been akin to worship. But as I said, aide him and you'll be a traitor as well. Turn around now and leave this dirty business to me."

"Listen to him," Greg implored. He settled a pleading stare upon her. "Please. Go."

Elizabeth shook her head and took another bold step forward. She kept her attention secured on the dagger held against Greg's throat. "Don't do this."

Her concern for Greg's life increased as the blade was pressed harder against his neck. Blood trickled from where the sharp edge of the weapon met his flesh.

Desperate, Elizabeth gave it one last try. "Uncle, I beseech you. Don't go through with this."

"Go!" Sidetracked by his niece's intrusion and underestimating the danger it posed, Salvatore foolishly removed the weapon from Greg's neck. He pointed it at her instead. "Get out of here before I kill you both!"

Elizabeth shot Greg a look of warning and seized her opportunity to attack. He must've understood, because as Elizabeth swung the pouch over her head in one swift, circular motion, Greg elbowed Salvatore in the stomach and twisted out of his grasp.

With Greg out of the way, Elizabeth sent the projectile soaring through the air. Just as she claimed, her aim was first-rate. The rock smashed into her uncle's forehead, and his lifeless body slumped to the ground.

Without Salvatore to lean on for support, Greg staggered from side to side.

Elizabeth dropped the weapon and lunged forward to catch him. "Don't fall." A noticeable tremor warped her voice as her imagination supplied a morbid picture of the arrow's shaft snapping in half as Greg's body crashed into hers.

To her great relief, Greg managed to stay on his feet long enough for her to get behind him. She hooked her arms under his. "Lean back. I've got you."

His legs gave out the moment the go-ahead left Elizabeth's lips.

"Shit." She grunted as she scrambled to keep his weight from pulling her down with him. It took all her strength to slow Greg's descent, but she succeeded. Once he was eased onto his side, she sank to her knees beside him.

"That was…a bit rough." The corners of his mouth twitched into a tight smile, but it was immediately swept away as a pained grimace crossed his face. He turned his head to look at their uncle. "Is he…dead?"

Elizabeth checked his pulse and nodded, gaping open-mouthed at the corpse next to her. Salvatore was sprawled out on the ground beside his intended victim, but if he'd taken her seriously, he'd still be alive. A woman with a rock sling can be just as dangerous as a man with a dagger.

"He would've killed you. I had to do it."

Greg coughed, unable to keep his eyes open as more blood leaked from the hole in his side. Even the excruciating pain he endured wasn't enough to hide the gratitude in his weakened voice. "I know. Thank you."

Tears welled up in Elizabeth's eyes, but when she peeled

her gaze away from her uncle and focused her full concentration on Greg, her gut balled up in the tightest knot.

She choked back a sob as she inspected his wound. Her hands trembled, and she was about to pull the arrow out, but she stopped herself when it dawned on her that doing so would tear his insides apart.

"I don't know what to do…" Elizabeth gaped at the injury as a combination of desperation and vomit worked its way up her throat. "Greg, I need you to tell me what to do."

"Bess."

The resignation in that one syllable was all it took to make her heart burst. Even in her panicked state, she could still comprehend what it, and the vacant look in his eyes, meant. "No. No, no, no. I can fix this if you tell me how."

"Elizabeth, you can't–"

"I can! Just tell me what to do!"

Greg reached over and grabbed her hand. His grip was remarkably stable for someone on the brink of death. "Breathe."

"Tell me how to help you," she whimpered.

Greg squeezed her hand in his, as if he thought he could transfer some of his calmness over to her. "Stay." His voice was faint, his tone soft. It wasn't a demand for her to stay, but he wasn't begging her to either. "Don't leave…me…alone."

"I won't." Elizabeth shook her head, still in a state of shock. "I'm not going anywhere, but please. Tell me what I can do. There has to be something."

"Not…this time."

Elizabeth leaned over him, careful not to bump the tail-end of the shaft as she examined his back. The tip of the small, triangular arrowhead poked through the skin.

"I can't break it. That would leave the rest of the arrow still inside. What should I do?" She used her sleeve to sweep away the snot that dribbled down from her nose, searching Greg's drawn face for answers that weren't there. "Greg? Look at me. You have to stay with me, please."

He reopened his eyes a fraction. "Thank you…for coming…back."

Elizabeth shushed him. The effort it took for him to speak through his labored breathing strained his face. "You shouldn't try to talk right now. Just rest. I'll go get help."

Greg tightened his grip on her hand before she even moved a muscle. "You said…you…would stay."

Elizabeth's head felt like it weighed a ton. Her throat was scratchy, and her eyes were so wet she couldn't see. But in that instant, all she could think of was saving his life. "I know, but I need to get a physician."

"I'll be…dead by the…time…you get…back."

"Stop! You're going to be fine. You've fought battles. I bet you've seen hundreds of men survive worse injuries than this, right? How did the field surgeons save them?"

Greg bit his lip. "I'm so sorry…for what I said. You're my…best friend, Bess. You didn't deserve–"

"That's enough. It's in the past now, all right? I've already forgotten it. Besides, what you said to me is nothing compared to what I did. I never should've left your side. I'm the one who's sorry. Terribly, terribly sorry."

Greg gifted her with a quivery smile, and his eyes fluttered shut.

Tears poured down Elizabeth's cheeks as her brother's grip on her hand grew weaker…and weaker. "Greg?"

She slapped his face in a desperate attempt to prevent him from closing his eyes for good. It was no use. There was no response, not even a stifled moan of discomfort upon receiving the strike. "Wake up. Damn it, Greg! Open your eyes!"

Frantic, she grabbed his shoulders and shook, hard, but even that wasn't enough to jolt him back.

Elizabeth let out a helpless wail. Never in her wildest dreams had she thought he could be brought down. She'd always believed he was invincible.

But Greg wasn't invincible. He was human. And now he was gone.

"I'm so sorry." Sobbing, Elizabeth scooped her arm under his neck and pulled him into her, cradling his head against her. Time slowed to a crawl as she grieved. What was probably only a few minutes felt like hours.

The arrow shifted as she held him in her shaky arms, but it didn't matter anymore. Greg was free from the agony that had tormented him in his final moments.

At least, that's what Elizabeth thought until she heard a small, almost imperceptible moan. Her eyes popped open, and she glanced down at his face.

To her astonishment, Greg's facial muscles weren't relaxed and unburdened as one would expect from a corpse. His eyes were closed, but the area around them was tightened, his brow lowered. Was it possible he wasn't dead, but had passed out for a while?

"Greg?"

"Mm?"

"You're alive!" That meant he had a chance. She glanced around for anything that would help.

The blankets! It'd be painful, and possibly fatal, but if she could get him on top of one of them she could have Lavender pull him to Mary's house. Mary was Greg's only hope for survival. She'd know what to do.

Elizabeth's knees wobbled as she dragged him onto one of the blankets, taking special care not to disrupt the arrow protruding from under his ribcage.

"Just hang on, Greg. You're going to be fine."

A quiet groan was his response.

Elizabeth held one corner of the blanket in her hand and mounted the horse. She started out at an extremely slow speed, but once she was certain Greg was secure and wouldn't roll off, she quickened the pace.

Mary will save him. She has to.

CHAPTER 13

The fire in the hearth blazed, and it wasn't long before the water in the kettle boiled. Elizabeth dropped strips of cloth into the pot and rushed back to her brother's side.

Now shirtless and supported by a mound of pillows on Mary's bed, Greg hadn't stirred much since they got here. Surviving the bumpy journey to the cottage was an extraordinary victory in itself, but his true test of endurance was yet to come.

"He needs to consume a bit of this." Mary whirled around the cottage like a spinning top as she handed Elizabeth a long brown root, then scurried over to the wash basin to rinse her hands. "It's mandrake."

Elizabeth's brows drew together as she eyed the oddly shaped root. "What's the purpose of–"

"It'll help numb the pain."

She tipped her head to the side and scratched her chin, contemplating how the hell that was going to be possible. "Mary. He's passed out. Even if he was lucid enough to chew on it, it'd break his teeth. How do you expect–"

Mary jerked around to face her and gave an exasperated little tut. "Grind it up, and *then* he can drink it." She pointed to a mortar and pestle on the shelf. "Use that."

Elizabeth set straight to work. Her dread solidified in the pit of her stomach as she pulverized the mandrake in preparation for the frightening procedure ahead.

Meanwhile, Mary brought a pot of wine to a boil. "That's enough for now, child. Too much will kill him." She took a spoonful of the powder and added it to the wine. A few minutes later, the beverage was ready.

Elizabeth tilted the cup into Greg's mouth. She was careful not to give more than a few small sips at a time and was impressed to learn that although he was unconscious, his swallow reflex was triggered by the liquid.

"Make sure he drinks it all," Mary advised over her shoulder. "This is going to hurt. He's incredibly lucky the arrow didn't pierce an organ or hit a bone, but that won't make removing it any less painful."

As if the ominous words could traverse the plains of consciousness, Greg began to rouse. He groaned in discomfort, and Elizabeth grabbed his hand, giving it a gentle squeeze. "Greg, can you hear me? You've been shot, but we're going to get the arrow out."

His eyes twitched open. He tried to speak, but a small moan was all that escaped his lips.

Encouraged enough by the attempt, Elizabeth dabbed the sweat from his damp forehead. "Don't worry, you're in good hands. Mary knows what she's doing."

"Go take one of the cloths out of the water." Mary shoved her aside and knelt down beside the bed, her expression serious as she examined the injury. "This is going to be more difficult now that he's awake. Mandrake root doesn't prevent *all* the pain."

"Should we wait until he passes out again?" Elizabeth handed the lengthy strip of fabric to the old woman and stooped down beside Greg's head. She placed what she hoped was a comforting hand on his forearm and added, "He looks about halfway there already."

"There's no time." Mary's voice harbored a finality so severe it made Elizabeth hesitate to argue. "Prince Gregory, if you can hear me lift your right finger."

Elizabeth's gaze shot to his hand, relieved to see the movement. "He did it!"

"Well done, my boy. Now, I'm going to tie this piece of fabric to the end of the shaft. It won't be pleasant, but as the cloth passes through it will remove any debris that got inside. This will lessen the chance of your wound going bad. Lift your finger if you understand what I've just told you."

"He did it again." Elizabeth forced a smile of encouragement. "You're doing great, Greg."

"You certainly are," Mary concurred with a smile that didn't quite reach her eyes. "Once the cloth is attached, I'll slowly push the arrow through. It may take a few minutes, but you *must* stay still the whole–"

"Mary." Elizabeth placed an ear to Greg's chest and let out a huge breath when she heard the glorious sound of a heartbeat. "He passed out."

"Good. I'll take it from here. You take the rest of the cloths out of the kettle and rub the poultice I made of honey and barley onto them. I want those bandages ready to go by the time this arrow is out."

"Yes, Mary." Eager to help in any way she could, Elizabeth gave her brother's hand one last squeeze and went over to the table to complete her task. This was all her fault, and if she could help save him, perhaps he'd be able to forgive her. She *needed* him to forgive her.

As instructed, Elizabeth dipped the spoon in the mixture and spread the poultice over the long pieces of cloth, one by one. She'd just finished the fifth bandage when Greg's cry pierced through the silence of the cottage.

A flush of panic swept through Elizabeth as she reeled around to see the point of the arrow exiting the small hole in his back. As Greg screamed out in pure agony, Mary was hunched over the side of the bed, her face inches from his ribcage as she drove the arrow out little by little.

The pain of the extraction was too much to bear, and as Elizabeth stood there, petrified, she wrestled the urge to sprint out the door and shield herself from his torment. Ashamed at her cowardice, Elizabeth gathered her nerves and dashed back to Greg's side. *Don't you dare abandon him again!*

He was coated in sweat as he rolled about without control. He howled as though every inch of his body was on fire, and when Elizabeth grasped his hand in hers, she was forced to raise her voice in order to be heard.

"Greg, I'm right here. I know it hurts, but you must try to calm down. Please." She grabbed a washrag out of the basin, rung the cool water out, and shoved the cloth into his mouth.

The ability to chomp down on the gag brought an end to Greg's shrieks. It did not, however, help control his crazed movements.

"I know it's difficult, but you *need* to be still," Elizabeth whispered, inserting as much confidence into her voice as she could under these circumstances. Her own body quivered with horror as Mary forced the long shaft through the hole in Greg's lower back. "Shh. Mary's going to get it out, but you can't move while she works. Please, Greg."

Mary pinched her lips together and threw her hands up in frustration. "Unless he stops flailing about, I can't remove it."

"You can't give up!" Elizabeth could tell by the immediate scowl she received that her voice was far too shrill for Mary's liking. She sweetened her tone and tried again. "Mary, please, I'm begging you. Don't let him die."

The tension in Mary's jaw loosened, and the irritation in her eyes melted away, leaving nothing but remorse and pity in its wake. "I'm sorry, but if he keeps this up, I'll end up doing more harm than good. There's nothing I can do unless he relaxes."

"Greg. Greg!" Elizabeth pushed up her sleeves and leaned in, cupping her brother's face in her hands to force him to look directly into her eyes. Her tone became urgent and commanding. "Listen to me. If you don't stop moving, you're going to die, do you hear me? The arrow is almost out, but you need to stay still and let Mary finish. I know you can do this. Stay still."

Greg's fingers curled into fists as he inhaled deeply through his nose, almost as though he was channeling the strength he needed from the air itself. He tightened his jaw, and his wild thrashes died down.

"Perfect, Greg." A smile spread across her lips as she clasped onto his hand in a show of support. "You're doing great."

"Yes, it's almost out." Mary pulled the arrow the rest of the way through with great care. Once the object was removed, blood instantly poured from the hole.

"Mary!" Elizabeth cried as she gaped down at the gush of crimson fluid rushing from Greg's body. "Do something!"

"It's all right, child."

"It most certainly is not!"

"Bleeding is necessary. The wound is cleansing itself."

Still skeptical, Elizabeth watched the blood flow from the hole in Greg's back. The burgundy stain on the bed expanded at a rapid rate, too rapid. "I think it's clean enough!"

Mary pressed one hand against the opening to staunch the blood flow and used the other to point to a miniature iron shovel beside the hearth. "Stick the broad end into the fire and hold it directly into the flames. Take it out right before it starts to glow red."

Following her orders without question, Elizabeth stood in front of the fireplace and waited for the shovel to heat up. It felt like an eternity. She didn't take her eyes off Greg for more than a few seconds at a time, despite the fact that he'd fallen back into oblivion.

"You'll want to cover your ears," Mary said. "He's unconscious now, but in a moment, he won't be."

The hairs on the nape of Elizabeth's neck spiked, along with the volume of her voice. "What the hell does that mean? What are you going to do?"

Mary beckoned Elizabeth over to her. "That's good enough. Give me the shovel."

Once again, she obeyed. However, she soon regretted her compliance, for the moment the iron tool was in Mary's hands, a fierce look of determination creased the old woman's brow. Before Elizabeth could question her intentions, Mary pressed the heated iron against Greg's back.

At the touch of the shovel, he awoke and let out a bone-chilling cry of anguish as his skin was seared.

"Stop! Mary! Stop!" Elizabeth wrapped her arms around the woman's torso, dragging her backwards away from the bed. "Have you gone mad?"

"This will seal the wounds closed. Let go of me, child. I must stop the bleeding."

"Sew it shut!" Elizabeth was irate as she tried to grab the hot iron from the woman's hands. "Let go! I won't let you burn him!"

"This is the quickest way to mend the holes, but I must do

it now, before he loses any more blood and bleeds to death. There's no time to sew it."

Elizabeth crossed her arms in front of her and took a reluctant step back, biting her lip as Mary pushed past her to reheat the shovel. "Your methods are barbaric."

"My methods will save him," Mary retorted.

"They better." Beset by both dizziness and nausea, Elizabeth pulled one of the short stools away from the table, placed it next to the bed, and settled in beside Greg.

As he whimpered into the pillow, Elizabeth dabbed the sweat from his forehead and whispered more words of encouragement into his ear. Her gaze continuously darted over to the hearth where Mary was heating the shovel in preparation for the second round of torture.

"It's ready."

Elizabeth blanched and reached for his hand. Deep down, she knew it was done more to comfort herself than for Greg's benefit, but she was too exhausted at this point to feel bad about that.

By the time Mary had finished cauterizing both the entry and exit points, Greg had drifted back into the world of unconsciousness. Elizabeth was close to joining him.

Mary shuffled over to the water basin and scrubbed her hands of the blood. "It's time to pour the alcohol over his injuries and bandage him up. I know you've been through a lot today, but I suggest you pay attention, dear. The bandages will need redressed with a fresh mixture every hour, so we want to make sure you know how to do it properly. Cauterizing is a faster way to stop the bleeding and close a wound than sewing, however it's just as likely to swell and ooze pus if we're not careful. The poultice and fresh wrappings will reduce the risk drastically, though."

Battling to keep her stomach contents where they

belonged, Elizabeth watched the old woman demonstrate how to wrap the bandages. Greg remained unconscious the entire time, a concern she quickly gave voice to.

"Don't fret, my dear. The mandrake root is starting to take effect. It's a shame it didn't happen sooner, but now that it has, he'll sleep much more peacefully. I don't expect him to wake up for at least a few hours, and even then it will only be for a moment or two. He'll probably fade in an out of consciousness for the next few days."

Elizabeth's eyebrows shot up as her stomach plunged down. "Days?"

"Don't worry," Mary said with a lighthearted chuckle. "That's to be expected after such a traumatic injury. In all honesty, it's for the best. In his moments of wakefulness, he'll be quite disoriented, not to mention in a great deal of pain. He needs to sleep as much as possible."

"So now what do we do?"

"Keep him comfortable as best you can and make sure he gets enough to drink. Every so often, give him tiny sips of the boiled wine. Remember to change his bandages in about an hour's time. The supplies are in the cupboard beside the hearth. I'll be back–"

"You're leaving?" Elizabeth's posture went rigid as she straightened on the stool.

"I must go into town for some ale. He'll certainly need it when he regains consciousness." With a gentle smile, Mary headed for the door. "Let him rest, dear. I'll only be gone a short while."

Elizabeth gulped. Despite her strong desire to oppose her friend's decision to leave her in charge of Greg's wellbeing, she didn't have the strength it'd take to do so.

"You've done well, child. You saved your brother's life today, and I know he'll be proud of you. Relax and take a nap. You've certainly earned it." With that, Mary took her leave.

Although the idea of a nap was appealing, Elizabeth couldn't possibly fall asleep while Greg's life hung by a thread. Instead, she clutched his hand in hers, and bowed her head to pray.

$$\sim$$

The cottage door creaked, and Elizabeth peeled her weary gaze off her brother.

"How's the prince doing?" Mary inquired as she approached the bedside. "Any changes since I left?"

"No." Elizabeth directed her gaze back to Greg and watched as his chest rose and fell with each peaceful breath. "He was asleep the whole time, just as you said."

"I'm happy to hear that."

Father Timothy dropped his sacks on the floor and joined the women beside the bed. Elizabeth let go of Greg's hand and stood up, giving the priest room to examine him. "My sister claims the injury has been treated, but I have to check for myself." He lifted the bandages with as much care as his old fingers would allow and studied the fresh wounds for a good minute. "Our father was a physician, you know."

"Mary mentioned that last night. How does it look?"

"Better than I imagined," he admitted, "yet the wound could easily become inflamed." The priest reapplied the fabric and held the back of his hand against Greg's forehead. His lips pulled into a frown that made Elizabeth's breath hitch.

"What's wrong?" Her voice was riddled with concern. "Does he have a fever? I just felt his head a few minutes ago, but–"

"He has a *slight* fever, yes. To an untrained hand, it would be barely noticeable, Your Highness. Now, while a fever is nothing unusual after such a distressing ordeal, it can become dangerous if it rises too high. My guess is that it'll get much worse before it gets better. The next week or so will test your mind, body, and faith, but it's my firm belief that in time, Prince Gregory will make a full recovery."

"Thank you, Father."

"You're welcome. Regrettably, I have some rather unpleasant news to share with you." Father Timothy's tone was casual, yet there was a note of disquiet in his eyes.

Elizabeth opened her mouth to ask what was wrong but was silenced when the priest pulled a scroll from his robe and held it out to her. She glanced over at Mary, who nodded in encouragement. "Go on, child."

Her mouth went dry as she unrolled the document and read aloud. "His Majesty, King Charles of Caracalla, orders anyone with knowledge as to the prince's whereabouts to come forth and give their testimonies. Prince Gregory has been declared a traitor to the Crown, having aided in the rebellion in the north and assaulted a member of the nobility. The exiled prince is hereby sentenced to death."

Elizabeth looked up at Father Timothy, her pulse racing. "The king wrote this?" Upon receiving a solemn nod from the bald man, she turned and cast Mary an accusatory look. "You said he'd change his mind. You said all would soon go back to normal."

"That was before I knew your brother attacked a noble, dear." Mary's tone was gentle, yet the words she spoke next shook Elizabeth to the core. "That's a crime punishable by death."

"Perhaps for citizens without noble lineage themselves,

but Greg's the prince! Surely His Majesty can't do this to his own son!"

"He who wears the crown makes the rules," Father Timothy lamented. "Go on, keep reading."

Elizabeth glowered, but continued. "Anyone who is caught housing, supporting, or helping the traitor in any way will in turn be deemed a traitor and also sentenced to death. A sizeable reward will be given to anyone with knowledge as to the traitor's current location. The people of Caracalla must band together to rid our nation of the poison within."

Elizabeth's throat burned as her eyes threatened to spill over with tears. "Where will we go?"

"To Fincost Priory." Her face must've revealed the confusion she felt within, persuading the priest to elaborate. "It's a monastery on the northeastern seaboard where some of my closest companions reside. I've already sent word of your arrival." Father Timothy then pulled a long black habit out from his sack and handed it to Elizabeth.

Her mouth hung open. "I...I can't be a nun." Her heart hammered as she let her dismay fall from her lips in a scramble of words. "I want to get married and have children and...I'm not even Catholic. How can I possibly become a nun if I'm not Catholic? I won't convert and...why are you smirking at me?"

The pair of elderly siblings laughed together, and the noise caused Greg to stir in the bed. Mary sobered and lowered her voice. "It takes years of strict religious service and devotion to become a nun. No offense intended, Your Highness, but you don't have what it takes."

"I couldn't agree more." Befuddled, Elizabeth took a second look at the clothing. It all appeared to be real, but appearances could be deceiving. "I'll feign nunnery?"

Father Timothy nodded as his face tore into a wide smile.

"Precisely! Prince Gregory will play the part of a friar who has taken ill and must return to the monastery. It'll take a few weeks to get there but once you arrive, he'll receive the best possible care. I'll come back soon, and if your brother's lucid, I'll talk all this over with him in further detail. There's much to discuss."

"When do we leave?" Elizabeth asked, feeling hopeful. The plan was ludicrous. So ludicrous, in fact, that it might work.

Father Timothy shrugged. "That depends on his condition. However, you mustn't leave any later than the first of October."

Elizabeth glanced at Greg and wondered if he'd be well enough to travel by then. July was nearing its end, leaving him about two months to recover. "Where will we stay in the mean time?"

"Here," Mary answered with stern conviction. "You'll both stay right here with me."

Elizabeth chewed the inside of her cheek. She appreciated her friend's willingness to house them, but it made Mary a traitor to the Crown as well. "I can't let you do that for us, Mary. It's too dangerous. We should seek asylum in the church."

Father Timothy shook his head. "Dozens of people visit my church a day. You'd be seen. This is the safest place."

Elizabeth wasn't convinced. "My uncle's dead body was left down the road from here. Once it's found, they'll assume Greg murdered him, and they'll raid every home and business in this town until he's captured."

The priest and his sister exchanged a knowing look.

"What? What is it?"

"Mary told me about what happened with your uncle." Father Timothy ran an anxious hand over his head and plopped down on one of the stools beside the table. "It's been taken care of. He'll be buried in the church cemetery tonight, after dark. I also found a a knapsack and a red doublet near the body. I assume they belong to your brother?"

Elizabeth nodded. "The doublet does, and I brought the knapsack from the palace."

The priest motioned to the floor. Lo and behold, there was the knapsack, Greg's doublet, and even the pair of shoes that fell off Elizabeth's feet in her rush to get back to the campsite.

"No one will know you or the prince are in Gettsbury."

"What about Salvatore's horse? If it finds its way back to—"

"He is enjoying a nice, peaceful stay in my personal stable. Don't worry, Your Highness. I destroyed the campsite and scoured the area for any remaining evidence that you or Prince Gregory were there. You're safe."

Elizabeth lifted her chin into the air and closed her eyes as she exhaled a heavy sigh of relief. "Thank you both, so very much. I only have one more concern. What if someone stops by for a visit? I understand the risk is lower here than at the church, but we could still be discovered, couldn't we?"

"Allow me to ease your mind." Mary hobbled over to the rug in the center of the cottage and lifted the corner, revealing a trap door beneath.

Excitement tingled through Elizabeth as she scrambled to her feet and peeked inside the secret hole. The combination of sunbeams shining through the windows and the fire in the hearth provided enough light to see inside, and although the space was scarcely big enough for two people, she was uplifted by the sight. It wouldn't be a comfortable fit, but she and Greg would both be able to squeeze inside if necessary.

Thanks to the king and his unquenchable desire to inflict

pain and abuse, the royal siblings had plenty of experience hiding in small, dark spaces.

Goosebumps still appeared on Elizabeth's arms when she remembered her father's reaction the time she'd failed her third spelling exam in a row. When her tutor warned her that the king already knew about the failure and was waiting for her in her chambers, the ten-year-old princess fled straight to her brother's lodgings instead. Greg, being no stranger to his father's disappointment or the bruises it led to, jumped into action.

He dragged Elizabeth into his wardrobe closet and shoved her into one of his many trunks. Crammed inside the wooden chest among the prince's collection of hats, she waited, her heart thumping so loud she swore it'd give away her position. She hadn't been hiding long before King Charles stormed into his son's apartments and demanded to know where she was. Greg feigned innocence, but the king knew better.

Elizabeth later learned that Greg had earned a thrashing for his involvement in her concealment, but when the lid of the trunk was opened, he didn't greet her with anger or resentment. Instead, he gathered her into his arms and promised to always keep her safe.

Mary's voice pulled Elizabeth's wandering, heavy thoughts back to the present. "My papa built this hideaway during the famine of 1534 to store the meat he hunted illegally. We kept dried venison in here back then, but now it'll serve as a hiding place for you and Prince Gregory should the need arise. So, you see, my cottage will be the safest place for you both until he's well enough to travel."

Tears of joy sprang to Elizabeth's eyes as she met Mary's sweet gaze. She didn't know how she could possibly thank them for this. Father Timothy and Mary had given her hope, but more importantly, they were giving Greg a future.

CHAPTER 14

he trees swayed with the wind, and a wolf's eerie howl filled the night air. With the stone in her hand, she tiptoed toward the man in the mask who was asleep beside the fire.

Motivated by her rage, she bashed the rock against his skull and he screamed out in sudden agony. Furious, Elizabeth hit him over and over until he took his last breath and her trembling hands were soaked with his blood. Through the mask, she could see that although he was dead, her victim's eyes were still wide open in shock.

She pulled the black mask off his face and her heart stopped.

"Greg!"

Elizabeth's eyes snapped open. Her chemise was soaked with perspiration and stuck to her drenched skin. *It's not real.* She ran a shaky hand over her head as she took in slow, deliberate breaths to regain her composure. *It was just another nightmare. I fell asleep, that's it.*

Sitting guard at Greg's bedside day and night, she'd accumulated no more than twelve hours sleep total since he was shot five days ago. Even so, she wished she hadn't dozed off at all.

The vivid nightmares grew in intensity each time she closed her eyes, but this one in particular haunted her most of all. Her face in her hands, it was all she could do to keep from being sick.

"Bess?"

Elizabeth's head shot up. Despite her physical exhaustion and mental anguish, her mouth turned up in a smile as she slid off the chair and sat on her knees beside the trundle bed.

It hadn't been an easy feat to move her unconscious brother from the upper bed to the lower one, but with the combined strength of Father Timothy, Elizabeth, and Mary, they'd succeeded in giving Greg his own sleeping space. As the priest had pointed out during his visit, the last thing Greg needed was to get his injury elbowed in the middle of the night. The trundle bed offered the perfect solution.

"Good morning, Greg. It's good to see you awake."

She placed a tentative hand on his forehead, and her heart drummed as the heavy weight on her shoulders lifted. To her relief, Greg no longer burned with heat. In fact, although his skin was ashen and clammy, it felt no warmer than hers. All her efforts had paid off, and Elizabeth's elation almost prompted her to get up and dance around the cottage. "Your fever broke! I think you're out of the woods! How are you feeling?"

"I've been better," he choked with a grimace.

"That's true, but you've also been much worse." Elizabeth was unable to contain her smile. "I'll admit, you had me a bit worried."

"Where are we?" He scanned the unfamiliar room through wide, nervous eyes.

"We're in Mary's home. I haven't known her long, but don't worry. She can be trusted. She saved your life."

Greg's eyebrows squished together, but instead of asking the question that was so clearly on the tip of his tongue, he pushed up on his arms in a struggle to sit up.

Concerned by his groans, Elizabeth placed a restraining hand on his shoulder. "Don't exert yourself. You're still healing."

Greg winced and as his features twisted into a look of defeat, he settled back into the pillows. A bleak frown darkened his face as he asked, "What happened to me, Bess?"

"Well, let's start with the last thing you remember." Elizabeth sat on the floor and crossed her legs in front of her like a pretzel. "You've alternated between unconsciousness and a fever-induced delirium for the last few days, and this is the first coherent conversation you've been able to hold since we got here. I think it'd be best to let you start at the beginning and work from there. Where do your memories start to get hazy?"

"Um, after I got sick from the badger." His gaze clouded as the light of the fire reflected on his sweat-dampened face. "I remember you came and told me our uncle was after me..." The word *uncle* seemed to spark his memory and his attention shifted to his torso. "Salvatore. He shot me."

"Yes." Elizabeth made a rueful frown. "Do you remember anything else?"

Greg gave a slight shake of his head. "Bits and pieces. Most of it's a blur."

With guilt so powerful she was unable to meet his gaze as she spoke, Elizabeth took it upon herself to clear the fog in his mind. "After we parted ways, I was on my way to Ephrata when I saw Salvatore riding by, armed with too many weapons to count. I ran as fast as I could to stop him, but you were already shot by the time I got there. He was about to slit your throat so I...I..." Elizabeth couldn't complete the sentence.

"I remember." Greg offered her a sympathetic, yet weak smile. "You took our uncle's life to preserve mine. You saved me."

"I murdered him." Her tone was far off, distant as she worked hard to choke back the sobs. "I killed our uncle."

Greg lifted his arm as an invitation for Elizabeth to hug him and she accepted his offer, powerless to control the tears any longer. "I had to do it."

As he kissed the top of her head, she could already sense the apology forming on his lips. If there was one thing Greg was good at, other than giving lectures, it was apologizing for things that were out of his control. Bird droppings could fall in his hair, and he'd still find a way to place the blame on himself.

"I'm so sorry you were put in that situation because of me." His voice quaked as he cradled her to his chest in the same loving manner Elizabeth imagined her mother would, if she was alive.

The sixteen-year-old princess had never known the love of her mother, but Greg had always done his best to fill that void. Even after taking an arrow to the side, he was still the one offering comfort, regardless of the pain the physical contact likely caused him.

"This is all my fault," he mumbled.

Elizabeth removed herself from his embrace and put on her sternest face. "No, it's not. Don't mistake my tears for regret, Greg. I'd kill him again in a heartbeat if I had to. I offered him a chance to leave, but he refused. That's on him, not you. He sought you out and was strangled by his own rage. None of this is your fault."

Greg's eyes filled with an inner glow as he stared at her. "I wish you hadn't been forced to end a life to save mine, but I appreciate that you thought me worthy of saving. Thank you, Bess."

"You're welcome." Elizabeth sniffed back the tears. What else was there to say? She knew she'd done the right thing. If anyone had earned the privilege of a long, meaningful life and a peaceful death as an old man in his bed, it was him. "I'm sorry. I didn't mean to make this about me when you're the one who was shot." She wiped away the moisture on her face with her sleeve.

Though his expression was serious, his eyes shined with sympathy and understanding. "I wish there was something I could say to help you feel better, but I'm afraid the only remedy to this particular ailment is time. I know this from personal experience. The faces of all the men I killed in the rebellion haunt me every time I close my eyes. I hope eventually, after enough time passes, we will both be able to move on. We might even forgive ourselves one day. But until then, I'm here if you want to talk."

"Thank you for that, but I'd rather we never discuss it again. I did what needed to be done, and although I feel the burden of the life I took, I don't regret it at all. It's over, and I want us both to forget it."

"Are you certain?"

"I am."

Greg nodded, signifying his agreement to adhere to her wishes. "So, what happened next? How did we get here?"

Elizabeth squared her shoulders, hoping to look more at ease than she felt. "After the duke was…*dealt with,* I realized you were still alive and I brought you here on a blanket."

"Yes, Lavender dragged me." Greg made a second attempt to sit up, a mistake that sent a ripple of pain scurrying across his face. His hand hovered over the area where the arrow had entered, but Elizabeth reached out and grabbed his wrist before he made contact.

"It'll only hurt more if you touch it," she warned with a hapless smile. "Mary purchased a jug of ale to help with the pain. I'll bring you some, but please, stay still." She hopped up and retrieved the jug from the cabinet, pouring him a generous amount and keeping a close eye on him all the while.

When she returned to his bedside, Greg's hands were balled up at his sides and his labored breaths came out as hisses through clenched teeth.

"Here." She held the cup to his lips, and he drank the ale in less time than it took her to pour it. Once the alcohol was gone, Greg reclined back against the pillows, tension etched into every one of his features as he waited for the ale to do its job.

"Do you want me to let you sleep?"

"No," Greg answered, his voice strangled. "Talking is a good distraction."

Elizabeth smirked. "Lucky for you, talking is one skill I'm quite adept at. Where were we?"

Greg swallowed, his eyes still closed as he spoke in a strained whisper. "You were telling me how Lavender dragged me here on a blanket, but I remember that part. The pain from the movement was so severe I woke up during the journey, but only for a moment."

"I prefer to say she pulled you, but yes, essentially that's what happened." Elizabeth rose and went to the pot of chicken soup that hung over the fire. She used a ladle to scoop some broth into a bowl and returned to her spot on the floor beside his bed. "Now that you're awake you can finally get some nourishment. Here." She lifted the wooden spoon to his lips.

He frowned at the broth, unimpressed. "Have anything more substantial? Some venison steak, perhaps?"

Elizabeth's heart twinged with sympathy. "I'm sure you're starving, but we have to take this slow. You've been semiconscious and feverish since we got here. I think it's best to start with something light."

Greg rolled his eyes at her but opened his mouth in compliance. After the first spoonful was down, he continued. "So, you dragged me here on the blanket. Then what?"

"Mary and I carried you to the bed, and she set right to work removing the arrow. She tied a cloth to one end and pulled it out the other. Afterwards she used an iron shovel to seal the wounds. I totally objected to that, of course, but she insisted there was no time to sew them shut. Then we bandaged you up with a honey poultice."

Greg moaned. "I don't remember much from the procedure, but I do remember how agonizing it was. That, and your very intimidating demand to stop moving. I doubt I would've survived if you hadn't been there."

There was a thickness in the back of Elizabeth's throat that made it difficult to take in air. "It's my fault you were shot in the first place," she murmured, staring at her lap in shame.

"That's ridiculous."

She slouched. "No, it's not. If I would've stayed with you in the clearing–"

"We'd both be dead. You saved my life."

With her shoulders hunched and her chin dropped to her chest, Elizabeth made herself as small as she felt. "Perhaps, but I abandoned you when I knew someone was trying to kill you."

"You saved my life," Greg repeated, a smile of gratitude lighting his face almost as much as the crackling fire lit up the cottage. "Despite the coldness I showed you, you still went out of your way to warn me of our uncle's plans, and then you came back a second time when you saw him heading in my direction. Trust me, you don't share in any of the blame." He lowered his voice, his complexion losing the little color it had left. "Unlike you, I was the one to make a true mistake."

"What mistake is that?" Elizabeth asked.

"Deep down, I always suspected Lucy didn't love me," he disclosed, his voice frayed by a combination of regret and the physical pain inflicted by his injury. "But she pretended she did and oddly enough that was sufficient for me. When you told me what you saw in the labyrinth, it infuriated me because it meant everyone else would soon see the truth too. I allowed my humiliation to overshadow everything else, including you. I'm sorry for that."

"I don't understand." Elizabeth frowned as she recalled the hostility in his eyes when he'd declared she was dead to him. That was the cruelest thing he'd ever said to her, and quite frankly, his words had gutted her. "If you suspected her unfaithfulness all along, why did you defend her? Why did you accuse me of being a liar if you knew I wasn't lying at all? I was devastated when you told me I was dead to you."

"There's no excuse for my behavior and I regret every word I said to you." Greg pinched the bridge of his nose, his eyes closed as he spent a few moments stewing in silence. When he finally opened his eyes and spoke again, his voice was drained. "I hate myself for treating you that way. I suppose all I can say is I was determined to deny it because I didn't want everyone to think any less of me than they already did."

"It's no secret Lucy is a half-brained strumpet," Elizabeth pointed out. "She'd bed a weasel if she thought it might elevate her station. Why would anyone judge you for her impurities?"

"Think of what His Majesty would say once he learned I couldn't even manage to keep a woman content. I've always been a complete failure in his eyes. You and I both know he'd blame me for the failed relationship, which would have led to him once again questioning my ability to rule."

The accuracy behind Greg's assessment twisted Elizabeth's stomach. "You're right. I hadn't considered that."

"All my life, I've felt undeserving of the royal family I was born into, victimized by His Majesty's criticism and derision. I wanted so badly to avoid his disparagement that I ended up hurting the one person who would've stood by me had the truth come out. You didn't deserve that, no matter the reason. You're the only person who ever cared for me, yet I repaid your loyalty by slinging mud in your face. Can you forgive me?"

"I already have." Elizabeth dipped the spoon in the soup and held it in front of his mouth. "I may have gotten my feelings hurt, but you can't get rid of me that easily."

Greg took the bite and as a multitude of conflicting emotions swept across his face, his shoulders slumped. "I don't understand. I told you that you were dead to me, yet you still chose to leave home and warn me of the danger I was in. Here you are, right by my side, even though I've been charged with high treason and exiled because of it. No matter what I do, you always stand by me."

"Yes, and that won't ever change."

His face marked by an expression Elizabeth couldn't

quite decipher, Greg let his head fall back into the pillows as he stared up at the ceiling in silence.

"Greg?"

"You're the one good thing in my life, Bess." He lifted his head to look at her, a flush of heat coloring his cheeks. "Watching you grow has been my greatest joy, and although I don't always show it, I want you to know you've given me purpose."

Elizabeth's lips parted, but words failed her. A brief moment passed where the only sound was the crackling of the fire as she explored her mind for the proper response.

"I don't know what to say," she said at last, opting for honesty.

"I don't expect you to say anything, but I have to get this off my chest." Greg's voice was stern, and Elizabeth straightened in her seat. "No one ever believed in me the way you do, the way you always have. I've messed up more times than I care to confess, but for some reason, you see me as more than just my mistakes. You see what you think I can be, not what I am. No matter what I do, you stay by my side. I don't deserve it and those who don't deserve what they have are destined to lose it."

Astonished, Elizabeth stared at him. Of course, he deserved it. Greg rarely made mistakes, and if he did, he was quick to admit his fault. He was responsible, dependable, and he always did the right thing. Most times, it was him correcting *her* mistakes then lecturing her so she wouldn't repeat her error. He kept her in line. He was a mother, father, mentor, friend, and big brother all rolled into one person. Yet he thought he was the undeserving one?

"If I didn't know any better, I'd think you're delirious again," she teased.

"I'm not. Let me speak."

"Apologies." Elizabeth set the bowl of soup aside and gave him her full, undivided attention. "Go on."

Greg picked up right where he left off. "His Majesty once told us love is a weakness, and for a long time, I believed him. But I realize now that deep down I've always known it's the opposite. It makes us strong."

"I've always believed that." She emitted a shallow sigh and her breathing slowed as a lifetime of memories took over…memories in which Greg literally came to her rescue or helped her solve one problem or another. He was the embodiment of strength *and* love. Because of him, Elizabeth believed the two to go hand in hand.

"You say I'm the one good thing in your life and you don't deserve my loyalty, but have you ever stopped to think about what you've given me? You're my hero."

A flicker of disappointment glided across Greg's stubbly face. His voice cracked when he replied, "I used to be a lot of things."

Elizabeth barely stifled a chuckle. "Used to be? No, you still are. I think it's safe to say you always will be."

"Even after everything I've done?" His tone was incredulous, his brows drawn together. "I killed people. I treated you poorly when you tried to help me see the truth about Lucy. I allowed rage to drown reason and–"

"Mistakes, Greg. Those were mistakes. I know better than anyone that we're more than our flaws. We're also our achievements, our hopes, and our dreams. *You* taught me that."

"Regardless, I'm no hero."

"You are to me," Elizabeth assured him upon seeing the doubt in his eyes. "The court was filled with vicious wolves trying to rip each other apart. Our own family played a part in that. But not you. You were always true to yourself and those around you. His Majesty saw that as a weakness, as did Bernadette and many of the courtiers."

Greg's jaw twitched.

"But to me it was inspiration. You were the light. In a place of blackness, you showed me the world is more than a never-ending race to the top. You showed me kindness exists, and if it wasn't for you, I would've ended up just like Bernadette—cruel and unbearably selfish. *That's* why I stay by your side. You say you don't deserve it, but you're wrong about that. You're the *only* one who deserves it, and I'd gladly follow you into the fire if I had to."

Greg's mouth slackened as he gaped at her, his blue eyes filled with wonder. "Thank you, Bess. I love you. I hope you know that."

Elizabeth grinned, and although the admission itself surprised her, the meaning behind the words did not. "I've always known it. That's why I'm coming with you. You may have been banished, but that doesn't mean you're alone. We're in this together."

"Together?" Something in Greg's tone was off and for a moment, Elizabeth was certain she saw his bottom lip tremble.

Her eyes narrowed as she cocked her head to the side, desperately trying to get a better read on whatever emotion he was trying to suppress. "What's the matter? Is it your injury? It's about time I change the bandages anyway."

"It's not that. I mean, yes, my entire torso feels as though someone is holding a torch inside me, but that's not the problem."

Elizabeth appraised him. "So, what is it?"

Greg cleared his throat and gritted his teeth as his expression morphed right before her eyes. He'd been smiling mere moments ago, but as he looked straight through her now, his features were stony and unfeeling. "Are you certain this is what you want?"

It was an innocent question, but it still knocked the wind out of her. "What?"

"Have you even considered how much you'll be giving up? There's no comfort to be found in exile. If you choose to join me, you'll be trading your life of extravagance for one of hardship and destitution." Greg's countenance remained inscrutable as he stared down at his hands, but the snag in his voice gave him away. He was scared. "How long will it be before you resent me for dragging you into my hell?"

As Elizabeth stared at him, she tried not to bristle at his maddening inability to comprehend how deeply her loyalty to him ran. She just told him she'd follow him into the fire. What didn't he understand about that?

Even if it took five years in exile for Greg to gather the men and resources he'd need to defend his birthright, Elizabeth wouldn't abandon him again. When the time came to fight, she'd stand by his side and help him rip the crown right off Bernadette's head. That was assured.

"Greg, I thought I made it clear...I'm on your side no matter what. You're my big brother, my family, and where you lead, I'll follow. You're not *dragging* me anywhere. I'm here of my own volition."

Greg's brows knit together, but his eyes glimmered with hope. "You're sure about this? You'll be aiding in the escape of a traitor, and chances are the bad days will far outnumber the good ones. It'll be dangerous and–"

Elizabeth dismissed his words with an unconcerned flick of her wrist. "I've already made up my mind and nothing is going to change it. Like I said, you can't get rid of me that easily. Besides, Mary's brother is a priest and has arranged for us to travel to a monastery in the northeast. We'll be safe there. You'll be able to recover without having to look over your shoulder, and once you're better, *then* we can worry about what our next step should be."

"Bess...I don't know what to say." Greg stared at her, a combination of joy and uncertainty on his face.

Elizabeth gifted him her most radiant smile. "Then don't say anything. It'll be a grand adventure."

Tears of gratitude welled in his eyes, and he eagerly drew her into his arms. "I'm glad you're here, Bess. Thank you."

CHAPTER 15

*G*regory eyed the jug of ale on the table and licked his lips, wishing he would've had the foresight to ask Elizabeth to pour him a cup before she went outside to hang laundry.

With a huff of air, he glanced at the door. How long had it been since his sister went out? Twenty minutes? An hour? Immobilized by his wound and confined to this trundle bed, it was impossible to measure time. The hours dragged on and the days blended together.

His gaze drifted back to the ale, his throat dry as the summer heat that spilled through the open window. It'd be easy enough to call out and summon Elizabeth back inside, but the last thing he wanted was to be any more of a nuisance.

I'll get it myself. With a deep breath, Gregory pushed himself up on his elbows. A surge of pain slashed through him, and he wilted back into the mountain of pillows, winded.

He clenched his jaw as he glared up at the wooden beams of the cottage's ceiling. The view was one he'd become quite familiar with these last couple days and he longed to possess enough strength to do more than lie around.

Mary and Elizabeth labored all day. Each night, the latter fell asleep before her head even hit the pillow. Meanwhile, Gregory remained about as useful as a rowboat in the desert. His inability to help out grated on him, and although she didn't say so, he could tell it bothered Elizabeth as well.

Knock knock. Knock.

The rhythmic thudding snapped Gregory's gaze to the door, and his blood ran cold.

Something was amiss. This was Mary's home. She wouldn't knock before entering and neither would Elizabeth.

No, whoever stood on the opposite side of that door was a stranger.

The warmth of the fire filled the room but even so, goosebumps crawled up Gregory's arms. He reached for the paring knife he'd used to cut strawberries earlier, gripping it tight as he waited to see who crossed the threshold.

"He's probably asleep, Father." Elizabeth's voice, smooth and lighthearted, flowed in through the window along with the afternoon breeze. "Perhaps you could come back tomorrow?"

His posture relaxed and the tension in his jaw eased. *The priest.*

"It's been a week," the man replied in a deep, impatient tone. "This can't wait any longer. I'll simply have to wake him."

In the next instant, the door swung open and a stout man clothed in the showy, elaborate robes of a Catholic cleric sauntered in. "Wonderful. You're awake."

Gregory loosened his hold on the knife. A little. "I am."

The stranger bowed, the top of his bald head shining in the firelight. "It's an absolute honor to meet you, Prince Gregory. I'm Father Timothy, Mary's brother and your faithful servant."

Gregory's shoulders sagged as the final vestiges of apprehension evaporated from his chest. He cleared his throat of the lump that'd settled there and motioned toward the chair. "My sister mentioned you'd be paying me a visit. It's a pleasure to meet you, Father."

"Trust me, the pleasure is *all* mine." The priest lowered himself into the chair in front of the hearth, his spine straight as a board as he gawked at Gregory. His eyes gleamed, filled with all the wonder of a child visiting the seaside for the first time. "So. Tell me, Your Highness, what are your plans?"

Taken aback by his business-like attitude, Gregory faltered a moment. "For?"

"The future, of course. How many men do you wager will join your ranks? I've spoken with the members of my parish, and there are at least sixty able-bodied men who are willing to take up arms and fight for your cause. I've sent letters to the churches in all the neighboring towns and have already heard back from—"

"What are you talking about?" Gregory let go of the knife at his side and brought his hands to his lap. "What cause?"

Father Timothy's eyes narrowed, but he didn't dither. "To take the throne. We can have an army assembled within a few—"

"Army?" Gregory scoffed. "I have no intention of raising an army."

"Of course not. I don't expect you to do it from the road." Father Timothy's lips curved up in the proudest grin as he scuffed his chair closer and leaned in. "Leave it to me," he said, the weight of his hand pressed atop Gregory's shoulder. "It'll be my honor to assemble men on your behalf. Then, once you arrive at the monastery, you can—"

"There will be no army," he declared, lacking even a shred of doubt. He knew firsthand the sort of torment one endured when they stood between Bernadette and the power she believed herself entitled to. It was a dangerous place to be, and now that he'd been pushed aside, he couldn't ask anyone else to stand against her in his place. He wouldn't spill other men's blood for the *chance* to be king.

Despite the lies Bernadette spread about him, he cared a great deal for the people of Caracalla. How could he tear the kingdom apart for a crown, a crown he wasn't even sure he'd ever wanted?

The cheerful song of a wren floated into the cottage as Father Timothy blinked. "I-I beg your pardon?"

Gregory raised his chin and crossed his arms over his chest. He met the priest's questioning gaze and hardened his tone. "I refuse to start a civil war over this."

Father Timothy drew his hand away, his eyes bulging so much Gregory half expected them to jump from their sockets. "Tell me you're not serious," he pleaded. "I've already sent word to my peers."

Gregory pressed his lips together in a firm line and glared at him.

"You're not thinking clearly, my boy." To the priest's credit, he didn't shrink beneath Gregory's glower. "You're destined to be king. I assure you, our Holy Father will support you in this endeavor."

"The answer is no."

Father Timothy's jaw tightened, and his fingers flexed, but he calmly rose to his feet and headed for the door. "This is a mistake, Your Highness. You'll see." Making no effort to disguise his antagonism, he cast a dark frown over his shoulder, then stepped outside and slammed the door behind him.

~

The cottage door shut with a bang, causing Elizabeth to flinch and nearly drop the freshly laundered chemise to the ground. She peeked around the garments hanging on the clothesline to find Father Timothy, his face twisted in a scowl, stomping toward his mount.

She exchanged a curious glance with Mary, who shrugged her shoulders and pulled another clump of weeds from the vegetable garden. "Something wrong, Timmy?"

"Nothing you ladies need to concern yourself with," he retorted, his wild eyes blazing as he climbed into the saddle. "The men have it handled."

Elizabeth's ears grew hot as she watched him ride off. "Is that typical?"

"Is what typical, dear?"

"For him to dismiss you like that."

Mary tugged another weed out of the dirt and tossed it to the side, unphased by the affront. "My brother believes women have their place and men have theirs. He doesn't tell me much."

"Doesn't that bother you?"

Mary chuckled, her wrinkled skin glowing in the sunlight. "You're young, but when you get to be my age, you learn to choose your battles. If my brother wants to keep his secrets, so be it."

"But aren't you curious what he and Greg were talking about? Whatever it was clearly angered him."

"Leave the men to their schemes and plotting. You and I have chores to do."

Elizabeth rolled her eyes and resumed her work, fully intending to ask Greg what he and the priest had discussed.

However, by the end of yet another exhausting day, Elizabeth fell asleep having forgotten all about Father Timothy's visit and the questions it raised.

CHAPTER 16

The scorching summer sun bore down on Elizabeth as she followed the road into town. The muddy mess created by the rainstorm had dried up, leaving the path covered in a thin layer of dust that stirred to life and clouded the air whenever anyone disturbed it.

She coughed with each inhalation, unable to prevent the dirt from getting into her throat. It was a downright miserable day, and without a single cloud in the sky to shield her from the heat, Elizabeth's mood was about as low as the temperature was high.

She lumbered across the square, grumbling as she pushed the shop's door open and stepped inside. Her scowl deepened as another drop of sweat rolled down her temple. To her utter disbelief, it was as hot inside the bakery as it was outside. The shutters on the window had yet to be fixed, which allowed the humid air to enter the building and blend with the high temperature produced by the oven inside.

"Good day," came Joshua's cheerful greeting. His back was to her as he stuck the peel into the oven and pulled out a loaf of bread, but when he turned around and saw her, he did a double take. "It's you."

Elizabeth's breath got caught in her throat. With great effort, she marshaled what she hoped to be a relaxed smile. "Indeed," she replied in the smoothest voice possible. "You know who I am?"

"I recognize you." Joshua blushed beet red as he wiped his hands on the apron around his waist and approached the counter. "You were in the crowd on the morning of the break-in. My father called you a good-for-nothing criminal."

"Oh, I remember," she scoffed. "But just to be clear, that was the first time you've ever seen me, correct?"

"Yes, and I thought for sure it'd be the last time, too."

All the tension in Elizabeth's body was released, allowing the relief to sink in and take its place. Her identity was still safe, and as the imaginary noose around her neck slackened, the beginnings of a smile touched her lips.

Joshua, on the other hand, was serious as could be. "I'd like to offer my most humble apologies for the insult my father threw at you. He can be a bit…explosive at times."

She rubbed the sweat off her brow with the back of her hand. "We're all subject to the tempers of our fathers," she said, her tone cushioned with deep understanding as her gaze wandered around the interior of the bakery. "Goodness, how can you stand it in here? It's dreadfully hot."

"It is rather warm today," Joshua agreed, displaying a wide grin even as Elizabeth narrowed her eyes and fixed him with a rigid stare.

"Rather warm?" Like Greg, the baker was clearly one of those agitating people who liked to understate problems. "No, it's bloody blazing."

Not at all ruffled by her poor attitude, Joshua emitted a lighthearted chuckle that instantly made Elizabeth forget all about the heat. "Bloody blazing, indeed. So, tell me, what brings you in today? Yesterday's baked goods are half price."

Bouncing on her tiptoes as she admired the scrumptious treats, Elizabeth licked her lips at the sight of a particularly tantalizing lemon tart.

"My tarts are the best in the kingdom," he proudly told her, "but might I suggest you try something slightly less common?"

"Such as?"

"Look over here." Joshua scooted along behind the counter and beckoned for her to follow along in front. Unable to wipe the eager grin off her face, Elizabeth complied. "These are maize scones. I'll bet you never had one of those before."

Elizabeth shook her head as she ogled the treats, surprised to admit that she hadn't. Maize was a foreign, strange food brought over from the New World. Like tomatoes, which Bernadette insisted were poisonous, corn was one food Elizabeth had yet to try.

"Scones made from maize?" Her eyes grew wide. "Who thinks up these outlandish recipes?"

"I believe the natives over in the Americas have been making bread from cornmeal for hundreds of years. My supply was purchased directly from His Majesty's personal privateer, a Dane by the name of Alexander Donahue. It was my idea to bake it in the form of a scone."

Elizabeth quivered, once again unnerved by the length of her father's reach. How far would she and Greg have to travel before these mutual acquaintances stopped? She worked to keep her face neutral and her voice steady. "Pray tell, how does a baker become acquainted with a pirate under the king's employ?"

"If there's one good thing about my father becoming a

baron, it's the quality and selection of ingredients I now have at my disposal." Joshua reached into the basket, grabbed one of the yellow scones, and held it out in front of her. "Try it. I promise you won't be sorry."

Elizabeth swallowed the saliva gathering in her mouth as she appraised the small cake. "I'm afraid I'll have to decline. I have no money to–"

"It's free of charge. Consider it an apology for my father's insults."

"Are you sure?"

Joshua laughed. "Yes. Take it."

A smile stretched across Elizabeth's face as she reached out and took the scone. "It smells wonderful." Her taste buds danced with pleasure the moment she bit into the delicious pastry, and her expression must've revealed her approval because the baker beamed at her.

"See? They're even better with butter."

Once the last bite was in her stomach, Elizabeth brushed away the crumbs that dotted her bosom. "I've tried many foreign foods in my lifetime, but that was surely one of my favorites. I wish I had a way to pay you back."

"Don't think twice about it," he said with a firm shake of his head. "At the end of the week my father eats whatever discounted leftovers the farmers haven't bought for their pigs, so you're probably doing his wardrobe a favor. His buttons are about to burst."

Elizabeth giggled, enjoying Joshua's company. "Well, I'd be glad to help if you ever need me to." Even as she spoke, her gaze shifted back to the plethora of pastries before her. The scone had been a real treat, and she was grateful, but it also served as a reminder of how hungry she really was.

While Greg was free to eat as much as he wanted, she and Mary had been reduced to eating scraps. Greg's bowls of soup were filled with most of the vegetables and meat, leaving mostly broth and an odd carrot or two for her. Her stomach growled nonstop, and for the first time in her life, Elizabeth knew what it was like to go to bed hungry. It was awful.

"Is there something else I can get for you today?"

Her mouth watered again as she gawked at the many choices teasing her from atop the counter. Not long ago, her tables had been covered with all this and more. Stuffed chicken smothered with cheese and seasoned with herbs, boar sweetened with plum sauce, and fresh peaches served on a platter with sugared apricots. It was all within an arm's length of her seat at the bountiful banquets, and the desserts were even better than the main entrées.

But now all she got to eat was a single slice of rye bread and a bowl of broth. The little portions she did get tasted like parchment. Meanwhile, Greg ate as much as his stomach could hold and snacked on fresh strawberries Mary bought especially for him. Elizabeth loved her brother and would do anything for him, but she never imagined her stomach would pay the price for her decision to join him in exile.

"How much would one English Shrewsbury cake cost?" she questioned, fully aware that she couldn't buy one no matter what the answer was.

"A penny." Joshua's tone was pained and conveyed what seemed to be an apology.

It was a fair price, a low one. Deep down, Elizabeth knew that, and she bit her lip, considering her options. The worst part of it was that she had the money to make the purchase. She fingered the tuppence coin Mary had given her as she struggled to resist temptation.

She wanted one of those cakes more than words could say, but if she used the money to buy herself a treat rather than send a letter to Clara, then both she and Greg would probably be doomed. Furthermore, if Greg found out she had used the woman's money to satisfy her appetite, he'd be livid.

So, with a heavy sigh, Elizabeth ruefully shook her head. "Perhaps tomorrow," she murmured, knowing full well she couldn't have one then either. "Today, I need to send a letter. I was told you double as Gettsbury's postal service."

"That I do. However, the post has already been sent out for the day."

Elizabeth pulled the letter from her pocket and handed it to him. "That's fine. Can you send it tomorrow morning?"

His voice dropped, and a remorseful expression flickered across his face. "It's doubtful. The messenger probably won't return from delivering the other letters until tomorrow evening. It'll have to wait to be sent out with the next batch, which won't be for a few days. I'm sorry it can't be any sooner."

"You have no reason to be sorry," said Elizabeth sweetly. "You're doing me a great service by sending it at all. And that scone was wonderful, truly. I'm in your debt."

"You owe me nothing but your name," Joshua replied in a rush of words that, judging by his crimson cheeks, came out faster and with more enthusiasm than he would've preferred. He cleared his throat and stuck his hand over the counter. "I'm Joshua."

"It's a pleasure to meet you," Elizabeth bubbled as she extended her own hand.

Joshua grasped it gently, then leaned over the counter and planted a soft kiss atop her skin.

"And your name?"

"Dorothy," she lied, although somewhat against her will. "I'm sorry, but I really must be leaving now." She gave Joshua the tuppence coin. "When a response comes, please have it sent to Mary Watson's cottage. I'll be staying with her for a few weeks. I'll check back soon to see if the letter has been sent."

"Come back tomorrow," Joshua suggested with a smile in his voice. "Perhaps I'll have another new item for you to try."

Elizabeth's heart skipped a beat. "I'd like that. Good day, Joshua."

"Good day, Dorothy." The edges of his mouth were raised in an expression of equal cheer as she turned and left the shop. "See you tomorrow."

Despite the tornado of dust engulfing her, Elizabeth skipped down the path as she made her way back to the cottage. The brief interaction in the bakery had lifted her spirits so much that she no longer minded the sunlight burning down on her. Nor did she care about the heat or that the next few hours would be spent waving flies away from Greg's wound.

Now, she had something to hope for, something to look forward to. Tomorrow she'd go back to the bakery to see Joshua again and soon the letter she wrote to Clara would be sent.

At first, Greg had rejected Elizabeth's idea to write to their cousin and ask for monetary assistance. He claimed it was unwise to take such a huge risk, but Elizabeth trusted Clara absolutely and knew her dearest friend would never betray them. It took some time, but she eventually managed to convince Greg that Clara was their only hope. She'd send them the money needed for their journey to the monastery, of that Elizabeth was certain.

All she had to do was wait.

CHAPTER 17

*W*ith a heavy sigh, Elizabeth dried the last supper bowl and stacked it atop the rest on the cupboard's top shelf. She was appalled by the wrinkles left on her fingertips whenever she washed dishes, but she had to admit there was a small sense of accomplishment upon completing the chore. She couldn't disclose that to Greg, though. Not unless she wanted him to assign more tasks for the 'betterment of her character.'

"I suppose that's enough scripture for today." Mary closed her precious book and got up from her chair beside the hearth. While Elizabeth had washed their soup bowls, Mary read aloud to the siblings. The Gospel wasn't Elizabeth's first choice of reading material, but at least it offered something for her to think about other than her own miserable situation. "I must be on my way. The choir is practicing tonight, and I offered to play the organ for them."

"How long will you be gone?" Elizabeth dropped the rag in the basin with a splash and pointed out, in a somewhat crabby manner, that it was almost dark. "After a long day of hard labor, I'm in *dire* need of a bath. Can you at least help me carry the tub out to the barn before you go?"

"I'm running late as it is, but I'd be happy to once I get home." Mary wrapped herself up in her cloak and tied the strings. "Perhaps while I'm away, you could lend me a hand with the dusting? You can use the leftover dishwater to wipe down the shelves."

Elizabeth's veins ran hot as she bit back the unsavory words poised on the tip of her tongue. "Mary. I'm tired and–"

"She'd be happy to do it. Wouldn't you, Bess?" The steel edge to Greg's tone matched that of an authoritative parent, and Elizabeth knew immediately she didn't have a choice in the matter. He wasn't asking if she'd be kind enough to dust for the old woman, he was telling her she would.

"Certainly." Elizabeth's voice was tight with bitterness. "Nothing would please me more."

The sarcastic remark rendered no reaction from Mary whatsoever as she said her farewells and floated out of the cottage, a triumphant smile plastered across her wrinkled face.

"I don't know why she thinks I'm her personal slave." Elizabeth crossed her arms as she stood in front of the window and watched Mary hobble down the path toward the church. "I spent hours pulling weeds in the garden today. Plus, I chopped all the vegetables for supper *and* washed the dishes. Now she wants me to dust shelves, too?"

"She's giving us…a place to stay," Greg stated, his voice rickety and weak. He was propped up on a mound of pillows to lessen the pressure under his ribs, but even with the extra support, his distorted expression told of the pain he was in. "The least you can do…is help with some of…the chores."

"I know that." She scowled as she grabbed the washrag from the dirty dishwater. To her great aggravation, she sensed Greg's watchful eye as she removed the jars of spices and herbs from the shelves, then wiped the dust away.

"I can feel your eyes boring into my back, but I assure you it's quite unnecessary. I'm being thorough. See?" Elizabeth spun on her heel and held the filthy rag up. "Look how disgusting this thing is. Just look at it. This very well might be the first time these shelves have ever been washed."

"What do…you want, Bess? An award?"

A tremor of anger ran through her. "No, I don't want a damn award. I'm dusting the shelves, as instructed, but I don't remember anyone telling me I had to be happy about it." She shot him one last dirty look, then returned to her work in a huff.

After a few more minutes, she concluded the shelves were clean enough, carried the bucket of foul water outside, and dumped it in the grass. She then made her way back inside and slumped into one of the two chairs in front of the fireplace.

"That was a tedious waste of time," she carped as she stretched her arms in the air with an exaggerated yawn. To her surprise, Greg didn't reprimand her for whining. She expected another lecture about earning her keep but when she glanced over at his bed, she was concerned to see him struggling for breath.

She leapt off the chair and dashed toward the cabinet where the jugs of ale were stashed. "I'll pour you a drink."

With his teeth gritted and eyes clamped together as he pressed the back of his head into the pillows, Greg clutched at the blanket draped over his legs. "It feels…like someone is shoving…a…mace into my side."

"I wish there was more I could do to help," she said. Greg winced as she handed him the cup of alcohol. "I'm sorry this happened to you, but I know you're strong enough to get through it. Nothing can keep you down."

"This might." He knocked back the entire cup of alcohol in three long gulps and as he emptied a second and third cup as well, the stress on his face gradually slackened. Once he'd guzzled four servings of the potent drink, all traces of his earlier pain were gone, and he sighed with contentment. "That certainly did the trick."

"How could it not?" Elizabeth gaped at him, her voice strained. "You chugged that down as though you haven't had a drink in days."

Greg took an audible breath through his nose, his narrowed eyes searching hers. "I know you disapprove, but drunkenness is the only way to extinguish the constant burning in my side. The best way to achieve that is to drink as quickly as possible."

Elizabeth's heart thumped as she watched him wipe the back of his hand across his mouth. "Are you certain four cups is enough? We don't want to leave any chance of sobriety." Her cynicism earned her a sharp look of irritation.

"No, we don't. Not when sobriety equals excruciating pain." The finality of Greg's declaration made pressing the matter unthinkable, and Elizabeth bit down on her tongue to bridle her argument.

She understood the ale helped him feel better, and she was glad his pain could be eased, yet that did nothing to stop the chill that slid down her spine every time he used alcohol to lessen the ache.

Of course, drinking alcoholic beverages was nothing new. Everyone consumed them on a daily basis, but back at the palace, her brother usually stuck to Malmsey wine, and when he did choose to enjoy drinks of a stronger nature, he stopped after one serving. He never consumed enough to lose control of his inhibitions. Things were different now.

Ever since his fever broke six days ago, Greg quaffed ale by the jug, and although Elizabeth didn't necessarily fear *him*, the effects of alcohol terrified her.

Her skin crawled every time he finished off a cup. Nevertheless, she couldn't deny it was selfish of her to expect him to suffer on account of her own insecurities.

"You're right. I'm sorry. If intoxication stops the pain, who am I to judge how much you have?" Although Elizabeth's attempt to voice support lacked enthusiasm and sounded more forced than she intended, her brother rewarded the effort with a half-smile.

"I know people who drink in excess scare you, and my own habits of late haven't been ideal, but I can promise you this: I'll never allow alcohol to guide my fists or influence my behavior the way it does His Majesty. You're safe, Bess. Even if I drained every jug in that cabinet dry right now, it still wouldn't be enough to make me hurt anyone, certainly not you. I give you my word."

Comforted by the sincerity in Greg's pledge, Elizabeth composed her lips into a grateful smile. "I'm fully aware that my fears are silly but thank you for humoring me."

"You're welcome. Now I want you to promise me something in return." A shade of gloom crept across Greg's face. "If something happens to me–"

"Nothing is going to happen to you." Elizabeth stomped across the small room and plopped back down in front of the hearth, crossing one leg over the other as she slouched into the chair. "It's been almost a fortnight since you were shot, yet you're still here. Mary says you're recovering much faster than she expected, and as long as your wound doesn't go bad and become inflamed, you'll be fine. It may be agonizing for now, but I'm certain with consistent cleaning and fresh bandages, you'll be back to yourself in no time. Planning for your death is pointless. We're past that."

"We're never past that," he disputed crisply. "So, if anything should happen to me in the future, near or far, I want you to go back to Crompton Palace."

The ridiculous notion almost made Elizabeth laugh out loud, and although she successfully stopped the smile from reaching her lips, her light tone exposed her amusement. "You can't be serious. I've been gone too long at this point. Even if Clara covered for me and said I was visiting her this whole time, how would we explain why none of her servants saw me? We'd spend a fortune bribing them to go along with our story."

"Then claim you were ambushed on the road, abducted, and held against your will. With that excuse, any length of time would easily be explained away."

She was powerless to swallow her sniggers. "You're jesting."

"No. I'm not."

Elizabeth peered into his grave face, expecting to find a hint of mirth in his eyes. There was none. All that reflected back was angst, and she checked herself at once.

"Greg, I doubt anyone would believe that. I struck Bernadette in front of the entire court, during her succession ceremony no less. Trust me, I made my allegiance to you quite obvious. I may have been able to explain why I was gone for a few days, but two weeks have passed since I left the palace. His Majesty is bound to know I joined you in exile."

"Not if you deny it." Greg's voice carried a heavy insistence as he shifted his gaze to his hands, which were clenched together so tightly his knuckles had turned white. "In the event that I don't survive this injury, I need to make sure you'll be taken care of. Crompton Palace may be swarming with people who adore Bernadette and despise me, but you'll be safe there if they believe you're one of them."

"Have you gone mad?" Her voice flared with dissension. "This could very well be the most doltish idea you've ever had."

Greg sucked in a deep breath, then slowly exhaled as he surveyed Elizabeth with a stare so caustic, she all but flinched. "If I die, whether it's tomorrow, next week, or three years from now, you will go back and convince His Majesty and the nobles that you believe I'm nothing more than a traitor. Say you're ashamed of what you did to Bernadette. Beg their forgiveness if you have to."

"I will do no such thing!"

"This isn't a request, Elizabeth." There was a note of resignation in Greg's tone as he continued, "His Majesty will accept your claims so long as you mention what I said to you in my apartments. Tell him you hate me for the vile words I spoke. If he needs more convincing, spread a few lies of your own creation to traduce my character. Make sure he knows you generated them."

"No! There's absolutely no way I'm going to slander your name. My loyalty lies with you, now and forever. You can't possibly ask me to pretend otherwise."

"I'm not asking." Greg pinched his lips together and lowered his voice to almost a whisper, yet somehow, he sounded even more commanding than before. "I need you to do this. Promise me you'll say whatever you need to in order to persuade them you're on their side."

"I don't understand why we're even discussing this. You're not going to die."

Where was his strength? Whenever Elizabeth's world fell

apart, whenever the shadows would creep in on her light, she looked to Greg for encouragement. His strength was her inspiration, her support. How could she hold onto her faith if he'd already lost his?

"Maybe not. I very well might pull through, but it's prudent to plan for the worst. I hope to live, however it's my responsibility to consider what'll happen to you if I don't. This is for your own good, as well as my peace of mind. I need to know you'll be safe even if I'm not around to protect you. For that to be possible, you must return to court, tell everyone you were taken hostage on the way to Clara's estate, and publicly denounce me as a traitor. Promise me you'll do that."

The cottage sizzled with tension as he waited for her to acquiesce to his demand.

Elizabeth ran both hands over her face, her stomach roiling. How could she stomp on his honor in front of the entire court when she'd spent the last sixteen years building him up? Greg may have her best interests at heart, but he had no idea what he was asking of her.

"Betraying your hero isn't something one easily agrees to," she muttered.

A bleak smile broached Greg's lips, and for a moment she saw a speck of joy warring with the concern and sorrow in his eyes. "Even so, I need you to promise me."

"Fine. I promise. If something happens to you, I'll go back to the palace and tell everyone I believe you're a traitor, but *only* if something happens. Otherwise, we're in this together."

CHAPTER 18

*E*lizabeth tossed the feed onto the ground and was assailed by a hoard of clucking chickens within seconds. "Be patient," she grumbled as she threw more grains into the midst of the huddle. "I know you're not starving. I just fed you last night."

Tending to the animals, *all* the animals, was one of the many household tasks she'd been charged with these last few weeks. A little over a month had crawled by since Greg was shot, and although Elizabeth saw a fraction of his strength return with each day, his recovery remained slow. For this reason, Greg insisted that a steady schedule of chores would be a beneficial way for her to pass the time until he was better.

Beneficial my arse. Elizabeth's lips curled into a scowl as she chucked a handful of feed at the rooster's head. Every morning that damn bird woke her up at the break of dawn, and after half an hour of forced prayers, Mary would put her straight to work.

While Greg remained immobilized by his injury and slept

the majority of the time, Elizabeth labored alongside Mary from sunrise to sunset like a common peasant. She was at the old woman's beck and call and was often asked to help water the garden, fill the wood box, wash the laundry, and prepare supper.

As if those odds and ends tasks weren't enough, Elizabeth's main and constant responsibility was to look after the livestock. This included feeding them, gathering the eggs from the coop and selling the extras to Joshua at the bakery, milking the cow, churning butter, and worst of all, cleaning the stable. Everyday.

Each afternoon Elizabeth went into the barn, dragging the shovel behind her. That particular job was disgusting and could very well be considered a form of torture, yet no matter how many times she made her suffering known, her troll of a brother refused to bend. He claimed the hard work would build character. Well, Elizabeth was still waiting to build up anything other than exhaustion.

Her hands were blistered, and although she was grateful for a place to stay and a warm meal every evening, she couldn't pretend to find the physical labor therapeutic. This new life was equivalent to hell.

Elizabeth ground her teeth as she dumped the rest of the grain in the dirt and stomped over to the coop. While the hens were occupied, she took the opportunity to grab the fresh eggs from their roosts. She placed them into the basket one by one with as much care as her grouchy disposition allowed.

Once all the eggs were collected, she took them inside the cottage and set the basket on the table. A quick glance down at the trundle bed confirmed that Greg was asleep, as usual.

"Lucky bastard." Elizabeth pressed her lips flat and sprinkled flour on the table. "I wish I could get a full night's rest once in a while. Must be nice."

She turned her attention to the bowl of dough Mary had left out to rise and her scowl deepened. "Rye again, how shocking." She wrinkled her nose in distaste as she removed the dough and plopped it on the tabletop. "I'm so sick of this shit. There are plenty of other types of bread to eat besides rye. Manchet, cheat, even wheat would be better than this!" She lifted the glob in the air and slammed it onto the table, causing flour to scatter everywhere.

"Fie!" Elizabeth backed up and looked down at her dress, the front of which was now covered in the white powder. With a roll of her eyes and stomp of her foot, she released her aggravation in a long, throaty groan. "Why didn't I wear a damn apron? Blast this horrid day!"

"Ahem."

At the sudden reminder of Greg's presence, Elizabeth's heart flipped, and she swiveled around to face him, a fake smile pasted on her face even as she caught his reproachful frown. "How long have you been awake?"

"Long enough to hear you call me a lucky bastard and spit out half a dozen curse words."

"Oh." Elizabeth's cheeks burned, and she wanted nothing more than to melt into the floor, but as Greg continued to study her with those narrowed, judgmental eyes of his, her shame curdled into frustration. "Wait. You've been spying on me?"

He harrumphed. "Don't be ridiculous."

"You were! You could've let me know you were awake, but instead you chose to lay there and watch me like some sort of ghastly gargoyle. You live to chastise me, don't you?"

As he crossed his arms over his chest, Greg drew his mouth into a taut line. When he finally decided to grace her with a response, his voice was gruff with anger and each word came out slow, deliberate. "Need I remind you that I'm confined to this bed? Don't accuse me of spying when you're the one who decided to throw your little fit in my presence."

"*Little fit*?" Elizabeth let out a snort of dismissive laughter. "I was *not* throwing a fit."

Greg arched a single eyebrow. "No?"

"No."

"Interesting. You could've fooled me."

A wave of heat rose in her chest as she rushed to defend herself. "Well then, you're an idiot. Besides, what does it matter if I was? I'm entitled to a few minutes of griping after all the work I've been doing. In case you haven't noticed, I'm the one earning our keep. While I'm outside washing laundry or chopping firewood without a moment's rest, you get to lounge around all day. So yes, I called you a lucky bastard. You have no idea what I'm going through."

Greg's lips twisted in disapproval and his eyes darkened, letting Elizabeth know at once she'd said the wrong thing. "Yes, and I'm sure that bit of flour on your dress is quite the added burden." Although his voice was smooth, there was a definite fire burning beneath.

"Be quiet. It's not just the chores. It's everything." Elizabeth collapsed onto one of the stools at the table and with her eyes fixed downward, she resumed kneading the dough. "Since your banishment, I live in constant fear we're going to be discovered. I understand you're not yet well enough to travel, but we've been here far too long. The more space between us and Crompton, the safer we'll be. I'm eager to expand that distance."

Greg's expression warmed, and his tone gentled. "So am I. If I could wish myself better I would, but–"

"That wouldn't solve the problem," Elizabeth blurted, becoming more impatient by the moment. "Even if you could get up and walk out the door right now, it wouldn't do us any good. I have yet to receive a reply from Clara, and unless she sends the money I asked for, we'll starve before we even reach the monastery. Don't you see? We can't leave unless we somehow scrounge up the funds it'd take to get us there. We're damned no matter what we do, but instead of opening your eyes to the direness of our situation, you prefer to scold me every time I refuse to jump for joy at the chance to clean up cow shit."

"I don't expect you to jump for joy," Greg shot back as he pinned her beneath a frosty glower. "But is a touch of civility really too much to ask? Your incessant whining is grating."

"Well, I beg your pardon, but not all of us have it as easy as you do." Elizabeth regretted the tactless words as soon as they flew off her tongue and it took all her restraint not to shrink away from the scathing glare they engendered from Greg. In a false show of poise that belied the nervous tingling in her chest, she lifted her chin and forced herself to look him straight in the eye.

"You think this is easy for me?" His jaw was rigid, and his hands curled into tight fists at his sides, a gesture that would've provoked her to flee the scene if this clash was with anyone else.

"No," she backtracked. "I shouldn't have devalued your suffering. Anyone can see you have it worse, but please, can't you at least try to see this from my point of view? The amount of stress I'm under is–"

"Nothing compared to mine," Greg interjected, his usual equability nowhere to be found as his eyes pierced through her like spikes. "Do you honestly think I don't have night-mares about one of His Majesty's henchmen breaking down that door and arresting you? You and Mary are both aiding and abetting a traitor, a crime punishable by death. I live in constant fear that your attachment to me is going to be the ax that severs your head."

Elizabeth blanched. "Damn, Greg. Don't mince your words on my account."

"The point is, you're not the only one who worries about that. But unlike you I can't use chores to distract myself from those gruesome thoughts. I'm stuck in this bed with two methods to pass the time. I can either dwell on those fears and flinch at every noise, or I can sleep. I choose to sleep."

"I understand, however–"

"However, you still think I'm the *lucky* one." His tone was even, but Elizabeth detected the fury looming behind his words. "You said it yourself."

"The word lucky may have been…an exaggeration."

Greg scoffed. "Our own uncle tried to murder me. He shot an arrow clean through my torso, but you go ahead and complain about the type of bread we're fed and the time you get to spend outdoors. I'm sure all that sunshine and fresh air is incredibly difficult to bear."

Elizabeth compressed her lips together in a conscious effort to lock in the unsavory retort threatening to break through. As she stared him down, she wrestled with the desire to scream every vulgar curse she knew at him. The intense amount of stress, constant hunger, and sleep deprivation had been pushing her to her limit for days. Now, thanks to Greg's unwillingness to admit her frustration was at all warranted, Elizabeth had reached her breaking point.

"You're so insensitive," she muttered under her breath, feeling the rage bubble in her gut as she shoved her fists into the rye dough. She was suddenly quite grateful Mary had charged her with the kneading because otherwise, it might just be Greg's smug face she pounded instead.

"If you have something to say to me, speak up."

Don't tempt me. "I don't."

"Obviously you do. Say it."

So you can yell at me some more? No thanks. "It's not important."

"Just say it!" Greg demanded, his tone stronger and more commanding than it'd been in weeks.

"Fine! If you must know, I said you're an insensitive ass, and if I have to spend one more minute in your company, I'm going to lose my damn mind! Happy now?" Propelled to her feet by the force of her ire, Elizabeth snatched the dough off the table and heaved it at the wall above Greg's head with all her might. It fell to the floor with a *splat* and before he had time to say a word about it, Elizabeth ran out the door.

Elizabeth plucked a peach off the limb of the tree and collapsed onto the damp ground. Biting into the fruit, she leaned back against the thin trunk and lost herself in dreams of the glorious world she'd left behind at Crompton Palace.

Two months ago, she resided in her own private state-rooms and slept peacefully in her canopied four-poster bed. Now, she shared a bed with Mary, the world's worst blanket hog.

As a princess, Elizabeth had a marvelous life with no responsibilities. There were no cows to milk, no weeds to pull, no shelves to dust, no dishes to wash, no fences to paint, and certainly no wounds to clean.

Her life had been one of pure pleasure and endless smiles. She attended jousts, danced with handsome nobles, and visited the many shops and theaters in the capital city of Lyndbridge. She strolled through the vibrant gardens that surrounded the palace, chatting with her ladies in waiting whose sole purpose was to do her bidding.

I gave it all up and now look at me. Elizabeth tore another bite from the peach with a jerk of her head. She felt a sharp pang of woefulness as it dawned on her that she was nothing more than a servant in a dirty, flour-covered dress at this point. She may be the king's daughter, but her royal blood did her no good out here. At the palace she was someone of great importance, revered and adored by everyone.

Well, almost everyone. Elizabeth's insides squirmed at the image her mind created of her father's face which was often scarlet-hued and pinched in extreme displeasure. Although she reminisced on many of her days at court with a sense of nostalgia and longing, quite a number of them were shadowed by the king's violence.

In almost every one of those painful memories, Greg stood tall at the forefront. As Elizabeth flipped through the pages and pages of abuse in her mind, she was reminded just how often he stepped in and shielded her from the king's wrath. When it was impossible for Greg to take the blame for whatever indiscretion had earned Elizabeth's punishment in the first place, he'd intervene on her behalf. As a result of his altruism, many of the bruises meant for Elizabeth landed on Greg instead.

That was who Greg was. That was the hero she'd left the palace to protect, the man she *chose* to support. He was the reason she gave it all up, and despite her complaints, Elizabeth didn't regret that decision one bit. She wasn't here under duress or out of obligation. She was here on her own accord...but lately she was doing a poor job of showing it.

Elizabeth chewed her lower lip as a swell of remorse crashed down upon her. The adverse, yet irrefutable truth was she had to go back and apologize for her childish behavior. It was providential then, that cleaning the animal feces from the barn had already taught her a thing or two about humility. It was time to swallow her pride once more.

CHAPTER 19

*E*lizabeth took a deep breath in preparation for the onslaught and lifted the latch on the door. She entered the cottage to find a stone-faced Mary hunched over the table, picking pieces of filth off the mound of rye dough.

She forgot all about the apology she came back to deliver as her gaze darted to the dusty spot on the floor where the glob had landed earlier. Her nose scrunched up in disgust.

As if capable of reading Elizabeth's thoughts, Mary's tone was sharp and defensive. "We can't waste food. There's barely enough to eat as it is." She didn't bother to look up from her task, which gave Elizabeth time to rearrange her revolted expression into one of contrition.

"I understand." In dire need of Greg's aid, she looked to the trundle bed where he was propped up on some pillows, chugging a cup of milk. If only he knew how disgusting it was to squeeze the cow's udder, perhaps he wouldn't be so quick to guzzle the drink.

Greg used his sleeve to wipe away a white mustache as he eyed her with a mixture of disappointment and sympathy. He mouthed the word, *apologize.*

Elizabeth nodded. After all, that had been her plan all along. "Mary?"

"Yes?"

"I'm sorry I lost my temper." She paused, but since the old woman still refused to make eye contact or say anything, Elizabeth figured her apology hadn't yet been sufficient enough to pacify her friend's discontent. "It was childish and uncalled for," she went on. "I should've been more considerate and respectful of the limited resources you have to share with us. I'm deeply sorry."

A tense and uncomfortable silence hovered over the cottage as Elizabeth's apology lingered in the air, unanswered.

Unsure what more there was to say, she stood rooted on the threshold, wringing her hands as she waited for the old woman's forgiveness to be granted. It never was. "Um. Can I help with anything?"

Mary's response was curt and to the point. "Change Greg's bandages."

"With pleasure." In an inflated show of cooperation, Elizabeth painted a smile on her face and leapt into action. She gathered clean cloths from the cupboard, hustled over to Greg's bed, and knelt to peel the old wrappings off his swollen wound.

Despite the care and time she took in pulling the cloth away, he grimaced as his reddened skin was lifted up along with it. It was obvious by the way he forced his head back deep into the pillow that the procedure was agonizing.

"I'm sorry," Elizabeth said with genuine sympathy. "I'm doing this as gently as I can."

"It's fine." His hoarse whisper and occasional shudders were drastic contradictions to his words, but Elizabeth didn't press the issue. To her amazement, Greg didn't utter a single word of complaint throughout the entire redressing of bandages.

It was his demonstration of courage and strength that allowed Elizabeth to fully grasp how different she was from him…and how inferior. She knew if she were shot, she'd complain day in and day out. To grouse and whine were her ways of dealing with her troubles, and she did it often. Greg, on the other hand, never complained. He was the type of person who held his head up no matter what. Being around him was a constant reminder of the type of person she wasn't and probably could never be.

However, as vexing as it was to compare herself to his perfection and fall short, she knew it forced her to be a better person. Usually.

Weighted by the humiliation of how she'd behaved in front of him, Elizabeth's cheeks flamed. Greg was the one who was shot, he was the one in pain all the time and cooped up indoors, yet she was jealous because he got a few extra hours of sleep? She was mad because she had to do some chores? That was nothing compared to what he was going through.

From this point forward, I'm going to be more like him. Elizabeth held her chin high, determination fluttering in her chest as this new goal was set. Of course, she'd made this vow countless times in the past, but this time she truly meant it. One day soon, Greg would be proud of her.

"Thank you, Bess." The tension on Greg's face eased as Elizabeth gathered the old bandages into a pile and dropped them into the basket on the floor beside her. They'd need to be scrubbed clean and hung out to dry in order to be reused tomorrow, but that could wait until later.

"Glad to help." Hoping to appear more at ease than she sounded, Elizabeth straightened her back and squared her shoulders. "I owe you an apology as well." She folded her hands in her lap and made a weak attempt at a smile. "My behavior has been unacceptable lately, and I'm sorry. I'll do better. I promise."

"And I promise to stop acting like an insensitive ass."

Elizabeth squirmed to have her words repeated, but swore she saw a flicker of amusement in Greg's eyes. "I shouldn't have said that."

"No, but I'm glad you did."

"You're glad?" Her eyes narrowed. Elizabeth examined his face for irritation. She found none.

"I can be a bit self-absorbed at times," he admitted. "Your struggles aren't the same as mine, but they're just as valid. I apologize for pretending they're not."

"I, um…thank you." She rose to her feet and shuffled over to the water basin. She was in the middle of rinsing her hands when the silence in the cottage was shattered by an abrupt and thunderous knocking at the door.

She felt a great leap of panic, and her mouth went dry as leather. The thuds were those of a stranger, not the secret knock used by Father Timothy whenever he came to visit.

Elizabeth's eyes flashed to Greg, whose ashen cheeks and tight shoulders showed his own fright as he motioned to the rug on the floor. It was a silent reminder that they were to hide in the cellar beneath, but the urgency with which he pointed to it did nothing to calm her.

"I'll be right there," Mary greeted in a steady voice as she bent down, tossed the rug aside, and opened the hatch. "Be patient with me, my friend. I'm an old woman, and you've woken me from my nap. My legs aren't as swift as they once were."

Meanwhile, Elizabeth had already lifted Greg to his feet. With his left arm slung around her shoulders and her right one wrapped around his waist, she half-carried him over to the trap door. She descended the steep staircase first, then offered her hands and helped ease him in after her. Once he made it off the last step, Greg collapsed onto the mattress Mary had placed on the cold, damp floor. He leaned back against the wall, out of breath and wincing from the strenuous transfer.

Mary poked her head into the dim cellar. "I don't expect you to be down there long," she whispered. "But I've stashed a jug of ale and some cheese in the corner just in case. See it?"

Elizabeth spun around and sure enough, the provisions were situated at the foot of the padded bedding. Her lips parted to confirm the finding, but no words came out.

"Here." An encouraging smile touched Mary's lips as she held out a lit candle.

Eyeing the flame with misgiving, Elizabeth climbed back up the wooden stairs to retrieve it.

"Don't worry, child. The light can't be seen once the hatch is closed. Besides, I have no intention of letting our guest cross the threshold. I'll step outdoors to speak with him. Just keep calm and all will be well."

Still struck mute by her fear, Elizabeth nodded and hurried back down with the candle in hand, settling onto the mattress beside her brother. With a parting smile, Mary closed the hatch, shutting the siblings inside the chilly, underground hole.

CHAPTER 20

*E*ven through the dim candlelight, Gregory saw the strain of terror around Elizabeth's wide, glossy eyes as she trembled beside him. She sat against the wall with her knees pulled into her chest, her arms wrapped around her legs in such a way that made him think she was desperate to hold herself together.

"We're safe down here," he whispered. His veneer of bravery contradicted the stab of dread in his gut. "I promise."

"If they find us, we're dead." Her lip trembled.

Gregory leaned in closer, straining to hear her subdued voice.

"How can you be so calm?"

He nearly laughed. *I'm not calm. I'm petrified.* His head filled with gruesome images of his sister's corpse swinging from the gallows. Sweat beaded on his forehead and bile crept up his throat. As he'd done so many times before, Gregory locked his true emotions deep within and scooted closer to Elizabeth to pull her into a side hug.

Biting back the groan that the movement created, he did his best to sound blithe. "We're going to be fine. I'll bet it's just someone asking for directions." He studied her face to gauge whether she bought the explanation and to his relief, her features loosened.

Gregory grinned at her, equal parts thankful and dumbfounded by the ease with which Elizabeth took him at his word. Flaming arrows could rain down on them, but as long as Gregory assured her she was safe, Elizabeth would believe it.

"You're probably right." Her shoulders seemed to relax a little, but she didn't shake his arm off. "How long do you think we have to stay down here?"

On the surface, her question was innocent enough, but to Gregory it was a punch in the stomach that reminded him of Elizabeth's eighth birthday.

"Quick. Get under there." Gregory lifted the edge of the green cloth and shoved his sister under the table. Once she was safely hidden, he crawled in after her and pulled her into his embrace. "We're safe now, Bessie."

"How long do we have to stay under here?"

"Just until His Majesty tires of the hunt. Now please, be quiet."

"He's going to kill us," Elizabeth cried, burying her tear-dampened face deep into his chest. "I told you we shouldn't have come in here."

She was right, of course. Entering the armory was a grievous mistake. If they were discovered in here and beaten for this late-night excursion, the fault would lie on his shoulders.

He knew the weapons room was off limits, yet he was so eager to lay eyes on the sword his ancestors had used to seize the throne that he pressured Elizabeth into coming with him anyway.

The height of his folly was in believing none of the night watchmen had seen them enter. Now, a group of guards was assembled at the bottom of the staircase, and King Charles was on his way to deal with his miscreant children himself.

"Shh. Don't make another sound."

"There aren't that many places to hide in here, Greggy. He's going to find us, and when he does, he'll use that stupid sword to chop our heads off."

"I'm not going to let that happen." Gregory gave her a tight squeeze. "As I've told you before, I'm your indestructible shield, and a sword is no match against a shield. His Majesty won't—" The words evaporated into the night as the clamor of footsteps echoed throughout the tower.

Elizabeth brought both hands to her mouth, but just to be sure she kept silent, Gregory placed his hand atop hers.

As the door to the armory crashed against the wall, he gulped down his breaths to stay quiet. Elizabeth flinched, but didn't make a sound.

"Gregory! Elizabeth!

He burrowed his face into her head to muffle the sound of his heavy breathing.

"Perhaps Princess Bernadette's eyes deceived her," one of the guards offered.

"The candle is lit," King Charles barked. "They're in here."

Gregory's heart plummeted. He should've blown that out!

"Your Majesty. Are you certain—"

"Get out!" The king's voice boomed throughout the armory, sending a chill down Gregory's backbone as he realized this time, hiding wasn't going to be enough. His Majesty

was intoxicated, but he wasn't yet near the point of passing out.

There was a shuffle of feet as the guard fled, leaving the pair of royal siblings alone, in a room full of blades, with their bloodthirsty father.

"Elizabeth, my darling." King Charles adopted an eerily soothing tone as his footsteps drew nearer. "It's your birthday. Don't make me punish you. If you come out now we can forget this even happened."

Gregory tightened his hold on her. She'd fallen for her father's tricks many times before and not once had she gotten away scratch free. No matter what the king said, there was always a punishment, usually a painful one.

"This is no way for the future king to behave, Gregory. Stop hiding and face the consequences for your actions. Now, coward!"

Gregory swallowed, ashamed. His father was right; he was a coward.

The king's boots echoed throughout the armory, and Gregory held his breath as his father's shadow became visible on the floor beside them. Any second now they were going to be found and punished. There was no way they'd both get out of this...but maybe he could spare Elizabeth.

His stomach in knots, Gregory let go of her and crawled to the far side of the table. There was a tug on his doublet, and he glanced over his shoulder at Elizabeth. Her eyes bore into him, a silent plea for him to stay. With a shake of his head, he put a finger to his lips, and before he lost his resolve, he slipped out from under the table.

"I'm right here," He faced his father head-on. "Elizabeth went to bed hours ago. It's only me up here."

King Charles let out a guttural roar and grabbed Gregory by the front of his doublet, dragging him into the center of the room. With a fierce shove, he sent his son flying backwards.

Gregory landed with a thud and scooted away as his monster of a father clomped toward him, teeth bared. He didn't make it far.

"How dare you!" The vein on the king's neck pulsed. He wrapped his fingers around his son's throat. "You're a pitiful excuse for a prince!"

Globs of spit sprayed on Gregory's face as he thrashed about, clawing at his father's hands.

The stench of alcohol was heavy on the king's hot breath as he squeezed.

"Let him go!"

Elizabeth's voice made Gregory freeze. He turned his head, and through the black spots distorting his view, he saw her point a rapier at their father. A rock formed in the pit of his stomach. He tried to speak, to tell her to run, but the hand digging into his throat prevented him from making any sound at all. All he could do was watch.

Elizabeth swung the weapon in front of her. "Let him go right now!" At eight years old and no more than four feet tall, she looked about as intimidating as one of the butterflies embroidered on her gown. The tremor in her voice didn't help her cause either. "Don't make me stab you in the eyeball!"

King Charles loosened his grip on Gregory's neck as he gawked at his youngest daughter. He got up slowly, one side of his mouth quirked up in a smirk. "You dare point a blade at your king? That's treason."

With the pressure on his neck removed, Gregory took in a raucous, noisy breath. "Leave–her–alone," he croaked. Coughing, he pushed himself onto his hands and knees. "She didn't even–want–to come up–here."

King Charles ambled over to Elizabeth and snatched the

weapon from her hand. "I'm impressed by your bravery." His voice was tinged with a note of pride, one that Gregory was a stranger to. "But if you ever threaten me again, I'll chop you into pieces and feed you to the hounds. Am I understood?"

The color drained from Elizabeth's face. "Yes, Your Majesty."

"Consider this act of mercy your birthday gift, Elizabeth. Don't test me again. I guarantee you'll regret it."

"You're letting us go?"

"This time."

Elizabeth's face was mottled with skepticism. "Both of us? Me and Greg?"

"Yes."

She swept into a deep curtsey. "Thank you, Your Majesty."

King Charles whipped his head around and shot Gregory a scorching look. "You're lucky your baby sister was here to save you. If you ever step foot in this chamber without my permission again, I will end you. I don't care if I have to do it right in front of her." With a parting glare and a haughty swish of his cloak, King Charles departed from the armory.

Gregory was shaken from his memories by the creaking hinges of the trap door and as light spilled into the cellar from above, Mary's face appeared over the edge.

"All is well," she announced, beaming. "Come on up."

Gregory turned to look at Elizabeth, whose joyous smile split her face in half as she clapped her hands together and cheered, "Thank Heavens!"

≈

Once Elizabeth had helped return Greg to the trundle bed and handed him a cup of ale, she spun around to face Mary. "Well? Don't leave us in suspense. Who was at the door?"

The woman's wizened eyes danced with merriment. "Go outside and see for yourself."

A sliver of curiosity rose in Elizabeth's chest.

"No. She's not leaving my sight." Greg gave Mary an icy stare, his features blighted by sudden distrust. In the next instant, he sprung to his feet. His muscles tensed and his gaze flickered to the bread knife on the table. "My sister isn't stepping foot outside this cottage until you tell us *exactly* who came to call."

Flabbergasted by the open suspicion Greg now harbored toward the old woman, Elizabeth glanced back and forth between the two as they stared unblinkingly at one another.

Greg's shoulders were thrown back and his feet were planted in a wide stance, as though energy coursed through his body in preparation for battle. Mary, on the other hand, appeared less intimidating than ever. Her back was hunched, more so than usual, and her frown made the creases in her face even more pronounced. She seemed to age another fifty years right in front of them.

Elizabeth's heart bled with sympathy for the poor woman. "Greg, why don't you take a deep breath and–"

"Who was at the door, Mary?" Greg's no-nonsense tone and the sharp set of his jaw made Elizabeth think twice about suggesting he calm down. Doing so would have the opposite effect, no doubt.

She could practically taste the tension in the room as Mary held a piece of parchment out for him to take.

He snatched the letter and even as he unfolded it, his narrowed eyes bounced from Mary to the door a few times before they finally landed on the piece of parchment in his possession. As he examined it, the flame in his eyes petered out and the hostility on his face softened.

"What is it?" Elizabeth questioned.

Greg didn't say a word, but his expression was pinched into one of great remorse as he handed the parchment over to her.

Elizabeth tuned out the sound of Greg's strained voice as he issued a swift apology to Mary and focused instead on the handwritten note in her hands. She'd recognize the calligraphy anywhere, for she'd written it herself.

"This is the letter I sent to Clara." She scratched her cheek. "But if it's here, that means…" A rush of excitement fizzed through her and before she could stop herself, Elizabeth was out the door.

CHAPTER 21

*W*armth spread through Elizabeth's chest as she embraced her beloved cousin, soaking in the sweet, floral scent of Clara's perfume. "I can't believe you're here."

"Me?" Clara let her arms drop to her sides and stepped back. Her nose wrinkled as she eyed one of the chickens pecking at her feet. "What are *you* doing here?"

"I left Crompton to warn Greg about Salvatore." Distracted by the extravagance of Clara's garments, Elizabeth didn't realize she'd reached out to touch them until she sensed the smooth fabric beneath her fingertips. The lavish clothes momentarily allowed Elizabeth to forget her current plight. For the briefest second, she was a princess again.

"You explained that in your letter. Although I must say, I expected your accommodations to be a bit less...rustic. And is that flour on the front of your...can that even be classified as a dress? Where did you find such a drab kirtle? Zounds, Bess."

The judgment in Clara's voice dragged Elizabeth out of her reverie and her body went hot as she was put on the defensive. "Greg was shot. I explained that in my letter as well." She crossed her arms over her chest and endeavored to maintain an even tone. "So while our accommodations may seem *rustic* and this *drab kirtle* may be less than flattering, let me assure you we've been focused on more important matters. Greg is alive so all in all, I'd say we've been very well looked after here. In fact, he'll soon be well enough to travel."

Clara's lips turned upward. "I'm glad. As it happens, that's precisely why I'm here."

Elizabeth glanced over at the unmarked carriage Clara had arrived in, pleased that her cousin had enough discretion and common sense to travel covertly. Her irritation melted away, and the corners of her mouth lifted into a joyous grin. "I only asked you to send some money for our journey, but as always you've gone above and beyond. Thank you, Clara. This visit is an unexpected, yet welcome surprise."

"This isn't just a visit." A light came into Clara's eyes, and she grabbed both of Elizabeth's hands, giving them an eager squeeze. "I've decided to accompany you. I need to get away, and Greg's banishment offers the perfect opportunity to do just that."

Elizabeth's smile faded, and she jerked her hands away. "Tell me you're not serious." The words flew off her tongue faster than she could think to control them. "Have you gone mad? You can't come with us. Greg has been accused of high treason, and we can only assume I have as well. His Majesty wants him dead, and if you join us–"

"I know, I know. I'm well aware of the risks involved, I saw the notice. But how could I call myself your closest friend if I let you commit treachery alone?"

"I'm not alone." Elizabeth rubbed her temples and paced a few steps before spinning back around to face her senseless cousin. "You realize this is a life-altering decision, don't you? You'll have no choice but to embrace poverty. Plans have been made for Greg and I to seek refuge in a monastery while he recovers from his injury, but we have yet to discuss what will happen after that."

"Do you think he'll defend his crown?"

"I assume so. But as I said, we haven't talked about it."

"Why not?"

Elizabeth crossed her arms, grated by the slew of questions. "He hasn't brought it up, and I don't want to press him. Right now, he needs to focus on getting better. We'll decide what our next move should be *after* his wounds have healed. What I want to know is why you would even consider joining us in exile when your whole life would be flipped upside down."

"The life I have isn't the one I want."

Elizabeth noted the quick, sideways glance Clara snuck at her carriage driver. She also noticed the brief smile that touched his lips in response. "But exile is?"

"I'm ready to start fresh somewhere else, even if that means leaving everything I own behind."

Elizabeth drew her lips into a tight line as she scrutinized her cousin's freckled face. She'd known Clara her entire life. Their fathers were brothers, and if there was one thing Clara loved, it was her luxurious lifestyle. If she was willing to leave that behind, there was something her cousin wasn't telling her. Something big.

"You're running away from something."

Clara expelled a nervous little laugh. "That's absurd."

"Is it?"

A tense silence thickened the air.

"You were always annoyingly perceptive." Clara sighed and looked down at her feet, kicking up the dirt in a cloud of dust that made the chickens scuttle off. "Very well, you're right. I'm running away." She lifted her chin. "But I have a good reason."

Elizabeth scoffed. "What possible reason could you have for–"

"It's a matter of the heart."

"The *heart*?" Elizabeth lifted her eyebrows as her cousin's gaze once again flitted back to her carriage driver. It was then that it dawned on Elizabeth how pleasing he was to look at, for a servant anyway, and judging by the rosiness of Clara's cheeks as she peeked at him through her lashes, this was an observation she'd made as well. "Care to elaborate?"

"I've been betrothed to the baron of Akrim," Clara finally spit out. "Can you believe that?"

Halfheartedly listening to her cousin's complaints, Elizabeth watched from the corner of her eye as the man who'd driven Clara here clenched his jaw and curled his fists in a visible struggle to remain temperate. Servants weren't meant to have opinions, but it was obvious this one did.

"That ogre doesn't deserve my hand! When I marry it'll be to a man of my choosing, not some–"

"Wait." Elizabeth turned back to Clara, somewhat flustered. "Did you say he's a *baron*? That's the lowest rank of nobility! You're the king's niece. Your marriage should be to a foreign prince, or an earl at the very least. Does he have a lot of land?"

"It's not about lands or his title, Bess. It's the idea of it. Why should I be told who I'm to spend the rest of–"

"The baron of Akrim?" Elizabeth's brow crinkled as she searched her mind's library for any indication she'd heard the title before. "What's his surname?"

"Garland." Clara grimaced, saying the name as if she was

chewing on a rock. "And I'm assuming by your frown that you've never heard of him either."

"The name Garland is unknown to me. How could the king's only niece be affianced to someone so...irrelevant? Surely there's been a mistake."

"I heard Akrim suggested the union himself," the carriage driver snarled from beside them, speaking for the first time since their arrival. "The milksop basically believes himself a royal already. His head is so big his tiny neck can hardly hold its weight."

"Yes, big heads are a common trait among the nobility." Elizabeth smiled through the hatred that the sudden image of Bernadette's snooty face sent through her veins. The servant swallowed and stared down at the ground, and she realized her candidness made him uncomfortable.

She changed the subject to put him at ease, intentionally adding a touch of sugar to her voice. "What's your name?"

"Channing, Your Highness. We've met before."

Elizabeth felt a rush of shame at this news. Unlike Bernadette, she didn't believe servants deserved to be treated like rubbish, but unlike Greg, she didn't go out of her way to acknowledge their existence either. She rarely noticed their presence and clearly, Channing was aware of that.

"Yes, I remember. Good to see you again." Elizabeth cleared her throat and willed the heat out of her cheeks as she returned her focus to her cousin. "Clara, I'm confused by your father's choice of a husband for you. I simply don't understand why he'd choose a baron. Did you do something to displease him?"

"Not that I know of." She looked pensive a moment, then shook her head. "His reasoning isn't important. I don't care what possessed him to make the match. I need to get out of it.

The wedding is in less than a month, so you see now why I had to leave home. I'd rather die."

Elizabeth wrestled with the urge to roll her eyes as she swept errant strands of hair out of her face. Clara was being overdramatic, as usual. However, Elizabeth could relate to the feeling of being auctioned off to the highest bidder. She might've considered running away too, had Greg not prevented her own marriage to Ernest of Austria four years ago. Not to mention, the idea of her cousin marrying so far beneath her station was sickening.

If Clara wanted an escape, who was Elizabeth to deny her one?

"You say that now, but if you're caught in our company, you'll be executed as a traitor along with us. You know that, right?"

"Better to die young than live a long life with a man I don't love." Clara's voice was soft, yet solid as stone.

"And what about him?" Elizabeth motioned toward Channing, who was doing a poor job of pretending not to eavesdrop as he stroked the snout of the mare hitched to the carriage.

Clara feigned ignorance with an exaggerated shrug. "What about him?" Her voice rang with false nonchalance, and her pasted-on smile wavered.

Elizabeth narrowed her eyes, now fully convinced there was more to the story. Although she decided to table her suspicions for now, she was fairly certain Channing had a greater role in all this than Clara let on. "Is he willing to risk his life as well?"

"I'm experienced in sword play." Channing stepped forward and patted the weapon hanging from his side. His chin was lifted high into the air, higher than a servant's ought to be. "I've sworn my life to Lady Clara, and I'll die before I let any harm come to her. You have my word." His promise sounded sincere, but it was the sparkle in his eye that left no room for doubt. Channing was infatuated with the Duke of Ephrata's daughter.

What a waste. There was no denying Channing was handsome. He was tall, muscular, and his green eyes were bewitching. Nevertheless, he was a servant. Without a title or lands or wealth, he was no match for a duke's daughter. Any feelings he had would be better spent on a scullery maid or seamstress. Clara could never be his.

As though Elizabeth had voiced these thoughts aloud for Channing to hear, the man's confidence appeared to dwindle along with the puff in his chest. "You don't think I'm up for the task." There was a challenge in his eyes despite his slackened posture.

She chewed her lip, wondering exactly which task it was he was referring to. She supposed it made no difference. Wiping the emotion from her countenance, she smoothly replied, "My opinion is of no consequence."

A contemplative crease appeared on Channing's brow, and as rays of sunshine beamed through the treetops, the brass buttons on his uniform glistened in the early morning light. The sight made Elizabeth's pulse spike. Clara had been sensible enough to travel in an unmarked carriage, but she neglected to have her driver change out of his livery.

Damn it, Clara! Elizabeth's gaze darted around the yard, checking for any onlookers who may have happened upon Mary's home in the woods. That livery bore the insignia of the Duke of Ephrata and would put them all in danger if it was recognized.

"Take off your doublet. You'll get us killed if anyone sees you in that."

Channing seemed on the point of questioning her, but

then his eyes widened in understanding, and he set to work removing the telltale sign of his service to the king's younger brother. "Apologies, Princess Elizabeth. I should've changed out of my livery."

"I'm sorry too, Bess." A frown puckered Clara's face. "That was a foolish mistake."

"I don't think either of you understand the gravity of our situation." Elizabeth ran a frazzled hand over her forehead, but the stray locks of hair fell right back in front of her eyes. "Channing says he'd rather die than let anything happen to you, and you claim death would be a better alternative to marrying Akrim. Now you've partnered carelessness with all this loose talk of death, leading me to believe neither of you take the threat of it seriously."

"We do take it seriously," Clara insisted. "We want to come."

Elizabeth gritted her teeth against a surge of irritation. This wasn't a life she'd wish upon anyone, yet these two idiots were *choosing* to partake in it? *Free will at its finest.*

"Very well," she surrendered, letting out a heavy sigh of defeat. "If this is what you want then so be it, but the decision isn't up to me. You can *try* to convince Greg to let you come along while Channing takes your horse into the barn."

Clara cracked a triumphant grin. "Lead the way."

Gregory rubbed his brow, unable to ward off the headache Clara's voice was giving him. They'd been debating the pros and cons of her request for some time now, yet he was no closer to convincing her it was a bad idea than when she first entered the cottage.

"If you think it's so dangerous, then why are you willing

to let Bess flee with you?" Clara's pout transformed into a satisfied smirk during the silence that followed. She crossed her arms and tilted her chin up, clearly pleased with herself. "Is my life more important than hers?"

"Of course not." He pressed his lips into a thin slash and glared at his pugnacious cousin. She had a point, and a quick glance around the room confirmed everyone knew it.

"Then I'll ask again. Let me come."

Gregory ground his teeth. "No. I already murdered one cousin. I won't be responsible for ruining the life of another.

"Murder?" Clara tilted her head to the side. "Are you referring to Thomas? He's not dead. He made a full recovery."

"He did?" Gregory's mouth went dry. Since Hawthorne, he'd tried his best to convince himself that although Thomas's death was an accident, it was also well deserved. However, as an unexpected rush of tension left his body upon learning of his cousin's survival, Gregory couldn't deny the relief this news brought. He shared a happy glance with Elizabeth, then returned his focus to Clara. "You're certain he's alive?"

"Yes. The cut wasn't that deep."

He sagged against the pillows and emitted a shaky laugh. "I can't believe it."

"Last I heard, he was assembling men to look for his father," Clara said. "No one has seen or heard from the duke since he left the palace over a month ago."

"I see." Gregory's gaze slid back to Elizabeth, who squirmed in her seat and pulled at her sleeve. "Well, I can't say I'm sorry to hear it. After all, he did shoot me."

"*Salvatore* is the one who shot you?"

"Yes."

Clara's mouth hung open as she rounded on Elizabeth. "You didn't mention *that* in your letter!"

"I…it didn't seem…" Elizabeth floundered, her cheeks void of color. "He…"

"I assume Salvatore thought I was dead because he left immediately afterwards. By the time Bess got there, he was gone."

Her attention still locked on Elizabeth, Clara squinted. "You didn't pass him on the road?"

Elizabeth shook her head, chewing her fingernail. Guilt was written all over her face, which she kept directed at the floor.

"He must've taken a different path," Gregory cut in. "What does it matter?"

"It doesn't." Clara shrugged. "So. Can I come with you?"

"Even *if* I agreed, you'd hate every minute of it."

"And Bess doesn't?"

"We're not talking about Bess." He didn't bother to hide his combative tone. "*You* aren't cut out for the life of an outlaw, Clara."

"I've already offered to sell my carriage and use the profits to buy a cart to haul you in. Bess said you'd be traveling in disguise, and I'll wear a nun's habit, too. I've been nothing but cooperative. Besides, you're in no condition to protect her on your own. Like you said, it's dangerous out there. Channing's presence could prove beneficial."

"That's true," Elizabeth piped in from her chair beside the hearth. She made an attempt to look apologetic when Gregory cast her a censorious frown, but it wasn't convincing.

"It never hurts to have an extra man around," Mary affixed.

"Oh, come on, Greg. Let them come with us."

With a coarse grunt, Gregory threw his hands up. "Fine.

I'm tired of arguing, and I'm clearly outnumbered here." He turned back to Clara, fuming. "If you want to do this, I can't stop you. You have my permission to throw your life away."

Clara let out a squeal so high-pitched it made Gregory cringe. He regretted his agreement straight away.

"I know I was against this at first," Elizabeth chimed as she bounced up and down alongside their cousin, "but now I can't control my elation. This is going to be so much fun!"

Fun? Gregory scoffed. *There's nothing fun about any of this.*

"Well, it's settled then." Mary's knees cracked as she rose from her spot at the table and hobbled over to the chest where she kept her savings in a little pouch. After handing a few coins to Elizabeth, she made her way toward the door. "There's much that needs done in preparation for your departure, so let's get to it. Channing, why don't you drive us ladies into town? We'll drop Elizabeth at the square so she can purchase some provisions for your trip. Meanwhile, I'll head to the church and ask my brother to donate two more disguises."

"What can I do to help?" Clara turned back to fix Gregory with a boastful grin. "I'm eager to contribute."

"Was your offer to part with your carriage sincere?" Skepticism rang in Mary's voice, and Gregory was gratified to learn he wasn't the only one who perceived Clara's exaggerated goodwill to be a show.

His cousin's cheeks took on a grayish sheen and she looked to Channing, visibly unsure if such a sacrifice was warranted. After a slight nod from her driver, Clara raised her chin once more, her tone firm with conviction. "It was."

Mary placed her hand atop Clara's shoulder. "Your generosity is much appreciated, child. In that case, you and

Channing can accompany me to the church. I'm sure my brother has a farmer's cart he could trade you for it."

"A trade?" Clara's face lost its color. "I'm to trade my carriage in for a simple wagon? That hardly seems fair."

"It may not be fair, but a wagon would be much more suited to transporting a wounded passenger. You'll need something Greg can comfortably lie down in. Not to mention, it'll attract far less attention than your fancy carriage."

Disgruntlement flashed in Clara's eyes, but she didn't protest. "Very well."

Elizabeth flung her arms around their cousin. "Thank you!"

"Happy to help." Clara's tone conveyed anything but happiness.

"Come on then." Mary opened the door and ushered the others outside.

As the cottage emptied, Gregory remained in his bed. He was so troubled, he didn't notice Elizabeth hadn't left with them until she'd ambled over to his side.

"Brooding again, I see."

He looked up and returned her sympathetic smile with a frown. "I know you're excited to have Clara here, but this isn't a good idea. She can barely part with her carriage without bursting into tears. What makes you think she'll be able to handle life as a peasant? We have no money, no luxuries. Every day will be a fight to stay alive, and I doubt Clara has what it takes."

Elizabeth knelt down and handed him an apple, showing no signs of discouragement. "Give her some time to get used to this new life. I haven't exactly handled it with grace either, but eventually I'll come around and so will she. We'll adapt."

Gregory gave a resigned sigh. "Sooner rather than later, please."

"I'll do my best." Her eyes danced with mischief, and as she crossed her arms, her lips quirked up in an impish smirk. "Fate has awarded you the perfect opportunity to practice patience, wouldn't you say?"

Despite his earlier frustration, a small chuckle escaped as Gregory realized Elizabeth had used his own words against him. A few nights ago, she'd been trying to darn a pair of stockings, huffing and puffing all the while about how difficult a task it was and how much simpler it would be to buy new ones. Gregory's response? *"Fate has awarded you the perfect opportunity to practice perseverance, wouldn't you say?"*

Elizabeth had been livid then, but there was no trace of anger coloring her face at present. She was teasing him, and Gregory's reservations slipped away in response to her buoyancy.

Her carefree personality might have been difficult to tolerate at times, but it was that same joviality that often brought a smile to his face even when his world seemed to be caving in. When Gregory stood alone in the dark, Elizabeth came to him with a torch. Gratitude expanded in his chest as her keen chatter continued.

"This will be good for all of us," she insisted. "I know you have your doubts, but there's safety in numbers, and I think having Channing around will put both our minds at ease. Don't you?"

As Gregory bit into the apple, he wrestled to curb any trace of emotion that might creep into his voice. "I suppose it won't hurt. As Clara pointed out, I'm in no condition to protect you."

Although both his tone and countenance were perfectly controlled, acknowledging the servant's value out loud slashed Gregory's own sense of worth to pieces. He'd always been Elizabeth's protector, an indestructible shield, and now he was forced to rely on a carriage driver to fulfill that role. He couldn't help but feel useless in comparison.

"I recognize that expression, the forced indifference in your eyes. Don't tell me you're beating yourself up over this."

"Over what?" He feigned ignorance.

"Over your *temporary* inability to wield a sword."

"It doesn't bother me." Gregory fought to keep his face inscrutable, but he sounded less persuasive than he'd hoped.

Elizabeth's raised brow showed she didn't believe a word he said. "You perceive yourself to be weak, don't you? I implied that Channing might be an asset, and now you've convinced yourself you're inadequate."

Gregory gave an undignified snort as a gush of heat raced up his neck, burning his cheeks. *How does she always manage to hit the nail on the head?* "No."

Elizabeth studied his face a second, but clearly didn't buy the lie. "Greg. You were shot in the torso and *survived*. Do you realize how extraordinary that is? You overcame an injury that would've been fatal to any other man, yet you doubt your strength? What the hell is wrong with you?"

Gregory didn't know what to say, but it didn't matter because Elizabeth didn't pause long enough to let him fit a word in edgewise.

"It'll take time to recover, and while you do, there's no shame in letting Channing help pick up the slack. You're no less valuable now than you were a year ago."

"I know that."

"And you know I have full faith in you, right? With Channing, we have an extra set of eyes and a sword at our side, but even without him, I firmly believe you'd never let any harm come to us. Stop doubting yourself. No one else is."

Once again bolstered by his sister's encouragement and unshakable support, Gregory's face broke into a smile. "Thank you, Bess."

"Don't thank me, it's the truth. Now, back to the topic at hand."

"The topic being?"

"Clara." At Gregory's irritated sigh, she persisted, "I don't know why you're being so obstinate about her coming with us. I understand you think she's making a mistake. Part of me even agrees with you, but she wants to run away, and I'm guessing she'd do it whether you agreed to let her come with us or not. At least with us, she'll have a disguise. We'll all be wearing them, so I'd say our chances of being discovered are rather slim."

"*Rather slim?*" Gregory repeated, his tone a tad sharper than he'd anticipated. He dulled it a notch before continuing, "Rather slim isn't good enough, Bessie. Even in a friar's robe, I could still be recognized, and if that happens, the rest of you will be found out as well. It's bad enough I've placed your life in danger. I can barely stand myself as is. Now Clara and Channing are–"

"Clara and Channing made their choice, same as I did. I know you feel responsible, but our lives aren't in your hands. We're all adults, capable of making our own decisions."

"You've never been good at making the right decision." His tone was light, and he wore a grin he hoped would soften the criticism, yet Gregory knew Elizabeth detected the seriousness lurking behind his words.

She sucked in a sharp breath and spots of color bloomed in her cheeks, but to Gregory's relief, his barb didn't goad her into losing her temper. "Perhaps it's time we stop looking at your banishment as a punishment and start viewing it as a second chance," she suggested with unexpected optimism.

"We have an opportunity to be happy, truly happy. We're free now, Greg. Free of His Majesty's fists *and* Bernadette's constant attempts to humiliate you. This journey can be whatever we make of it. I'm going to make it fun. What about you?"

"I'm going to make it survivable."

Elizabeth shook her head at him, but a small giggle exposed her amusement. "I suppose that's what makes us a perfect team. You keep us alive, and I'll make sure we have a reason to live." She gave his arm a pat and stood up. "Now, get some rest. We're finally getting out of here." With a farewell wave, Elizabeth sped off to join the others in the carriage outside.

Left alone inside the cottage, Gregory had little to do but drift off to sleep. His nightmares continued as usual…only this time there were two more corpses dangling by their necks beside his sister.

CHAPTER 22

*K*nock knock. *Knock.*
Gregory rubbed his brow as his gaze alighted on the cottage door. *Father Timothy's secret knock. I should've known he'd come back.*

Without waiting for an invitation, the priest barged inside, deposited his bag on the floor beside the table, and plopped himself onto one of the stools.

"Your Highness." His toneless greeting held none of the enthusiasm he'd harbored at the beginning of their previous encounter, nor was he wearing his fanciest garments this time. Clothed in a simple black robe, he was no longer dressed to impress. "You're looking much less poorly."

"Thank y–"

"Do you know why I'm here?"

Gregory schooled his expression, careful not to show his irritation. "I could hazard a guess."

"Mary came to the church less than half an hour ago and requested two more disguises."

"Yes."

Father Timothy arched a brow and tapped his fingers

207

against the table, obvious gestures for Gregory to elaborate. When he didn't, the priest let out a loud breath. "Your cousin and her servant were there as well, to trade a carriage for my wagon."

"Yes."

"I hear you're leaving for the monastery. Today."

"It would seem so."

"You're in a talkative mood this morning," Father Timothy remarked, sarcasm heavy in his tone. He reached across the table for the jug of ale and poured himself a cup, his sight fastened on Gregory all the while. "You see now I was right, don't you? People will flock to your side in support of your claim. This is only the beginning."

Gregory stifled a snort. "Father, I'm afraid you've misunderstood. Clara isn't here because she wants to fight for me. She's merely trying to avoid marriage and my banishment awarded her an escape, or so she says."

"And the servant?"

"Love may be the reason Channing's here, but I assure you, it's not love for *me*."

"Oh? Well, it doesn't matter. You have no shortage of supporters." Father Timothy reached around the folds of his robe and dug inside the bag at his feet, producing a stack of papers at least three inches thick. "Letters are pouring in from churches all over." He stood up, shoved the parchment into Gregory's hands, and returned to the stool with a gleam in his eye. "Take a look."

"What is this?" Gregory flipped through pages and pages of what he assumed were signatures, most of which were illegible scribbles.

"Almost every priest in Caracalla asked the men of his parish to sign a declaration of loyalty to you." Father Timothy's teeth were displayed through his huge smile, and he fidgeted in his seat, clearly too excited to sit still. "Each name you see belongs to a man who's ready to lay down his life in service of his prince."

"Burn these!" Gregory gritted his teeth and fought through a wave of pain as he rearranged himself into an upright position. He'd need to appear authoritative if he had any chance of being taken seriously and lying on his back with his head on the pillow was not the answer. "Burn them, Father."

"Your Highness–"

"Every name listed here will belong to a *corpse* if Bernadette gets her hands on these papers."

Father Timothy blew out a peal of laughter. "I'd bet my left leg she couldn't make out a single one of those signatures."

Gregory rolled his eyes. "She wouldn't need to. Each priest wrote the name of his church at the top. See?" He lifted one of the declarations and pointed to the heading. "Church of Saint Peter, Reethdale." He held up a few more pages of signatures. "Saint John the Baptist's Church at Chorley, Saint Mary's Church in Leslie. Church of Saint–"

"I've been to Leslie." The priest sat up straighter, a glow lighting up his face. "Three years ago, I attended their annual raspberry festival. Have you ever been?"

"Father, you don't comprehend the danger these people are in." The parchment crinkled as Gregory waved it in front of his face, all traces of patience gone. "Bernadette won't take the time to decipher the names written here. She'll simply send men to these towns and round *everyone* up, whether they signed this or not. She won't take chances. She'll slaughter every man, woman, and child if she believes doing so will eliminate the threat against her. You need to end this before you dig yourself, these men, and their families in any deeper."

"They all knew the risks when they made their mark."

"*Hundreds* of innocent people will die, and if you're identified as the spark behind this plot, Bernadette will make sure you suffer the most. It's not worth it."

"It is." Father Timothy squared his shoulders. "I'd die a hundred deaths if I thought just one of them would keep her off the throne."

Momentarily ruffled, Gregory scratched the back of his neck. "Even so, I've made it clear that I don't share your...passion."

"I'd wager Princess Elizabeth does."

Gregory's lips curled as heat flushed beneath his skin.

"Now I've got your attention." Father Timothy's face screwed into a smirk. "Perhaps I'll ask her how she feels about–"

"Keep my sister out of it." Gregory hurled his most intimidating scowl at the priest as he gripped the blanket in his hands, twisting it with so much force he half expected the fabric to rip. "Or I'll involve yours."

Father Timothy's triumphant expression melted away in a trice.

"I take it Mary isn't aware of any of this either. How do you think she'd react if she knew of the danger you've placed yourself in?"

Skin flushed, the priest focused his attention on the corner of the room and sipped his ale in absolute silence. Once he'd drained the cup, he cleared his throat, pasted on a smile, and returned his reluctant gaze to Gregory. "On second thought, women are prone to fits of distress and are, therefore, better suited to ignorance. Perhaps we shouldn't involve them."

"You shouldn't have involved *anyone*," Gregory snarled. "End this now, or you'll get us all killed."

"There's something else you must see before you make up your mind." Anger burned in Father Timothy's voice as he yanked another sheet of paper from his bag and thrust it at Gregory. "Surely this travesty will motivate you to take up arms against Bernadette!"

Gregory's pulse leapt and his lips pulled back as he studied the vile poster.

There were no words on the page, but the sketch spoke volumes. It showed a hippogriff, Bernadette's royal emblem, lifting its back leg to take a piss upon Gregory's symbol, the Tree of Life.

While that offensive image alone was enough to send fire through his veins, it wasn't the true source of his rage. No, what really got under his skin was the addition of a little bird, a blue tit, to be exact, happily perched upon the hippogriff's shoulder. As Princess Elizabeth's official insignia, the blue tit was meant to represent her.

"Where did this come from?" Gregory asked through his teeth. Nostrils flaring, he scrunched the poster up and squeezed it with all his might.

"Does it matter? Someone who hates you clearly has access to a printing press."

He chucked the ball of paper into the fire. "It's deplorable!"

"It certainly is. Not only does it debase your character, but it also implies that Princess Elizabeth has turned on you and joined up with Bernadette."

Gregory's skin tightened, the muscles in his forearms flexing as he opened and closed his fists. Heat flushed through him as he worked to regain his composure. It wasn't easy though, not when Elizabeth's loyalty to him was called into question. It was common knowledge throughout all of Caracalla that Prince Gregory's little sister was his greatest ally. To show her like that, in league with Bernadette, was a deliberate attempt to portray him as an outcast with no support.

"It's a decent strategy, no matter the truth. If Princess Elizabeth is seen to have jumped ship, what's to stop the rest of your supporters from doing the same? You can be sure whoever created this poster will print more just like it. Sketches like this will continue to circulate throughout the whole kingdom, and as they do, you'll lose your allies one by one. That is, unless we put an end to it right now. Stand up to Bernadette and prove—"

"No." Gregory lifted his chin and pushed up his sleeves. "They can distribute all the drawings they wish, it doesn't matter. I've made up my mind and nothing will change it."

Father Timothy's eyes were dark as storm clouds.

The pair sat in silence, each man waiting for the other to give in, but neither would bend. Neither would yield.

Although Gregory wanted to hate Father Timothy for being such a sharp, persistent thorn in his side, he couldn't. Infuriating as the priest was, the man firmly believed he was doing the right thing for the kingdom. He was wrong, of course, but his motives were understandable, and Gregory appreciated his devotion even if nothing would come of it.

As his gaze fell to the heap of signatures in his lap, a faint smile came to his lips. Every one of those names represented a Caracallan man. A man who, like the priest, was loyal to Gregory and was willing to die beneath his banner. Honored and uplifted by their support, he imagined life at Crompton would've been a lot more bearable had he known more people believed in him.

Gregory issued a heavy sigh. "Listen, Father. I appreciate–"

"It's a shame you still haven't come to your senses," the priest said, his tone full of venom. "You truly intend to walk away from your birthright and leave this kingdom at the mercy of your elder sister? She's evil incarnate."

Gregory sucked in his cheeks. *Can't argue that.*

"Well?"

"I intend to walk away from the bloodbath you're suggesting we create."

"Don't you see? I'm trying to *prevent* a bloodbath. Your whole family is Protestant, and that's fine, but Princess Bernadette openly detests Catholics. If she becomes queen, she'll burn us all."

As understanding dawned, Gregory leaned back against the pillows and ran his hands through his hair. "That's the reason behind all this, the reason you and so many priests want me on the throne."

"Yes," Father Timothy confirmed, matter-of-factly. "Your Highness, you donated funds for the rebuilding of my church. You're a friend to us. I'm certain that with you as our sovereign, the people of Caracalla will know true religious freedom. Please, do not turn your back on us. Fight for the crown, Prince Gregory. Fight for your people."

With a sinking feeling in his stomach, Gregory once again glanced down at the sheets of parchment in his lap. This time, he considered Father Timothy's side of things. His insides squirmed as he weighed the pros and cons of challenging Bernadette.

If he did this, thousands of men would die on the battle-field in his name. If he didn't, Bernadette would have complete control over the realm. Either way, the citizens of Caracalla would suffer.

Gregory closed his eyes, rubbing the middle of his fore-head. He knew Father Timothy's opinion, but the one he valued most was Elizabeth's. He already knew what she'd say though. Without hesitation, his little sister would take up arms and fight for him, right alongside the rest of his army.

That tragic image, Elizabeth mounted up and clad in a suit of armor as she charged through enemy lines, put an immediate end to Gregory's indecision. Picturing the soldiers who'd fall beneath his banner was difficult enough to stomach, but he'd never risk his sister's life on the battlefield.

After watching the emotions play across Gregory's face, Father Timothy bowed his neck and pressed his lips flat. "You've made up your mind then? There's no changing it?"

"No," Gregory announced, his voice steady. "What you're suggesting would cost thousands of lives. I couldn't live with that, not even if it all worked out, which I have my doubts about."

"I can't believe this…"

Gregory held his chin high. "You've arranged for us to stay at Fincost Priory while I recover from my injury, but if your kindness is dependent upon my fight for the crown, we'll go elsewhere."

The priest's head shot up. "I did that because it's the Christian thing to do," he spat. "Just because you're too stubborn to–"

"Then I thank you, Father. You're dismissed."

"Excuse me?"

"Unless there's another matter you wish to discuss, you're dismissed."

Father Timothy leapt off the stool and snatched the declarations from Gregory's grasp.

"Don't forget to burn those," Gregory commanded.

"You're a fool, boy. You're damning this kingdom to hell

and mark my words..." He leaned in close enough for the rank stench of his sweat to pollute the air. "You'll pay for this."

Just then, the door creaked open, and the priest slid away from the bed seconds before Elizabeth came inside.

"Good to see you again, Father. Have you brought–"

"The habit and friar robe my sister requested are in there." He made no effort to temper his tone as he motioned toward the bag on the floor. "Farewell, Your Highness. I'll pray for your soul and that of your bull-headed brother."

Elizabeth's lips parted, but Father Timothy pushed past her and stormed out of the cottage before she could utter a sound. The door slammed shut with such force, the vase of yellow poppies on the bedside table rattled in his wake.

Wide eyed, Elizabeth gaped at Gregory. "What was that about?"

"Nothing you need to concern yourself over, Bess. Where is everyone?"

"They'll be back soon." Elizabeth approached the table and poured two cups of ale, her eyebrows drawn together as she handed him one. After sitting down on the edge of Mary's bed, she grew still and sipped from her cup, observing him.

Gregory pretended not to notice as he took a casual drink of his own ale. "How's the weather? Good day for travel?"

"You're really not going to tell me what just happened?"

"I told you, it's nothing to worry about."

"Somehow, you riled a priest. *You*. What were you two talking about before I–"

"Elizabeth. Drop it." He shot her a scowl that warned against further inquisition.

She tucked her lips in and stared at him a moment, then rolled her eyes and exited the cottage.

CHAPTER 23

With the evening light casting the forest in a brilliant orange glow, a rare sense of tranquility washed over Elizabeth as she breathed in the fresh, woodsy air. She couldn't have asked for better weather, and although her heart panged at the memory of her emotional goodbye with Mary, she knew the parting was long overdue.

Elizabeth flicked the reins and rode up beside the wooden cart. She looked over the side, disheartened by the creases of pain dug into Greg's brow. They'd been traveling most of the day now, yet he hadn't uttered a single word of grievance since they left Gettsbury.

Clara, on the other hand, expressed often and with no shortage of dramatics that they'd already spent far too much time on the road for one day. Elizabeth's sore bottom was a testament to that and worse, she'd lost all feeling in her legs hours ago. However, it was her determination to follow Greg's supreme example that prompted her to keep her complaints to herself. Besides, with Clara around, the role of whiny moaner had already been filled, and the last thing Greg needed was to put up with gripes from both of them.

She massaged her upper thigh and expelled her own problems from her thoughts. *Just a little while until we can stop to rest.* Until then, she'd focus on Greg. "Are you comfortable enough in there?"

"As comfortable as can be expected." Reclining on a few pillows and snuggled up in blankets like a newborn babe, Greg lifted one side of his mouth in a half smile. "I wouldn't refuse a sip of ale, though."

"Hold on, I have it right here." Elizabeth untied the jug from her pack and handed it down to him with a playful grin. "We packed plenty, so you might even be able to have *two* sips."

"Nah, I wouldn't want to spoil myself."

Elizabeth chuckled. "No, we wouldn't want that."

The uneven path jostled Greg around the hull, and as he tried to take a drink, ale dribbled down his chin. The cart was rickety as could be, and Elizabeth knew that despite the thick padding of wool beneath him, her brother felt every bump.

"Channing," he called with a grimace. "Stop a minute."

The servant, who was squished in beside Clara on the wooden bench in the front, brought the wagon to a standstill and glanced up at the setting sun through the treetops. "It'll be dark soon. Shall we find someplace to rest for the night?"

Overjoyed that someone else broke down before she did, Elizabeth did her best to appear disinterested as she awaited Greg's response. It didn't work out as well as she would've liked. Her eagerness to dismount the horse and call it a day was heard in every rushed word she spewed. "What do you think, Greg? Are you hungry? There's a nice spot over there to light a fire. Channing could do that while I set up the tent."

He opened his mouth to answer, but was interrupted when Clara emitted a loud, theatrical gasp. Her hand flew to her chest, and she twisted around in her seat to peer at Elizabeth, her face white as a corpse. "*Tent*?"

Elizabeth bit back a snide remark but failed to keep the exasperation out of her tone. "Yes, Clara."

"You're planning to have us sleep outdoors?"

"Where else would we sleep?" The question belonged to Greg and was spoken in a most fractious manner. "We warned you this wouldn't be–"

"There's a village up ahead," Channing interjected. "*Warrick*, I think it's called. It must have an inn."

Greg shrugged. "So?"

"So, we can sleep there! There could be scoundrels and pagans lurking behind every bush and boulder." Clara's wide-eyed gaze bounced from tree to tree, her face marked with sudden horror as she pulled her cloak tighter around herself. "We can't possibly stay out here all night!"

An icy chill swept over Elizabeth at the word *pagan*, and her imagination painted a nightmarish picture of the tattooed heathens gulping a cup of fresh blood. Her blood. She shuddered, but when her gaze returned to Greg, she was somewhat comforted by his apparent lack of fear. To her puzzlement, she discerned only vexation in his narrowed eyes.

"Isn't that why Channing's here?" he growled. "To offer protection from such threats?"

Clara pursed her lips. "Oh, Greg, don't be an idiot. You know full well Channing's sword is ineffective against magic."

"Magic?" Greg snorted, his humorless laughter turning Clara's face a deep shade of purple.

"Yes, magic. Everyone knows pagans are flesh-eating devil-worshipers who use curses and jinxes to destroy their enemies. How do you expect Channing to fight an enemy like that? No, no. I'm not doing this. You're a dullard if you expect me to sleep in a tent in these woods. A daft, incorrigible dullard!"

Greg inhaled and his nostrils flared as a raw and potent anger mottled his skin. It was no secret that Clara enjoyed dancing on his last nerve, and although her insults were generally harmless, Elizabeth knew they made Greg's blood boil. The mutual dislike between the two was palpable, and it'd been that way for as long as she could remember.

Nevertheless, Clara was the one who'd provided the means of travel for this trip. Without her, they'd still be stranded in Gettsbury, waiting for Greg's wound to heal enough for him to ride a horse. She may be a nuisance at times, but she'd earned her right to be here.

"Clara, there's no need for insults." Elizabeth deliberately spoke loud enough to drown out the sound of whatever retort Greg intended to deliver. His fists were tight, and he was taking in deep breaths through his nose, clear signs that the final tether restraining his temper was about to rip. "I agree our sleeping arrangement isn't ideal, however–"

"I *refuse* to sleep in a tent, Bess!"

"Listen, I understand your qualms." Elizabeth infused as much softness into her voice as possible, as though she was trying to sooth a youngster in the midst of a temper tantrum. It occurred to her that this was probably how Greg felt whenever she was in one of her moods, but she shoved that uninvited revelation from her mind the second it formed. "Believe it or not, I share your fears. No one *wants* to sleep in the woods. However, I'm afraid we don't have a choice."

"How can you say that?" Clara's eyes flashed and her shoulders stiffened. "Of course we have a choice. Did you not hear Channing say we're close to a town? What's the point of wearing these ghastly religious clothes if we aren't going to use them to hide in plain sight?"

"It's not about being seen. You're right, the purpose of these disguises is to let us pass through crowded streets without calling attention to ourselves. That's not the issue here."

"Then what is?"

Elizabeth sighed, her command over her composure waning. "When I wrote to you asking for financial assistance, it was because we needed it. I'm happy you're here, truly, but the few coins Mary gave us won't last long. Every penny we have needs to be put toward purchasing food on our way to the monastery. Surely you can see how lodging at an inn is a waste of our funds."

Clara blinked at her. "That's what this is about? Money?"

"Not entirely," Greg cut in. His quarrelsome expression confirmed that the sole purpose of his objection was to needle her.

"Yes." Elizabeth hurled a look of admonishment in her brother's direction, hoping it would express her desire for him to shut up and let her handle this. "Entirely."

Her cousin's lips twitched up in a smile. "Then I think there's something you need to see." Ignoring Elizabeth's confusion and Greg's aggravated grumbles, Clara stood up and pulled her cloak open to reveal a sizeable satchel hanging from her waist.

Elizabeth's heart gave a leap as she ogled what she could only assume was the solution to all their financial woes. "That looks heavy."

Clara giggled, her green eyes glimmering. "Of course it's heavy. Did you honestly think I came here empty-handed?"

"Well, yes. How much is in there?"

Clara shrugged, sporting a victorious grin as she removed the satchel and held it out for Elizabeth to take. "See for yourself. There's definitely enough to avoid sleeping in a tent."

Elizabeth fumbled over the drawstrings, too enthused for her fingers to work properly. When she finally managed to open the purse, her jaw fell open and tears of relief sprang to her eyes. "Greg! Our problems are solved. See?" She poured a pile of silver and gold coins into her hand, marveling at their sparkle. "There's at least a hundred shillings here!"

While Elizabeth counted the coins in a hurried attempt to get a more accurate estimate, Clara sat back down beside Channing. Eyes aglow and chin high, she smirked at Greg over her shoulder. "Now, if there's no further argument, I think it's time we find ourselves a decent place to sleep."

CHAPTER 24

*E*lizabeth chewed her lower lip as she scurried after Channing into the crumbling stone building. The village of Warrick's one and only tavern had fallen into a deep state of disrepair, yet despite its outward appearance, it was alive with activity.

Every table was crammed with intoxicated men who were either gambling their coins away or trading them in for the company of one of the many promiscuous, underdressed women prowling about. One of those women seemed particularly unashamed of her profession, for her naked breast hung out overtop her bodice and was being suckled by the man upon whose lap she was perched. When the harlot caught sight of Elizabeth's lingering gaze, she spread her legs wide open and lifted her skirts to her knees, exposing her privates for everyone to see.

The tavern erupted in hoots and cheers.

Elizabeth's cheeks flamed and she turned away, but not before noticing the lewd smirk that'd appeared across the woman's face. Careful not to make eye contact with a single patron from that point forward, she leaned into her cousin's side and whispered, "I don't think *decent* is the right word to describe this place."

Clara grunted to show her annoyance but had the good sense not to argue.

The sinful behavior they witnessed while Channing paid the innkeeper was appalling, but the late hour left them little opportunity to let the scandalous sights alter their decision to stay there overnight.

Once they'd been given their rooms, Clara and Channing carried their belongings upstairs while Elizabeth returned to the stable where they'd left Greg waiting with the wagon. Despite her brother's best efforts to convince her to stay with him, she'd ignored his request and ventured into the tavern with Channing and Clara instead. Like most people, Greg didn't appreciate his wishes being disregarded. The scowl he'd worn as she departed attested to that.

"You can stop fretting now." Elizabeth skipped up to the cart and peeked over the side, grinning so wide it made her face hurt. "The mission was a success."

"I'm glad." There was a definite thread of impatience in his tone, but his jaw loosened a bit as the anxiety on his face converted to relief.

Elizabeth set out to further ease his mind. "We didn't get into any trouble, I promise. I have to warn you though, this place is unsavory! Of all the inns we could've come across, this has to be the worst one of all. I counted half a dozen ladies of the night in there. One of them intentionally exposed herself to us and she wasn't wearing any drawers. I saw *everything.* Who shows their privates to a nun? I'm not a real nun, of course, but she doesn't know that! Perhaps I should've stayed with you after all."

Greg crossed his arms as he glowered back at her.

Elizabeth cleared her throat. "But like I said, we're

perfectly safe. See?" She took a step back from the wagon, held her arms out to the side, and spun around in a full circle. "No visible wounds. The only harm done is the image burned into my brain. That's a scar that'll never heal."

She'd intended for her lighthearted words to be taken as a joke, but Greg didn't appear the least bit amused. He didn't say a word, yet his thoughts were conveyed well enough through his reprehensive gaze and compressed lips. Desperate to dodge a blast of anger from him, Elizabeth wiped the smile off her face and fell into submission.

"Anyway, Clara and Channing already took our knapsacks and all the provisions up. You'll share a room with him, but there's a trundle tucked under the master bed so you'll each have your own sleeping space. I requested the chamber just across the hall for me and Clara. That way, I'll be close by if you need anything."

Greg's lips parted, and for a moment it looked as though he was going to protest something, but he seemed to think better of it. "That was thoughtful," he murmured instead. "Thank you."

"You're quite welcome. Now, let's get you inside."

It took some time and a good deal of effort, but Elizabeth managed to help Greg up the stairs and into one of the rooms they'd rented. It wore them both out.

Elizabeth's eyelids were heavy, and she staggered a bit as she handed Channing the basket of supplies Mary had put together for the care of Greg's wound. "Can I count on you to change his bandages tonight? I would, but I'm about to topple over."

"Yes, I'll do it right now."

She released a sigh, grateful for the servant's willingness to lend a hand. "Thank you. Be sure to wash out the wound with clean water before applying the poultice. And don't forget to change the one on his back as well."

"Don't worry, Your Highness. I can handle it."

"Splendid, and please, call me Elizabeth. We should dispense with the formalities in order to keep our identities a secret."

"Yes. As you wish...Elizabeth."

She searched his face, and her worries evaporated upon seeing the genuine friendliness that hovered behind his smile. His emerald eyes shined, warm and bright, and for a second, she toyed with the possibility that perhaps Channing was worthy of Clara's affection.

Was it plausible that a penniless servant could make for a better husband than a baron? She was beginning to think so. Money didn't guarantee happiness, but perhaps poverty didn't guarantee unhappiness either.

"I'll bid you both goodnight then," Elizabeth spluttered, dumbfounded by her shifting notion of love and the restrictions placed upon it. "I'll see you in the morning." With that, she scampered off to find her own bed.

Drained and aching from too many hours spent atop a horse, Elizabeth struggled to keep her eyes open as she removed her habit and snuggled into the bed beside her cousin. The wooden frame creaked under the added weight, and she cringed, certain the worn-down legs would shatter. The bed, along with everything else in this ratty, old tavern, seemed to be on the brink of decay.

"This thing must be at least a hundred years old," she surmised, unsure herself whether or not she was joking. She rolled over onto her side in search of a more comfortable position, creating such a racket it *almost* rivaled that of the drunken caterwauling coming from downstairs.

"Still better than a tent," came Clara's immediate retort. It was a point even Elizabeth couldn't dispute. "Bess?"

"Yes?" She yawned and her eyes fluttered shut as she tugged the blanket up to her neck, leaving only her head exposed to the stuffy air.

"You do realize we never ate supper, right? I do hope that doesn't become a habit."

If Elizabeth's eyes had been open, she would've rolled them. "It won't."

"I'm famished. And thirsty. Aren't you?"

"Yes. Now go to sleep." Paying no heed to the grumbles of discontent her demand evoked from her cousin, Elizabeth nuzzled her head deeper into the lumpy pillow. Normally she would've been put off by the faint scent of mildew that lingered there, but she was far too tired at present to care. Instead, she imagined a steaming cup of wassail and a plate laden with delicious sweets as her drowsiness took hold at long last.

Elizabeth's eyes shot open when the awareness that she'd forgotten to give Channing the honey for Greg's poultice crashed over her like a ruthless wave. Despising herself for being so forgetful, she rubbed the sleep out of her eyes and dragged her sore body out of the ancient, squeaking bed.

Her lips parted with the intent to express regret for disturbing Clara's slumber, however the apology was forestalled when the light from the hearth revealed there was no one there to apologize to.

Elizabeth took a quick scan of the room, which was no

bigger than her wardrobe closet back at Crompton, and arrived at the conclusion that Clara must've ventured downstairs in search of refreshments.

She couldn't know for sure whether she'd been asleep for two minutes or two hours, but as she wrapped herself up in her cloak and slipped her shoes on, she decided it didn't matter. The honey was necessary to prevent inflammation, and she needed to take it across the hall regardless.

It didn't seem too late though, for the ruckus coming from the tavern below was just as deafening as it'd been when they'd first arrived. Whoops, hollers, and energetic music assaulted her as she tiptoed into the hallway and hovered outside her brother's room.

"Channing?" Mindful of Greg's advice not to call any unnecessary attention to herself, Elizabeth spoke in a whisper and kept her face down. "Open the door. It's me, *Dorothy*."

There was no answer, and she felt a pang of guilt for having to wake them up. She raised her voice and tried again, knocking this time to ensure she was heard over the distasteful song currently being bellowed by a disreputable passerby in the hall. "Don't leave me standing out here all night, Channing. Let me in."

The stranger's singing came to an abrupt end, and in the resulting stillness, the commotion downstairs seemed to drift away. Elizabeth's heartbeat, however, thundered in her ears.

Panic ripped through her and she froze, sensing the drunkard's stare draping over her like a net. Her breath stuttered, and a cold chill shot down her spine as she stole a sideways glimpse at him.

The man had stopped dead in his tracks, licking his lips. "Well, ya sure are a purdy one." His glossy gaze raked over her with shameless appetence.

With a gulp, Elizabeth returned her attention to the

wooden door in front of her. In her fatigued state she'd lacked the good sense to put her disguise back on, a doltish mistake for any woman in an unruly cesspool such as this.

"How much fer a moment of yer time, my sweet lil' rose?" The lanky oaf dug in his pockets as he shuffled toward her, his anticipatory grin revealing a mouthful of rotted teeth. "I've a shilling 'ere. T'will that be 'nuff ta gain entry ta yer bed?"

Elizabeth suppressed a gag. "No, I'm not a–"

"No?" Offended, the presumptuous newt glowered at her, but that didn't halt his steps. "Ya think ya be worth more?"

"Yes. I mean, no. Apologies. You misunderstand…" She stumbled over her words as the space between her and the randy stranger diminished. "I'm not…this isn't happening! Good night, sir!"

Forced to abandon all sense of propriety by the urgent need to escape the drunkard's unwelcome advances, Elizabeth lifted the latch to Greg's room and pushed herself inside uninvited. She then slammed the door shut, barricading herself behind it.

For a brief spell, she stood glued to the spot, silent and motionless. She didn't relax her rigid stance or release the breath she'd been holding until the man's footsteps thumped off down the hall.

"Bessie? Are you alright?"

Elizabeth sucked in a deep gulp of air, arranged her face in a smile, and circled around to Greg. He must've seen through her pretense though, because he leapt to his feet so fast her heart skipped a beat.

"What happened?" All traces of drowsiness slipped from his eyes and his jaw locked, his injury forgotten as he curled his fists in preparation for a war with whatever entity had her so frightened. "Did someone try to hurt you?"

"No, I'm fine. Calm down."

"Your face is white."

"And now yours is red, but I told you nothing happened. Relax, please." Thinking on her feet and hoping to set her brother at peace, Elizabeth concocted an excuse that would defuse him. Her voice was velvety smooth as she fibbed, "I had a nightmare, that's all. It was about our father."

It wasn't uncommon for her to seek Greg out whenever her inner demons reared their ugly heads. She exploited that fact, and although she could taste the dishonesty on her tongue, Greg's shoulders sagged, and a small amount of hostility lifted from his eyes.

"I'm sorry. Do you want to sit in here awhile?"

The genuine sympathy Greg exuded created a lump in her throat, and as the guilt of the lie charged through her, she shook her head. "Thanks, but it wasn't that bad. I wouldn't have come over at all if I hadn't forgotten to give this to Channing." She held up the jar of honey as her gaze wandered about the room, but like Clara, the servant was missing. "Where is he?"

Greg shrugged as he climbed back into the bed. "He was here when I fell asleep."

"That's odd. Clara isn't in bed either."

"*Odd?*" he echoed, a smirk splitting his face in two. "They were all but holding hands at Mary's breakfast table."

Elizabeth bit her tongue and ignored the inappropriate comment altogether. "Here's the honey." She set it down beside the basket of bandages, determined not to dwell on the questionable feelings her cousin harbored for her servant. "Speaking of breakfast, we skipped our evening meal. Do you want me to fetch you something to eat? I know it's late, but–"

"No. I don't want you going downstairs. This is no place for a young woman to roam unchaperoned." Greg's words, which were most certainly true, brought an instant pout to Elizabeth's lips. "That doesn't mean you can't eat," he clarified. "If you're hungry, *I* will go get you something."

She emitted an impatient huff. "Don't be ridiculous. You can't use the steps alone."

"Which should stress to you how serious I am about my desire for you to stay put." His voice was low, and she could've sworn she heard the hint of a threat in it. "I mean it, Elizabeth. Do not go down there."

A spark of defiance ignited in her gut and she gritted her teeth, vexed by his incessant need to control her every move. "I'm not a child. If I want to–"

Greg held his hand up in a deliberate interruption, one that inflamed her temper close to the point of eruption. "Let me rephrase that," he requested with equanimity. "I'm asking you, *please* don't venture down there. I don't need to tell you how viperous men with too much ale in their bellies can be. It's true, you're not a child, yet you know full well children aren't the only victims of a drunkard's belligerence. I went against my better judgment and accepted your decision to join me in exile, but when you made a promise to support me, I made a promise to keep you safe. I implore you, help me uphold my end of the deal."

Elizabeth's scowl dropped as shame slipped in to replace her earlier rage. Greg's change of wording made all the difference, and she crossed her arms, embarrassed for letting her pride and selfishness eclipse his concern for her safety. "You have my word," she muttered to the floor. "I won't go downstairs. Goodnight."

CHAPTER 25

*R*avished, Gregory tore into the tray of food the second it was placed in his lap. The bread was stale, and the cheese was spotted with mold, but after what Channing had just told him, the freshness of his breakfast was the least of his worries.

"What do you mean the wheel's broken?" He used his knife to cut away the undesirable pieces of cheese and popped one of the better bits into his mouth. "How much will it cost to replace it?"

Channing sat down on the chair in front of the hearth and scratched his temple, pensive lines creasing his brow. "It'll take a few days, and I'll need help from the local blacksmith, but I can repair it myself for a fraction of the price."

"Then we'll do that," he said around a mouthful of cheddar. "We shouldn't deplete our funds unless it's truly necessary."

With a troubled frown, the servant agreed. "That solves the problem yet does nothing to explain how it happened. I inspected all four wheels before we left, and all the spokes were in pristine condition. There's no reason this should've happened, especially after only a single day of travel."

Gregory flung another chunk of cheese into his mouth. "The first of many mishaps, I'm sure. You'll soon learn that fortune and I aren't on the best of terms." Recognizing the familiar emotion of self-doubt loitering behind Channing's stupefaction, Gregory aimed to relieve him of his guilt. "No need to worry, friend. Accidents happen."

Channing shook his head, deep in thought as he slumped further into the chair and drummed his fingers on his cheek. "That's just it, though. I don't think it was an acci–"

A knock sounded on the door then, interrupting the servant's speculations. Channing made a move to get up, but Elizabeth stormed in before his bottom left the chair. With a look of fierce determination pinching her features, she marched across the room and planted herself beside the bed.

Clara trailed in after her, head hung and eyes on her feet.

"Good morning, Bess. Clara." Gregory looked back and forth between the two women. "Is there a problem?"

"As a matter of fact, there is." Elizabeth gritted her teeth. "Ask these two what they were doing last night." She placed her hands on her hips, her elbows sticking out as she eyeballed their cousin with severe reproach. "Tell him, Clara."

Her cheeks taking on a pinkish hue, Clara murmured something in an inaudible whisper.

"I don't think he heard you," Elizabeth spat at her.

Clara made a second attempt, louder this time. "We went dancing. In the tavern."

"In the *tavern*." His sister's face was marred by an uncharacteristic darkness. If Gregory had to take a guess, he'd say jealousy was the cause of her pursed lips and discoloration. "While I honored my promise and stayed in bed with nothing to do but listen to my stomach rumble, these two idiots were down there carousing with the whores and drunks."

Yes, definitely jealousy. "Bess–"

"Don't *Bess* me. Are you going to scold them or not?"

Gregory took in a lungful of air, considering his next words very carefully. "I'll admit, it wasn't the wisest decision. We're supposed to be lying low."

Elizabeth's mouth twisted in impatience. "However?"

"However, they're both adults."

"As am I," she bristled, a visible flush in her cheeks. "Clara's three months younger than I am."

"Clara isn't my responsibility."

Elizabeth's jaw twitched, and she plopped down on the foot of the bed. She focused on the ceiling and inhaled through her nose, then slowly released it in a commendable effort to keep her composure. The briefest smile touched Gregory's lips as he watched this, pleased that she was at least trying to control her temper. That was new.

When she spoke again, her voice was a few degrees warmer. "Help me understand why I'm expected to follow the rules and they're not." Her confused gaze sought his. "You basically forbade *me* from leaving my room last night, and yet you don't care that they paraded themselves about for everyone to see? They didn't even wear their disguises."

"Why would we?" Clara snorted. Now that it was clear she wasn't in trouble, she held her chin up in her typical lofty fashion. "A friar and nun dancing together would attract every eye in the room. We were being discreet."

Elizabeth jerked her head to the side and cast their cousin a scornful glower. "Discreet? Have you already forgotten that Greg has a bounty on his head?"

Clara tutted. "I'm well aware he's a wanted fugitive, but

that doesn't necessarily have to be *my* problem. No one wants *me* dead. There's no reason why I should have to hide myself away, too."

"Not your problem?" Elizabeth's mouth fell agape, and her gaze darted to Gregory, as though checking to see if he took issue with Clara's insensitivity. He shrugged it off and in the next instant, she exploded. "We're talking about your life here!"

Clara's green eyes were alight with insolence. "No, Elizabeth, we're talking about a few harmless dances. You're jealous because while I'm free to do as I please, you still have Greg here to boss you around."

Elizabeth's brows pulled in as she opened and closed her mouth. While it was clear she wanted to argue their cousin's insight, it was also clear that she couldn't.

Gregory's heart cramped.

"I understand your concern." Channing sounded polite enough as he gave Elizabeth a gentle smile. "Perhaps it was irresponsible of Clara and I to mingle with the locals, but–"

"But you're overreacting," Clara finished for him.

"No, I'm not." After throwing her cousin another glare, Elizabeth returned her attention to Gregory. "What about you, Greg. Do you think I'm overreacting?"

Silence permeated the room, and all eyes shifted to Gregory, the expectation of his reaction pressing against his chest like a brick wall. He spoke directly to Elizabeth, maintaining a level tone and neutral expression. "I think it's complicated. While it's true that all four of us should stick to the shadows whenever possible, the risk of you or me being recognized is far greater than it is for Clara. We're members of the royal family, the king's own children, and as she so tactlessly mentioned, my face is the one associated with treason."

Elizabeth tensed. "So, you approve?"

"Sounds to me like he does."

"I didn't say that." Gregory sent a fierce look in Clara's direction, then turned back to Elizabeth. "Bess, you being seen wasn't my concern last night. I thought you understood that I told you not to enter the tavern because it's not safe. Clara had Channing with her, but you were alone. That's the difference."

She squinted, fiddling with the sleeves of her habit as she sifted through his words. "If that's the case, then could I have joined them? If I'm under Channing's care, can I go dancing at the next inn we stop at?"

"I don't think it'd be wise for you to go dancing." Despite the remorse he infused into his speech, the refusal put a pout on Elizabeth's face. "It's not an activity most nuns partake in. You're the king's daughter, and as such, you could be recognized without a disguise. You must wear the habit at all times. That said, I see no reason why you can't sit at one of the tables and order yourself a meal. As long as Channing is nearby to keep an eye on you and it's not too late, I see no reason why you have to be confined to your room."

"See, Bess?" Mockery resonated in the elevated pitch of Clara's voice as she leered at Elizabeth. "With Channing around to be your wet nurse, you're permitted to have a little taste of freedom as well. So long as it's not past your bedtime, that is."

Gregory's pulse spiked and his belly roiled as he watched Elizabeth clasp her hands together, squeezing them with such force each of her fingers turned red. It didn't escape his notice that she'd been on her best behavior since they'd left Mary's house, but proud as he was of her, Gregory doubted she'd be able to take much more of Clara's prodding. It was only a matter of time before her temper got the better of her, and quite frankly, their cousin was working on his last nerve as well.

"At present, the only thing I want to taste is some break-fast." Elizabeth's voice was silky, belying the anger that was certain to be festering below the fake smile she'd painted on. "I'm starved." She leaned over and filched a slice of bread off his plate. She wrinkled her nose after the first nibble, but to Gregory's amazement, she kept whatever complaint she had to herself as she crunched into it again. "What time are we setting out today?"

"Turns out we're stuck here for a few days," Gregory answered, in awe of his sister's sudden maturity. "One of the wagon wheels broke."

She tilted her head to the side. "So? Let's buy a new one and get going."

"Channing says he can fix it. It'll take time, but it's worth it for the money we'll save."

"How long will it take you?" Elizabeth asked Channing.

"Under normal circumstances, a few days–"

"Then how will that save money? If we stay here longer while you fix it, we'll have to rent both rooms for additional nights." Elizabeth's brow furrowed. "Wouldn't it be cheaper to buy a new wheel?"

Gregory did the math in his head. "You're right. I'd forgotten to factor in the cost of the rooms."

"As it happens, both hostlers went home sick this morn-ing," Channing cut in. "So the innkeeper offered to give us a generous discount if I clean the stables and tend to the horses in their absence."

"How generous?"

Channing answered Clara's question with a triumphant grin. "Our room is free, and yours is half-priced. Even with the extra nights, it'll still cost less than it would to get a new wheel. Spare parts are incredibly expensive."

"Why would he give us such a bargain?" Elizabeth's puzzlement echoed in her tone.

"I think it helps that I'm dressed as a friar. He must be Catholic."

"So we're staying here?"

Gregory gave his sister a nod. "Yes."

"In that case, I'm heading back to bed." Elizabeth snatched two more slices of bread off the plate and hopped to her feet. "Do *not* wake me before noon."

Later that afternoon, Elizabeth's grin was wider than the sea and there was a bounce in her step as she walked down the street alongside Clara and Channing. The tantalizing aroma of smoked sausages drifted into her nose, and she licked her lips, making a mental note to purchase a few after their visit to the blacksmith.

Merchant carts clamored through the streets and a throng of people danced to joyous music in the square, but clad in their religious clothes, the three outsiders escaped the notice of the busy townsfolk. Being overlooked wasn't something Elizabeth was accustomed to, yet it was liberating to explore without fear of being exposed. The habit, itchy and ugly as it was, offered a sense of protection she hadn't felt since leaving Crompton Palace.

"Oh!" Clara's face brightened, and she broke her stride to peer inside the window of the mercer's shop. "Look at that fabric. It's divine." She twisted around to face Elizabeth, her green eyes luminous and urgent. "We should shop while Channing goes to the forge."

"I don't think that's wise."

Clara jerked her head to the side and wrinkled her nose at the servant's words.

He wasn't dissuaded by the look of vexation Clara threw at him. "Greg put me in charge of Elizabeth's welfare. He'd have my hide if I let her out of my sight."

A naughty little smirk slid across Clara's face. "We don't have to tell him. I've been known to keep a secret or two."

Channing shook his head, but there was a twinkle in his eye that led Elizabeth to believe he wasn't as perturbed as he let on. "Clara–"

"The innkeeper said the smithy is at the end of the lane. Bess and I can stay here and browse while you find out if he's willing to help you repair the wheel. We'll be fine. Won't we, Bess?"

Excitement flickered inside her, but Elizabeth buried it. "I promised Greg we'd stay together. That's the only reason he let me come along."

"*Let* you?" Clara crossed her arms and scrutinized Elizabeth, ridicule written into every one of her facial features. "Greg has been giving you orders since the day you were born, that's nothing new, but since when do you obey them?"

Try as she might, Elizabeth couldn't keep the impatience out of her voice. "Disregarding his *requests* could lead to a rope around our necks. And what would two nuns be doing in a fabric store, anyway? It's not as if we can wear anything made of silk so why bother looking at it? We should stay with Channing."

"He'll be right down the street," Clara huffed with a dramatic roll of her eyes. "Besides, I've never heard of anyone dying while they browse through some textiles. Stop being such an uptight stick-in-the-mud. Greg already has that trait spoken for, and saintliness doesn't suit you, Bess."

Elizabeth shot her cousin a scornful glare. She was well aware she was being baited and therefore, refused to let her resolve taper. "The answer is no." Like Clara, she folded her arms and the two stood nose to nose. "Either we stay together or go back to the inn. Your choice."

"Channing?" Clara's voice was unnaturally sweet as she blinked up at the servant through her lashes. "You're no longer under my employ, so I won't *order* you to leave us. However, I'd appreciate the opportunity to shop without feeling like I'm some sort of prisoner. Give me a few minutes of freedom, and I promise, I'll find some way to thank you later."

Elizabeth's mouth hung open. Greg may be the prince and she may be the princess, but there was no way in hell their wishes carried any weight when matched against Clara and her womanly wiles. "You can't be serious. That's what you're resorting to?"

Her flirtatious cousin paid her no mind as she stood on her tiptoes and planted a lengthy kiss atop Channing's cheek. The servant flushed and aimed a nervous glimpse at Elizabeth, as if to measure her reaction.

"Damn it, Clara." Elizabeth glanced around their perimeter to make sure none of Warrick's townsfolk witnessed this public display of intimacy. Luckily, it didn't appear anyone had. "You're supposed to be a nun. Nuns don't kiss friars."

Clara's affectionate gaze remained connected to Channing despite the steel edge in Elizabeth's tone. "Please? It'll only be for a few minutes."

"Very well," Channing acquiesced with a resigned sigh, "but don't leave this shop until I come to collect you."

"We won't." Clara kissed his cheek again, this one landing dangerously close to his mouth. "I promise."

His jubilant grin split his face in half as he scuttled off in the direction of the forge without another word.

"Get back here!" Elizabeth's command fell on deaf ears, and she rounded on her irresponsible, selfish turd of a cousin. "What the hell is wrong with you? Why would you do that?"

Clara shrugged. "Go with Channing to the smithy or come shop with me. Your choice." With a devilish smirk, she sauntered into the store.

Fuming as countless curse words poised themselves on the tip of her tongue, Elizabeth struggled to keep her temper in check as she jogged to catch up with Channing.

CHAPTER 26

*L*aid up and left to his own devices while the others were out, Gregory once again whittled away at the piece of wood he'd been shaping into a bird pendant during his moments of solitude. Wood shavings sprinkled his lap, and as he carved the final details into the tail feathers, the silence of the room was disrupted by Elizabeth's entrance.

Gregory flinched at the sudden disturbance but was quick to pull the blanket over his legs and conceal the small pendant before his sister could take note and ruin the surprise.

"We have a problem," she blurted out as she barged into the room. Channing and Clara were right behind her, and all three of them were soaked from head to toe, dripping puddles of water onto the floor.

"I see you got caught in the storm." A chuckle tickled Gregory's throat as he set the knife on the bedside table, but the fear in Elizabeth's eyes sobered him right up. His gaze bounced from face to face, each one graver than the last. Anxiety tightened his chest. "What happened?"

Without a word, Channing removed a damp piece of parchment from his robe and held it up for Gregory to see.

"Come closer. I can't read…" His pulse stuttered as he realized that he didn't need to read it because the picture in the middle was worth a thousand words. A very detailed and accurate drawing of Clara was in the center of the parchment. The heading read *MISSING!* in big letters at the top of the poster.

"Where did you get that?" Gregory's voice quaked. "Are there any more like it?"

"It was nailed to the door of the apothecary." Channing looked as though he was about to retch. His hands shook as he handed the parchment over to Gregory and stepped back, the color sapped from his cheeks. "I didn't see any others."

"We must've checked every door in town," Elizabeth told him. "This was the only one we found. That's a good sign, isn't it?"

"Possibly. It says here Lord Akrim is offering a reward to have you returned to him." Gregory looked at Clara, who hadn't made a sound since they came in. "That's who you're betrothed to? The Rising Loaf?"

"The what?" Clara and Elizabeth chorused together.

"The Rising Loaf. I've never met him, but I heard plenty of gossip while I was fighting in the north. Lord Akrim is infamous."

Clara visibly swallowed and when she next spoke, her voice held all the ferocity of a mouse. "Infamous for what?"

"For climbing to the top of the social hierarchy overnight. Rumor has it he was once a baker."

"A baker?" His cousin's eyes were wide and frantic as they shifted to Elizabeth for confirmation, but his sister's jaw had dropped, giving the impression that she, too, was stunned by the news. Clara returned her attention to Gregory. "Why would my father marry me off to a baker?"

"I don't know how accurate the story is, but I heard one

of Akrim's distant relatives died unexpectedly. I think of typhoid. Or was it malaria? I can't remember exactly–"

"Get to the point!" Clara cast him a nasty glare, and wrong as it was, Gregory found enjoyment in his cousin's plight. There were plenty of well-bred noblemen for her to marry, yet she'd been matched with one who lacked even the smallest drop of royal blood. Her father certainly hadn't considered the damage this would do to her hubris when he'd agreed to the uneven match. "Greg! We're waiting!"

"Alright, I'm getting there. For Christ's sake woman, loosen your corset."

Elizabeth snickered at his words, but upon earning a scornful glower from Clara, she muffled the sound with her hands. "Sorry," she choked, a smile lingering in her eyes.

Clara wasn't amused. "You were saying?"

"Akrim's incredibly wealthy cousin succumbed to the disease, whatever it was. Apparently, he didn't have any immediate family members, so his profitable Italian winery was left to his closest living relative by default, allowing the baker to go from peasant to a wealthy member of the gentry overnight."

"I still don't understand." Elizabeth's eyes were creased in bafflement as she leaned against the wall, scratching at her neck. "How did he become Lord of Akrim? That's a Cara-callan title, not an Italian one. The dead cousin wouldn't have been able to give him a barony here if he was from Italy, no matter how successful his winery was."

"You're right," Gregory replied. "His Majesty is the one who gave him the title and land. It's not often a peasant inherits something so valuable, but when it happens, the king likes to keep a close eye on things. Giving Garland the barony of Akrim was his way of keeping the man in his pocket, as well as making sure the money earned by the winery is close at hand. With Garland as an ally, His Majesty has a better chance of dipping into those funds. The king is a sneaky devil."

"Surely the winery isn't *that* profitable." The strangled murmur came from Clara, who didn't appear to realize she'd spoken aloud. Redheaded and covered with freckles, her pale complexion was nothing out of the ordinary, but at present her skin was chalky-white. She looked like death.

"Perhaps you should sit," Gregory counseled.

Clara didn't move. Channing, however, shuffled closer to her. His arm hung loose at his side as he allowed his hand to brush against hers, just soft enough to be noticed. When Clara looked up at him, she was rewarded with an encouraging smile that erased all traces of stress from her face. Her posture relaxed and she blushed, red as a rose.

Quick to avert his gaze, Gregory cleared his throat and pretended not to notice the private moment that'd passed between them.

Elizabeth, on the other hand, was too lost in her own thoughts to see any of it. "I suppose I understand His Majesty giving the baker a title, but to also give him the hand of his own niece in marriage? It doesn't make sense. Clara is descended from kings; she deserves to be married to a duke or an earl at the very least."

From the corner of his eye, Gregory could see the effect Elizabeth's insensitive dictate had on the servant. Channing winced, his shoulders low as his mouth turned down.

"I *deserve* to marry who I want," Clara revised. Her gaze was fixed on Channing with such intense longing that Gregory was forced to look away again.

"Of course you do," Elizabeth muttered, still oblivious to what was happening right in front of her. "But a legitimate title would be a good start, wouldn't it?"

Gregory shook his head. "I'm telling you, Lord Akrim's purse is already much fatter than that of any earl, and his wealth continues to grow with each bottle of wine his workers produce. To be honest, I'm shocked he chose to stay here and keep his bakery running despite his mounting wealth."

"Why doesn't he move to an Italian villa and hire servants to do everything for him?" Elizabeth removed the sopping wet wimple from her head as she approached the clothes rack, then hung it to dry before taking the habit off as well. The familiar brown kirtle beneath had darkened in a few places where the water soaked through, but overall the dress had survived the rainstorm. With a noticeable shiver, she strode over to the hearth to warm her hands over the fire. "Why keep the bakery open at all?"

"He lives in a manor a few miles from the town he grew up in, but he forces his son to keep it open, presumably to fill his belly with pastries." Gregory shook his head in disapproval. "He doesn't bestow a penny upon his son that wasn't earned."

"Joshua!" Upon receiving strange looks from everyone in the room, Elizabeth took her enthusiasm down a notch and rearranged the smile on her lips into a stoic line. She cleared her throat and lifted her chin up, poised once again. "Believe it or not, I met both the baron and his son in Gettsbury."

Elizabeth picked up one of the iron rods beside the hearth, a faraway look in her eyes. "What a small world." The sparks danced wildly as she poked at the scorched lumber. "I can't believe Josh is going to be your stepson, Clara. He's our age."

Clara scrunched her nose. "If his son is our age, Akrim must be elderly...and grizzled."

"He's too old for you, that much I can confirm. He's mean, too. On the morning the broken shutters were discovered, he was screaming at everyone. He even accused *me* of—"

"Elizabeth." Gregory cast her a glower. "How's this helping?"

She gnawed her lip and shrunk into herself, then perked right back up and continued with her chatter. "If it makes you feel better, Josh is one of the most generous souls I've ever met. He always brought a smile to my face no matter how miserable I felt when I first walked through the door. A few times, he even slipped me a pastry free of charge. Did I tell you he's the one who taught me how to make lemon tarts?"

Clara's expression turned even more sour, if that was possible. "Who cares?"

Elizabeth dismissed the remark with an idle wave of her hand. "I think it's wrong that Joshua should be forced to keep working even after his father received such a profitable inheritance. I had no idea; he was always so cheery. He never uttered a single complaint about his predicament, despite how unfair it is."

"Unfair?" Clara scoffed. "You want to talk about what's unfair? How about the fact that I'm being forced to marry his father? Zounds, Bess. The way you're carrying on about how wonderful Joshua is, it's almost as though you fancy him."

Watching as his sister's skin crimsoned, Gregory suspected Clara was right.

"He's not of noble birth," Elizabeth pointed out, as though that vague response was enough to discredit the accusation. Her tone was silky, a little too silky not to be construed as forced, but she said nothing more about it and rerouted the conversation back to Akrim instead. "There must be more to the story. No matter how wealthy this Garland fellow is, without noble lineage and proper breeding, he's not a suitable match for you. It's confounding."

"It's not," Gregory argued. "The bottom line is that His Majesty wants full control over his subjects, especially if they have enough resources to hire their own private army. By giving Garland a title and a coveted wife of noble birth, he's ensuring that the wealth brought in from the winery doesn't cause him to forget his place and rise up against the Crown. He's keeping him close. In theory, if Garland is happy and well taken care of, he'll have no desire to use his wealth against the king. Now do you understand?"

"I suppose so, but I hate Clara's role in all this. She'll be disgraced and humiliated by such a preposterous match. She's merely the bone thrown at the wolf to make sure he's too distracted to attack. It's wrong to be paired with someone so far beneath her."

"His station isn't the problem," Clara seethed. Her arms were straight, her hands locked into fists despite their close proximity to Channing's. "It's that I don't love him."

"So you've said." Elizabeth frowned at her in a pitying way, which appeared to worsen the state of their cousin's already fragile temper. "But you and I both know love has no place in royal marriages. A husband should provide both wealth *and* prestige. Akrim can only offer you one and there-fore, isn't suitable. This is an affront against you, and quite frankly, I don't understand why you aren't more upset about it."

"Her father wouldn't have agreed to the match unless there was something in it for him," Gregory pointed out. "Garland must've paid a hefty sum in exchange for Clara's hand."

"What does any of this even matter?" Channing ques-tioned, his voice no more than a tortured whisper. "She doesn't have to marry him. That's why she ran away."

"It matters because according to that poster, Akrim has

the mind to chase her down." Elizabeth glimpsed at Gregory, anxiety soaked into every inch of her face. "That puts all of us in danger."

"We were already in danger," Clara snapped.

"Yes, because last night you ditched your habit and flaunted yourself around for the entire tavern to see. For all we know you've already been recognized." Elizabeth's voice rose with each word, her brown eyes cold. "You've ruined everything!"

Gregory gaped at Elizabeth with a ripple of pride. In light of this poster, it was obvious her concerns were valid. He had his doubts about their cousin, but at least his sister seemed well equipped for a life on the run. "Bess isn't wrong, but we'll address that problem in a minute." At the sight of Clara's hardened expression and curled lip, he forged ahead. "There's one more thing about Akrim I think you should know."

With a heavy sigh, Clara crossed her arms across her chest. "Go on, then."

"Last I heard, the king planned to appoint him as the commander of the Special Task Force. If it's true, Akrim will soon have even more resources at his disposal. The STF is a prestigious cavalry squadron of the Royal Forces. They're the ones responsible for traveling throughout the kingdom and *cleansing the land of undesirables.* While he's at it, he'll be able to search for you. If your betrothed has a militia behind him, that complicates things for all of us."

Elizabeth's brows knit together. "Who are the *unde-sirables?*"

"Pagans," he clarified.

"I see." Elizabeth poked her tongue into her cheek and stared at the flames. "I know they worship the devil and dance around fires without any clothes on, but isn't killing them a bit extreme? I should think converting them to Christianity would be more humane."

Stunned and appalled by the grossly inaccurate image Elizabeth had of the pagans, Gregory realized an educational conversation was in order. The topic could be tucked away for the time being, but he'd need to come back to it later. It was obvious their father's prejudices had dribbled down to her.

Clara let out an explosive breath that jolted him back to the problem at hand. "Who cares about the pagans? Akrim is coming after *me*. He could be on his way here as we speak!"

Channing took on a strangely calm disposition, and though his voice was laden with conviction, it remained gentle enough to soothe Clara's current dithers. "I won't let him take you, Clara. I promise." With a hesitant, yet cordial smile, the servant opened his arms to her.

It seemed that was all the invitation she needed, for in her next breath, Clara had twisted sideways and stepped into his waiting embrace. "I can't marry him." She buried her face in Channing's chest. "I can't."

"You won't." His voice lacked even a shred of doubt as he comforted her with a light kiss atop her head. "I love you, Clara. Marry *me*. If you'll take me as your husband, I vow to spend the rest of my life running alongside you."

"Yes! Of course, I'll marry you! You're the only man worthy of–"

The servant tilted his head down and pressed his lips against Clara's, halting her declaration with all the force of a hurricane. It was as if they'd forgotten Gregory and Elizabeth altogether.

Elizabeth's line of sight flew to Gregory, and they shared an uncomfortable look before she dropped her gaze and busied herself with stoking the fire. A smirk ghosted on her lips as she made an obvious effort not to stare at the couple, despite the show they were putting on.

"Um…" Gregory cleared his throat. The room suddenly felt much smaller than it had before. "Now that you've settled that – congratulations, by the way – I've reevaluated the decision to fix the wagon wheel. Despite the additional cost, we should buy a new one and leave Warrick as soon as possible. I suggest we set out the second it's attached to the wagon, no matter how late the hour. There's no telling how many people saw the notice and recognized Clara."

Channing agreed. "I'll go see if anyone has a spare they'd be willing to sell." He lifted the hood of his drenched friar's robe over his head, a silly smile spreading across his face as he readjusted the wooden cross that hung from his neck.

"I'll come with you."

Gregory was about to call Clara out for her asininity but was beaten to it by Elizabeth.

"Are you daft? Your face is the reason we have to rush out of here. You should stay indoors and stick to the shadows."

Clara straightened her back and pulled a disgruntled look but took a few coins from her satchel and handed them to Channing without protest. "This should cover the cost. Hurry back."

"I will." After receiving a long parting kiss from Clara, the servant ventured back out into the downpour, gleaming.

CHAPTER 27

"*W*ell, that was interesting." Elizabeth lowered herself into the chair beside the hearth and leveled a wide grin at her cousin. "Care to explain how *you* of all people fell in love with a servant?"

Clara squirmed. "I need to change out of these wet clothes." Her cheeks colored as she slipped from the room without further comment.

Elizabeth started to get up and follow her out, but when Greg held his hand up in a motion for her to stay put, she fell back into her seat. *Fantastic. Another lecture.* "Yes?"

"Don't tease her, Bess."

"Me?" She pressed her hand over her heart in mock insult. "I would never."

Greg smiled, yet he looked a trifle uneasy. "I hope not, because love isn't something that should ever be judged or criticized. Is it?"

"No. It's not." That belief was one of the major differences between Greg and their father, and Elizabeth would rather spend a night in the stocks than share that opinion with the latter. "I promise not to poke fun at her about it."

"Good." Greg's whole disposition brightened, and a genuine smile engulfed his face. He straightened his back and thrust out his chest. "I have a surprise for you."

"You do?" Elizabeth's line of sight shot to his hands, and it was then that she noticed the way they were cupped together, hiding something. She leaned forward for a better look, but her brother was careful not to let whatever it was show through his fingers. As her gaze bounced to the bedside table, her excitement increased tenfold at the sight of the knife.

While Elizabeth was praised for her realistic landscape paintings and musical talents, Greg's skills at woodworking and sculpting were unparalleled. Give him a block of wood and a blade, and he could whittle anything you wanted. Elizabeth's toy chest back at the palace was filled with wooden animals he'd gifted her over the years.

It was most unfortunate she'd left them all behind, but her emotions soared at the prospect of receiving a new one now. "Did you carve me something?"

"I did."

Elizabeth clapped in effervescent enthusiasm.

"I wanted to do something to express my gratitude."

"Gratitude?" Her gaze flicked from the mysterious object cradled in Greg's hands up to his face, which was still split in half by a boyish grin. "For what?"

"For your loyalty. You left all your personal belongings behind when you left the palace, even your lute. Although you haven't mentioned it, I'm sure it bothers you not to have anything to call your own anymore. My hope is that this token of my appreciation, little as it is, will help with that."

"But where did you get the wood?"

"From Mary. I mentioned the enjoyment I found in whittling and she provided me with the materials." Greg's eyes glowed as he extended his hand. "Here."

Elizabeth shot out of the chair and dashed to the bedside. Her mouth hung open as she lifted the treasure from his palm.

"What do you think?"

"It's marvelous!" With a pleasant sensation of dizziness, she examined the bird's immaculate details up close, mesmerized. "The blue tit is my royal symbol!"

Greg chuckled. "I'm aware. I made it flat and threaded a length of twine through the loop on top of its head so you could wear it as a necklace."

Elizabeth didn't hesitate to put it on. "How does it look?"

"Great," Greg answered, his face rippled in cheerfulness.

"Thank you!" Overjoyed, Elizabeth enfolded him in a bone-crushing hug. "This is the best gift imaginable. I'll cherish it always."

CHAPTER 28

"*T*his is delicious." The early morning light trickled in through the window as Gregory grabbed another slice of bread off the breakfast tray beside his bed. "Clara better get up soon or there won't be any left for her."

"I've already set some aside." Elizabeth spread a heaping glob of butter onto her third slice. "If she's not up within the hour, I'll have to wake her. Channing's down in the stable now, and I'm guessing he'll have the new wheel attached soon."

"Not soon enough. We should've left last night."

Elizabeth sipped her perry and *ahhed* in pleasure. "I agree, but the weather is out of our control."

"There was *some* rain yesterday, yes, but enough to cover the road?" Gregory's skepticism resonated in his tone as he searched Elizabeth's face for any sign of mutual distress. It seemed he was alone. "Don't you find that unlikely? What town only has one road leading in and out?"

"Why would the innkeeper lie? To keep us here longer? This place is packed, Greg. I doubt he was desperate for the money our second night brought in."

"Still." He glanced down at his torso in frustration. "If I wasn't an invalid, I could've checked it out myself to confirm the road was flooded over. The whole thing seems odd to me."

Elizabeth's slumped shoulders and dull eyes pointed to the fact that she didn't share his doubts. "Now you sound like the blacksmith." Bored, she chomped into her bread.

"How so?"

"Apparently, he agrees with Channing."

"About?"

"That the fracture in the wheel could've been intentional."

As a gush of sudden infuriation coursed through him, Gregory was tempted to snatch the food out of her hand and chuck it out the window. "And neither of you felt the need to mention this to me? That didn't concern you at all? What if it *was* done on purpose?" His voice intensified and additional beads of perspiration formed on his brow with each question he churned out. "What if whoever it was recognized Clara from the poster and aimed to stall our departure? What if they sent word to Akrim?"

For a moment, Elizabeth looked as though she was about to laugh at the notion, but in the next instant, her eyes widened and understanding dawned on her face.

Gregory's muscles tightened. "Go wake Clara. Now."

Elizabeth sprang to her feet. Before she made it to the door, it flew open with a thunderous bang. Channing barreled inside, panting for air.

"You have to help me! He took her!" Covered in sweat, the servant bounded forward. He snatched Elizabeth's wrist, giving it a tug so fierce she nearly fell on her face.

"Ouch! Let go of me!" Dragged against her will toward the exit, Elizabeth fought to gain footing. Her stockings slid across the wood floor like it was made of ice. "Channing! Stop!" With a quick twist and yank of her wrist, she escaped his firm clutch.

Being the prince's little sister had its benefits, one of which was that she was his practice partner whenever he wanted to perfect his self-defense moves. She'd never used the counterattack on anyone other than Greg and was shocked to discover it actually worked. She'd always assumed he was going easy on her.

Channing was undeterred. He reached out to reclaim his victim.

Elizabeth backed up, terrified by the menacing gleam in his eyes and the cluster of spittle that'd collected at the corners of his curled lip.

"Come on! Clara needs our help!"

Before Channing had the chance to grab her again, Greg leapt to his feet, knocking the breakfast tray and wine jug over with a clatter. He paid no mind to the shattered shards of crockery that now littered the floor as he rushed to position himself between Elizabeth and the crazed servant. In preparation for their departure, Greg already had his boots on. Had he not, his feet would've been sliced open.

"Back off." He glared at her attacker. His nostrils flared, and he locked his jaw. "Touch her again, and you'll be sorry."

Shielded behind her brother, Elizabeth watched in silence as the two men sized each other up.

"Take a breath and tell us what happened." His tone was a smidgen lighter than before, yet a threat loitered just below the surface. If Greg's side caused him any pain, he hid it perfectly.

Speaking slower and with less insistence this time, Channing obliged. "Clara came down to bring me a drink and check on the progress of the wheel. I'd just gotten it attached when Akrim and three guards ambushed us. They took her away, and I tried to fight back, but I was outnumbered. If you come with me, we might be able to catch up to them and get her back."

Elizabeth exchanged a guarded look with her brother. To engage in a skirmish with Akrim would lead to Greg's death, and possibly hers as well. Clara was destined for the altar, but they'd be the ones to suffer if they tried to intervene on her behalf. Elizabeth's spirit wept for her cousin, knowing it was a lost cause.

Channing must've detected their shared reluctance, because his eyes took on a deadly glow. "You *will* help me."

Elizabeth licked her lips. A crushing weight stunted her ability to breathe. She shifted from one leg to the other, her knees no longer strong enough to hold her steady. "Channing, how could we–"

"Did you not hear me?" He took an aggressive step toward Greg, and it became apparent he wasn't going to take no for an answer. "Clara's gone. I need your help to get her back!"

Greg tensed and even with his wound, his clenched fists and puffed chest showed his readiness to take the servant on. Although both men were just over six feet tall and close to the same age, Greg was much more muscular. Nevertheless, only a little over a month had passed since the arrow pierced his torso. Despite his combative stance, Elizabeth knew he was in no condition to fight.

Greg and Channing knew it, too.

"Do you have a plan?" Elizabeth asked, endeavoring to distract the servant from the fight he seemed determined to provoke.

Greg's shoulders were thrown back and his mouth was twisted in an intimidating scowl, but the beads of sweat that'd developed on his temple didn't escape Elizabeth's notice. She also saw the quick spasm of discomfort that flitted across his face. Hard as he tried to hide it, he was in tremendous pain. If Channing were to challenge him now, Greg would most certainly be brought down.

She refused to let it come to that. "You said Akrim has three armed men with him? How do you propose we tear Clara away from them? You're the only one with a weapon, and Greg is still recovering. What do you expect us to do?"

"We'll liberate her tonight while they sleep," Channing answered after mulling over his choices.

Elizabeth shook her head but made sure to keep her tone smooth as butter. "Akrim's estate is in Gettsbury, which is less than a day's ride from here. They won't stop to rest."

Channing snarled, his teeth bared like a hound awaiting the signal to start the hunt. "I'm open to suggestions."

"I don't have any," Elizabeth confessed as she snuck a glance at Greg. His pallid color and unsuppressed grimace verified his weakness. If he wasn't careful, this exertion would compromise his recovery. He needed to get off his feet. "Perhaps if we all sit down and discuss our options, we could come up with some sort of solution."

"Elizabeth." Greg waited until their eyes met. "I know how deeply you care for Clara, but you can't have any part in this. It's too great a risk." His voice was heavy with regret. "You know that, don't you?"

"Yes." Tears pricked the backs of her eyes. "I do."

At her admission, Channing erupted. "After all she's done for you!" Spit sprayed in every direction. "You'd turn your back on her?"

"We're not turning our backs on anyone," Greg argued.

There was a slight tremor in his voice that made Elizabeth's heart wrench. "Clara isn't in any danger. We can't risk our lives simply to prevent a marriage."

"He's right. Look at the state he's in, Channing. How can you even suggest he involve himself in a fight against four other men? Even if he were to join you, the odds are still two to one."

"I don't give a damn about the odds!"

Elizabeth's lip quivered. "I wish you and Clara could be together, I do. However, if the contract has already been signed, this wedding will happen. I'm sorry."

Channing emitted a wry laugh, his face drawn with fury. "She's your best friend, and you're going to abandon her? You won't even try to help me rescue her from that demon?"

"It's out of our hands," Greg concluded. "Any attempt to rescue Clara would get us all killed. It's not worth it. It's a wedding, not an execution."

"You're cowards," the servant bellowed with a glower that scorched Elizabeth to her core. "The both of you!"

In Elizabeth's next breath, Channing was gone.

Greg crumpled to the floor.

CHAPTER 29

*A*wakened by the creaky floor as his sister entered his room with a tray of food, Gregory yawned and rubbed the sleep out of his eyes. He squinted out the window. To his bafflement, the last rays of the afternoon sun had given way to evening.

That can't be right. He checked again, but the sky outside still glowed as orange as the hearth. Had he slept the whole day away?

"I'm glad you're awake." Elizabeth set the tray down beside him and offered a cup of ale. "Feeling better?"

Gregory tried to sit up but fell back into the pillows with a groan. "No. How long have I been asleep?"

"A few hours." Her features were dimmed by a vacant expression. "I tried to wake you, but–"

"A few hours?" He pushed himself up again, determined this time to ignore the jolt of pain that shot through his torso. "Why would you let me sleep that long? We need to get out of here."

"As I said, I tried to wake you. You wouldn't budge. Standing up to Channing must've taken a lot out of you."

Elizabeth's voice cracked and sympathy blunted Gregory's previous irritation.

"We made the right decision, Bessie. There's nothing to be done about Clara's upcoming nuptials. Channing's on a fool's mission, and if he doesn't back down, he'll either be killed or imprisoned for his folly."

Elizabeth's chin trembled, but she said nothing more about it. Instead, she squared her shoulders and held her head up in what Gregory perceived to be a false show of indifference. "Speaking of folly, it seems putting the coin satchel in Clara's possession was the height of ours. When I went to get the money to pay the cook for our supper, I couldn't find it anywhere. Clara must've had it with her when she was taken. Her horse is gone as well. I assume Channing took it."

"All the money's gone?"

"Yes."

"Even the coins Mary gave us?"

Elizabeth's face drooped. "Yes."

Gregory leaned back and rubbed both hands over his head, his fingers going numb as panic shot through him. He took a deep breath. Then another one. As expected, they did nothing to soothe him. "Clara's money was a bonus, but Mary's was supposed to hold us over until we reached the monastery. If all of it's gone…" He stopped, unable to articulate the grim thoughts flouncing through his head.

"Greg?"

"Give me a minute." He buried his face in his hands as he considered their options. There weren't many.

"Why don't we turn around and go back to Gettsbury?" Elizabeth calmly suggested. "I'm sure Mary would—"

"Mary has done too much for us already." His chest tight, Gregory looked up to meet his sister's gaze. Though his own blood pressure was rising, Elizabeth was a picture of composure. "I'm a fugitive, Bess. I won't ask her to put herself at risk for me again. We need to move forward, but without that money, I don't see how we can."

"We'll find a way," she assured him. "I know you're worried, but everything's going to be fine. We'll figure it out. I'll go hitch Lavender to the wagon and give you some time to think. All right?"

With his head spinning and a painful lump in his throat, Gregory nodded. "Wait." He uncovered his face and looked up at Elizabeth, who was halfway to the door. "How did you procure our supper without the means to pay for it?"

She spun around, eyes narrowed. "Is that an accusation I hear in your tone?"

Gregory pursed his lips. "I'm not in the mood for your games, Elizabeth. How did you pay for the food?"

"If you must know, I made a deal with the cook. I earned it in exchange for manual labor." Her eyes were wounded, and it was clear she was offended by his suspicion. "He agreed to feed us if I took care of the massive pile of dishes that needed washing. He even provided us with a few meat pies and apricots for the road. Contrary to what you so obviously believe, I didn't steal anything."

Relief and pride lifted his spirits, as well as the corners of his mouth. Perhaps everything was going to be fine after all.

"What on earth are you grinning about?"

"We had a problem and you solved it, properly and through hard work. Well done, Bess. I'm proud of you."

She blinked at him in surprise but soon enough, an appreciative smile graced her face. Her eyes lit up like stars, brightened by the verbal applause she'd been given. "You're welcome. The weight of this isn't yours to bear alone. Remember that."

CHAPTER 30

*W*hen the door creaked open a few minutes later, Gregory glanced up from his supper. "Finished alrea–" All the blood rushed from his head the instant his gaze landed on the visitor, not Elizabeth returning from the stables as he'd assumed.

It was Father Timothy.

Gregory struggled to swallow his mouthful of pottage as the priest entered the room with two familiar faces in tow and closed the door behind him.

"What the hell are you doing here?"

Despite the rancor in Gregory's tone, Father Timothy's cheeks glowed pink with pleasure. "I've brought callers, Your Highness."

"I see that." Gregory glowered at the priest, then turned his attention to the pair of noblemen who'd shuffled in behind him. Lord Fowler and Lord Melbourne, both of whom were earls and respected members of the king's court, lowered their noses to the floor in a deep bow. "Why?"

"Your Highness." Lord Fowler, a well-fed man with

crooked teeth, straightened and approached the bed. "Father Timothy told us you were shot clean through and that it was God's will for you to survive. We're here to witness this miracle ourselves." His eyes narrowed, as though he was hesitant to believe it. "May I see the wound?"

"No," Gregory growled. He shifted atop the mattress, uncomfortable under the earl's intense stare. "Father, what's the purpose of this?"

The priest cleared his throat. "These men have come to pledge themselves to you. As devout Catholics, they wish to see the crown upon your head. I've brought them here as further proof of the support you have, not just from the lower class, but among the nobles as well."

Melbourne nodded and tugged on his ginger-colored beard, unable to take his gaze off Gregory's torso. "God truly is on your side. As are we, Your Highness." He knelt down to one knee, and Fowler, though less graceful, followed suit. "We vow to serve–"

"Stop!"

The room fell silent in the wake of Gregory's outburst.

He snapped his gaze to the priest. "I told you, I'm *not* doing this!" His vision flashed as shards of rage scattered beneath his skin. "I'm not challenging Bernadette!"

"Father Timothy informed us of your reservations." Fowler's quivering voice held all the strength of a feather. "However, you're the rightful heir, and Princess Bernadette is wicked. This kingdom needs you, and you need support. We're here to show you that you have it. All the Catholic noblemen are on your side."

"As well as the Duke of Gleason," Melbourne put in, a slow smile spreading across his face.

"The Duke of Gleason?" His jaw agape, Gregory processed this information. Surely they were mistaken. Or it was some kind of trick. There was no way the king's youngest brother would align himself with a traitor to the Crown. Gleason was a powerful man with more wealth than could be spent in a lifetime. He wouldn't risk losing that. "He's not Catholic, why would he care—"

"Even Protestants can see what a disaster it'd be for Princess Bernadette to sit on the throne." Father Timothy dragged one of the chairs away from the hearth, placed it at the bedside, and took a seat. "Don't you see? You have friends in high places, Your Highness. All you have to do is say the word, and we'll begin assembling an army."

Gregory harrumphed. "To what end? The king is still very much alive so none of this even matters. Until Bernadette sits on the throne, all this talk of overthrowing her is premature. It could be twenty years until then."

"And this is how you plan to live in the meantime?" Fowler swept his gaze over the small room, dry washing his hands as a grimace overtook his face. "This place is brimming with filth and disease. No, Your Highness, exile does not suit you. We must build your army now. Your place is at Crompton, and even if it requires overthrowing King Charles to get you there, we mean to ensure your victorious return."

His breath knocked out of him, Gregory's thoughts were thrown into chaos. "You would have me kill my father?"

"A preemptive strike would ensure Princess Bernadette never rules," Fowler went on. "Your Highness, you could put an end to all of this right now. You could be king."

Gregory bowed his head in a futile effort to steady himself. "This is madness," he said through tightly clenched teeth. "As I've already told Father Timothy, there will be no army. All three of you are to go home and never speak of this again, am I understood? This meeting never happened."

"But Your Highness—"

Cutting the priest's objection short, Gregory rose from the bed. "Get up."

Father Timothy slipped his hands into the pockets of his robe and licked his lips as he reluctantly got to his feet. A good head shorter than Gregory, the priest trembled in his shadow. "Your Highness, I–"

"Shut up." From the corner of his eye, Gregory caught a glimpse of the look of shock shared between the two earls. To speak to a man of God in this way was detestable. Even so, Gregory couldn't help the satisfaction doing so brought him.

Father Timothy was a stubborn fool, and his incessant attempts to change Gregory's mind were growing in both boldness and carelessness. To bring members of the nobility here was a huge risk, one that not only put their own lives in danger, but Gregory's and Elizabeth's as well. Enough was enough.

"What must I do to get this through your thick skull? I will *not* fight for a crown I don't want. Do not come to me again, Father, or I swear to God, the next time I see you, I'll put your head through a wall."

Melbourne gasped and Fowler made the sign of the cross over his chest, both wearing twin expressions of horror.

Gregory rounded on them next, his cheeks hot as the flames dancing in the hearth. "If either of you hear even the faintest whisper of a rebellion in my name, you snuff it out. You tell the other Catholic nobles I will *not* raise an army and I will *not* seize the crown. My patience is gone. The next man who has the audacity to tell me what to do will lose his tongue. Do you understand me?"

"Yes, Your Highness," Fowler and Melbourne chorused together.

"Leave. Now."

Without the customary parting bow, the earls left in a huff.

Father Timothy, however, remained rooted to his spot beside the bed. His features were loose, his eyes lackluster. "Was that necessary? They are on *your* side."

"There are no sides," Gregory hissed. "How dare you bring them here! What if they're spies?"

"They aren't."

"Speaking of spies, is that how you found me? Are you having us followed?"

The priest gave a noncommittal shrug, but the determination with which he avoided Gregory's eye was an answer in itself.

"That ends. Now. Do Fowler and Melbourne know Elizabeth's with me?"

"I saw no point in mentioning that."

"What if they would've seen her? If it's confirmed she's with me, she'll have a bounty on her head to match mine. Do you realize how much danger you put her in?" Gregory's voice grew louder with each word, as did the thumping of his heart.

It took every ounce of control he had not to pound his fist into the priest's face. That'd teach him to put his nose where it didn't belong.

"How could you think it's acceptable to bring them here, to me? If they go back to Crompton and tell anyone where we are…" Gregory paced the length of the room, desperate to keep himself moving. If he didn't get his temper in check, there would be a priest-sized hole out back come morning. "I've let this go on for too long, Father." Gregory stopped, pinning the man beneath a murderous glare. "I meant what I said. Do not let me lay eyes on you again."

Father Timothy ground his teeth. "Perhaps it's for the best. Apparently, you're more like Princess Bernadette than I thought. May you rot in Hell."

Gregory clenched his fists so tight his fingers went numb as he watched Father Timothy stalk from the room.

CHAPTER 31

*T*he next three days of travel were a blur in Elizabeth's mind; a miserable blend of hunger, boredom, and fatigue. The nights were even worse. Trying to fall asleep beneath the stars while an owl hoots into the darkness might be peaceful to the pagans, but not to her.

At one point she'd considered throwing a stick at the damn bird but changed her mind when she realized she'd have to leave the warmth of her blanket to do it. To say she was exhausted would be a severe understatement.

As the wagon passed through the forest, a gentle breeze sent leaves spiraling from the trees. One landed on Elizabeth's shoulder and in a snit, she flicked it off and ripped her teeth into a chunk of bread. Chewing as loud as possible in a deliberate attempt to annoy her ingrate of a brother, she cursed herself for sharing the food with him. He didn't deserve a single crumb after the way he'd yelled at her. Had she known he'd react the way he did, she would've let him starve.

Their stomachs had been rumbling nonstop since yesterday, when they'd finished off the food provided by the cook in Warrick. So earlier this morning, Elizabeth had taken initiative to solve the problem. While the sun just barely peeked over the horizon, she'd ridden Lavender to a nearby farm and asked for some bread. Since she was dressed as a nun, the farmer gladly offered her two whole loaves, plus four hardboiled eggs, and three plums.

She'd been under the impression that her display of dependability and resourcefulness would please Greg. Oh, how wrong she'd been! Thanks to her, he now had food in his belly, but rather than express an ounce of gratitude, he'd scolded her. He was so unappreciative, it made her blood boil.

Elizabeth glared at him over her shoulder as she fantasized about the next meal. Tomorrow, she'd obtain something even tastier to eat. Perhaps a glazed ham. Or a couple turkey legs. She imagined herself eating a steamy bowl of rabbit stew right in front of him, just out of spite. No matter how much he begged for a bite, she'd refuse to share. That would teach him to be so ungrateful.

Distracted by these devious thoughts, Elizabeth didn't see the danger up ahead in time. Her skin bristled as the large rock came into view.

To drive over it would send a wave of vibrations throughout the wagon, resulting in an agonizing experience for Greg in the back. She could entertain thoughts of withholding food to teach him a lesson all day, yet when it came down to it, the truth was that she'd never do anything to bring more pain into his life. Today was no exception.

She gnawed on her lower lip as she made a frantic attempt to maneuver around the stone. Although Lavender was quick to obey, she wasn't quick enough. Elizabeth cringed as the back wheel rolled directly over it, causing the entire wagon to shake back and forth like an infant's rattle.

"Good God." Rocking side-to-side on the mattress, Greg

let out a hiss as he swayed with the movement. "Damn it, Elizabeth."

"Sorry! There was a huge rock in the road. I tried to avoid it."

Though his voice was unsteady, Greg somehow found the strength to hurl another lecture her way. "Pay attention, would you? Keep your eyes on the road."

Elizabeth's veins ran hot, and her remorse turned over into defensiveness. "It appeared out of nowhere. You wouldn't have seen it either."

Greg's snort foretold his disagreement. "I assure you, I would've. Unlike you, I don't let my mind wander when I'm supposed to be working. Stop daydreaming and–"

"If you think you're so perfect, why don't you come up here and drive this thing yourself? Oh wait, you can't!" Heat rushed to Elizabeth's face as she tightened her grip on the reigns. She squeezed them with all her might. "You're in no position to be criticizing me. Who are you to talk to me about work anyway?"

She threw a scowl over her shoulder. Encouraged by Greg's flaring nostrils, she pressed on. "I do everything. Who takes care of Lavender and makes sure she's well fed? Me. Who lights a fire every night so we don't freeze? Me. Who washed your clothes in the stream yesterday? Me. Do you have any idea how foul your socks are? You never even walk, and they smell as if a rat crawled inside them and died. And then, when we ran out of food, *I* went out and got us more. I was being responsible, and how did you thank me? By calling me a naive, foolish little girl."

"What you did *was* foolish!" Greg's tone was charged with emotion, and although Elizabeth's eyes were directed ahead and she couldn't see his face, she felt his glower on her back. "That farmer could've recognized you, and if he did, you can be sure a messenger is on his way to Crompton this very minute. If it's discovered that you're consorting with a traitor, you'll be executed for treason, too. How many times do we have to go over this?"

Elizabeth whirled on him. "I'm wearing *this*!" The distaste she held for the wimple resounded in her tone as she pointed to her head. "The purpose of these disguises is to let us go out in the open. I did nothing wrong!"

"You did everything wrong! Why can't you see that? Your inability to understand the seriousness behind all this is infuriating! You snuck off while I was still asleep, neglecting to leave a note behind to explain your whereabouts."

"A note?" Elizabeth scoffed and flicked her gaze upward. "We have no parchment or ink. What did you expect me to do? Write it in blood?"

Although Greg overlooked her sarcastic remark, when he spoke again his voice had an even sharper edge to it. Elizabeth didn't need to see his face to detect his rising temper. "I'd woken to find you vanished, gone without a trace. As if that wasn't bad enough, you knocked on a stranger's door and *asked* for food. How thoughtless can you be?"

"Thoughtless?"

"Yes, thoughtless! The safer option would've been to tiptoe into the garden and take a few vegetables. Maybe an egg or two from the coop. You easily could've trespassed without being seen, but instead you thought it'd be better to march right up to his door and talk to him, face-to-face."

"Are you saying you'd have preferred me to *steal* the food?" Elizabeth twisted around once more. She needed to read his expression, for surely she misunderstood. Greg didn't condone stealing. Ever.

And yet, his face was stone cold and unapologetic. "Don't

look so distraught. No one would miss a few carrots. You wouldn't be hurting anyone."

"And I suppose you weren't hurting anyone when you broke the window to Joshua's bakery?"

Greg stiffened. "I did what I had to in order to survive."

Elizabeth's brow furrowed as she struggled to process what she was hearing. "You're the one who told me that decent, honorable people don't take what doesn't belong to them. I thought I was doing the right thing by asking for food rather than taking it. I honestly thought you'd be pleased."

"His Majesty wants my head on a pike and the entire realm is filled with those who'd happily give it to him." The color of his throat and cheeks rose along with the resentment in his tone. "Things have changed."

"No. You've changed." She spared a quick glance at the road ahead, and then returned her attention to Greg. "Basically, what you're saying is that it's acceptable to steal when it's convenient for you?"

He ran his hand through his dark hair. "Sometimes in order to survive it's necessary to do things you know are wrong. The honorable path isn't always the advantageous one. I know full well you agree with that statement."

"And I know full well the man who raised me wouldn't. You've always said integrity is the most important quality to strive for."

Greg forced a laugh. "*Now* you choose to listen to me. Who would've thought you'd be the one preaching to me about ethics?"

Again, Elizabeth rolled her eyes. "What you're saying now goes against everything you've taught me in the past. As a matter of fact, just a few days ago, you said you were proud of me for obtaining our food properly, remember? You were relieved I didn't steal the food from the kitchen. What's changed since then? Why are you so upset now?"

"Stealing from an establishment such as the inn is a far bigger risk than taking a handful of vegetables from someone's garden." Greg seemed drained of all energy as he went on. "I realize it's impossible to avoid all contact with others, but we need to keep our heads down and limit exposure as much as possible. Let what happened to Clara serve as a lesson of what can happen to us if we show our faces too often. Had she stayed in the room instead of going down to the tavern to dance with Channing, they might still be with us."

"I agree that was foolish of her, but–"

"She chose to show her face one too many times and paid the price. Learn from that. Every time you knock on a door to ask for handouts you increase the probability that someone will identify you. We can't take that chance. We need to be more careful than Clara was, and if that means stealing a few radishes here and there to avoid being seen, so be it."

"I don't see what the problem is." Elizabeth held her head high, still quite proud of herself regardless of his dismal outlook and needless disapproval. "The outcome was positive, was it not? What he gave us was far more filling than some dirty radishes would've been. Why must you be so combative all the time?"

"I'm done arguing about this," Greg grumbled with finality. "It's done, but next time, I expect you to think before you act."

Elizabeth adjusted the cloth headdress that covered her hair and turned back to the road. "Times are rough, I realize that. His Majesty cast you out, but the good people of this kingdom had no part in that. I refuse to steal from them. I'm not a thief, and neither are you."

"I hope that thought comforts you when you're swinging from a rope."

The sinister comment pushed her over the edge. "If I'm executed, it'll be because I chose to help *you!* Perhaps you're right and I am a fool, but it's not because I won't steal. It's because I was daft enough to join you on this wretched journey in the first place! Of all the foolish things I've done, jumping off the comfortable cloud that was my life into the muddy pig sty that it is now definitely tops the list."

In the loaded silence that followed her eruption, Elizabeth took in deep gulps of air and worked to recompose herself. Her hands ached from gripping the reigns so tight.

After a long while, Greg's voice pierced the quiet. "You're right."

Upon hearing the dejection in his response, Elizabeth glimpsed over her shoulder at him. The anger from before had vanished from his face and moisture glistened behind his gloomy eyes. She'd spoken in agitation, yet it was clear Greg took her words to heart. She instantly regretted her tactless outburst and infused a touch of sweetness into her voice to make up for it. "You know what tops your list?"

"What?"

"When I was twelve, His Majesty planned to arrange my marriage to the Archduke Ernest of Austria. Remember that?" At Greg's solemn nod, Elizabeth went on. "I begged you to prevent it, and without hesitation, you boarded a ship and traveled to Austria."

Greg grimaced. "I spent the entire voyage with my face in a bucket."

"Yes, but that didn't affect the outcome of your journey. Any chance you're ready to tell me how you convinced the archduke to refuse the marriage contract?"

"As I said four years ago—"

"It was a business negotiation, I know." Elizabeth's gratitude pulled her lips into a smile. "Well, whatever you did, it saved my life."

"That's an exaggeration."

"Even so, His Majesty had a lot riding on that marriage, and he would've skinned you alive had he known you were behind the archduke's rejection of it. You took an enormous risk, and at the time, I was too blinded by my panic to see it. I never should've asked you to intervene."

"I'd do it again," Greg declared with fervor. "Even if I knew His Majesty would learn of my involvement."

A sharp pang of repentance prodded Elizabeth's chest. "You know what you told me once?"

Greg narrowed his eyes. "What do you *think* I told you?"

"When you came back from the rebellion in the north, you told me that everything we do is a choice."

"I did," he admitted, cautious. "And?"

"And ever since we were children, you've made countless choices to put me first. Think about it. Every time you did something risky, it was done in an attempt to help me in one way or another. You've made sacrifices for me my entire life."

He shrugged. "That's what older brothers do." He was matter-of-fact about it, as though he believed having a younger sibling meant he was forever responsible for carrying the weight of her life on his shoulders.

"Well, that sentiment should go both ways. As your sister, I'm required to support you. That's what I'm doing here. Don't think for a moment that I shouldn't have come with you. Perhaps it was *a bit* foolish, but I'd do it again in an instant. You risked your life for me on countless occasions. It's about time I risk mine for you."

A look of fear slipped into Greg's eyes, but he was quick

to cover it up with an odd little half-smile. "I appreciate your loyalty, Bess, but you're wrong. The last thing I ever wanted was for you to place your life in jeopardy on my account. Although I'm glad you're here, not a second goes by that I don't question if it's a mistake. Sometimes I think it'd be best if I set my selfishness aside and sent you back to the safety of the palace."

Elizabeth's heart dropped. "You wouldn't!"

"You just said yourself being here is a risk."

"A slim one!" Even to her own ears she sounded desperate.

Greg must've noticed too, because a touch of amusement tugged at the corners of his mouth. "Listen, when I woke up this morning to find you gone, I was terrified. I had no idea where you were or what happened to you. Nevertheless, it was wrong of me to take that fear out on you. I shouldn't have lost my temper like I did. I know you were only trying to help, and truth be told, you did good."

Elizabeth's chest swelled. "So I'm not a fool?"

"No."

"Or naïve?"

Greg chuckled. "What I said to you was wrong. *I* was wrong. Stealing isn't right, and I'm glad you've held onto your values despite living in exile. Just promise me next time you go off in search of some breakfast, you'll let me know first. Promise me that, and I'll end all this talk about you going back to Crompton. Deal?"

"Deal!"

CHAPTER 32

*S*eated in the back of the wagon as the evening sun glistened over the barley fields in the distance, Gregory chomped on a berry until it was mush in his mouth. He wanted to savor the sweet taste as long as possible, for once it was gone, there was no telling how long it'd be before they happened upon their next meal.

"Another one." Elizabeth extended her arm behind her back, cupping her hand for him to place another handful of blackberries into. "Don't be greedy, Greg."

"Hold on." He reached beside him and fingered the vacant bottom of the wicker basket. "They're gone. Those were the last ones."

"You're joking!" She glimpsed over her shoulder, wide eyes centered on the basket in his hands. "Please tell me you're not serious."

Gregory held it into the air as proof. "See?"

"How can they be gone already?" Her mouth turned down in a frown. "How many have you been eating back there?"

"They were divided evenly," he lied. "I had the same amount you did."

Taking him at his word, Elizabeth heaved a dejected sigh and turned back around to watch the road. Little did she know, the berries *hadn't* been shared equally between them. The truth was, Gregory had given her double the amount he'd given himself, and his belly despised him for it. The berries had been a decent snack, but that's all they were. A snack. They needed more.

"I understand now what possessed you to eat that badger. I might've done the same in your situation." After further consideration, she amended, "Although, I would've made sure it was cooked all the way through."

"Trust me, that's one mistake I'll never make again." Gregory's stomach lurched at the mere thought of it. "I'd rather starve."

"Don't joke about that. Unless we find something substantial to eat soon, starvation might be in the cards for us." Elizabeth sucked the remaining berry juice off her stained fingers.

Gregory agreed. Four days had passed since Elizabeth received the food from the farmer, and all they'd eaten since were the blackberries she'd found growing beside the road yesterday morning. Now that those were gone, their situation looked grim.

That is, until about an hour later when a stately stone building became visible further down the road. Gregory straightened his back and squinted his eyes. The wooden sign located at the entrance of a private lane read, *Blackmore Abbey, Home for Children.*

"Do you see that?" Elizabeth's voice burst with joy as she, too, peered into the distance. "It's an abbey! Do you know what that means? The disguises Father Timothy provided will no longer be of use. What a stroke of luck!" She pulled back on the reigns and brought the wagon to a standstill. Then, with all the grace of a three-legged dog, she climbed over the seat to join him in the back.

Gregory arched his brow, puzzled. "How's that a good thing?"

Elizabeth eagerly pulled the habit off to reveal her chemise beneath. "Because we can toss aside our religious attire and dress like normal people for a change! We can't impersonate a nun and friar here, they'd know we're lying. Now, where's the green kirtle Mary gave me?" She dug through her own rucksack, also a gift from Mary, with enthusiasm etched into every inch of her face. "Here's my hairbrush, I'll need that. Ah-ha!"

Gregory watched as Elizabeth dislodged the dress from the sack with a fierce yank, then put it on over her long-sleeved chemise. Once clothed, she climbed back to the driver's seat and gazed at him expectantly.

"Well? Are you going to change?" She ran the brush through her wavy, chestnut-colored hair, wincing as she untangled the knots. "If we hurry, we may get there before supper's over. Surely they can spare two servings of whatever it is they're dining on this evening. After all, it'd be the Christian thing to do."

"It's not a good idea." Gregory rubbed his neck and pretended not to notice the growls in his gut.

"What's not?"

"You know what."

Elizabeth's smile slipped. "Greg, we're starving. Not the 'I haven't eaten since breakfast' kind of starving, but legitimate starvation. I counted each berry I put into my mouth yesterday. Do you know how many I ate?"

Sixty-four. And I ate forty-eight. "No."

"Sixty-four. All we ate yesterday were sixty-four berries. Do you know how many we had today?"

You had fifty-three. I had twenty. "No."

"Fifty-three. We're going to waste away if we don't get proper nourishment. Besides, the distance between us and the palace is extensive now. I doubt a group of nuns and the orphans in their care will recognize us."

"Clara probably thought the same thing about the patrons at the tavern."

"She had a poster with her likeness on it," Elizabeth huffed as she gathered her hair over her shoulder and divided it into three sections, then interlaced them together into a single, thick braid. "The notice His Majesty circulated about you didn't have a drawing attached so unlike hers, your face is still unknown."

"Did you already forget the conversation we had about keeping our heads down?" Gregory's voice hummed with disapproval, belying his internal strife. The rational portion of his brain knew what Elizabeth suggested was ill-advised, but he was hungry. They were both hungry, and the abbey was the first sign of human life they'd come across in hours. "This is the opposite of limiting our exposure."

"Nun is synonymous with recluse. All they do is stay inside, singing hymns and reading the Bible. They basically live under a rock. I'm the first nun I've ever seen…and I'm a fake. Plus, this abbey doubles as an orphanage. On top of all their religious duties, they have the children to care for. They're too busy to worry about our identities."

Gregory tugged on his bottom lip, his conviction fading despite his best efforts to remain obstinate. Hunger was a powerful motivator.

The gleam in Elizabeth's eye confirmed that she'd spotted his weakness. "You know I'm right. Even if they did know you're wanted for treason, they'd never be able to identify you. Nuns care about God and virtue, not politics or the royal family. They'll have no idea who we are. Please, Greg. We need food and they have it."

"We can't make a habit of thinking with our bellies rather than our minds. Hunger can't lead to recklessness. Am I understood?"

Elizabeth's face broke into a grin, for Gregory contradicted his own words as he took off his disguise. Once the scratchy robe was removed, he was left wearing the blue doublet Elizabeth brought from the palace and the black breeches he'd been wearing when he was expelled from court.

"There. Is this better?"

She scrutinized him, her lips bunched together as she plaited her hair into a loose braid. "Erm…Mary made this dress for me. It's plain and therefore, ordinary. You're clothed in an outfit from your own wardrobe."

Gregory didn't detect a hint of jealousy in her tone, which astonished and pleased him in equal measure. "You're right. You could be anyone, but dressed like this, I'll have to come up with an explanation for my affluent appearance. Perhaps I'll say I'm a knight."

"A knight? Pray tell, what part do I have in this story you've concocted? Am I to be your lowly servant?"

"You can be my sister. We don't need to lie about everything."

"Well, clearly I'm your *poor* sister." Again, Elizabeth surprised him when she expelled a little laugh, rather than the envious scowl he'd expected. She truly was changing for the better, and that awareness sent a surge of pride through him. "It might be more inconspicuous if you take the doublet off. Do you have your white undershirt on underneath?"

"I do."

"Good." Elizabeth spun back around. With a snap of the

reigns, the wagon jolted to life as Lavender pulled it toward the abbey.

Meanwhile, Gregory heeded her advice and removed the doublet. He kept his movements slow and controlled as he slipped it off, careful not to provoke his wound in the process. His side hurt more than usual, but he refused to acknowledge it. If he ignored the pain it would go away. He was certain.

"It'll be getting dark soon," she observed. "I wonder if they'll allow us to rest here for the night." Hope rang in her tone.

"First let's see if they're willing to feed us," Gregory countered, endeavoring to prevent Elizabeth's premature excitement. "Then we'll take it from there."

"Do you think their kitchen is well stocked? I'm so hungry I could devour an entire mince pie all on my own. Maybe two. What about you?"

"I'd rather not get my hopes up." Gregory rubbed his stomach in anticipation. "That said, I wouldn't say no to a plate of grilled salmon."

~

Why's it so lumpy? Elizabeth grimaced as she stirred the thick mush. She lifted the spoon and tilted it sideways to allow the chunky goo to run off. It landed back in the bowl with a disconcerting *splat.*

"If you find your porridge unappetizing, I'd be happy to eat it for you." Greg eyed her with a censorious look as he reached for another spoonful, but with a sharp grunt and a shudder of pain, he dropped the utensil into the bowl.

"What's the matter?"

"Nothing." After a deep breath, the tension was released from Greg's face. He adopted an expression of perfect placidity as he stiffly reclined into the arrangement of pillows behind his back. "I'm fine."

Despite the fake smile her brother wore, Elizabeth knew something was off. "People don't cringe if they're fine. Is your wound bothering you?"

"No. I bit my tongue."

"You bit your tongue?" Elizabeth cocked her head to the side as skepticism fluttered in her gut.

"Yes, now eat. Your porridge will taste worse if it gets cold."

Seeing the wisdom in his words, Elizabeth took a big bite of the white glop. She was in mid-chew when a quiet tapping sounded behind her, and she turned to find Sister Margaret hovering in the doorway.

With a plump midsection, protuberant eyes, and small, yellowed teeth, the middle-aged nun possessed one of the oddest forms Elizabeth had ever seen.

Stranger than her outward appearance, however, was the manner in which she conducted herself. The peculiar, almost childish way she talked and acted made Elizabeth believe she possessed the mindset of an adolescent rather than the maturity her actual number of years would imply.

Nevertheless, Sister Margaret had been the one who welcomed them into the abbey, no questions asked. Then, during their long, tense meeting with the Mother Superior, it was Sister Margaret who quoted numerous Bible verses and ultimately persuaded the stern abbess to permit the siblings to stay the night. For that, Elizabeth couldn't be more thankful.

"Sorry to interrupt." The woman ogled Greg, a lustful glow in her bulging eyeballs.

"You're not interrupting." Elizabeth picked up the cloth napkin she'd spread across her lap and used it to wipe her mouth. "Come in."

The nun stepped into the room with a jar of brown powder in hand, her line of sight still glued to the bed where Greg sat supported by the mountain of cushions she'd provided. "I hope you're comfortable, Mister George. If you need more pillows, I'm sure a few of the children could go without for tonight."

"That won't be necessary."

"I brought my secret stash of cin'min. Would you like me to put some on your porridge?"

Greg answered with an appreciative smile. "That's very thoughtful."

Sister Margaret shuffled over to the side of the bed. A blush painted her cheeks scarlet as she dumped a spoonful of the spice into what was left of his boiled oats.

"Thank you. That's enough."

She didn't stop. "My mother used to say cin'min makes anything edible, and you deserve the best."

"Thanks. That's plenty."

"Don't be silly. Just a few more scoops."

Greg chewed at his lip. "I assure you, I'm quite satisfied with the amount you've given me."

"Almost done…"

Disappointment registered on his face as the woman continued to add more and more powder to his porridge. Yet even as his meal was ruined, he couldn't bring himself to be anything less than polite. He was gracious to a fault, and though Elizabeth admired his discipline, sometimes she'd rather see him stand up for himself than internalize his discontent. Just once, she wished he'd say what he wanted to say…to someone other than her.

"There!" Sister Margaret deposited one last heap into Greg's bowl and stepped back, a wide grin sprawled across her chubby face. "That's perfect."

Greg swallowed hard and stared down at his supper. Visible reluctance slowed his movements as he mixed the mass of powder into the oats. When it wasn't plausible to stall any longer, he inhaled through his nose and took a wary bite. "Delicious," he choked, his brows pinched together in a grimace. "Thank you."

Sister Margaret thrust her chest out. "You're quite welcome, Mister George." Almost as an afterthought, she turned to Elizabeth. "Do you want some?" The dullness and lack of volume in her voice betrayed her unwillingness to share her precious cinnamon with anyone other than Greg. Elizabeth considered that a blessing.

"I'm quite alright," she tittered as her brother attempted to eat the pile of cinnamon inside his bowl. She'd much rather eat the bland oats as they were. "But thank–"

The woman's gaze bounced back to Greg in a trice. "Is there anything else I can do for you before I retire for the evening? Would you like a fresh cup of milk?"

There was no answer. Elizabeth glanced at Greg, who was too focused on swallowing his powdery porridge to notice the fanatical nun was speaking to him.

"Mister George?"

Upon hearing the fake name he'd given himself, Greg looked up from his bowl. His cheeks were filled with food, and he struggled to chew faster. Coughing on the powder, he put a finger in the air as an indication to wait a moment.

Elizabeth's ribs hurt from trying so hard not to laugh. "I think some milk would be splendid," she snickered.

A few minutes later, Sister Margaret returned with a single cup. For Greg.

While he chugged the drink in enormous gulps, Elizabeth held her tongue and slumped deeper into her chair. Although she was thirsty as well, she'd learned long ago not to take offense at the exorbitant amount of favor shown to Greg by members of the fairer sex.

Even back at the palace his appearance had attracted the attention of many awestruck ladies, both young and old. In fact, Margaret of Valois, the Queen Consort of France, had once described him as "a Greek god with well-defined cheek bones, expressive cerulean eyes, and the biceps of a black-smith." She wasn't alone in that assessment. There were few females who didn't find him beguiling, and apparently, nuns weren't immune to his charm either.

That was probably the driving force behind the Mother Superior's initial reluctance to let them stay here. Greg had the face of a lady's man, a definite cause for concern in an abbey full of virgins.

"Tell me about yourself, Mister George. Do you have a wife?"

"Not yet."

Sister Margaret's hand flew to her chest and her mouth fell agape. "You mean to tell me a handsome man such as yourself has no one to keep him warm at night?" The flagrant infatuation she had for Greg made Elizabeth want to laugh, but by some miracle she managed to restrain herself. "Had I not already taken my vows, I'd remedy that right now."

A strained smile broached Greg's lips as he avoided the woman's amorous gaze. His face flushed pink and he opened his mouth to speak, but no sound came out.

Unable to control herself any longer, Elizabeth collapsed into a fit of sniggers. The situation alone was hilarious, but Greg's reaction was best of all. She made an effort to feign a cough upon catching his repressive glare, but she could tell it wasn't believable.

Luckily, Sister Margaret was too busy gawking at Greg to notice anything Elizabeth did. She could probably climb up the walls and hang upside down like a spider without the besotted woman taking note.

"Well, I suppose it's time we head to bed." As her own announcement summoned a regretful frown to her face, the nun spared a quick glance at Elizabeth. "The children usually wake up before sunrise. I expect you'll be getting up bright and early to help me serve them their bret-fist?"

Elizabeth nodded despite her disinclination to do anything of the sort. "May I ask where I'll be sleeping tonight?"

Sister Margaret showed no signs of having heard the question as she informed Greg they'd be having apples and cheese for the morning meal. "However, if you'd prefer some eggs and sausage instead, I'd be happy to make them special for you."

"I appreciate the offer, however, I don't require any special treatment. Apples and cheese would be great. Thank you."

"Sister Margaret?" Elizabeth raised her voice to be sure she was heard this time. "Where will I sleep?"

"Mother Superior says you're my responsibility." She didn't bother to peel her eyes away from Greg, who appeared determined to ignore the advances she made toward him, as she explained, "You'll stay in the dormitories with me. I share a chamber with two others, but Sister Alice is in the infirmary. You'll take her bed."

Elizabeth balked. "Oh?"

"Sweet dreams, Mister George. If you need anything, the dormitories are located in the north wing. Second door on the right. My bed is the one closest to the window."

With an unrefined snort, Elizabeth pressed her fist against her lips and turned away to collect herself. It was a good thing she didn't have any milk, for surely she would've spewed it across the room.

"Good to know, but I should be fine." To Greg's credit, he kept his voice flat. "My sister and I are grateful for your generosity."

"Not as grateful as I am for your company," the woman gushed, batting her lashes at him. "You're welcome to stay as long as you desire. See you in the morning…or sooner should you need me." She winked, but given her advanced age and bizarre appearance, the gesture was more disturbing than flirtatious.

Elizabeth compressed her lips together as hard as she could in a futile effort to lock in her amusement. Take this woman out of her habit and reduce her age by about a decade, and she was basically Lady Charlotte. The comparison brought forth an additional snort from Elizabeth's mouth, which she swiftly turned into another cough. Again, not convincing.

"Do you need a drink?" Sister Margaret's enormous eyes crinkled in concern.

Now she asks me. Elizabeth shook her head and patted the base of her neck, where her blue tit pendant hung, trying to recover from an imaginary coughing spell. "I'm fine–*cough*– Thank you–*cough*."

Greg rolled his eyes. "I'll see you both in the morning," he stated with remarkable decorum. "Good night."

"Good night." Her lips set in a pout, the nun placed her hands on Elizabeth's shoulders, which shook with silent giggles, and steered her toward the doorway. "Come now, Miss Dorothy. Let's get you cleaned up and ready for bed."

CHAPTER 33

A steady tide of water poured from the thunderous sky as Elizabeth tried to escape the inevitable reach of the Blind Man. Her breaths were ragged, and the rainfall blurred her sight. Though she knew it was no use, she put every speck of energy she had left into the run.

It made no difference. He was too fast, the ground too wet. It wouldn't be long before her pursuer closed in on her.

The tag was unavoidable.

"Blind Man's Buff!" David ripped the blindfold off, his victorious grin creating the cutest dimples in his cheeks. "Miss Dorothy is *It*!"

Elizabeth dropped to her knees in the tall, soaked grass. Her cheeks ached from the permanent smile the children put there. Over the course of two days, she'd become one of them.

Sure, she swept the floor after their meals, changed the soiled linens of the littlest ones, and offered guidance when the older children got into a disagreement, but the task she enjoyed most was being their constant playmate. Most of her assignments couldn't even be classified as work. She enjoyed every song she sang, game of marbles she played, and story she read to them. Besides, who could find fault in a system where hugs were considered a form of payment?

Submersed into darkness as the blindfold was tied around her head, Elizabeth tried not to dwell on her upcoming departure. She'd grown to love it at Blackmore Abbey, and it pained her to abandon the little darlings. However, it was her adoration of them that allowed her to see the benefit of moving on. Every day Greg was here put them at greater risk.

Don't think about that now. Play! Elizabeth shook the unpleasant thoughts from her mind and returned to the moment, for it was a marvelous one. "Here I come! One… two…three!" She scrambled to her feet and followed the sounds of squeals and giggles.

Elizabeth laughed along with them as she chased the orphans around the meadow, guided by their jovial chuckles. She slipped and slid in the damp grass, falling to the ground more times than she cared to admit. Her dress was sullied by sweat and mud, but she didn't care. That was part of the fun.

If her prissy old governess, Lady Duncan, could see her now, she'd roll over in her grave. The notion birthed an instant smirk on Elizabeth's lips.

"Anyone there?" There was a high-pitched shriek to her right, and she changed directions, headed straight for the joyous noise. "I hear you, Corah!" Her fingers grazed the fabric of the child's dress. After a quick burst of speed, she tagged her.

"Blind Man's Buff!" Triumphant, Elizabeth removed the blindfold and tied it around her captive. She then ran off to join the others, pursued by little Corah.

That was when she noticed Sister Margaret.

The woman waved her arms in the air over her head as she wobbled at full speed toward the meadow. "Miss

Dorothy!" A mixture of perspiration and precipitation dripped from her forehead, and she was wheezing by the time she reached Elizabeth's side. Physical exertion wasn't something the voluminous nun was accustomed to, that much was apparent. "You…must…come…inside."

"What's wrong? Are you unwell?"

Doubled over and unable to catch her breath, Sister Margaret shook her head. "Not me…Mister George."

A shard of panic sliced through Elizabeth's chest. She spun around and sprinted toward the abbey as fast as her legs would carry her.

Gripped by a fear so powerful it made her question her ability to breathe, Elizabeth stood rooted to the threshold. This had to be déjà vu. Either that or she'd somehow traveled back in time to revisit the deplorable morning Greg was shot. The difference was that at present, it wasn't the agony of the arrow's extraction that caused her brother to scream and flail about on the bed like a raging madman.

"Let go of me!" He rolled around in a frenzy as he fought to escape the hold of the orphanage's physician, John. Greg's sallow complexion was void of all color and sweat soaked his hair, streaming down the sides of his face. "I'm not a traitor!"

"What's happening to him?" Unable to comprehend the chaotic scene before her, Elizabeth trembled in the doorway, watching her brother's body thrash around in a desperate attempt to escape the doctor's restraint. "Why are you–"

"Come hold him down!" Determination boomed in John's voice as he leaned over Greg and pinned him beneath the weight of his body. "Now!"

Suspicion and uncertainty kept Elizabeth in place. "Let

him go," she murmured, wondering if doing so would actually be beneficial.

"Let me go!"

"Fever controls his mind!" John had to holler to overcome Greg's shouts, which reverberated off the walls in deafening volume. "Help me!"

That fatal word, *fever*, propelled Elizabeth to the bedside. Shaken by the heat emanating off her brother's body in fiery waves, she couldn't bring herself to do anything other than stand there and stare. "He's hotter than the hearth," she gasped. "You have to do something!"

At the sound of her voice, Greg froze. His gaze sought hers, and for the briefest moment, he seemed to recognize her. Beads of sweat accumulated on his furrowed brow as he stared at her, his expression shadowed in confusion. But all of a sudden, a nasty glint emerged in his eyes and that confusion curdled into a fresh serving of hatred.

"You bitch!" Hysterical and driven mad by fever, Greg once again flopped around with all the rage of a shark that'd been caught in a fishermen's net. "I'll kill you for this, Bernadette!"

"Bernadette? No, I'm not Bernadette. I'm–"

"For God's sake, woman, you're making it worse!" John looked up at her, his face twisted in frustration. "Get out or help me hold him down!"

This time, Elizabeth didn't dither. She grabbed Greg's arms and forced them to his sides. Like the physician, she, too, leaned over Greg and it took all her strength to do so.

"I should've slit your throat when I had the chance!"

Elizabeth stiffened, but didn't lessen her grip. "You're hallucinating. Whatever you see, it's not real."

"Liar!"

"I'm not lying." A rush of sickness churned over in Elizabeth's belly as she struggled to keep Greg's arms at his side. "You're safe!"

"Shut up! Shut the hell up!" His furious eyes smoldered with the heat of the sun, but instead of being burned, an icy chill swept down Elizabeth's spine. "Let me out of this cell, or I'll smash your brains out!"

Elizabeth squeezed her eyes shut and choked back the sob that threatened to tear from her throat. In all her life, she'd never known Greg to harbor such horrendous animosity and seeing it now shook her to the core.

This, right here, was the secret side of him he normally kept caged within. It'd festered too long. Incapacitated for a month and a half, Greg was forced to tuck his emotions into the deepest recesses of his mind, and at present, his fever allowed all that pent-up aggression and inner rage to claw its way out.

Elizabeth and the physician were witnessing the consequences of that firsthand.

"I'm not a traitor!" Greg's voice ripped through her moment of reflection. "I'll have your head for this, Bernadette!"

"It's me!" Elizabeth's eyes pricked with tears as she tried, and failed, to reach him through his fevered madness. "No one wants to hurt you. We want to help!"

"He's blinded by delirium." A rag in one hand and a bottle of vinegar in the other, John spilled the liquid over Greg's torso in his effort to wet the cloth. "I need to lift his shirt and clean the wound. Don't let go of him."

Elizabeth bit her lip but nodded in understanding.

To her relief, Greg appeared to have worn himself out. His breaths were loud and irregular, but for the moment, the yelling and thrashing had ceased.

As the physician dabbed the rag on his wound, Elizabeth

was unfortunate enough to catch sight of the vile thing and immediately wished she hadn't. The point of the arrow's entrance was inflamed and oozed a yellow pus that reeked of death.

Her stomach roiled and a foul taste entered her mouth. "I think I'm going to be sick."

"Don't you dare let go of him," John demanded, unsympathetic to her discomfort. "Help now, retch later. Understood?"

Elizabeth shut her eyes as tight as she could and willed her stomach contents to stay down. It worked. She reopened her eyes, careful this time to avoid looking at Greg's torso.

"It's gone bad?" She knew it was a stupid question before she'd even gotten it off the tip of her tongue. "I told him something was wrong when I was changing his bandages yesterday, but he insisted he was fine."

"You should've trusted your instincts. Never trust a patient's judgment."

"Her instincts are that of a demon!" Hit by his second wind, Greg made another vehement try at rolling off the side of the bed.

John blocked him and sent a stern glower Elizabeth's way. "You let your guard down!" Annoyance tinted the doctor's face purple as he continued his futile efforts to cleanse the area below Greg's right rib. "Vigilant as a newborn kitten, aren't ya? I can't clean this if you don't hold him."

"I'm *trying*," Elizabeth said through clenched teeth. "He's too strong!"

Greg proved that to be true when, in a desperate attempt to get away, he sat upright and twisted around to face her. In an unavoidable flash of movement, he balled his hand into a fist and sank it into the side of her face with tremendous force.

The violent strike sent Elizabeth soaring backwards and she crashed into the table, taking the doctor's medical supplies with her as she tumbled onto the floor in a mortified mess. Her upper cheek throbbed, and black spots clouded her sight, like little ants crawling across her eye.

"Damn it!" John darted to the spot where she'd previously stood and shoved Greg back down. "Enough! George, that's enough!"

"My name's not George! You can't keep me here!"

Disoriented and unnerved, Elizabeth used the toppled table to pull herself back onto her feet. She wavered, still struggling to regain proper vision as she tried to make sense of the trauma she'd just endured. She pressed her hand against her cheekbone. Had Greg aimed for her nose, he would've shattered bone.

"You all right?"

"Splendid," she lied in a tremulous voice that resembled the croak of a frog.

"Good. Before I sent her to get you, I had Sister Maggie mix sleeping powder into a jug of ale. It's on that shelf." He pointed across the room. "Grab it."

She limped over to retrieve the jug. "We should've started with this."

"Hindsight," John grumbled, a strain of irritation around his eyes. "Now get back here."

Elizabeth was on her way over when she noticed Sister Margaret in the doorway.

"I've returned." The woman's unblinking gaze was targeted on Greg, her expression now void of the lust that once lived there. Only fright remained. "Do you still require my assistance?"

"Excellent timing. Yes, we'll need all the hands we can get." While the nun scurried forward and used her excessive weight to fasten Greg to the bed, John's hands were free to pry his mouth open. He almost lost a finger or two in the process. "The ale, Dorothy. Pour it in his mouth. Quick."

Though riddled with trepidation, Elizabeth complied. Greg, however, did not. He spat the liquid out, along with numerous threats so disturbing they raised the hairs on the back of her neck. "He's not swallowing it."

"Of course he's not." The physician smirked at Elizabeth's bafflement. "That's why I had Sister Maggie triple the ingredients. It'll work. Just give it a moment."

Lo and behold, Greg stopped fighting, and his screams quieted into hoarse whispers within minutes. "You've poisoned me," he slurred.

John placed his hand on Greg's shoulder. "It's not poison. It'll help you sleep so I can get this swelling under control."

Elizabeth knelt beside the bed and grasped his clammy hand in hers, giving it a gentle squeeze. "It's medicine. We're at the abbey, remember? John is the physician we met last night, and he's going to help you get better. Your wound has gone bad and you have a fever, but you're going to be fine. Do you know who I am?"

Greg stared at her a moment through squinted, clouded eyes. The sleeping powder pulled down on his eyelids, which probably made it even more difficult for him to recognize her through his delirium. "Bessie?"

Elizabeth flashed a wide grin but cleared her throat when she saw the speculative look on John's face. To confirm the name could give away their true identities, but to deny it would confuse her febrile brother even more. She chose neither option. "You're safe here. Get some rest."

"No. No, no, no. You can't be here." He jerked his hand

away from hers, a look of anguish on his sweat-dampened face as he fastened his gaze on the exit. "You have to go. If Bernadette sees you–"

"Bernadette isn't here. We're both safe."

Greg shook his head, haunted. "We'll never be safe. Never. You need to leave."

Elizabeth looked up and was met by John and Sister Margaret's questioning stares. "This is a powerful fever, huh? I can handle it from here though, thanks. I'll come find you once he's asleep."

The two shared a look of apprehension.

"I'll be fine. Please, give us a moment."

As they bustled from the room, their matching expressions of mistrust formed a rock in Elizabeth stomach. Her breath hitched.

They knew. They had to.

All the same, she waited until the sound of their footsteps disappeared down the hall and lowered her voice to a whisper. "You're sick, Greg. Fever controls your mind and makes you see things that aren't here. This is an abbey, not a prison, and I promise Bernadette has no idea where we are."

For now, she stopped herself from adding. After what they'd just heard, the nun and physician would have to be dense as jelly not to suspect the truth.

"Don't drink the ale, Bess. They've poisoned it."

Elizabeth once again assured him it wasn't poison. "You can trust me, Greg. You're safe."

Whether he believed this or not was unknown, for he soon succumbed to the sleeping powder and fell deep into oblivion.

CHAPTER 34

The trills of crickets spilled through the open window as Gregory sat upright, hissing through the pain that shot through his side. "Good evening, John."

Without preamble or the faintest hint of friendliness in his hardened eyes, the sour-faced physician approached the bedside and rolled up Gregory's sleeve. "I must rid your body of the evil humors. Lift your arm."

Gregory swallowed the saliva that flooded his mouth. There were only two methods he knew of to expel bad humors, and neither of them were pleasant. His arm suddenly carried the weight of a dozen bricks as he lifted it up for John to place the bowl underneath.

"Now that the fever's gone and you've recovered, bleeding is the final step to cleanse the last traces of sickness from your body." The physician's lips twisted into a strange smile, and he removed a small blade from his tool kit. "Ready?"

Gregory squared his shoulders and put on a brave face for Elizabeth's benefit.

She was seated in a chair in the corner, and although she

appeared to be transfixed on the book of sonnets in her hands, he knew her well enough to recognize her stoic expression as forced nonchalance. Elizabeth hated the sight of blood, and she hated it even more if Gregory was the person bleeding.

"I'm ready," he announced with as much confidence as his own anxiety allowed.

The second the words were out of Gregory's mouth, John sliced his forearm. A river of red streamed into the bowl and although the time he spent in the north ensured he was no stranger to gore, Gregory turned away. "Isn't there a better way to guarantee the bad humors are eliminated?"

"I can fetch the leeches if you'd prefer them over the blade."

"No." A nervous chuckle escaped him. "This is fine."

"Fine?" Elizabeth slammed the book shut and glared at him, her scarlet face contorted with rage. "You think this is fine?"

"Erm—"

"This wouldn't be necessary if you would've listened to me in the first place! How could you be this daft?"

Gregory met her heated gaze head on, and although he didn't approve of the excessive volume or the ring of hostility in her tone, he kept a lid on his temper. In doing so, he gave himself a chance to notice the exhaustion on Elizabeth's haggard face.

Until now, the shadows under her heavy eyes were eclipsed by the fresh bruise she'd received while playing with the children. In truth, her black eye was a distraction from how tired she looked.

That's no excuse. Upon realizing how oblivious he'd been, Gregory further inspected Elizabeth's troubling appearance. Half her hair was gathered to the side in a braid while the rest hung at her shoulders in disarray. In addition to that, her olive-green dress was covered from top to bottom in dried mud stains.

She was about as well put together as someone who'd spent the last hour wrestling pigs. This level of carelessness was abnormal; even in exile, Elizabeth never neglected to make herself presentable.

How had this escaped his notice?

"I told you something was wrong," Elizabeth screeched at him. Her eyes were like needles piercing into his. "The day after we got here, while I was changing your bandages, I said your wound was swollen and the coloration was strange. I begged you to let John examine it, but you assured me you felt fine. Are you really so stubborn and bull-headed that you couldn't admit you were in pain?"

Gregory exhaled a puff of air. Although he longed to scold Elizabeth for losing her temper like this in front of a stranger, he couldn't deny she was right.

Unwilling to accept that his recuperation was in jeopardy, he'd lied to her face. In truth, the agony caused by his injury was almost unbearable, but he'd hoped if he convinced Elizabeth everything was all right, his mind and body would be tricked into believing it as well.

That foolish notion was the reason he now had a bleeding gash in his forearm.

"Look where that got you!" Her face rippled in vexation. "Maybe next time you won't be so quick to dismiss my–"

"All right." Gregory winced as John rubbed vinegar on the fresh cut. "Next time I'll listen."

Elizabeth rolled her eyes and folded her arms. "I doubt it."

Gregory's jaw clenched as he resisted the urge to release a retort. He understood Elizabeth's concern, but she was taking it too far. So, he'd gotten a fever and needed to be bled, it wasn't nearly as serious as she made it out to be.

There was such a poignant, unnecessary display of angst lurking in Elizabeth's features. Couldn't she see he was better? The fever broke yesterday morning. The redness and pus on his wound were practically gone. He'd recovered.

"I share your doubts, Miss Dorothy. Men often think they're tougher than they are. It can blind them to the danger at hand. Your brother fell victim to his pride."

"Excuse me?" Gregory's pulse spiked as he swept his gaze over John's unapologetic countenance. "I survived, didn't I?"

"Barely!" Elizabeth shot out of the chair, sending the book of sonnets to the floor with a thud. "Don't you understand? You almost died, again!"

"Well, I'm fine now."

"Now," she echoed in a voice that quaked. Her lips trembled as though she was about to cry, yet her features were ravaged by fury. "You're fine *now,* but for three days you drifted in and out of delirium. Three days! You were so sick you didn't even recognize me."

Doubting this information, Gregory looked to the physician for confirmation.

John, however, nodded in agreement. "Miss Dorothy's statement is accurate. You were very unwell."

"I had no idea." Gregory scrubbed the back of his neck with his hand as remorse trickled through him. He heaved a sigh and opened his mouth, but his apology was thwarted by Elizabeth's somber continuation.

"John told me not to entertain too much hope for your survival." Her anger slipped away as her eyes welled with tears. "You teetered on the brink of death for days. It was terrifying."

"I don't remember anything—"

"Well, I remember it all," she spat, her ire returning in the blink of an eye. "You might not give a damn about your life, but I do! You had one foot in the grave and all of it could've been avoided if you'd let John take a look at you, like I suggested!" A tide of rage streamed down her cheeks as she marched out of the room with a swish of her filthy dress.

Gregory was astounded by the news, but it didn't erase his embarrassment. "Allow me to apologize for my sister's behavior. She can be overly theatrical at times."

"Perhaps." John stopped redressing the bandage on Gregory's arm and directed his intense gaze to his patient instead. "However, this time she's not overreacting. I fear you don't comprehend the magnitude of your illness, Mister George. There's a new burial plot in the cemetery, dug especially for you. I truly believed you were going to die, and preparations were being made for your funeral."

Gregory's eyes widened and a chill slid down his spine. "It was that bad?"

"Yes. I was ready to summon the priest so your last rites could be read, but Miss Dorothy wouldn't hear of it. She remained at your side even as delirium overcame you. You woke in chaotic fits, screaming and threatening anyone who came near you, yet your sister stayed. I honestly think you'd be dead if she hadn't tended to you so carefully. I know I wasn't quick to come to your aid after you threatened to gauge out my eyes and feed them to the crows."

"I said that?"

"Among other things."

Gregory's heart plunged into the pit of his stomach. "Why? Why would I threaten you?"

"You accused us all of trying to kill you. Your fever made

you believe you were the exiled prince. You thought this was a prison."

"I see…"

"But that's enough talking for now. You need rest." The physician finished wrapping the bandage and was on his way out the door when Gregory finally conquered the rock in his throat.

"I'm sorry I threatened you," he said, his voice scratchy. "Please know I'd never behave like that while in my right mind."

John stopped in the threshold, his hand on the latch. "Yes, Miss Dorothy assured us it was quite out of character for you. Besides, the threats you directed at me were empty ones. I'm not the person you should apologize to."

Anxiety swirled in Gregory's stomach and goosebumps broke out across his skin. "Are you saying…did I hurt someone?"

"You did. She's fine, though. I took special care to–"

"Who? Sister Margaret?"

The physician scoffed. "No. Sister Maggie refused to come back in here after you threatened to smash her head against the wall until it was *soft as a boiled apple.*"

"*I* said that?"

"Yes, and that was one of the tamer threats."

"Then who did I hurt? If it wasn't you or Sister Margaret, then that leaves..." Gregory's gullet closed up, and his sister's name got stuck on its way out. Dread tightened his chest.

"I gave her my word," the physician whispered as he checked to make sure the corridor was empty. "I promised not to discuss this with you."

"What did I do?"

John shushed him, displaying a look of urgency. "If you

must know, you struck her. Fortunately, she doesn't blame you for your actions."

"She told me…" Gregory's voice broke as his practiced exterior of composure faltered. "She said the black eye was a result of a collision with one of the children. Tell me that wasn't–"

"A lie? Yes. It was. She seems to think the truth would destroy you. Hence, my promise to keep my mouth shut."

I hit her? In the face? Gregory's heart split as the weight of this unfathomable realization crushed every organ in his body. The walls caved in, pressing against his chest with such force, he felt sure his ribs were breaking under the pressure. The air was pushed from his lungs, and his mind emptied of everything other than this debilitating panic. "I– can't–breathe."

John darted to his side and poured a cup of ale. "Drink this."

Gregory took a sip between labored gasps but tasted nothing.

Although his mind raced, there were no thoughts in his head. All he had was fear. Harsh, unyielding fear. Sweat glided down his temples and he quivered, still unable to take in oxygen as he struggled for breath.

"Calm yourself."

"Can't." Gregory shook his head, his rapid heartbeat pounding in his ears. "I'm–supposed to–protect–her."

"Forget I told you this. I promised I wouldn't speak a word of it. You were sure we were trying to kill you, and as I said, she knows the hallucinations were to blame."

"She–must–hate me." Nausea threatened to expel the three helpings of cabbage pottage he'd eaten for supper. He clamped his mouth shut and looked around for something to vomit into.

John fetched the chamber pot and thrust it at him just in time.

Bile spewed from Gregory's mouth, his throat burning as he heaved into the pot.

"There you go. Let it out." The physician gingerly patted Gregory's back.

Gregory continued to retch as the minutes passed, his stomach convulsing to rid itself of everything within. Once there was nothing left to bring up, he wiped his mouth with the back of his hand, out of breath.

"I suppose that's another way to expel the bad humors," John said with a nervous chuckle. He covered the contents of the chamber pot with a cloth, then carried it out to the corridor. "I'll dispose of that later." He returned to Gregory's bedside and handed him the cup of ale. "Feeling better?"

With a stiff nod, Gregory sipped his drink. As his shallow breaths began to deepen, his heart rate slowly went back to normal.

"Good." John put his medical instruments back in his bag, then swung the strap over his shoulder. "Get some sleep and I'll return at first light to check on your injury. Again, I implore you not to mention this conversation to Miss Dorothy." Without waiting for a guarantee, he slipped from the room.

Gregory leaned back against his pillow, his thoughts in turmoil.

According to the physician, Elizabeth didn't hold him responsible for his actions. That was horse shit. Of course he was responsible. He'd been feverish when he hit her, and yes, fevers could cause disorientation, but they don't make good people violent. All it did was unlock the cell, releasing the inner demons he kept imprisoned within.

Ever since he murdered those men in the north, Gregory

knew he wasn't the decent man he'd always pretended to be, and now, thanks to his delirium, Elizabeth knew it too.

She'd deny it until her last breath, but it was inevitable that she'd see him for what he truly was: a monster.

Gregory's worst fear had come to pass. The darkness inside him was exposed, and Elizabeth was the victim of it.

CHAPTER 35

*W*ith her brother's breakfast plate in one hand and a hot beverage in the other, Elizabeth kicked the bottom of the door in an awkward attempt to knock. "It's me. May I come in?"

"Yes."

That single word was enough to twist Elizabeth's stomach. She couldn't be certain, but she thought she detected a degree of agitation in Greg's tone. Mentally preparing herself for the lecture she was about to receive, she threw her shoulders back and plastered a smile on her face as she pushed the door further open and crossed the threshold.

"Good morning." She held up the steaming cup of mulled cider. "I brought you this. Don't tell anyone, but I added extra nutmeg to yours. What good is a peace offering without proper flavoring?"

"I'm not thirsty."

"Well, you must be hungry." Elizabeth glimpsed over at the window. Both shutters were wide open, inviting the September breeze to come inside and make itself right at home.

"I'm not."

"At least take a bite." Determined not to let her smile slip, she ignored Greg's moodiness and deposited the food on the bedside table. "I accidently burned the bread, but it should taste fine if you spread enough marmalade over it."

"I said I'm not hungry."

"Very well." Elizabeth took a deep breath and swiveled around to face Greg. "I want to apologize for my behavior last night. I shouldn't have yelled at you or stormed out like I did." She sat in the chair, folded her hands across her lap, and gave him her full attention. "So, go ahead."

Greg's brow crinkled, but he kept his gaze averted. "Go ahead with what?"

"I'm sure you have a scolding prepared for me. I deserve it, and I'm listening."

His head shot up, and for the first time since Elizabeth's arrival, he looked her in the eye. "You think I care about that?"

"Um…yes. Don't you?"

"No. Your fit of temper was completely justified."

Elizabeth's jaw almost dropped, and it took her a moment to recover from his baffling dismissal of her childish actions. "No, it wasn't. I shouldn't have spoken to you like that, especially in front of John. It was disrespectful, and I'm sorry."

"Don't you dare apologize to me, Bess."

Rendered speechless by the ice in Greg's tone, Elizabeth waited for him to break the uncomfortable silence he'd fathered. It didn't take long.

"Not after what I did."

A stab of alarm pierced her in the chest and her heart skipped.

"Tell me how you got that bruise. And this time, tell the truth."

"I…" *John must've squealed. That big-mouthed imbecile.* "It was…"

"It was me. Say it."

Caught off-guard by Greg's directness and unable to formulate a believable lie, Elizabeth crossed her legs and wilted into the chair. "You were sick," she muttered at her lap. "Incredibly sick."

"Damn it, Elizabeth. Don't make excuses. This pedestal you've placed me on isn't doing either of us any favors. I'm not perfect and it's high time you stop imagining otherwise. I'm going to ask you one more time and for both our sakes, I want you to admit the truth. How did you get the black eye?"

She shifted her weight in the chair, unable to find a comfortable position. She glanced at the door in desperation, but when no interruption came, she leveled a disheartened gaze at Greg. "You punched me," she confessed.

A shadow fell across his face, regardless of his prior knowledge about what he'd done. "Exactly. Don't you see? Normal, healthy-minded people don't become violent monsters when a fever strikes." Moisture sparkled in his eyes and his chin bobbed. "Something is terribly wrong with me."

Elizabeth shook her head in denial, but when her lips parted to argue his dismal self-assessment, she found herself at a loss for words. Her mouth went dry, and she bit her cheek, ruffled by the tense silence that descended upon the room.

"I can see it on your face. You know I'm right."

She hastily adjusted her expression into a neutral one, but it was too late. If eyes were the window to the soul, she'd just given him full access to her thoughts. Regret engulfed her and she lowered her gaze once more, hoping Greg wouldn't be able to read her emotions if she kept her head down.

He forged ahead in a strangled voice, no doubt appreciative of Elizabeth's unwillingness to meet his tearful gaze. "The fever opened the door for all my inner demons to escape through, and you were right here to meet them. What I did to you was awful, and I can't live with myself unless something changes. What you witnessed, what you *suffered*, was the accumulation of twenty-two years worth of suppressed rage. His Majesty has been cultivating the darkness in me since the day I was born and now, thanks to the fever, it's become impossible to ignore that darkness any longer."

Elizabeth's throat burned with stifled sobs, and as she lifted her head to look at Greg, her heart twinged in reaction to the tears that now leaked down his cheek. She longed to offer him words of comfort, but he didn't pause long enough for her to fit one in. That came as a relief, for she hadn't the slightest idea what she'd say to console him.

"You've seen it. Your blackened eye is the result of it."

She still felt the urge to contest this, but as the legitimacy of Greg's comments sank in, her disagreement was squashed before she had the chance to give voice to it.

Difficult as it was for her to admit, Elizabeth knew he spoke the truth. It was silly *and* unfair of her to pretend he was above reproach when it had become obvious that he was besieged by the same feelings of resentment, fury, hatred, and fear as everyone else. His veneer of self-control and perfection had fractured, exposing the flawed man beneath.

Greg was badly damaged, and that realization struck her like a fist to the belly.

"There can be no more justifying my actions. I hurt you. I need to know you see the enormity of my mistake, as well as my accountability behind it. I can't properly own up to my faults if you won't acknowledge their existence."

It was the deep earnestness in his voice that compelled her to choose the path of candor. "Yes." She wrung her hands, wishing she had something to squeeze. "You hurt me, and although the fever was the channel in which the darkness emerged, I realize now it was there all along."

"I appreciate your honesty." His measured tone was at odds with the tension in his facial muscles. He gulped and took a controlled breath. "Thank you."

"So now what?"

"Now it's time we face this problem head on." Greg's expression wavered between nervousness and something else. Enthusiasm? "I tried to hold it all in and you were the one who paid the price. Nothing like this can ever happen again and after thinking about it all night, I think I know how to ensure that it doesn't."

A heavy weight materialized in Elizabeth's chest, but she tried not to show it. "How?"

"I've stopped denying the deep-seated animosity that dwells within me," he announced. His demeanor lightened and as his slumped posture returned to its usual dignified state, his tone swelled with what Elizabeth could only perceive as optimism.

"I've acknowledged my demons and now, I can finally let them go. The suffering His Majesty and Bernadette caused was extensive and terrible, but it's all in the past. Since my banishment, I've been so busy looking over my shoulder that I haven't stopped to consider what the future has in store for us. Have you?"

"Of course I have." She blinked at him in confusion. "We're going to the monastery, aren't we?"

"Yes, but then what?" Greg examined her face, which she could only imagine displayed her bewilderment. "Not once have we discussed what we'll do once my wounds are healed. We've been so focused on surviving that we failed to devise a plan for the future."

Elizabeth squinted her eyes at him. "I always assumed this was temporary."

"What is?"

"Your exile," she answered with a tad more bite than she'd anticipated. "Aren't we going back someday?"

"Back? To court?" His pitch raised an octave, a perfect match to the shock portrayed by his open-mouthed stare. Once he recovered, each word that rolled off his tongue was unhurried and articulate, as though he thought her a child who was incapable of understanding simple logic. "Elizabeth. I was accused of treason and banished."

"Don't speak to me in that condescending tone," she growled. "I know what happened. I was there. That said, I thought we were only going to seek refuge at the monastery until His Majesty's death. He won't live forever, and by the time he expires, we'll have gathered enough men and support to wage a war against Bernadette. Wasn't that your plan? To take back what rightfully belongs to you?"

Greg released a laugh but cut it short and checked himself when he caught sight of the scowl Elizabeth threw his way. "Y-you're not joking?"

She pursed her lips. "No."

"You honestly thought we'd go to war over this?"

"Yes." The word passed through her gritted teeth in a prolonged hiss.

"Do you have any idea how many lives would be lost if we tried to dethrone her?" Greg's pointed stare was filled with such censure and incredulity it was as though she'd announced her intent to fly to the moon. It was apparent the two things were equally unrealistic in his mind.

Goaded, she was about to unleash the full measure of her impatience upon him when he cast her a scowl so severe, she was persuaded to take pause.

"No. War isn't an option. I have no interest in a power that must be paid for with the blood of other men." His tone was laced with the undisguised authority befitting a king.

If only Greg could see that...

"This is precisely what I was talking about," he went on, reproof lurking behind his narrowed eyes. "We need to let this go. All of it. I'm no longer Prince Gregory of Caracalla. That part of me is gone and with it, all the pain I've amassed in my life. I don't want to be that man anymore."

Elizabeth took in a sharp breath of air through her nose and her next sentence came out with an unladylike spray of spit. "What the hell are you talking about? You *are* that man! You're the future king! You can't turn your back on the crown. *Your* crown. The people of this realm deserve–"

"The people of this realm deserve to live," he finished for her. His jaw was set in resolution as he reached for his mulled cider, which was sure to be tepid by now, and took a sip. "There's no telling how many of my supporters would have to die in order to secure the throne. I won't risk their lives. It's not worth it."

"Not worth it?" Elizabeth's cheeks flamed. Her fists were clenched so tight she felt the tips of her nails digging into her palms. She couldn't believe her ears. After all the misery Bernadette had caused Greg over the years, he wanted to fold? The notion of it made Elizabeth's skin crawl. "What are you talking about? You were born to be king."

"No. I was born *to* a king." He assumed an air of casualness, serenity even, as he set the cup on the bedside table and returned her glare with a weightless gaze.

His unperturbed attitude made her pulse quicken.

"The power and responsibility carried by a ruler is a terrible burden, one I was *obligated* to inherit. Now I'm off the hook."

"In your absence, Bernadette will obtain everything that belongs to you, everything you've spent your entire life proving yourself worthy of. You mean to tell me all our efforts were wasted?" Elizabeth worked hard to maintain her temper, however her caustic tone was irrepressible. "You don't care about any of it?"

"I did feel cheated at first," he confessed after a brief moment of thought. "My misconduct while feverish is evidence of that. I could only see the life that was stolen from me. But now I'm choosing to focus instead on the new one I've been gifted with. I'll never sit on the throne and truth be told, I'm relieved."

Elizabeth's mouth hung open as she attempted to sift through Greg's words, failing to comprehend their meaning. "You really have no intention of opposing Bernadette? Ever?"

"None whatsoever."

"This is lunacy!" She shot to her feet and threw her hands in the air. "We can overthrow her. If this is because you're afraid you won't have enough support–"

"Elizabeth. The answer is no."

"But you would win!"

"At what cost? Thousands of lives?"

Elizabeth paced the length of the room, too riled up to remain seated. "It's unavoidable that some lives would be lost," she lamented. "However, those lives would be willingly given. For you."

Greg scoffed. "You think I want that on my conscience?"

"Of course not, but–"

"Let's say you and I do start recruiting soldiers to rise against Bernadette in my name. What do you think would happen if she got the slightest whiff of a plot to dethrone her?"

As her lips compressed into a thin line, Elizabeth lifted

her shoulder in a half shrug. "I don't know." It was a lie, poorly delivered and judging by the dubious look on Greg's face, easily seen through.

"You do know. If she found out what we were trying to do, she'd slaughter anyone who has ever voiced a positive opinion about either of us. In addition to the soldiers we'd lose on the battlefield, Bernadette would go after everyone we care about. She'd murder them out of pure spite, just to hurt us."

Elizabeth's resolve began to deflate, yet she kept her expression blank as she stalked over to the window and breathed in the crisp morning air.

Several children were playing leap-frog in the yard below, and as their unfettered giggles reached her ears, Elizabeth's heart panged with nostalgia as memories of her own childhood at Crompton Palace swept over her. Some of her favorite pastimes involved playing bowls in the garden with Greg, searching for tadpoles in the pond with Clara, and dispensing humorous pranks on the courtiers with Henry. Her life as a princess had its share of problems, most of which stemmed from Bernadette and the king, but in general, Elizabeth had been happy there.

Is there truly no chance of going back? Ever? Tears sprang to her eyes, but her back was to Greg so, thankfully, they fell unnoticed.

"Anyone who has ever befriended you or helped me in any way would be seen as a threat." The graveness of his tone yanked her out of her trance and sent a frisson of dread up her spine. "She'd execute each of our contacts without hesitation. Lady Jane. Henry. Mary. Father Timothy. Joshua. Clara."

"You've made your point."

It was obvious he disagreed as he mercilessly continued listing people who'd find themselves in Bernadette's sights should he choose to reach for the throne. "Channing. The blacksmith in Warrick. The farmer who gave us food. Sister Margaret. John. The children in this orphanage."

Elizabeth grew more distressed with each name he rattled off, but it was the callous mention of their youngest, most vulnerable friends that drove her over the edge. Infuriated, she spun on her heels and bellowed, "I said you made your point!"

Greg didn't even flinch. He'd struck a chord and he knew it. "All of them, killed because they showed us support. Picture little Corah's face and tell me her death would be worth it."

An unfathomable coil of fright rose up and constricted Elizabeth's throat. She wanted to lash back and proclaim that he was an idiot for suggesting Corah was dispensable, but the ability to talk eluded her.

Greg must've noticed, but he didn't withdraw. "Would you trade her life just to put me on the throne? How many people would have to die before the risk outweighed the benefit?" His tone was harsh and unyielding as he pinned her beneath a frigid scowl. "Ten? Fifty? Three hundred? Six thousand?"

"Shut up!" She plopped into the chair beside the hearth as the faces of all the innocent, loveable children she'd gotten to know these last few days flashed through her mind. The answer was obvious. Zero. No life was expendable.

Bernadette was the most vindictive, hellacious monster on earth. She'd massacre everyone who stood between her and the power she believed was *her* birthright. There was no question about it. Even if Greg were to succeed in ousting her, his conscience could never shoulder the weight of the carnage enacted in his name.

The awareness that King Gregory would never exist cut

through Elizabeth like a knife, and she scrunched herself further into the chair, resigned to this unexpected revelation. There would be no army. No plot to usurp Bernadette.

That door was closed to them, and it was with an unnatural pairing of remorse and joy that Elizabeth accepted the truth. Conflicted by these two vastly different emotions, she wiped the dampness from her cheeks.

"This is the way it has to be," Greg concluded, an apology in his voice.

"But is it what you *want*?"

"Yes," he answered without a second's thought. "In an odd sort of way, it's what I've always wanted. The backstabbing and scheming at court drained me, and even as a king, I never would've been able to escape it. I'd never be permitted to relax or let down my guard. The constant stress would've sent me to an early grave. This banishment is my one chance at happiness. I realize now it's a gift, one I fully intend to make the most of."

Elizabeth leaned back in the chair with a sigh. Any trace of argument left in her was wiped out, turned to ash by Greg's words. If this was his way of letting go of the past and overcoming his inner demons, then who was she to stand in his way?

"Very well," she said. "We let Bernadette have the throne."

CHAPTER 36

*G*regory's smile stretched across his face as he spread a generous heap of marmalade over a slice of bread and offered it to his sister. "Here you go."

"Thanks." Elizabeth took a nibble and leaned back in the chair. She crossed one leg over the other as she tilted her head to the side, studying him. "You already seem different," she observed, her brow furrowed in thought. "There's a gleam in your eyes I've never seen before."

Gregory nodded and chomped into his breakfast, unable to stop grinning. "I'm free, Bess. Now that you've come to terms with my decision to relinquish the crown, it feels as though the invisible shackles chaining me to the past have finally been broken. I know it wasn't easy for you to accept my renunciation, but you did it anyway. You've given me your full support and because of that, I can put the past behind me, once and for all. It's liberating."

"Well then, here's to broken shackles." Elizabeth lifted her cup in the air and once Gregory did the same with his, they bashed them together, spilling mulled cider all over themselves in the process.

"Now look what you've done," Gregory teased.

"Me?" Elizabeth's cheeks shined, and with a playful smirk, she ripped off a corner of her bread and tossed it at his face, smacking him right in the forehead. "Take that!"

Gregory caught it as it fell to his lap, then, with a triumphant laugh, he chucked it back at her.

She ducked. "Ha! You missed."

He tore a piece off his own slice and was rounding up for another toss when he caught sight of a hooded figure in the doorway. He sobered at once.

"Isn't this a picture of carelessness?" Father Timothy crossed the threshold and pulled the door shut behind him. Donned in a long, black robe, he lowered his hood and glared at the siblings. "Having fun?"

"Father Timothy!" Elizabeth's voice was light, and unlike Gregory's, her smile had yet to be extinguished. "What are you doing here?"

"I'm here to talk." His voice was smooth as cream as he reached into his pocket.

Gregory tensed.

Though the priest's scowl was directed at him, the wheel-lock pistol he'd concealed in his robe was now aimed at Elizabeth. "And this time, you're going to listen."

Elizabeth gasped.

Gregory's insides shriveled. He made a move to get up from the bed but froze when the priest poised his finger on the trigger.

"Think again. One wrong move and she's dead." The crazed glint in his eyes confirmed his threat to be real. "Don't provoke me."

"Alright." Chest tight, Gregory held his hands up. Panic shot through his blood vessels and beads of sweat anointed his brow. "I'll listen. *After* you let Elizabeth go."

"No one's going anywhere. Get up, Princess. Now."

Gregory gulped and spared a glimpse at his sister.

Stark white, Elizabeth stared down the barrel of the gun as she followed his order to stand. She didn't dare make a sound.

"Let's all stay calm." Hard as he tried, Gregory failed to quell the tremor in his voice. "Put the gun down. Then we'll talk."

Father Timothy's lips curled into a nasty sneer. He set his jaw and pushed his shoulders back, lifting his chin to expose his neck. He squeezed the handle of the gun so tight his hand turned white. "We'll talk *now*."

Gregory's breaths quickened. Against his better judgement, he slowly rose from the bed. Shocks of pain shot through his body, but he fought through them, determined to mask his weakness.

"I said don't move!"

"Your issue is with me." Keeping his hands in the air and his eyes trained on the priest's trigger finger, Gregory took a hesitant step toward Elizabeth. His pulse raced and the sound of his heartbeat thrashed in his ears, but he refused to cower on the bed while his sister was held at gunpoint. "I'm the one you should be pointing that thing at."

"That's true." His voice jagged, Father Timothy bared his teeth. A vein in his neck throbbed. "You're the reason Mary's dead."

The room fell silent as the priest's news sank in.

Mary's dead? Sweat coated Gregory's skin as he inched closer to Elizabeth.

"My devotion to you was rewarded with fire." Devastation marred Father Timothy's face. His hand shook and with it, the pistol. "Last Sunday, Princess Bernadette's men barred the doors of my church during mass and set it ablaze. Everyone inside perished."

Gregory's stomach roiled. His gaze darted around the room, searching for anything that could stand a chance against a loaded pistol. There was nothing.

"I see now the carnage you leave in your wake." Father Timothy cast him a dark glare. Bubbles frothed at the corners of his mouth. "I thought you were an angel, sent from God himself to be our salvation. But I was gravely mistaken. You're a demon!"

Gregory's mouth went dry as sand, but he kept his eyes fixed on the weapon. With one more agonizing step, he reached Elizabeth's side. A fraction of the stiffness in his muscles loosened as he carefully pushed her behind him and extended his arms out to block her.

Now positioned between his sister and the pistol, Gregory released a quiet exhale. He would be the one to take the hit should Father Timothy pull the trigger. Wheellocks only fired one shot. They took at least a minute to reload. Elizabeth would have plenty of time to escape.

"All you had to do was say the word," the priest spat. He didn't appear to notice, or care, that his target had changed. "You had legions of men willing to defend your claim, but you chose cowardice. You're no better than the mud on the bottom of my shoe!"

Gregory's mind raced to calculate the amount of time it'd take him to close the distance between himself and the weapon. No matter how fast he was, he'd never make it across the room before the shot rang out.

"Every Catholic in Caracalla was prepared to pledge his allegiance to you. I showed you the written proof of their support, yet you refused to assemble them." His bitterness oozed through tight lips and a murderous scowl. "You turned your back on me, on all of us. Your diffidence led to the deaths of every Catholic in Gettsbury."

Gregory pursed his lips and ignored the pang of guilt in his gut. "What happened to them was tragic, but I'm not the cause. Their deaths could've been avoided had you listened to me and—"

"I was trying to defend your birthright!"

"But I told you not to." Aggravation burned through Gregory like wildfire. His cheeks and neck were hot as the logs in the fireplace. "I made it perfectly clear that I wasn't going to lead the rebellion. I ordered you to stop, but you went ahead with your plans anyway."

"I thought you'd change your mind! I wanted to have your troops ready to march the moment you called upon them." Father Timothy's shoulders fell, and the passion leaked from his face. "But none of that matters now. It's over. Somehow, Princess Bernadette found out I was attempting to raise an army in your name. She must've assumed I'd be leading Sunday mass and planned for me to die there, alongside everyone else."

A poignant silence fell over the room.

Colorful spots danced in front of Gregory's eyes, his breaths shallow and erratic as another surge of pain seared through his side. Shoulders rigid, he focused every morsel of energy he had into staying on his feet.

"Princess Bernadette believes I'm dead, and I might as well be. You know what will happen to us Catholics without your support. She'll murder us all."

"Only the ones who continue to oppose her," Gregory countered.

"No." Father Timothy's body sagged. "All of us."

Gregory eyed the pistol.

"Without your protection, all hope is lost." His voice was

thick, choked with emotion. The priest's shoulders hunched and as a vacant look warped his face, the last spark of light vanished from his eyes.

Gregory's pulse sounded in his ears. No creature was more dangerous than a man without hope. "Father Timothy—"

"Mark my words, you'll burn in hell for this." He pulled the trigger.

Gregory cringed and his heart stopped, but the only noise the firearm made was a quiet little, *click.*

Shielded behind Gregory, Elizabeth let out a raspy breath.

Father Timothy's eyes were wide in alarm as he squeezed the trigger again. *Click.*

Gregory lunged.

Elizabeth's scream sliced the air.

He slammed into the priest, propelling him backwards onto the floor. They fought for control of the pistol, and when the weapon went off with a deafening bang, the force of it threw the men apart.

A cloud of smoke engulfed them.

The pressure in his head was so intense, Gregory thought his skull had split in half. He rolled over and pressed his hands against his ears, desperate for the ringing to cease.

"Greg!" His sister's voice sounded a million miles away.

He opened his eyes, squinting as he tried to make sense of the grisly scene before him. The pool of crimson on the floor seeped closer to him. He wondered who it belonged to. If the sharp and biting ache in his torso was any indication, the blood was his.

"Greg?" Elizabeth tugged on his arm, dragging him to his feet. "Can you hear me? Were you shot?"

Dazed, Gregory glanced down at his blood splattered

clothes. His existing injury screamed in agony, but there didn't appear to be any fresh wounds. "I…I don't think so."

Elizabeth's frantic gaze swept over him, top to bottom. He must've passed her inspection though because in her next breath, she threw herself upon him and pressed her face into his shoulder.

A hiss of air escaped his lungs at the impact, but he didn't pull away.

"I thought you were dead," she cried, shaking as sobs racked her body.

As the throbbing in his ears gradually receded and his hearing returned to normal, Gregory ground his teeth and glanced down at Father Timothy.

Or at least, what was left of him.

Gregory suppressed a gag and turned away. He squeezed his eyes shut, his arms tightening around his weeping sister. His legs wobbled, but the anxiety pumping through his veins helped keep him upright. "It's alright, Bess. We're safe."

At their feet, the priest was sprawled out on his back, unrecognizable as blood continued to gush from the gaping hole that used to be his face.

As a man of the cloth, Father Timothy wouldn't have known that unless properly maintained, wheellock pistols were prone to malfunction.

CHAPTER 37

*C*hilled to her bones and unable to shake the horrific image of Father Timothy lying on the floor with his face blown off, Elizabeth rubbed her arms and watched the door. The children seated at the table around her were oblivious to her torment as they sang a ridiculous song of dancing pigs, at top volume.

Assembled in the hall while Greg and John dealt with the body and cleaned the mess left behind by the priest's gruesome death, the orphans and nuns lacked even the slightest inkling anything was amiss. They continued to play their games and sing their tunes, unaware of the terrible event that'd occurred right under their noses more than three hours ago.

Three hours. That's how long Elizabeth had been sitting there. Waiting.

"Miss Dorothy? Do you want it?"

Elizabeth dragged her gaze from the entryway and focused instead on Francis. "Huh?"

"My cloak. Do you want to borrow it?"

"Oh. Um…" She stole another glimpse at the door. *Where is he?*

"You look like you're freezing." Francis, a sweet little boy of no more than seven years, removed his outer garment and lovingly draped it over Elizabeth's shoulders. "There. That's better." He beamed at her, his eyes aglow.

"That's very thoughtful of you, Francis." Elizabeth's chin quivered as she reigned in the tears that'd gathered in the corners of her eyes. "Thank you."

"Dorothy?"

At her brother's strained voice, she looked up.

Greg's posture stooped as he settled a weary gaze upon her. Dark circles shadowed his cerulean eyes and though he seemed a bit unsteady, he was standing. On his own.

"You're back." She straightened in her seat. "Where have you been?"

She realized right away what a stupid question that was.

"After John and I…" Greg's voice cracked. "After we cleaned up, Mother Superior insisted I have a bath. And a shave." He ran a hand through his dark hair, which was significantly shorter than before. "And a haircut."

"And a new wardrobe," Elizabeth observed. Not only was Greg sparkling clean and well-groomed, but he was also dressed in a fresh pair of breeches and a spotless, moss-green doublet she'd never seen before.

Greg tugged the borrowed doublet more firmly into place. "She's lending these to me while mine get washed."

"I see." It'd take a whole bar of soap to scrub all the grime out of his old attire. Not to mention the blood…

"She offered to have both your kirtles cleaned and mended as well." Greg looked down on her with a strained smile. "Sister Margaret was instructed to draw you a bath later, after supper. Leave all your clothes with her, and they'll be good as new come morning."

Elizabeth hoped she looked more pleased than she felt. Under different circumstances, she would've been thrilled by the prospect of a warm bath and freshly laundered clothes. However, all she could think of at present was Father Timothy's harrowing end.

"What did you and John do with…" She let the question fall away when she noticed that Francis and a few of the other children were hanging on her every word. She cleared her throat.

"Let's go for a walk," Greg suggested.

Without protest, Elizabeth rose from the bench and returned Francis's cloak. "Thank you. That warmed me right up. Was it weaved of magical thread, perhaps?"

"Maybe!" A smile spread across the boy's face and he turned to his neighbor. "Miss Dorothy thinks it's magical!"

Greg wrapped his arm around her shoulder. "You're great with them, you know."

"Thanks." Her gaze directed down as she walked and she noticed the shoes on her brother's feet were not his own either. These boots, although a bit too small for him, didn't leave bloody footprints in their wake.

As she allowed Greg to lead her out of the hall, Elizabeth bit her lip and fought to ignore the stickiness on the bottoms of her own shoes. None of Father Timothy's blood had sprayed her clothes, but it was obvious to her now that she hadn't been very careful where to step.

"Where are we going?" she asked, choked by a wave of nausea.

"Outside." Greg gave her a lopsided smile but said nothing else as they made their way out the front door and headed toward a cluster of trees in the distance.

The crisp wind twisted at her dress, yet despite her shivering, it felt good to get out of the abbey. She did wish she'd kept Francis's cloak on though.

Once the siblings came to a fallen log, Greg clutched his rib and sat down. "I guess this is where we stop," he grimaced with a hollow chuckle. "Seems as good a spot as any."

The calls of a chaffinch rang from the treetops and beams of light shined through the leaves, shimmering on the ones that'd already fallen in surrender to the changing seasons.

As good a spot as any. Elizabeth flattened the back of her dress and sat onto the log beside her brother.

He took in a great breath, his face twisted in discomfort.

"We shouldn't have walked so far." She fiddled with the blue tit pendant that hung from her neck, unable to control the vibrations in her hands. "You're still recovering."

"I know, but I wanted to converse in private. Not that I have any idea what to say."

"I've seen someone die before, remember?"

A spasm of grief slid across Greg's face. "Yes, but that doesn't make it any easier."

"No." Elizabeth gripped her necklace tighter and stared at the ground. "It doesn't."

"I owe you an explanation."

I'd say so! Biting back a scoff, she was tempted to smack her brother upside the head for keeping his conversations with the priest a secret. Greg had supporters, men willing to defend his claim. How could he hide from her?

She longed to rip into him. However, just hours ago Greg had voluntarily placed himself between her and a firearm. For that, he deserved some patience.

"You owe me nothing," she murmured, half believing it.

"The man had a gun pointed at your head, Bess. The least I can do is tell you why."

"From what I gathered, he came to you and asked you to fight for the crown. You told him no, but he didn't listen. Bernadette found out. People died. Did I miss anything?"

The sharpness of her tone made Greg wince. "I should've told you."

Yes! You should've! With a tightness in her jaw, she reminded herself to calm down. "Yet you didn't. Why?"

He clamped his lips together, pressed so tight Elizabeth doubted he'd answer. He ripped pieces off a leaf that'd fallen into his lap, either unwilling or unable to meet her gaze.

"Because I knew you'd agree with him," he confessed at long last. He threw what was left of the leaf on the ground, then shifted atop the log and looked her straight in the eye. "I figured as long as you thought raising an army was out of the question, you wouldn't expect it of me. However, if I told you about my meetings with Father Timothy, you'd know I had support. You'd know there were men out there willing to fight for me, and you'd expect me to take advantage of it."

Elizabeth held her tongue. He was right, of course.

"If it became clear to you that I had the opportunity to gather the forces needed to oppose Bernadette, yet still chose to relinquish the crown, you'd lose all respect for me. And I couldn't bear that, Bess. I need you on my side."

She drew in a deep breath, then, with a long exhale, released her irritation about being kept in the dark. Once again, her brother's need for approval made itself known, and as usual, she took it upon herself to ease his mind.

"I'm always on your side, Greg, even when we don't see eye to eye. Yes, I would've questioned your decision. Did I not do so when you told me about it this morning? But the bottom line is that this wasn't my choice to make. It wasn't

Father Timothy's either. It was yours, and you made your stance clear. Even if you could have an army of a million men, why bother when the prize their fighting for isn't one you want? Why let them die for nothing?"

The corner of Greg's lip twitched.

"I understand why you feel the way you do, and I respect your decision to stand down. I respect *you*."

A flush rose on Greg's cheek and as his smile grew, the tension on his face lessened.

"I do have one more question, though."

His smile fell.

"Father Timothy was so desperate to keep Bernadette off the throne that he was driven mad by your refusal to fight for the crown. He believed if Bernadette becomes queen, she'll execute every Catholic in the kingdom. Obviously that fear pushed him over the edge." The chaffinch in the tree above them emitted a sudden trill, and Elizabeth flinched. With a gulp, she returned her gaze to her brother. "But surely he was wrong," she muttered, her voice raw. "He wasn't right in believing Bernadette could do that, was he? I know she hates them, but even a queen can't eradicate a major religion. She would need a reason for each execution she ordered, right?"

"Yes. Besides, at least half of Caracalla is Catholic, and to actively move against them would land her at the feet of yet another rebellion. Not to mention, it would put her at odds with Rome and Spain. I highly doubt she'd take such a risk. But whether he was right or not, Father Timothy blamed my choice to stand down as the reason he lost everything he loved, including Mary."

Their friend's name was a blow to the heart. Unable to stifle the anguished sob that flared within her chest, Elizabeth allowed the tears to fall freely down her face as she wept into her hands.

Greg pulled her into his side and uttered words of comfort, but they went unheard as Elizabeth grieved for the old woman who'd welcomed them into her home and given them a place at her table. Every breath Greg took was a gift from Mary, and Elizabeth wished now she'd expressed more gratitude. She'd planned to shower her friend with riches once Greg took back the throne, but that was impossible now, in more ways than one.

"I'm so sorry, Bess."

Elizabeth wiped the final streams of water from her cheeks and pulled away from Greg's embrace. "It's not your fault," she sniffed. "Father Timothy should've respected your wishes. If he'd listened to you, Bernadette wouldn't have had any reason to lash out at him. The church wouldn't have been burned, and Mary would still be alive. It wasn't your decision that got her killed, it was Father Timothy's unwillingness to accept it. You warned him not to poke the viper; he chose to ignore you and got bit. You're not to blame, do you hear me?"

"I do."

Elizabeth frowned at the lack of sincerity in her brother's tone. "Is there something else bothering you?"

"No." Greg was careful not to meet her gaze as he absently twisted at his sleeve. A shade of uncertainty colored his face and he cleared his throat, but that did nothing to negate the tremor of nervousness in the speech that followed. "Well, yes. There is one last thing we need to discuss. Father Timothy's death was horrifying, but it gave me reason to stop and really think about what it was that he…and *you* expected of me."

"What do you mean?"

"In our conversation earlier today, it became clear you were under the impression my exile was temporary. You believed once our father was gone, I'd round up troops to depose Bernadette. You thought I'd win back the crown and someday, we'd return to Crompton." When Elizabeth said nothing, Greg arched an eyebrow. "Correct?"

"Yes."

"And now you know that's out of the question. You must be…disappointed."

Yes. Elizabeth picked at the specks of dirt dotting her dress. "A bit."

He went still and rigid. "You've been misled into thinking my banishment was just a hurdle, a brief pause from the life you had at the palace. It wouldn't be fair of me to expect you to stay now that you know the truth."

"What are you saying?"

"That I wouldn't blame you if you've reconsidered your decision to stay with me." Blinking way too much, Greg rose to his feet and walked a short distance away. "Now that you know following me into the fires of treason is a *lifelong* commitment, you should be given the chance to back out. You say you respect my decision and you'll always be on my side, but that doesn't-"

"I meant it," Elizabeth cut in.

"I know you did, but that doesn't mean you should suffer for it. This isn't the life you deserve and now that it's getting colder…" He returned to the log and plopped back down, his hands clasped together so tightly his fingers turned red. "It's not too late for you to go back, you know. You could still claim you were abducted on the road to Ephrata. Hell, you could even say Father Timothy was the one who held you captive all this time, and after he *died in the fire*, you were able to escape."

"He said the fire was a week ago. Even if I turned around now, it would take at least another fortnight for me to get back to the palace. How would I explain where I've been since the church burned down?"

"I'm sure we could come up with something." Greg's eyes flickered to hers. "Do you want to return to Crompton?"

Elizabeth pressed her tongue against the inside of her cheek. Indecision suffused her from head to toe, and although she despised herself for it, she allowed the question to flounder in her mind.

There was no denying the fact that Greg's banishment had turned her whole world upside down. Her life no longer consisted of lazy afternoons painting beside the pond, peaceful evenings in front of her harpsichord, or bounteous feasts in the magnificent Great Hall.

No, since leaving the palace seven weeks ago, she'd killed her own uncle, nursed Greg back from the brink of death twice, and experienced true exhaustion as she labored alongside Mary. She'd slept in a tent with nothing in her belly save for a few berries, and most recently, she watched a priest's face get obliterated when his gun, which had been aimed at her for a time, failed to shoot her brother and misfired.

Elizabeth had been flung headfirst over the palace walls and experienced the world's cruelty firsthand. And they hadn't even made it to the monastery yet.

Did she truly have the endurance she'd need to survive the rest of the journey there? Or better yet, the days that would come after? Was she strong enough for this life?

"Do you need some time?"

She spared a glimpse at her brother, who looked as though her brief moment of hesitation had leeched the life right out of him. For her, time had whizzed by as she rushed to reach a decision, but as Greg's dim gaze searched hers, she had the distinct impression it had felt more like ages to him.

Guilt ravaged her to the core, and she made up her mind right then and there. She'd promised to stand by him no matter what, and she wasn't about to waver now. "No. There's nothing to think about. I said I'd follow you into the unknown, and I meant it. Whether you're seated on the throne of Caracalla or not, I am with you. I don't care if you're the king or a cabbage farmer. Residing in a palace isn't a stipulation for my loyalty."

A slow smile graced Greg's face. "Are you certain?"

"Positive."

He brightened. "Good. Then from this point forward we look ahead, not backwards. Last night, John told me about the burial plot that was dug for me. Father Timothy's in it now, but as far as I'm concerned, the cemetery here at Blackmore Abbey is where Prince Gregory will remain as well. Forever. I refuse to spend another day as the tormented, banished prince living in constant fear of capture. Today is the day we turn our backs on the past and all the suffering it brought us. Agreed?"

"Agreed!"

Encouraged by her animated response, Greg's face broke into a wide grin. "Once we leave this place, we'll no longer be two royals in exile. The titles of prince and princess no longer belong to us. We're just George and Dorothy, two ordinary peasants. What do you say? Are you ready for a fresh start?"

Hope lifted Elizabeth's heart, and as a bud of excitement blossomed in her stomach, she nodded in affirmation. "Yes. I am. The fires of treason be damned."

AUTHOR'S NOTE

Thank you so much for reading The Fires of Treason! I hope you enjoyed Gregory and Elizabeth's story as much as I do. If you have a few moments to leave a review on Amazon or any other book site, it would be greatly appreciated. Reviews are like gold to authors, even short ones. They keep us going and encourage us to keep writing.

If you would like to be kept in the loop about updates on the sequel, please give me a follow on Twitter, Facebook, or visit my website at https://michelequirkewrite.wixsite.com/mysite. I love hearing from my readers and look forward to connecting with you!

ACKNOWLEDGMENTS

It's said it takes a village to raise a child. Well, ask any writer and they'd say writing a novel is similar to having a child. You pour yourself into it. Mind, body, and soul. Then, you throw it out into the world and cross your fingers for success. Like raising a child, publishing a book takes a village. I want to take a moment to thank mine.

To my husband, Ed: You made this possible. Without your constant love, support, and patience, I never would've been able to make this dream a reality. From the bottom of my heart, I thank you.

To my son, Greg: You are the light of my life, my reason for being. I love you so much.

To my family and friends: I can't tell you how much your encouragement has meant to me throughout this journey. You all mean the world to me.

To Jodi Jensen, the best critique partner ever: Wow, if it wasn't for you, I never would've had the courage to share this book with anyone. Your belief in me and this story pushed me to take the leap. Thank you so much for helping me transform the mess that was my first draft into the finished novel it is today. I can never repay you for all you've done for me!

To my beta readers: Thank you all for the advice and feedback you gave me. Because of you my novel has improved by leaps and bounds.

To my editor, Charlie Knight: Thank you so much for helping polish up my manuscript, particularly by catching a plot hole that slipped by the rest of us.

To my cover illustrator, Anna Klimova: I can't thank you enough for painting the gorgeous artwork of Gregory and Elizabeth. You brought my vision of them to life.

To my cover designer, Fantasy and Coffee Design: You captured the aesthetic I wanted for my cover perfectly. Thank you!

To my ARC team: Your excitement about reading the book before the official launch made my spirits sour and I am so thankful for the reviews you left on release day!

To the Twitter Writing Community: You are all gems. The support you've given me on the road to publishing has been vital. When I faltered, you inspired me. You've been by my side every step of the way. Thank you.

To my friends and fellow authors, McKenzie Austin, N. Malone, Hayley Reese Chow, and SD Simper: All four of you have been incredibly helpful when it comes to the many questions I had about publishing. Your advice and knowledge was a pillar for me as I ventured into the unknowns of publishing a novel. Thank you all so much!

To Dewi Hargreaves: Thank you for creating such an amazing map of the Kingdom of Caracalla. You took my ridiculous doodle and turned it into something wonderful!

To my formatter, N. Malone: I am so grateful to you for

making my manuscript compatible for eBook and paperback. I really could not have done that without you!

And finally, my readers: I wouldn't be here without you. Sharing Gregory and Elizabeth's journey with you is a dream come true and I hope you've grown to love the Cavendish siblings as much as I do.

ABOUT THE AUTHOR

Michele Quirke is an up and coming historical fiction author. She currently lives near Seattle, Washington with her husband, son, and their cat, Link.

The Fires of Treason is her first published novel.

https://michelequirkewrite.wixsite.com/mysite

facebook.com/MicheleQuirkeWrites
twitter.com/MicheleQuirke
instagram.com/michelequirke

Made in the USA
Middletown, DE
01 November 2020

23030526R00210